THE WIND FROM THE PLAIN
A Trilogy

I   THE WIND FROM THE PLAIN

Yashar Kemal was born in 1922 in a village on the cotton-growing plains of Chukurova, which feature in this novel. He received some basic education in village schools, then became an agricultural labourer and factory-worker. His championship of the poor peasants lost him a succession of jobs, but he was eventually able to buy a typewriter and set himself up as a public letter-writer in the small town of Kadirli. After a spell as a journalist he published a volume of short stories in 1952, and in 1955 his first novel, *Memed, My Hawk*. This won the Varlik Prize for the best novel of the year. It has sold over a quarter of a million copies in Turkey and has been translated into every major language.

Yashar Kemal was a member of the Central Committee of the banned Workers' Party. In 1971 he was held in prison for 26 days, then released without being charged.

Kemal, many of whose books have been translated into English by his wife, is Turkey's most influential living writer.

D0680043

Yashar Kemal

THE WIND FROM THE PLAIN

Translated from the Turkish by
Thilda Kemal

COLLINS HARVILL
8 Grafton Street, London W1
1989

Collins Harvill
William Collins Sons & Co. Ltd
London · Glasgow · Sydney · Auckland
Toronto · Johannesburg

BRITISH LIBRARY CATALOGUING IN PUBLICATION DATA

Yasar, Kemal, *1922-*
The wind from the plain
Rn: Kemal Sadik Gogcel
I. Title   II. Ortadirek. *English*
894'.3533 [F]

ISBN 0-00-271029-3

First published under the title
Ortadirek, Istanbul, 1960

First published in Great Britain by
Collins and Harvill Press, 1963
This edition first published by
Collins Harvill, 1989

© Yashar Kemal 1960
English Translation © William Collins Sons & Co. Ltd 1963

Printed and bound in Great Britain by
William Collins Sons & Co. Ltd, Glasgow

Chapter 1

The whirling thistle is here again. Go, take it to the villagers!

No, he tried to persuade himself, this can't be. These are only stray thistles. The cotton can't have ripened yet in the Chukurova plain. Something's wrong this year with the roots of these whirling thistles. The worms may have been eating the cursed things, or perhaps the field-mice have been at them. They keep breaking off and blowing over when it's still much too early for that.

He was sitting in the sun leaning against the wall of the house, his legs stretched out, a bitter expression on his long shrivelled face. His dirty white beard straggled over his breast and his grizzled tufted eyebrows jutted over his tiny green eyes, but his head was quite bald. The bones of his huge bare feet, tapering into black jagged nails, could be counted. His *shalvar*[1] and shirt of coarse hand-woven cotton had been patched so often that nothing could be seen of the original material.

A kid hovered around him and brushed his hand. Farther away, an excited hen was bustling about followed by a brood of almost immaterial soft yellow down that wriggled in the dust. Old Halil loved to watch the newly-hatched fluffy chicks warming up to the earth and the sun more than anything in the world. But now he only raised his head occasionally at the hen's clamour and grunted: "The plague on you, stupid fowl. What's all this fuss!" Then his chin dropped on to his breast again.

What if the whirling thistle blows right up to my door, he

[1] Baggy trousers worn by both men and women peasants in Turkey.

mused. What if the cotton bolls are bursting open in the Chukurova and the whole wide plain is overblown in white, there's no
strength left in my knees. I can't walk down to the Chukurova
plain this year. I just can't.

The day had mellowed into afternoon when he straightened
up painfully and called to his daughter-in-law:

"Woman, bring me some water."

There came no answer from within the house.

"Woman, may you remain fallow!" he cursed. "No one here
to give a man a drop of water. A body had much better die than
grow old!"

He went inside, filled a bowl and drank with trembling hands,
spilling the water on his beard.

At eventide he made his way to the top of the hill. A haze was
settling over the distant steppe and the vast stretches were turning
grey. He fancied he saw a cluster of whirling thistles being
tossed by the wind.

The whirling thistle's here again and there's nothing you can
do about it; the thought pursued him. If you don't let the villagers
know that the cotton is ripe in the Chukurova, then they'll eat
you alive, Halil, they'll make *kebab* out of you! Suppose they
arrive too late, long after the labourers of the other villages have
picked all the cotton. . . . What will you tell them, Halil? That
your reckoning went astray?

When the whirling thistle is blown over across the wide
steppe, Old Halil knows that the cotton is bursting ripe in the
Chukurova plain. Each year at this time, perhaps even earlier,
Old Halil picks up one of the thistles that have come drifting
from the steppe, examines its twigs and thorns and then heads
for the Muhtar's[1] house.

"Hail, son of the old Headman Hidir, the whirling thistle's
come. I've seen a mass of them soaring like a flock of cranes in

[1] Muhtar: the representative of the Government in the village, elected by the
villagers themselves. Replaces the former "headman" of the Ottoman Empire.

the direction of Mount Tekech. Tell the villagers to get ready within three days."

And each year at this signal the villagers pack off for the Chukurova cotton plain.

All through that night Old Halil was kept awake by a stream of disturbing images. Chilling autumnal winds licking the grey earth, birds cowering in their shelters, their necks drawn in . . . The twittering of partridges is heard no longer. Gone are the traces left by their red legs at the foot of the bushes. Whistling gusts are uprooting the thistles and hurling them from hill to hill. Huge thistles, basket-like, are swirling over the bare hill-tops in the pale sky, filling the valleys and glens and overflowing on to the roads and plains.

These villagers, have they no sense at all? he fumed. Have they no eyes, no ears, no judgment? What would they have done these thirty years without me? Just suppose Old Halil were dead. Just suppose. . . . Well then, you fellows, wouldn't you have gone down to the cotton just the same? Why, you beggers, not a single one of you has ever said to me, "Bless you, Uncle Halil, thanks to you we have always got down to the cotton in good time." Well, what if I went amiss this year. Any human being might. Am I what I used to be? You can see for yourselves how weak I've grown. How could I know whether the cotton's ripe in the Chukurova, how could I? I just can't, you cuckolds!

These thoughts nagged him till morning and when he rose, his eyes were red and smarting as if they had been rubbed with pepper. He looked out into the distance. A cold wind was blowing.

"The men in this village are all asses," he cried. "All asses!"

A man of over fifty with greying head and beard moved up to him.

"What's that, Father?"

Old Halil ignored him.

"Father, isn't the cotton ripe yet?"

Old Halil did not answer.

"For heaven's sake, Father, what's come over you these days? A knife couldn't pry your mouth open!"

Old Halil raised his brows menacingly and looked his son up and down.

"May Allah shower you with curses! Look at him, damn him, standing there and talking to me like that!" he cried out angrily. "If you'd been like other people's sons, would I have been in this state?"

Old Halil rumbled on and on until his son walked off exasperated and he was left alone with his thoughts.

The whirling thistle's here again. There's nothing you can do but take it to the Muhtar.

He rose and stretched his aching limbs. Then, leaning heavily on his stick, he hobbled off towards the village.

He decided to take a roundabout course to avoid going past the house of the Molla's son who would pester him again with that dirty smirk on his face: "Well, Uncle Halil, how many days left before your whirling thistles flock in? When do we start off for the Chukurova? We're all at your mercy, Uncle Halil. You could, if you wished, keep us from the cotton until it was too late, until mid-winter, eh, Uncle Halil?" The son of a bitch, raged Old Halil. If he's a man, why doesn't *he* try and tell us when the cotton's ready?

He was pausing for breath at every other step. Have I really grown so old, he asked himself. God knows, I must be over eighty now. But it isn't old age, it's hunger. That bitch of a daughter-in-law of mine doesn't feed me properly. Hides all the food where I can't find it. That's why I feel so weak. Down in the Chukurova there'll be water-melons, tomatoes . . . just what I need. But how can I get to the Chukurova? Ah, Ali, you're a good lad, you're the son of my old friend Ibrahim, but . . . If it weren't for that mother of yours, that old sow . . . She was the cause of your father's death, by Allah she was, the harridan!

As he drew near Long Ali's door he struck his stick twice against the ground. Ali's house had been built by his grandfather. It was a low, unplastered hut made of earth and large unhewn stones. He hoped Ali was alone. It would be no use talking to him when Meryemdje, his old whore of a mother, was at home.

"Ali, my child," he called softly. "Ali."

"Welcome, Uncle Halil," Ali called back as he came out immediately. "Won't you come in?"

Old Halil slumped down on a log. "Come here beside me," he said.

Ali sat down near him without a word. For over a week now the old man had been visiting him regularly. He had talked and talked, and then had left without coming to the point. Ali had guessed what he was driving at, but what could he do. . . .

"There's still plenty of time for the cotton," began Old Halil. "The weather's been cold this year and the cotton will bloom late. Late or early, how can I go down to the Chukurova, Ali, with these failing legs? Curse this old age! It's the greatest misfortune on earth. I'll never be able to make it. Even on my way here, I stopped ten times to get my breath. My legs shake as if caught in an earthquake, and they ache, and they twitch. . . . I'd like to see anybody else go down to the Chukurova in such a wretched state."

He paused, his eyes on the ground. A small thistle blown on the wind settled at his feet. He flicked it away and the wind swept it afar. When he raised his head, his small eyes were wet.

"Ah," he said in low quavering tones, "your father, may he rest in peace, may a plenteous light fall upon his grave . . . your father Ibrahim . . . ah, if he had been alive . . . Why didn't I die instead? Why didn't we both die together? I should never have survived my Ibrahim. A man can't count on his neighbour, or on his wife, or even on his own son. No, only on a friend. Such a virtuous man Ibrahim was! Virtuous and brave. And such a good thief too! He could steal a man's nose off his face while he slept! He used to take me with him on his thieving expeditions and it was he who taught me how to steal. Thanks to that I've always been able to live comfortably without depending on niggards. But now that I'm old, and Ibrahim dead . . . Curse this old age! A man should be killed before his back starts to bend. But there's no help for it. This is the way Allah made this world, and He should have known better. Look, Ali, I've thought of staying here in the village all alone, but people would think I'd gone crazy, and anyway I'd die of hunger. How can a man live all by himself in a deserted village? It's not just five days or ten days. Two whole months! A man may be attacked by the wolves. Even the ants can make a feast of him and pick his eyes hollow. Has anyone ever remained in the village during the cotton season? Not in my lifetime. Tell me, has anyone, ever?"

"No, never," replied Ali wearily.

Old Halil felt that Ali had been moved by his words. His voice rang triumphantly.

"Ah, if only I had died with my Ibrahim and not seen such days! Or if I had had a son like you. . . . But Allah only gave me that snivelling Hasan. A fat lot of good he did me! Hasan hasn't got a horse, or even a donkey which I could ride. Ah, I remember when Ibrahim first brought your pure-bred to this house. He had stolen it from a Circassian agha, way up on the Long Plateau, and with Allah's blessing it has served you well for years. Yes, Ali my son, Hasan hasn't got a horse like you have. I wouldn't call that good-for-nothing a son!"

He broke off and leaned forward expectantly.

Ali was scraping the earth with a twig. He could not bring himself to raise his head but he felt Old Halil's gaze piercing him like pointed nails.

At last the old man rose. He staggered away, more stooped than ever. Is there any good, he thought bitterly, any help at all to be expected from one born of that bitch Meryemdje? This can't be Ibrahim's offspring. Who knows by whom Meryemdje got him. . . . Ungrateful wretches, who was it brought that horse to you, eh? If no one else knows it, Meryemdje does. She knows her husband wouldn't have hurt a fly, much less steal a horse! Fie, you fickle world! May your wheel be broken, Fortune, to have reduced Old Halil to begging from door to door just for a short ride to the Chukurova! Go your way, you harlot world! Let those who enjoy your bounties sing your praise. Oh dear, my head is swimming! And my back! Oh dear, oh dear, my back's breaking!

Ali looked after him. The old man's legs were weaving into each other limply.

He can never go down to the Chukurova all the way on foot, he thought as he scraped the earth furiously with his twig.

At this moment he heard his mother's voice, fraught with pent-up anger: "What did he have to say this time, the old hound?"

"What could he say, poor man," replied Ali sadly. "He didn't put it in so many words, but he meant . . . You know."

"Never!" cried Meryemdje. "As long as I'm alive and breathing, that old carcass, that stinking pig carrion, will never ride my horse. Last year I let him, just for your sake. Then I saw my Ibrahim in a dream. 'Why you old Meryemdje,' he reproached me, 'how can you let that man ride my horse? I could not rest in my grave all the time he was on it.' 'Ibrahim,' I said, 'it's done now. It was your son's wish, how could I refuse it? Forgive me.' No, no Ali, never again. Not even if the Saint from the Hollow Rock were to rise from his grave and bid me do it. Go your way, Saint, I'd say, and mind your saintship. Don't go meddling with a poor mortal's horse. And anyway, Ali, the horse is sick. It's much weaker than Old Halil. I doubt if it will be able to carry me this year. Its ears are drooping and its nose is running. I warn you, Ali, you'll have to slit my throat open before you put him on my horse again."

Ali rose, brushing his *shalvar* trousers with his hand.

"He never even once asked for a ride, the poor fellow," he said with a deep sigh. "He only spoke about his failing strength."

Meryemdje's eyes flashed. "If he didn't ask to-day, he'll do so to-morrow. Mark my words. He's so brazen, he'll make me get off and ride the horse himself. He's the devil's own son, I know that and the great Allah above knows it too. There are things I've never told you, Ali. Don't make me speak. I just pray that his dirty heart be riddled with deadly bullets."

"Don't say that, Mother dear. I can't help pitying him with all my heart. How will the poor man ever walk all that long road? He might die on the way."

"Let him die," shouted Meryemdje. "I don't care what happens to him so long as he doesn't ride my horse."

Ali tossed away the twig impatiently. "If only I were sure that the horse could carry both of you I'd let him ride behind you."

At these words Meryemdje flew into a towering rage. It was impossible to make out what she was saying from the torrent of abuse that poured from her lips.

Ali was alarmed. "No, no! I won't put him on the horse," he cried, clasping her arm, "I swear I won't."

Meryemdje calmed down a little. "If ever you do, I shall go away to a country that neither you nor anyone else has ever heard of. I'll go, and the white milk you sucked from my breasts will be a curse to you."

She was a tall woman, but bent with age. Her features were handsome with high wide cheekbones tapering into a pointed chin, and her big black eyes must have been large and fine in her youth. Her face was a maze of little wrinkles and her cheeks sank into a toothless mouth. From under her headcloth a few wisps of white hair fell over her brow.

"Don't you ever utter the word horse again. That old pig can come and come again as often as he likes. That's that!" She stormed off into the hut.

Old Halil came back several times. With each visit he would complain even more about his health and would praise Ali's father still more highly, but each time he would find he was only butting against a wall.

There were four horses in the village. Old Halil visited the other three owners as well and plaintively recounted his misfortunes, but he would not humble himself to the extent of asking forthright for a ride, and not one of the owners made the offer he was expecting so eagerly. They would listen to him uneasily and then slink away shamefaced.

The days went by and Old Halil still scoured the village desperately like a drunken man. Death, he thought. Death would be better than this. It seemed to him that the villagers had nothing else to do but pester him.

"Isn't it time yet, Uncle Halil?"

"Last year at this time? Why, we'd been picking cotton for days!"

"Is it because the weather's been cold this year that the cotton's not yet ripe?"

"Uncle Halil, the valleys and glens are filled with whirling thistles."

"You may be wrong this year, Uncle Halil. Only Allah is infallible."

"Stop it, you fellows, don't pick on the man like this. When has Old Halil ever failed us? He must know what he's doing."

"Well, there's something fishy about all this. Old Halil has been acting funny this year."

"Nonsense, Old Halil never makes a mistake."

"Tell us, for heaven's sake, Uncle Halil, how much longer before we set off?"

He would parry the onslaught as best he could, lying, cursing or pretending he had not heard, but the thought was there, unremitting.

The whirling thistle's here again and there's nothing you can do about it. He was cornered. Screwing up his courage, he finally made his way to the Muhtar's house. Each year he would rush through the village, laughing and almost dancing with joy, brandishing the whirling thistle as he went. This time he was hard put to it to make a show of rejoicing.

The villagers watched him as he wended his way in a halting gait.

"Well, the cotton's ripe at last," they said. "It's ripe, yes, but the past year has told on Old Halil. He can hardly walk at all, the poor fellow, let alone run."

The Muhtar met him at the door. "How very late the cotton's been this year," he remarked, smiling pointedly. Then without waiting for an answer: "I didn't expect this of you, Uncle Halil. Conspiring against me with Long Ali and the others! Shame on you, shame on your white beard!"

"Mind your words, Muhtar," Old Halil growled. "You can't talk to me like that." In the past if anyone had spoken to him in this way he would have crushed him. But the old spirit was not there.

Each year as he handed the thistle to the Muhtar he would cry joyfully: "The whirling thistle's here again. I've seen masses of them gliding through the pale sky like a flock of cranes bound for Mount Tekech." The Muhtar would then joke: "What a story-teller you are, Uncle!" And the group of villagers around them would roar with laughter. Then the public-crier would be summoned to proclaim the news and the villagers would start making ready for the journey. But this time Old Halil's tidings dropped lifelessly from his lips, the Muhtar did not joke and the villagers did not laugh. The elders silently reflected that this was a sure sign of ill-omen. Even the voice of the public-crier as he called out the news was listless, with not a trace of the ringing tones of the past years.

The villagers were disturbed. "There's something afoot this year," they whispered to one another. "Let's hope it bodes no evil."

After this Old Halil shut himself up in his house and was not seen again in the village until the day of the big meeting.

Chapter 2

From late August to October the whirling thistles turn to red and at sunset the steppe appears to be swathed in a red mist. Like a long winding red road, like a phalanx of cranes, like a passing flight of screeching birds, the thistles break apart and close together again, they surge and sink, and are whipped to and fro by the boisterous, irrepressible winds that sweep the boundless steppe.

The whirling thistle is the only plant that grows freely all over the steppe. A soft green in the summer, it bestows life and freshness on this arid land. Its spines and roots are sturdy then, but as it dries up, the roots lose their strength, and by mid-autumn when the mighty winds begin to blow they have become so frail that the thistle is wrenched from the earth and swept away. Hundreds and thousands of thistles can then be seen hurtling over the steppe, whistling through the air.

"It is the whirling thistle that gives brightness and beauty to these dreary wastes," Old Halil would always say. "What would this lifeless steppe be without it?"

Rustling sounds come from the steppe. Old Halil puts his ear to the ground and listens to the murmur rising from deep deep down. The soil of the steppe is a good conductor. One can hear the creeping of ants in their heaps, the scurrying of birds in their holes. There is a bird of pure lustrous blue that makes its nest by delving deep down into cliff walls. One can hear it digging away in its tunnel. One can know when the roots of the whirling thistles are on the point of breaking by the special creaking noise they make. "There's nothing like the earth of the steppe," says Old Halil. "Why, it's better than the telegraph. Put your ear to it and you will hear all kinds of wonderful sounds. You will hear a shepherd piping at the other end of the world, you will hear a song that has never been sung before, laden with all the beauty of strange flowers. Yes, put your ear to the ground and hear the beat of horses' hooves a day's journey off. But it's not everyone can hear the voice of the earth. It needs a good ear, a discerning ear like mine, you ignoramuses!" Ever since he was a youth, it had always been Old Halil's favourite pastime to listen to these sounds for hours on end.

The peaks on the northern side of the Taurus Mountains level off in long slow undulations into a scorched, bleak highland that merges with the steppe. At the first breath of autumn all the villagers of this high land migrate down to the Chukurova cotton fields. The aged and infants, the sick and the lame, all have to go along. Nobody is left behind, not even a watchman, despite the grain hoarded in pits, the bedding piled in closets, the clothes left in trunks. The peasants know that no one would ever attempt to steal the slightest trifle, or even set foot in their village while it is empty. Only when they are back again will the forays of bandits, the pillaging and pilfering and abductions begin again.

A long time ago there roamed in these parts a band of brigands led by a ruthless outlaw named Jotdelek, who terrorised the countryside. When Jotdelek smelled money anywhere he would kill and cut to pieces anyone who stood in his way, were it his own wife or child. Well, it so happened once that this notorious brigand, being hunted by the gendarmes, managed to shake them off his trail as he fled far into the inner Taurus. There he chanced to come upon one of these empty villages. He was worn out, famished and thirsty, but this is what he said: "Comrades, we cannot steal food from this deserted village."

"Jotdelek Agha," his fellow bandits objected, "how can we afford to be noble now? We are dying of hunger, each one of us

19

is more dead than alive. There is food in this village. Let's go in and eat. There is bedding there of white Chukurova cotton. Let's go and have a good long sleep."

Jotdelek stood lost in thought for a while. Then he raised his head. Allah protect us from his wrath, flames were darting from his eyes!

"This cannot be, my friends," he cried. "You know that I never stop at anything. Let us plunder one of those inhabited villages farther off and lay it waste, butchering every living soul there, if you wish, raping the women and carrying off the fat and honey. But I'll never break into a deserted village and steal the food, however hungry I might be. I am so sleepy I can hardly stand. Were there a soft bed of white Chukurova cotton, I would lie on it and sleep soundly for a whole week. But I cannot be the first to violate this old tradition. A hundred, two hundred years hence, people will say that once upon a time, during the cotton picking, the empty villages of the Taurus were safe for wolf and lamb alike. Then came an evil man, a certain Jotdelek—and they will spit on my bones—who broke the custom and plundered empty villages. No, my friends, I will not have people saying that about me. I cannot have my name and bones execrated till the end of time. But if we spare the village, what will people say? They'll say: There was once a great agha named Jotdelek, a bloodthirsty bandit chief, but he died here of hunger on the threshold of this deserted village, overflowing with bread, butter and honey, rather than lay his hands on the paltriest rag. Good for the man, a thousand, two thousand cheers for the man who, together with his gallant comrades, is ready to lay down his life in the name of honour. May their graves be showered with light!"

These days Old Halil was cursing Jotdelek for all he was worth. If only that dog of a Jotdelek had looted at least one empty village, he thought, then people wouldn't all have gone down to the Chukurova. They'd have left the old ones behind. A curse on his bones. . . .

The Wind from the Plain

It is usual for village people in these parts to labour one or two months in the Chukurova cotton fields. For the inhabitants of the Long Plateau, the Chukurova is the principal source of income, much more important than their own crops or their sheep or goats.

All the villagers of the Plateau buy from Adil Effendi, the shopkeeper in the little town.

"How many heads are you?" Adil Effendi will ask.

"Ten."

"All able to pick cotton?"

"There is a little baby, my Agha,[1] born five days ago. A black-eyed little baby. . . ."

Adil Effendi does some mental assessing. Then he gives them a certain quantity of wares and enters the sum they owe him into his yellow book. He knows that on their return from the Chukurova nothing short of death or desertion will keep the borrowers from settling with him down to the last penny.

The village was all astir with comings and goings and shouting and swearing. There was considerable moaning and grumbling from the sick and the old, keening in some households and rejoicing in others. The watchman shuttled back and forth across the village, crying: "Hark village folk! Attend to my words and don't say you haven't heard. You have only two days left. Look sharp. Hurry, for the other villages have by now reached the Chukurova. All dawdlers will be punished by order of the village council and of our Muhtar."

But something unusual was brewing in the village this year. This was manifest on the faces of some of the villagers. "Be careful," their eyes seemed to say to one another, "don't let that snake-in-the-grass find out. He mustn't have an inkling or he'll do us dirt."

It was now five years that they had been debating the matter fruitlessly. But this year Long Ali, Tashbash and Lone Duran

[1] A title given to landlords and rich villagers.

21

had managed to rally a good number of the villagers to the point of action.

That morning Tashbash and Long Ali had been making a stealthy round of the village, calling at the homes of trusted friends. "We meet at Lone Duran's house," they had whispered and gone.

Lone Duran lived on the outskirts of the village. There was quite a crowd gathered there when Long Ali and Tashbash arrived, and everybody was speaking at the same time. Tashbash sat down on the threshold and took his yellow prayer beads out of his pocket. His long face was sullen as he scanned the crowd.

"Well, brothers," he began, "have you decided?"

"We have, Tashbash," called a voice from the back of the crowd, that of Gümüshoglu. "This is a matter of life and death."

"We cannot be cheated out of our rights any longer," cried another. "They've dipped their bread into our blood and sucked us dry."

"We must all go to the Muhtar together," continued Tashbash. "If we don't stand as one man, then he will crush us. We mustn't break the front."

"Never," they all cried.

"Will each one of you swear on the honour of his wife?"

"Yes, yes," the excited villagers cried.

Then Lone Duran started to speak. He was proud that his house had been chosen for the meeting.

"We must choose two spokesmen to plead our cause well. A Muhtar, they'll say, should be a father to the villagers, as was your father the Headman Hidir. But you have joined forces with that cuckold, Batty Bekir, and the two of you receive bribes from the owners of the most barren cotton fields to get us to work there. While other villagers gather a hundred kilos each a day, our people hardly make twenty-five. While other villagers return home with bags of money, we cannot even pay back what we owe Adil Effendi. Have you no heart, no conscience? Whatever bribe you get, we're ready to give you as much, but if you turn us down then we shall choose a field for ourselves. We'll never set foot in a field rented by that Batty Bekir again. . . . That's how they shall speak and we must stand firm behind them so they will not be afraid."

"Duran has spoken well," said Tashbash. "Let's choose two men. But who? They must be strong and fearless."

"Let one of them be Long Ali." Duran's voice was trembling with excitement. "He was the first to discover that the Muhtar and Batty Bekir were cheating us and were having their palms greased by the plantation owners. And for the past five years he has talked himself hoarse to get this truth into our brainless heads. We couldn't find a better man."

They all agreed.

"And I propose Lone Duran as the second man," said Tashbash. "He speaks like a politician."

Long Ali had been sitting a little apart from the others, listening dreamily. He straightened up now.

"No turning tail when the time comes," he said. "No retreating into a safe corner leaving us to face the music!"

Köstüoglu sprang up, his large body quivering with excitement. "We've agreed to repudiate our wives if . . . We can't turn back. This is how it behoves us, effendis."

They all laughed.

"That Muhtar of ours," said Tashbash, "is the devil incarnate. He has a thousand tricks up his sleeve. It won't be easy to get the better of him, and we should all realise that he'll do everything to browbeat us. To begin with, let me tell you, he'll denounce us to the aghas of the Chukurova. He'll accuse us of rising up against our good aghas, our government, our nation. . . . He won't let the plantation owners hire us. Yes, that scoundrel will stop at nothing. He'll work them up against us and we may not get a cotton field to pick this year. Brothers, can you see this through? If you can, then victory is ours. Next year we shall be able to choose the field we like. And with Old Halil to tell us when the cotton's ripe, we'll be down and working on the cotton before the other villages even get wind of it."

They all looked at each other solemnly, sitting with their hands held stiffly on their knees as if attending some ceremony.

Old Halil cleared his throat. This was his chance.

"Yes, he poked fun at me, that mangy son of the Headman Hidir," he began, speaking very quickly, "that crooked Sefer whom you have to address as Effendi now. Why, you scum, I said to him, just like that, that father of yours was headman of this village thanks to me. Times have changed indeed that a man like you can make light of me. You ought to be ashamed of yourself, robbing a whole village and scheming with a worthless fellow whose wife is the whore of this village. You'd better follow my advice and mend your ways or you'll get into real trouble with the villagers. I didn't get this white beard at the flour-mill."

Old Halil was in high form when Tashbash broke in: "Not one of you must breathe a word of this business until Ali speaks to the Muhtar on our way to the Chukurova. Not before!"

"We won't," they all cried.

Old Halil was writhing with annoyance, but he checked his impulse to hurl curses at Tashbash.

"This year, as usual," he declared, "I took the whirling thistle to him and said: I've seen a flock of them bound for Mount Tekech. And what do you think? He dared to jeer at me! Why you son of a bitch, I said, you bastard of a cuckold, may I see my wife dead before . . ."

There was a roar of laughter, for Old Halil's wife had been in her grave these many years.

Old Halil was incensed. "What are you laughing at, you whelps?" he glowered. The tendons in his scraggy neck had swollen and stood out thick as fingers. "Let me tell you this.

I took the thistle to the Muhtar long ago. Mark my words, you're late this year and don't shove the blame on me. It's been a fortnight now since I told him the cotton was ready. Muhtar, I said, don't trifle with me, don't trifle with the villagers. Give the signal to go. But he wouldn't listen. An old dotard, that's what he called me! I've grown old, there's no denying it, and that's why I can't walk down to the Chukurova this year. But I'll never go wrong about cotton picking time so long as there are whirling thistles on this plateau."

The others were arguing excitedly and not listening to him. He cast a glance at Ali. But Ali was not paying attention to him either.

"It's a bad business," sighed Güdük Murtaza, a small thin man in ragged clothes. "Suppose Sefer Effendi persuades the Chukurova aghas not to give us a field. What shall we do this winter? What about our debts? Adil Effendi will flay us alive."

"Let him," cried a new sullen voice, "we'll pay him back next year, plus interest."

Old Halil was quivering with exasperation as he attempted with one or two well-rounded curses to draw attention to himself.

"When I see the whirling thistle in the sky . . ." he began several times. He raised his voice and shouted: "For thirty years now, have I ever been proved wrong? When the whirling thistles come knocking at my door, when I see them spinning in the sky towards Mount Tekech, then I know that the cotton fields of the Chukurova are as white as if it had snowed and the cotton owners are looking out for the arrival of the labourers. Why don't you give the signal to the villagers, I asked the Muhtar. They'll starve because of you. That was a fortnight ago. So you see, it's all his fault. He grabbed my arm and said: If you tell the villagers, I'll denounce you to the police as a sorcerer dealing night and day with the devil, as a recidivist, a deserter from the Yemen wars, as a bandit from Aslan Agha's gang. I'll get a warrant for your arrest and have you thrown into the Adana[1] dungeon, and then to the rope with you."

There was a lull in the discussion and his voice rose above the others.

"Uncle Halil," Lone Duran interrupted him, "for heaven's sake cut it short and let us talk in peace. We've come here to discuss vital business and there you go prattling on."

Old Halil was nettled.

"Prattling on! You snivelling whelp, isn't my talk as good as anyone's? Instead of stopping me you'd much better open those ass ears of yours and listen to worldly-wise Old Halil. You think you've become somebody because the villagers are meeting in your house, but you're just a filthy . . ."

Some of the villagers came to Lone Duran's rescue.

"Oh, lay off, Uncle Halil," they protested. "We've got serious business to discuss."

Old Halil was disconcerted. "There then, I'm not talking any more," he muttered in an offended tone. "Go on, don't listen to me. We'll see who'll be the loser!" He withdrew into a corner in a childish huff.

Kümbetoglu had said nothing during the whole meeting. As everyone had put in a word, he felt he had to talk too.

"If they won't give us work, then we'll go to Tevfik Bey, the Party leader in the town. 'Didn't we give you our honourable votes, we'll say. Well, see now how your people are being treated by the Muhtar and the great aghas of the Chukurova!"

This started off a heated argument as to whether Tevfik Bey would side with the Muhtar or with the villagers. In the end they decided that if Tevfik Bey had a shred of sense—and no one doubted but that he was a well of wisdom, or how could he have been elected president of the Party branch—he would support the villagers.

Old Halil could stand his enforced silence no longer. "Don't

---

[1] County seat and principal town of the Chukurova cotton plain (Cilicia).

you see what a wretched state I'm in, you infidels?" he exploded at last. "You'll listen to me now and if anyone interrupts me I'll gouge his eyes hollow. How am I to get down to the Chukurova, that's what I keep thinking. My legs won't bear me any longer. How am I to walk? Muhtar, I said, you can't treat me like this, and as for the villagers they won't let themselves be stripped by you. If you can't find a horse for me, you, the powerful Muhtar, you, the man of the Government, then the villagers will. They can even get me a huge train, if they wish. They'll bring the train right up to this village and say, here you are Uncle Halil, get in!"

"What a whopper, Uncle Halil," cried Tashbash. "How can the villagers bring a train into these mountains?"

Old Halil's beard quivered. Still, he felt better now everyone was listening to him.

"They can too," he shouted, "once the villagers set their minds on something, you can't stop them. See here, Tashbash, don't you play the fool with me, or I'll tell how your father's bloody carcass was dragged around by hounds like a jackal's. Don't make me open my mouth now! Yes, I said to the Muhtar: Your father the Headman Hidir, may his bones rattle in their grave for having borne such a son, would heed the villagers' every wish. He'd look after the sick and the aged. And to me he would always say, Halil, you're a saint, the only true Moslem in this village. One day the bandits fell upon us. They were after Hidir, but I hid him in my house. No bandit ever dared even raise his eyes on my door. And that's how Hidir escaped being killed. You've saved my life, Halil Agha, he said to me, how can I ever repay you? And I replied, It's nothing Hidir, you're the headman of this huge village. . . . At that time, neither the Muhtar nor any of you had even been born. There was only Ismet Pasha and Abdulaziz Pasha in this world. At that time I had horses, ten of them. But we never went down to the Chukurova then to pick other people's cotton. At that time

I was in the prime of youth. Do you think I was like this then?"

He paused. Everyone was listening to him. Some were laughing outright, some winking at each other, but still they were listening.

"So I said to the Muhtar, don't touch the villagers or they'll make pulp out of you. I am the Old Halil of this village. I've grown weak, but I've lived more years than anyone's grandfather. If you're the Muhtar, if you're a man, then find me a horse. If you don't, your reputation won't be worth a kurush, for the villagers will bring a train right up to this village for me, and if not a train, then they'll find a horse, and if not a horse then a donkey. . . ."

Tashbash could not help interrupting again: "If not a donkey then a colt, and if not a colt then a greyhound. Now suppose we can't find a greyhound, what then, Uncle Halil?"

"Shut up!" shouted Old Halil, his face purple. "I shit right into your dead father's mouth! If they can't find even a donkey, then the youths will carry me by turns on their backs. Do you hear, Tashbash, you son of a whore? And there's Long Ali Effendi, the son of my dear dead friend. He wouldn't ever leave his Uncle Halil in the lurch. . . . Yes, Tashbash, I know every dirty detail past and present of your family, dogs every one of them. This isn't the moment to . . . I remember times when you came to kiss my arse. . . ."

"What a parcel of whopping lies," laughed Tashbash, "shame on your white beard! Now, don't you go and blab to the Muhtar about this meeting or I'll light a match to that beard of yours and burn it till you're like a plucked chicken."

Old Halil sprung up convulsed with rage and lunged out at Tashbash with his stick. The others, who were splitting their sides with laughter, managed to stop him just in time. The old man gave a long look at Aii and then stalked off in high dudgeon.

It seemed they were all firmly decided to go through with this business, come what might. However, Ali and Tashbash still had their doubts. It had been this way for the past three years, but each time the villagers had let themselves be won over by the Muhtar and had deserted Ali and Tashbash.

"Do you think they'll turn tail again?" mused Ali.

"Well, after all, they've sworn a solemn oath on the honour of their wives," said Tashbash.

"I hope to goodness no one will tell the Muhtar."

"Someone's sure to. If no one does, then that old dog will tell."

"Uncle Halil would never do that, I'm sure," protested Ali.

"Who called him to the meeting? Did you?"

"No. He must have got wind of it and just come by himself."

"Well, he did talk! How he buttered the villagers."

Ali shook his head. He sighed deeply. "The devil take old age," he said.

Chapter 3

They all rose long before dawn that day.

Tugging at his *shalvar* trousers Ali went to the dark stable, calling to his wife for a light. He saw that the horse had eaten only a few mouthfuls of the fodder and hay that he had given it the night before. He picked up the nosebag, filled it and handed it to his wife who was holding the torch of resinwood. Then he untied the horse and led it out of the stable.

Outside, in the twilight, the horse stood like a long gaunt phantom. Ali brought the saddle. It was a Circassian saddle that had come with the horse eighteen years ago. Then the horse's coat had glistened like polished silver. How had such a fine horse ever come to this humble home? This was something no one knew except Meryemdje and Old Halil. Whenever the old man set eyes on the horse, he would heave deep sighs. "Ah, my stupid head!" he would repeat. But now the horse was so old and lean that the comb stuck to its bones whenever Ali tried to curry it, and right in the middle of its back was a sore that would not heal. The Circassian saddle was in worse condition than the horse, with no leather left to speak of, its feather stuffing almost all gone, its frame standing out bare. Ali settled the saddle firmly on the horse's back and tied it securely with embroidered braiding made of goat hair. He then placed the bedding on top of it.

The village was awake now, in a ferment. Köstüoglu could be heard swearing in his house. Nearby a baby was whining continuously, a sick man was moaning. Dogs barked, a horse neighed and one or two donkeys started braying. The Muhtar's voice rang out above all the din.

The Wind from the Plain

Ali finished loading the horse and then lifted his mother on to it.

"Give me the girl too, my Ali," she said.

Ali hesitated, glancing at the horse's sagging legs.

The first streaks of dawn were about to break out in the east. Soon the crests of the distant mountains would pale with light.

"The horse is in bad shape, Mother," he said. "The girl can walk this year. She's grown up now."

Meryemdje pursed her lips. "What difference would a small child make!"

"Is everything in order?" Ali called to his wife. "Have you locked the door?"

"I'm ready," she replied.

The clattering of tin cans now rose above all the other noises. This meant that the villagers were on the move at last, leaving their village behind devoid of all human life, save for Spellbound Ahmed who, mad with love, roamed along secret paths in the mountains around. As the tail of the column emerged from the village, the noise suddenly diminished to a murmur, broken only by the occasional twitter of birds, the tramp of feet and the clink of cans and copper vessels tied to the donkeys.

Winding up the column was Lone Duran. He would always be the last one to leave the village as they set off for the Chukurova and the first to enter it as they returned.

The sun rose and hung over the village. A north wind was blowing and the dust stirred up by the horses, donkeys, oxen, goats and human beings spread in a cloud over the grey steppe. The caravan was advancing in great haste as if fleeing before a monster.

Lone Duran turned round towards the village.

"Hey," he shouted. "The village is out of sight!" It was his habit to give the news every year.

For a moment there was no sound. Then the din of voices

31

suddenly broke out again. Life flowed into the road. Long Ali pulled his pipe from his belt and started to play a lively skipping tune that made a man want to dance on the spot.

Ali was tall and very thin. His thick black eyebrows stood out in his narrow pale face and his chin was pointed like a woman's. His *shalvar* trousers and shirt were faded with wear. He was bending under the weight of the pack he carried wrapped in a goat-hair cloth.

He was proud of his horse and for years the entire household had gloried in it. As it grew old, Ali and the villagers had jokingly nicknamed it Küheylan, the Arab courser. It was now a very tall, rambling, camel-like horse whose legs would get entangled with one another as it stumbled along and this provoked hilarity among the villagers. Ali took the whole thing in good part.

"Hey, my thoroughbred, my young Küheylan! The brigand Köroglu himself never owned a horse like you. Hey, my sprightly wild-maned courser, bringing joy and good luck to our home! Heeey!"

An elderly woman, who was trudging along ahead of them, turned round and, shading her eyes, gazed at the horse.

"Good luck indeed! Very likely, the way you've loaded the poor creature. You'll meet with your good luck soon enough."

"Bless your sweet dreamy soul, Zaladja Woman," laughed Ali, as he played a few mocking notes on his pipe. "Did you see the horse's fate in your dreams? But this isn't a young swain to dream about, it's only an old horse, my beauteous Zaladja!"

This sally drew delighted giggles from a group of young girls who were walking barefooted, their young breasts swelling through their bodices.

Towards nightfall, leaving behind the bare highland, the caravan reached the foothills of the Taurus mountains and came to a stop in a wooded glen, where, beneath a cluster of lofty oak trees, was the Gurgling Fount, a spring surrounded by fragrant beds of mint. This would always be their first halt on the journey.

The village started to settle down for the night. Fires were lit and the bulgur wheat set to cook in large pans. The moon was setting behind the tall rustling oaks. The burning wet wood hissed and crackled, its pungent smell mingling with that of the mint.

Ali had unloaded under a plane-tree and had lit a large fire around which the two children were huddling, warming themselves. Meryemdje stood beside the horse, stroking its neck and trying to coax it into eating a little. Elif had balanced the cauldron of bulgur on three large stones she had placed over the fire.

A figure hovered on the fringe of the firelight. Ali could not make out who it was.

"Who's that?" he cried out.

There was no reply.

"What's it to you whether a body stands there or not?" said Meryemdje. "If he had something to say, he'd come up."

Ali peered into the gloom. "Why Uncle Halil!" he exclaimed. "What's the matter with you? Why don't you come and sit by the fire?"

Resting on his stick Old Halil advanced slowly towards the fire. Ali spread the goat-hair cloth on the ground for him.

"Sit down, Uncle Halil," he said softly.

The old man looked surprised. "Shall I, my child?" he asked as he sat down drawing his knees up to his chest. The light of the flames fell on his white beard, turning it to copper.

Meryemdje promptly drew away from the horse and sat down forbiddingly opposite the old man.

In the bright light of the fires the forest was like the teeming mouth of an ant-hole. Even the rustling of the trees had a different sound now that the village had camped there.

Old Halil had locked his hands under his beard and was staring straight before him into the flames. The others fixed their eyes on the fire too, each longing for someone to start talking. Meryemdje was chafing. Finally she could stand it no longer.

"My son," she said sharply, "you should know that the horse is dying."

Old Halil's beard trembled as he turned his head slowly towards Meryemdje and fixed his eyes on her.

"The poor thing hasn't eaten for three days," Meryemdje pursued inexorably.

Ali picked up a twig and started scraping the earth. Elif watched this silent struggle, feeling crushed. She knew that, whatever happened, Meryemdje would never relent.

"Think, Ali, think what will happen to us if our horse dies . . ." Meryemdje insisted.

Old Halil stroked his beard nervously as he spoke at last in a voice full of reproach.

"Doesn't Old Halil know how you came by the horse, eh, Meryemdje? Tell me, doesn't he?"

This was a stone cast at Meryemdje and she had no answer.

Ali kept raking the earth with his twig. Why did his mother hate the old man so, he wondered. It must be something rankling from the past, some grievance of long ago.

Meryemdje waited, unbending as a rock. As the silence of mother and son remained unbroken, Old Halil's anger rose and the veins of his neck swelled. He tugged at his beard and sucked his fingers. Suddenly he sprang to his feet with the agility of youth.

"Listen to me, Meryemdje! He who owns a horse and a field, he who lies in silk, he who tosses on a dry bed, he who drinks bird's milk, the ant on the earth, the bird in the sky, even you, even I, everything will go down into this black earth and become dust. Do you hear, Meryemdje?" He turned his back on them and wandered off.

Ali followed him with his eyes. The old man was making a big effort to walk quickly, but he was limping badly. Who knows, thought Ali, how tired he must be, how his feet are swollen, how his knees must crackle. Poor old man, last year he had

walked down to the Chukurova until there was only one more
day to go. Then he had not been able to take another step. So
Ali had made him ride Küheylan. How pleased he had been,
looking down at him from the horse with brimming eyes. But
Meryemdje had raged and made life impossible for them all.

"Do you remember those days, Ali? Ah, confound this old
age. . . . Your father and I would go down to the Chukurova and
bring back sack upon sack of water-melons, enough for us and
for all the village. Do you remember those days, my Ali? One
night your father and I were returning to the village with a load
of stolen cotton, and hot on our heels was the overseer of the
cotton field. He was riding a horse but still he couldn't catch up
with us! Yes, my Ali, the Osmanlis should draft all the old people
and send them into the Yemen desert. Rather than grow old, a
man should go off to die in the Yemen. Isn't that so, my Ali?
Once it was raining in torrents. Floods had overrun the cotton
fields, washing away the beds and pans, the tents and wattle huts.
Who was it saved the villagers from this calamity? Wasn't it
your father and me? And you, Ali, I found you cowering with
cold under a huge mulberry tree, up to your waist in water, your
teeth locked so you couldn't open your mouth. I took off your
wet clothes and held you close to my body to warm your limbs.
Do you remember? And then I carried you in my arms running
all the way to the nearest village, and there I made you drink
some hot tea. Do you remember Ali? You were very small then,
five or six years old. My beard was already as white as it is now,
but no one could have called me old. . . . Even if we have a horse,
a field and property, even if we drink of bird's milk, we shall all
become one with the earth, mingled with the dust. So will you,
so shall I. . . . When your father was alive, do you remember, my
Ali, how you used to steal juicy peaches for me from the distant
orchards?"

Ali's eyes filled with tears.

The fires grew smaller and smaller as the flames foundered,

35

studding the forest like stars. The camp was buried in a deep silence, broken only by an occasional snore, the crying of a baby or the wheezing of a horse.

Ali could not sleep. He tossed about listening to the sounds of the forest and watching the dying embers. He could not place the ache he felt somewhere within him.

Shortly after midnight a cock crowed. Ali rose and went to the horse. Its head was hanging and the nose-bag filled to the brim with fodder and straw touched the ground. He stroked its rump. There was not an ounce of flesh there. Küheylan had become all skin and bones. Groping his way in the dark, Ali gathered some grass from the forest and threw it before the horse, but it made no move to eat. Ali took hold of its head and thrust it into the grass, but still there was no reaction from the horse. Then he pried its mouth open and pushed a handful of grass into it. The horse did not even move its jaws. Ali gave it an angry push.

"Eat poison," he cried. "Eat poison and die, *inshallah*! And let me be. . . ."

Since that evening he had been boiling over, not knowing on whom to vent his rage. He went back to his bed.

This was the third time in his life that he was unable to sleep. The first time was during the flood, out of fear and cold. The second time was the night his father died.

Chapter 4

In the hush that falls before the break of dawn, when the gurgle of water springing from the fountain-head grows louder and mingles with the soughing of the trees, Ali rose from his bed and went over to the horse. The fresh grass he had placed before it the night before was untouched. He gave it a kick that sent the blades to settle in shreds on the bushes. A woodpecker flashed out of the trees and was gone. Birds were chirping in the distance. He could smell the scent of pine-resin, and the sharp fragrance of wild mint borne on the early morning breeze.

Elif was gathering up the bedding and the pans. Ali eyed the horse for a while, then he strapped the sacks of bulgur wheat and flour against its flanks, clapped the bedding on to the Circassian saddle and fastened some of the pots and pans to it.

New sounds filled the forest now. The rustling of its trees and the murmur of the spring were drowned in the hubbub of the awakening camp. As the dawn broke a flight of screeching birds sailed over from the east. A green haze settled over the woods and the air was suddenly laden with the odour of rotting bark.

Ali pulled the horse towards a low stump. Meryemdje stepped on it and he propped her up. She took the reins and drew herself up proudly. Then setting spurs to the horse, she rode on along the narrow forest path. A little farther down a man was beating a donkey and at the same time trying to hoist the pack that had fallen off its back. They were blocking the way and Meryemdje swung into a by-path among the trees to avoid them. Ahead of her the road was clear.

Far, very far, a mountain peak wrapped in mist was turning blue.

The children came next followed by their mother. Ali was the last to set out. As he plodded under the weight of his load, his eyes never left the horse's legs. When it stumbled, his face darkened. When it broke into a trot, he brightened up. The smell of wheat filled his nostrils. Vast fields of close-growing ripe wheat undulated before his eyes, the blazing light of the sun fusing with the golden ears.

He turned and smiled at his Cousin Veli who was walking beside him.

"Why, man, you're dreaming awake," cried Veli. "I've been walking beside you for the past half-hour and you never gave me so much as a glance. What's the matter?"

"Nothing," said Ali. "How's Fatma?"

"Don't ask!" replied Veli. "She hasn't opened her eyes since we left the village. What do you think it is? You've seen many sick people during your army service. What do you say, Ali?"

"What can one say?" sighed Ali.

Batty Bekir rode past them at a rapid pace, looking straight before him.

"There goes that snake-in-the-grass," muttered Ali. "Run on, you bedevilled old crook! Go and find us a field of cotton in bloom if you can!"

"Let him run, the cuckold," said Veli. "He doesn't know what the villagers have in store for him."

"He knows well enough," retorted Ali. "But he's counting on the Muhtar and doesn't care a damn about the villagers."

"Well, he'll see!" cried Veli. He stopped. "Fatma's behind. I must go and see if she's all right. I just caught up with you for a little chat. Farewell!"

The village moved on along the road in a long straggling column. The old women wore the customary long blue skirts of their age. The middle-aged ones had white headcloths bound over their heads. Those with the gold- and silver-embroidered little fezzes cocked over their braided hair were the married women. The young girls had tied their hair in bright coloured kerchiefs. They all trekked along, their bare feet leaving an intricate tracery on the white dust of the road. The men advanced in little groups, talking to one another and the children gambolled on the roadside.

When the sun rose, a maze of shadows darkened the road. Hasan held out his hands chafed by the cold for his father to see. "I'm glad the sun's up at last," he said. He was just seven years old.

Ali took no heed of him.

" What a sunrise it is!" insisted the child.

Ali did not reply. He was sick of looking at the horse's legs. Three of the hooves were bare and the fourth had only a piece of broken iron on it. For years Ali had wanted to have it shod, but he had never been able to manage it. He pressed forward, leaving the horse behind.

They were now out of the forest and going downhill into a grey treeless valley. Old Halil was leaning heavily on his stick as he hobbled along painfully. Now and again he opened his mouth wide and took in a deep gasping breath. Ali slowed down, anxiously wondering if he could find a way of slipping past without the old man seeing him, but Old Halil kept losing speed.

"Why are you lagging behind?" someone asked Ali. "Are you hurt?"

Ali pulled a wry face. "There's a pain in my side," he said as he doubled up.

His mother rode past. Then his wife. These villagers are a pack of infidels, he raged inwardly. Godless and faithless, all of them. Look at that old man's plight! How can anyone stand it? Damn this order of things, damn this life! He clenched his teeth.

By the time Old Halil reached the bottom of the valley the

rest of the caravan had climbed the opposite slope and was clearing the summit.

Ali sat down, darkly brooding. There's nothing, nothing I can do, he said to himself. The horse is sick, and there's only a dog's chance it'll get my mother down to the Chukurova. If I let the old man ride it as well, it's just looking for trouble. Damn it all, what are other people's concerns to me?

He sprang up and ran past Old Halil, trying to ignore the old man's wondering, pitiful stare. Half-way up the slope he stopped and turned round. Old Halil was hunched up over his stick, gazing after him. Suddenly Ali spurted on like a man possessed. The tiny wrinkled eyes were boring through his back like gimlets. Blindly butting into man and beast, he caught up with his mother, grabbed the horse's head and swung it around. His face was dark as thunder. He left the stunned Meryemdje there, holding the reins in her trembling hands, ran down to Old Halil and taking him by the arm almost dragged him up the slope. Then he hoisted the old man up behind his mother. Meryemdje flung the reins down in fury. Ali picked them up and thrust them harshly back into her hands. Then holding the horse by the head, he tugged it forward so savagely that the animal almost toppled over.

"What a good fellow our Ali is!" exclaimed the villagers when they had caught up with the rest of the caravan. "May Allah turn everything he touches into gold!"

"What a sweat you're in, Father," Hasan said, "and you've gone and put Old Halil on the horse too. Suppose it dies, what will Granny say?"

"Let it die!" thundered Ali. He spat on the ground.

They passed Tekkale and reached Serchelik. One of the worst stages of the journey was ahead of them for the road there dwindled into a narrow path studded with small sharp rocks through which they had to thread their way painstakingly.

Ever since Old Halil had mounted the horse Meryemdje had

kept up a steady muttering and now that the horse entered this rocky path she raised her voice so that Old Halil could hear every word she was saying.

"Don't come, brother. If you can't walk, if you're so weak, just don't come. Each year you have to ride our horse! Is it for me that you pick cotton? No, you pick it and that snivelling thing you call your son plasters it over his woman's fat hips so she should grow fatter and please the village youths still more! Don't come, you filthy-bearded pander! How my Ibrahim suffered at your hands. . . . Don't come, you ill-omened owl, you green-eyed dry toad, you dead snail. Don't come, since that whelp of a son of yours hasn't even been able to provide you with a little donkey. Stay in the village. No one's taken you by the hand and begged you to come. But you must come all the same, you accursed hog, and then, wailing that your legs can't support you, you must ride someone else's moribund horse. Why don't you go and ride on your son's back, you old muckworm? What you did to my Ibrahim . . . sullying his pure name . . . Haven't you any conscience? Haven't you thought that, if this beast drops dead under the weight of two persons, the poor lad will be stranded in these mountains with his mother, wife and children? Bah, you unscrupulous snake-in-the-grass! You've made our life one long stretch of misery. How could people know? I know. . . ."

Old Halil was chewing the tip of his beard in his toothless gums, itching to knock Meryemdje off the horse. And a good thing if she broke her neck, he thought, but what if she doesn't die? She'll tell everybody I pushed her off the horse. . . . It would mean prison for me.

He decided to ignore her and gazed at the soft blue mountains capped with shining violet clouds, trying to conjure up happy times of the past. The blue mountains, he said, the white clouds. . . . The blue-green and orange slopes of the Kusuk defile. . . . On this very road, long ago . . . It was no use. He could not shut out the continuous drone of Meryemdje's curses. He chewed

at his beard still more vehemently. A craggy mountain crest . . .
The men of Usurgan would go deer-hunting there, and there
were many who never returned. Yes, deer-hunting is a bad business, Allah protect us. On that mountain crest is a tall rock, three
times as high as the minaret in the Adana market-place. Its
surface is like marble and each spring the white rock blooms with
flowers, and over it the great eagles soar. . . .

The horse floundered and Meryemdje's voice rose to a higher
pitch.

"These vicious old drivellers! Spoiling everybody's peace
and quiet, the pests! The world won't thrive with them around.
But they will cling to it for dear life, as though people had any
use for them!"

Old Halil looked wistfully at the forest below. It was their
second halting place and the caravan would enter it late in the
afternoon. We should be getting nearer, he thought, but somehow the forest seems to be shifting away. The forest is cruel, just
like people, like Meryemdje. . . . How far it is, and receding
farther and farther all the time. But I smell a familiar, slightly
bitter scent, akin to wild mint, pines, mountain streams and
rotten apples. A very ancient smell, wafting gently. . . . Does
it come from the past, from a dream? God damn you, Meryemdje!
Shut your mouth a little and let me have some peace. Ah, if
there were someone to give me a smoke now! If only Meryemdje
would stop her jabbering. . . .

Ali came up to them. "Are you all right?" he asked softly.

Meryemdje did not answer.

"Bless you, Ali, my child," said Old Halil warmly, "may you
never see evil days."

Chapter 5

The Muhtar rode at the head of the caravan, swaggering on his black, perky-eared three-year-old donkey. His cap was askew with the peak slanting over his right ear. His two wives walked behind him in a respectful attitude, their eyes fixed on his broad shoulders, never once glancing at each other.

Köstüoglu was the first to catch up with the Muhtar. He started walking abreast of the donkey. Soon after, Lone Duran joined him and then Veli, Osmandja, Tashbash and Long Ali. Before long a group of thirty to forty had surrounded the Muhtar.

He scanned the crowd with a mocking smile. "What's this, Köstüoglu?" he asked composedly.

"Nothing, Muhtar Agha. . . ."

"Damn you and your Muhtar Agha!" muttered Tashbash.

Ali stepped forward resolutely. "Muhtar," he said, "I'm speaking for all the others. The long and the short of this business is that we've decided not to pick cotton in the field Batty Bekir has chosen for us. We've taken our oath on that."

The Muhtar's face changed colour at Ali's determined tone, but the mocking smile never left his lips as he turned to Köstüoglu. "Have you taken the oath too?" he asked derisively.

Köstüoglu was flustered. "Allah forbid! With all due respect to our Agha . . . What can I say? . . . It's like this. . . ."

Köstüoglu was a large, thick-set man. He had never worn shoes in his life. During his army service it had turned out that no size would fit him, so special shoes had been ordered for him.

But when it had come to wearing them, Köstüoglu had refused to take a single step. He had stood there as if fettered to the ground, his legs apart, shouting for help. Try as they would, the military had been unable to make him budge an inch with his shoes on. In the end they had allowed him to go barefooted for the rest of his term.

The Muhtar turned to Ali. "You're at the bottom of this, Ali. You've been hatching this business for the past five years and now you've egged on all the others. But do you think I don't know what you really have in mind, all of you? No one has forgotten the exhibition Lone Duran made of himself three years ago down there in the cotton field, in plain sight of everybody. I'll have you know that the business of a village cannot be conducted in keeping with your lewd pursuits. You want a field that has banks and ditches, shrubs and trees and convenient hiding places, eh? And truly this is shameful! And truly, in plain sight of everyone . . . it's indecent!"

"You're making all this up, Muhtar," retorted Ali firmly, "but no matter what you say, we're going to pick the field we choose. That's how all the villagers want it. We're not obliged . . ."

"Of course you're obliged," shouted the Muhtar, "do you expect the owner of the field to grow shrubs and trees on the level plain of the Chukurova? Is he to invent, especially for you, a strain of cotton that yields a thousand to one? And then plant a whole field of it? Just to please you? . . ." He choked with rage.

"That's not what we're talking about, Muhtar," Ali went on doggedly. "Batty Bekir is a bad man. Anyone can buy him off, and the next thing we know we find ourselves working in a field that hardly has a boll to a plant. His only care is to fill his own pockets."

For some reason the Muhtar controlled himself and spoke in a persuasive tone.

"Look here, Ali, don't try to fool me. You don't really care about how much cotton you pick. All you have in mind is that

44

fornication business. For that you'd let your children die of hunger."

Someone laughed.

"Oh, come off it, Muhtar! Why should we want to do that like bitches in the middle of an open field?"

"I know you never think of anything else," roared the Muhtar. "Well, think of your children a little for a change."

"Muhtar," said Ali, "it's because our children are precious to us that we have to make good money this year. Come, be on our side and let Bekir go. A Muhtar should stand by his villagers."

The Muhtar saw that he would have to change his tactics. He glared down at the crowd, cleared his throat and began: "Friends! My honourable village comrades! And, in truth, my good patriots! And, in truth, my very own lovers of Democracy. I have come here into your presence to say a few words to you!"

"Hear, hear!" Tashbash jeered, "now he's giving us Tevfik Bey's election technique, confound him! He's at it again, the old schemer."

"He's at it again!" echoed Osmandja.

"Where there is no Democracy, there can be no well-being for the people, and where there is no Unity of Speech, there can be no harmony, my friends. So heed me well! Don't follow Long Ali's lead for he's an enemy of Democracy and you'll all be committing a black sin in the eyes of the Government if you do. And truly, even I will not be able to save you. Disobedience to a Muhtar! Think of it! You all know what a clever man Bekir Agha is, sharp as a needle, wise in the ways of this world. During the war, his German friends said to him, Bekir, they said, if all the soldiers of the Turkish army were like you, this nation would conquer the world. No army could resist, neither the Germans nor the English. Which of us knows better than Bekir Agha how to speak to the Beys of the Chukurova, who can outwit them better than he? If other villagers are paid ten kurush a kilo, we get eleven. So we make a profit and all thanks to Bekir Agha.

Compatriots and beloved villagers, you who have from the very first given your hearts to Democracy, I warn you, it's a deadly sin to go against democracy. For that a man can burn right in the very core of hell! And truly, it is an intolerable thing to remain there in the flames of hell!"

Tashbash leaned towards Osmandja.

"The old fox is now aping the Imam from Karatopak, damn him. May he drop into the bottom of hell himself with his claptrap!"

"And truly, my fine friends . . ." The Muhtar had worked himself into a devastating rage. He jumped off the donkey and stamped his foot.

"Now he's imitating Captain Ali, the Kurd! Look at that pose!"

"Pose or not, he'll get what he wants," replied Osmandja, "you'll see!" Tashbash's face fell.

"You blockheads!" the Muhtar began anew, "it's clod you have in your heads, not brains, and arid worthless clod at that! All you do is prowl about ready to drop your pants! Damn you, can't you control yourselves for two months? Damn you, do it every day if you like when we return to the village. Get it into your heads that we're going there to work, not to fool around. Where do you want poor Bekir Agha to find you a field with ditches and hedges and running water? Control yourselves for a while!" He thrust his finger at Ali. "And truly, my friend, I'll not let you lead my villagers astray. Take your woman and go off to the seashore and loaf about to your heart's content." He raised his voice to a shrill pitch. The whole caravan fell silent. "There's plenty of water and shade for you there, but no cotton. Go there and starve to death. Yes, clear out of this village! Hey, watchman, come here! Proclaim this. It's an order of the village council. Ali Uzundja, born in 1922, son of Ibrahim and of Meryemdje, is to be banished from this village as soon as we get down to the plain. Since he holds our village in contempt . . ."

He turned and pointed accusingly at the crowd. "If there are any of you who hold our beautiful village in contempt, let them pack off right away. And truly, all those who don't like the field Bekir Agha chooses for us, and truly, all those who commit treason against our village, who defy our Government, who hurt our Democracy. Yes, it is because of these Long Alis that Democracy has come to grief. And in truth, they are the tools of that old dictator, of that Ismet Pasha!"

Ali was shaking with exasperation. Tashbash held his arm. "No use saying anything now, Ali. His dogs are ready to pick up a fight. And most of the villagers are besotted by his pretty phrases again."

The Muhtar sensed that victory was his. He stamped his foot again. "Listen, my countrymen, thanks to me and to the constant efforts of Bekir Agha, you've been blessed with the best cotton fields of the Chukurova and each year you've earned pots of money. How dare you say the contrary?" He stamped his foot again forcefully.

"Curse the man!" said Tashbash loudly, "he's going to break his foot. What a temper!"

The Muhtar pretended he had not heard. He usually avoided clashing with Tashbash, for the latter had important friends and relatives in the town.

"Ungrateful wretches! You dare accuse Bekir and me of taking money from the cotton owners? Do we look as if we needed bribes? And truly by the will of almighty Allah, this Bekir Agha's been a boon to us."

"Boon indeed! A worse bane . . ." Ali began, but Tashbash put his hand on his mouth.

"Hush," he said. "These matters can't be settled like this."

"Watchman!" bellowed the Muhtar.

The watchman stepped forward and stood to attention like a soldier.

"Watchman, when we get down to the Chukurova, you are

not to allow Long Ali into the field we're going to pick. If you do you'll be committing a crime. I've been Muhtar of this village for twenty years, you dirty sons of Adam, always ready to drop your pants, and I can make life miserable for you in the Chukurova. Don't drive me beyond endurance or I'll see to it that you pick no cotton at all, you traitors. Now be off with you!"

"Well!" said Tashbash, "how he has pelted us with his 'and trulies'. You'd think he was the Imam of the Great Mosque. But he's capable of playing any dirty trick on us, Ali. Let's hold our peace for the present."

"He's capable of anything!" The word passed around. They were all cowed.

The Muhtar had mounted his donkey and was already off at the head of the caravan.

Old Halil nudged Meryemdje. "Don't worry, sister," he said, hoping to mollify her, "that dog can't do anything to my Ali so long as I'm alive. Upon my word, I'll make mincemeat out of him!"

She only gave him a withering look. "These accursed, filthy old men," she growled with unabated vehemence, "these imbeciles! They don't think . . ." The horse slipped and Meryemdje hung on to the reins. She raised her voice: "Whoa, whoa, you unfortunate horse ridden by a pig carrion, an infidel, a mangy dog!"

A woman was suckling her baby and softly singing a lullaby as she walked on rapidly. The sheen of yellow down on her large breast caught Old Halil's eye. There, he thought, that's how a woman's breast should be. Then, "For shame," he remonstrated with himself, "you're just a doddering old fool!"

"Listen to me, my horse. You can't carry two persons down to the Chukurova. You'll die. Has he no pity at all? Why doesn't he get off now? His beard may be white and his face wrinkled, but he can walk right down to the Chukurova like a lad of twenty when he wants to. . . ."

48

"Gabble on, gabble on," muttered Old Halil, "you can fume and rave as much as you like, but I won't get off. It's the owner of this horse that put me on it. Would I have stood your dirty company if I could help it?"

Huseyin was hobbling beside them. Rabbit Huseyin, that's how they call him. He's still young, but so thin, nothing but skin and bone, and even that will shrivel and drop by the time he gets down to the plain. . . .

Farther away, Mangy Mahmut is resting on a stone scratching himself. He's had the mange for seven years now. If he could only get himself enlisted in the army! . . . They'd cure him there. . . .

And there's poor sick Home-Leave Memet standing in the middle of the road taking a deep breath. For the past nine years he's been trying to complete his army service. But he's been sent home on sick leave so often that he's still not done his term and the villagers have nicknamed him Home-Leave Memet.

What a din the pots and pans are making! And look, there's a long rent in Zaladja Woman's skirt. Her drawers are showing.

"Whoa, you poor horse ridden by an infidel! I've had enough of your stumbling. To think that my Ali's children are getting swollen feet on these rocks, all because of this mucky, lousy-bearded old hound who pretends he's deaf, may Allah pour lead into his ears!"

Meryemdje had become very skilful at tugging in the reins and steadying the horse just when it was on the verge of falling.

"Please don't die, my horse, until we get to the Chukurova! Let that old swine who's sticking to our backs like a leech die instead!"

She stole a glance at Old Halil. His eyes were screwed up and his face more wrinkled than ever. She was satisfied.

"Eh, my horse, this isn't for anyone to hear, only for your ears. If a man sees with his own eyes his daughter-in-law billing and cooing with the Molla's son, and then pretends he hasn't noticed anything, and only for a pound of grapes that the Molla's son gives him not to blab, then may that man be smitten by the wrath of Allah! Yes, my horse, this mucky-bearded old man, whom you're carrying on your back right now, saw his son's wife in an open cotton field, at daybreak, almost in broad daylight, saw her lying under the Molla's son. . . . And what do you think he said? Bless you, he said, good strength to your loins!"

She saw that Old Halil's beard was quivering now.

"Yes, my horse!" she gloated. "That season, the drawers of his daughter-in-law became the flying colours of the cotton field. His son couldn't bear it any longer. But this slimy old pimp forced him to stomach all this just for a pound of grapes. And now this filth is basking at his ease on your back."

Old Halil was chewing the tip of his beard desperately. He was crimson. Suddenly he exploded: "Good people, I'm going to burst! This whore . . ."

Meryemdje slapped the horse's neck. She felt elated. At this rate she would soon drive Old Halil off the horse.

"Burst, *inshallah!* And may your flesh be a prey to the bald vultures circling above us. If you burst this minute, I'll hold a thanksgiving fast for three months and then eat my meals with a mangy dog for three Fridays running."

Old Halil was tearing at his beard. "Meryemdje," he pleaded. "Meryemdje, I'd walk if I only could. I wouldn't listen to your foul words. If you love Allah and your religion, stop it, Meryemdje! Hush, sister!"

Meryemdje half turned, pulling in the reins. "What's that, my man?" she said with feigned surprise, "what's got into you? Can't a body speak to her horse any longer?"

Then she spurred the horse on again.

"Yes, my horse," she continued with relish, "that's how they are, these old pimps. They'd readily go to bed with their own daughter-in-law, if they could only do it. What's more, for two pieces of coloured candy they'd push all the youths of the village on to their daughter-in-law. Yes, and then sit back and watch!"

She stroked the horse's neck affectionately. "You don't believe me, my horse? It's because you don't know these dirty old swine. Don't be deceived by this one's age or his white beard. Instead of picking honest cotton in the Chukurova, he steals it and then gets caught. He's spat upon by everyone in public and swears he won't do it again. Then he does it again and throws all the blame on my Ali's innocent father. . . . And now he has the cheek to ride Ali's horse! And on top of that, he wallows in the muck old Meryemdje heaps on him, and never turns a hair! Why, if I'd said only half as much to a stone, it would have crumbled into pieces!" She stopped the horse. "Are you so thick-skulled? Don't you know when people shit on your beard and dirty it properly?"

Old Halil's agonised cry rent the air. "Ali! Aliii! Come quick and take me off this horse. Aliii! Help!"

His voice was so harrowing that the whole caravan froze for a moment into a dead silence. Ali ran up to the horse.

"For pity's sake, my child, take me down. This old whore's been sucking the very life out of me!"

Ali looked at his mother sternly.

"I didn't do anything at all, Ali," protested Meryemdje, "it's just that I was bored so I thought I'd have a little chat with Küheylan. He seems to have taken it to himself."

"Ali, help me down, for mercy's sake, or I'll jump off and break a bone!"

"Uncle Halil," said Ali soothingly, "Mother wasn't speaking to you, only to the horse." He turned to his mother. "And you, Mother, for heaven's sake, stop talking to the horse!"

"Since our Halil Agha takes offence, then I certainly won't, I promise you. What have I said to my Halil Agha?" She signalled to Ali to come nearer. "The horse is dying," she whispered in his ear, " it can't go on carrying the both of us."

Ali drew away brusquely. "Let it die!" he cried. "At least I'll be delivered. . . ."

Old Halil's eyes filled with tears. Another word and he would have burst out sobbing like a child. Something stuck in his throat, hurting him. His green childish eyes were bitter.

Were you the kind of man to put up with all this, Halil? he thought. This is how it is when wolves grow old. They become the butt not just of dogs, but of bitches like this one. Ah, if only my legs would bear me, if I could only jump off and not have to listen to this serpent. He wanted to beg Ali to take him off, but dared not open his mouth for fear of breaking down.

"Don't fret, Uncle," said Ali, "that mother of mine always talks to herself like this. Don't pay any attention. Let her talk on as much as she likes."

These words were like balm to his heart. What a good lad this Ali is. You'd never believe he'd sprung from that vixen. . . .

As soon as he felt a little better he called Ali, who was walking ahead of them.

"Thank you, my sweet child," he said, laying his hand on Ali's shoulder and squeezing it affectionately. "Your father was like you too. I've never taken grapes from anyone, Ali. And no one's ever spat on me down in the Chukurova."

Ali smiled. "The things you worry about, Uncle Halil! They can spit on us and kill us too. Those are the Beys of the Chukurova. They hold the seal of power, Uncle Halil. . . ."

"Look, Ali. Believe me, I never saw my daughter-in-law doing what they say. If that good-for-nothing son of mine lets himself be cozened by her . . ."

"It's his concern," replied Ali. "There's nothing you can do about it."

He heard Tashbash calling and waited for him.

"You see, my friend," Tashbash began, "you see how the villagers have gone over to his side again. Let's leave them, the two of us, and hire ourselves out on another farm."

"This Muhtar can stir up a lot of trouble for us," said Ali thoughtfully, "we have to wait until at least some of the villagers are with us."

"To think that they could still be duped by this ape of a scoundrel . . ." said Tashbash.

"If Köstüoglo hadn't funked at the very beginning . . ."

"Do you see that?" said Tashbash suddenly. Black rain clouds were gathering over the mountains in the north. "We mustn't get caught here in this valley by the rain that's coming!"

Ali scanned the sky anxiously. "This rain will be on us in less than an hour."

"Come, let's run to the Muhtar and warn him of the danger."

They hurried on and caught up with the Muhtar. Just then a cold rain gust stirred up the dust from the road and subsided again. The Muhtar was alarmed.

"Good God!" he cried. "Where did this spring from? For heaven's sake, tell the people to get a move on!" He prodded his black donkey hastily. The animal was tired, but broke into a trot at the sharp prick of the rod on its flanks. "Tashbash, you pass the word on to the villagers. Let them hurry. To the forest . . . If not we're lost. Quickly! Watchman," he shouted, "come here at once. You've got to call out a proclamation!"

The watchman's public crying would be superfluous, for the villagers, sensing what was threatening them, had already quickened their pace. But it was an old habit of the Muhtar's. He never did anything without the public crier.

"Hey, you village people! Attend to my words and don't say you haven't heard! Do you see that cloud? It comes way down from Mount Erjiyesh, growing darker and more ominous every minute. If the rain it brings catches us here in this treeless hollow, we'll all be swept away by the torrents. What's more, there's no firewood here and we'll all catch our death of a cold. So run for all you're worth to the forest. Spur on your horses and donkeys, and you, walking-folk, step lively. Now, don't say you haven't heard!"

The clatter of tin cans, the bawling of children and the general din increased as the caravan surged forward.

"Watchman!" The Muhtar's deep, powerful voice boomed out again. "You haven't called out this proclamation properly. You've omitted saying: you're to walk quickly by order of the council of elders and of our Muhtar. And you've forgotten the cattle. Now listen, Long Ali and Lone Duran are to go to the shepherds in our rear and tell them to hurry and herd the cattle into the forest. By order of the council of elders and of our Muhtar, don't forget!"

The watchman's voice could not rise above the hubbub. But Ali and Lone Duran had heard.

"The fellow's got his knife into us now," said Duran as they turned back. "He couldn't send Tashbash back. He's afraid of him because he's got powerful relatives."

"We have to make a stand against this man somehow," said Ali. "Elif," he called to his wife, "keep an eye on the horse."

The dark clouds were drawing swiftly nearer. Sudden fitful blasts of rain-heralding wind whipped up whirls of blinding dust. The villagers were huddled as if the rain was already upon them.

Küheylan sank down on to its knees again. Meryemdje shrieked: "Help, help! Save me, help!"

Two youths ran up, but Küheylan had somehow managed to struggle to its feet alone.

"Thanks be to Allah," said Meryemdje. She was almost in tears. "Didn't I say that this old horse can't carry two persons? But that pigheaded son of mine will never listen to reason. Perhaps if I got off . . . I'll try and walk. Hey, my lads, help me off the horse."

The two youths put her down.

Old Halil's cunning green eyes twinkled. "And while you're about it, my lads, lift me on to this saddle. My buttocks are just one big bruise from sitting on this horse's bony rump."

The two youths did as he asked.

"Allah be praised," he cried gleefully. "Bless this Ali. There isn't another one like him in this village. If I had a son like him,

54

I'd offer thanks to Allah night and day for having given me such an angel. I wouldn't scold and grumble as some ungrateful mothers do. Oh, my back feels so much better! What a soft saddle!"

Meryemdje looked up angrily at Old Halil. The old man was at ease on the horse and laughing up his sleeve. This infuriated her. She grabbed the horse's head.

"Boys," she cried, "for the peace of your departed ones, put me on that saddle again and this old man right back where he was sitting before!"

Smiling, the two lads lifted Old Halil on to the croup of the horse and then heaved Meryemdje back into the saddle.

The caravan was fleeing in disarray towards the forest. Loads toppled off the pack animals, were hoisted back again, or were hurriedly dragged on by their distracted owners. The Muhtar had lashed his black donkey to a canter and was leading the caravan, turning back every now and then to shout: "To the forest, march! Forward march! Forward!" The van of the column was nearing the forest, while its tail still straggled down in the valley.

A frenzied wind, cold as ice, suddenly whipped up eddies of dust and the caravan, strung out like beads, was shrouded in darkness. A few warm drops pattered to the ground. The thunderstorm broke out. A rumbling arose from the depths of the skies and the thunder clapped and echoed, while streaks of lightning picked out the rocky slopes.

Küheylan had been lagging far behind the tail of the column. Meryemdje kept urging it forward, but to no avail. Küheylan would break into a trot for a few steps, then slow down again. It had obviously been a very strong horse in its time.

Suddenly, amidst the dust and the pelting rain, Meryemdje caught a glimpse of the tail of the caravan disappearing into the forest. She thrust the spurs violently into the horse.

"Huh, huh! What kind of a horse are you anyway?" she

wailed. "Here we are stranded in the open wastes, under the rain, and what a rain! And all the folk in the forest by now and already putting up for the night! Oh dear, oh dear! What shall we do?"

"Spur it on, sister," replied Old Halil. "Spur it on!" He brought down his stick with all his strength on Küheylan's back. "Spur it on, sister. . . ."

Meryemdje flung out her legs and stabbed at the horse's belly with all her might. Again and again she plunged in the spurs while Old Halil, gritting his teeth, struck at the horse with his stick. Küheylan was roused into a canter. Old Halil clung to Meryemdje to keep his balance and Meryemdje clutched the pommel of the saddle. The horse was snorting disquietingly and its belly heaved and fell spasmodically.

A streak of lightning lit up the valley. As the thunder rolled in the skies, Küheylan pitched over. It tried to steady itself but slipped again and came crashing down. This time it lay quite still on the ground.

Meryemdje had been projected against a clump of thistles by the roadside. All her body was a-tingle. She scrambled to her feet and ran to the horse.

"Allah be praised!" she blurted out. "You're not dead." She clasped the horse's head in her arms and turned to Old Halil, who lay farther off moaning loudly. "The horse is all right," she muttered.

The rain was pouring down relentlessly.

"What sort of people are these?" cried Old Halil. "A fine new generation this is, abandoning us, two old folk in the mountains!"

Meryemdje said nothing. She sat there by the horse, her head in her hands, her teeth chattering with cold.

The downpour was letting up now, but an icy wind had risen that was piercing them to the very marrow. Old Halil rose and went to sit beside Meryemdje. His head was shaking like a leaf on a bough.

"Don't fret at all, sister. Not at all. The horse threw itself down because the storm frightened it. Thoroughbreds always sense danger. Just wait till these rain clouds blow away. You'll see how it'll get to its feet. It's afraid of the storm, that's what it is."

Meryemdje turned away from him. Old Halil was wounded to the core.

"Meryemdje, my lady sister, won't you listen to me? These thoroughbreds are always like this, and I know Küheylan is one. Ibrahim had stolen it from a fellow coming from Urfa and there was that certificate lying right there in the fellow's pocket. Ibrahim had said to me, if only I could lay my hands on that certificate, he'd said, I'd take this horse to the Merjimek stud and sell it there for a thousand liras. But if there's one thing in his life that he'd wanted to steal and had not managed to, it was that certificate."

Meryemdje was flushing with anger.

"Was there ever a one like Ibrahim!" Old Halil went on. "Why, I remember how we'd stolen cotton from all over the Chukurova plain, just so he could make enough money to wed you. . . ."

Stung to the quick, Meryemdje glared threateningly at the old man, then turned her back on him. Old Halil's tiny button-like eyes gleamed bitterly. His shivering had stopped while he was talking. Now it started again.

Swept by a violent north wind the clouds were speeding away towards the south and a whitish blue streak widened steadily over the mountain range. The nipping cold increased as the skies cleared.

Meryemdje was gazing at the fast-dimming eyes of the horse. She recalled the day it had been brought to their home. . . . Her husband, pure and staunch, mild and shy as a girl. . . . Afterwards they had secretly given Old Halil an embroidered *kilim* woven by her mother in exchange for the horse.

Ah those days, she thought, even this old hog was in the prime of youth then. . . .

Old Halil rose to his feet. He was pale as a sheet.

"Sister," he said, "my beautiful doe-eyed sister! Come, get up and let's start walking. We'll freeze here."

Meryemdje did not even lift her head.

"This north wind's a cruel wind. It comes from the land of the giaours way up and, by God, it can freeze a man to death. Come, let's get going. You can hold on to my arm."

Meryemdje did not bat an eyelid but sat on there huddled in the mud, her arms crossed over her breast and her hands nestling in her armpits.

He shook her by the shoulder.

"It's you I'm talking to, my lovely sister. Come, let's go. What's the good of staying here? You can't make the horse get up."

Meryemdje did not stir.

Old Halil lost patience. "Damn your stubbornness! What more can I do? You're the true daughter of Green-eyed Hadji, a mulish breed all of you."

He was off on the road.

Meryemdje slowly raised her numb head and gazed after him. Her mouth worked as she muttered something. Then she drew her legs in closer to her body, laid her forehead on her knees and remained crumpled in a frozen ball.

Old Halil had already walked a good way when he impulsively turned back to Meryemdje.

"My lady sister," he said plaintively, "my lady of ladies, come with me. The horse won't be the worse for waiting a little here. But if you stay, you'll die. I swear you will. Look, it's going to snow now. . . ."

He argued and pleaded in vain. At last, thoroughly exasperated, he fetched her a violent kick in the ribs.

"Have it your way then, accursed hag! Rot and die right here for all I care!" he cried as he left her again. "I hope to God they find your frozen corpse here, alongside that old carcass!"

The sodden clayish earth clung to his feet like glue and his wet clothes weighed on his back.

"The damned woman," he growled, "staying there to die in the mountains out of sheer pigheadedness! What shall I do now? I can't go back. Anyway it wouldn't do any good. She wouldn't come. I must make haste and get help for her!" He lurched on towards the forest. "The devil take her! She's made me spit blood, the old hag, just because I rode her horse a little. Well, let her freeze to death. Does she expect to take root on this earth for ever? At least now Ali will be rid of her."

The sun was setting as he neared the outskirts of the forest, mantling the little puddles left by the rain. From within the forest came the rumour of the camp. He heard laughter and cursing and the voice of a woman singing a lullaby, and was awakened to life again. He inhaled the dank smell of the forest with relief. For thirty, maybe forty years now, he had made the same trip down to the Chukurova and every time he had come to this spot the same odour had suffused it. For him each place on their way had its own particular smell, so that even at night in the pitch-dark he was able to recognise it. Here the Trilling Spring, there the first ford of the Forty Streams, the road passing below Akkale, the White Tower, the hill overlooking the Savrun Stream. . . . In the village they could blindfold his eyes, put him on a donkey so his feet would not feel the familiar paths, and swing him round and round until they were sure he had lost his bearings. But still his nose never failed him. This is Gökdogan's house, this the Muhtar's barn, this Lone Duran's straw-rick, he would declare unerringly.

As he was dragging himself towards the camp, a chilling thought arrested him: "Suppose they accuse me of having left her there in the wilds on purpose. . . . Suppose they think it's a put-up job. . . ." The only thing that would save him now was the dead rabbit act. It was an old trick of his. To avoid a flogging whenever he was caught thieving, he would throw himself to the ground at the first blow. Most of the time people were fooled and would give him up for dead.

He gave out a loud scream: "Help! A body's dying here. . . . Help, good Moslems!"

There was a commotion in the camp. Several villagers dashed forward. Osmandja was the first to reach him.

He's finished, the poor old man, he thought. Old Halil seemed to be stone dead.

The villagers drew up and stood in a sad silent circle. Then the Muhtar came up. He took in the situation at a glance and roared with laughter.

"Even a donkey when it blunders into a muddy path takes care not to take it again. And you are human beings and, with all due respect, not donkeys! Although Old Halil has served you his dead rabbit act a hundred times, you bite at the bait again. And truly, men are more brainless than animals. Animals copulate once a year in a certain month, but you men are ever on the prowl, ready to drop your pants! What's more, you badger me about flat and waterless cotton fields! And truly, my beloved compatriots, my noble jewel-hearted villagers, men are baser and more foolish even than animals."

He stamped up to Old Halil, seized him by the shoulders and heaved him violently to his feet.

Old Halil opened his eyes and blinked dazedly.

"Good Moslems!" he murmured in the faint sick tones of a man who has just escaped death. He tried to drop down again, but the Muhtar held him up mercilessly.

Old Halil knew there was no way out now.

"Good Moslems," he blurted out. "Meryemdje's freezing way back on the road near the fallen horse. She may be stiff dead by now. Help, good Moslems, quick!"

Then his knees sagged again, but the Muhtar tightened his hold.

"That's enough," he said, "no more fooling."

A group of villagers headed by Tashbash and Osmandja were already on the road. Elif ran after them, moaning and beating her breast. The two children were close on her heels.

The Muhtar remained alone with Old Halil.

"Look here, gaffer," he said, "other fools may be gulled by those ruses of yours, but I . . ."

"So help me God, Muhtar Agha, I was really done for! You've saved my life and I will never forget it." His green eyes glinted like glass buttons beneath the white overhang of brows.

"You've killed Meryemdje," insisted the Muhtar sternly, "and her horse too. Then you came here and pulled that dead rabbit trick on us."

"So help me God, I didn't kill her, agha of aghas!"

"I know she was cursing at you because you were riding her horse. So you pushed her off and killed her. I won't let you get away with this. And truly, justice will be done, my crafty fellow! So you were stirring up the villagers against me, eh? Saying I took bribes, eh?"

Old Halil threw himself at the Muhtar's feet.

"Let me be your slave, Muhtar Effendi! Your father and I were bosom friends. For pity's sake, for the sake of your dead father. . . . I begged that accursed Meryemdje to come. She just wouldn't budge. . . .'

The Muhtar shook him off. "I'll have you dragged from prison to prison. I'll have the gendarmes pluck your beard hair by hair! Watchman!"

"Here I am, Agha." The watchman appeared instantly from behind a big tree.

"Come here at once. Halil Tashyürek, born in 1884 of Mustuk and an unmarried woman, has murdered Meryemdje Uzundja, born in 1886, daughter of Green-eyed Hadji and of Ansha. I order you to arrest him. Bind his hands and we'll deliver him up to the first police station we come to, together with the corpus delicti. . . . And truly, this decree shall be enacted!"

"For mercy's sake, Muhtar! Your father's bones will start up in their grave with grief if you do this to his old friend. . . ."

"What are you waiting for, Watchman? Tie up his hands. And tightly too."

The watchman pulled a length of rope out of his pocket and trussed up the old man's hands behind him. Then he herded him towards the Muhtar's wattle hut and tethered him to a tree with a solid halter.

The Muhtar strode up and down in wrathful indignation, while the old man raised his voice in loud lamentations.

"Ah, for the good old days! Those days when Old Halil could fight back! When the wolves grow old they become a sport for dogs. Ah, old age!"

The crowd had reached Meryemdje where she lay in a hollow near the prostrate horse. Osmandja felt her limbs.

"She's alive!" he cried. "She's breathing, but frozen stiff. Quick, light a fire. Rub her hands and feet."

Elif started rubbing her hands and feet, trying at the same time to warm them with her breath.

When at last Meryemdje opened her eyes she saw a blazing fire near her.

"Find some soft grass and dry it a little over the flames," Osmandja was saying. "And when it's dry, lay it by the fire."

They held the grass over the fire, then spread it out and laid Meryemdje over it. Her eyes rested on the crowd gratefully. Then she looked at Elif.

"The horse, my daughter?" she asked weakly. "Is it alive?"

"Don't worry, it'll be all right. We'll light a fire for it too."

At these words a few villagers went off to gather more brushwood. Soon a big fire was roaring by Küheylan as well.

"Aunt Meryemdje," said Tashbash, "can you get up? We must go back to the camp."

Meryemdje's lips trembled. "Where is he? That renegade on whom I wasted my milk?"

"The Muhtar sent him after the cattle," replied Elif. "He hasn't come back yet."

"Let him see what he's brought upon me. I won't stir until he comes."

"Well, if you won't stir, I'll make you," said Tashbash, laughing. He attempted to take her on his back but Meryemdje burst into a flood of tears. She screamed and struggled so that he let go of her. "All right, all right, stay here until your son comes. I'm sure there's no one wishes to carry you on his back."

Meryemdje wept on silently. Elif pleaded with her, but she was deaf to reason.

"I'm going," Tashbash cried out impatiently, "it's getting dark and I'm freezing. Confound these old beldams!"

An icy moon had risen and the north wind was blowing cruelly. The crowd began to scatter in twos and threes. Soon only Elif, the children and Veli were left with Meryemdje. Icy cold shafts seemed to be streaming down on them from the low moon.

Suddenly Veli pricked up his ears at the sound of voices on the road.

"Aunt Meryemdje, my cousin's coming," he said happily as he recognised Ali's voice.

There was no reaction from Meryemdje.

As Ali's silhouette came into sight, Veli ran towards him. "There's been an accident, but don't be afraid, your mother's all right, brother. But I think the horse is done for."

Ali went straight to the horse and examined its eyes. Then he knelt over Meryemdje. "Are you all right, Mother?"

She did not answer him.

"I'm sorry, Mother. What could I do? The Muhtar sent me after the cattle. . . ."

Meryemdje tightened her lips.

"Why don't you speak? What have I done to you?" Ali shouted. "Veli, help me get her on my back. Come on, children. Come on, Elif. Go ahead. Veli, you stay here, I'll come back with some soup for you."

On the way to the camp, Ali spoke again: "Why are you angry with me, Mother? It wasn't my fault."

He pleaded with her to speak to him, to tell him how he had offended her, to forgive him. She never uttered a word.

Chapter 6

Day was breaking when Ali returned to the camp, his face dark with weariness from having sat up all night beside the horse. He found the villagers already astir and packing up.

"How's the horse faring?" Osmandja asked him.

"Just the same. Just lying there," replied Ali dejectedly. "I'd like to bring it here into the forest. Will you lend me a hand, Tashbash?"

Tashbash picked out a few men.

"You and you there . . . Durmush, you too. Come on. Quick, before the villagers take to the road. . . ."

They set off at a run.

Veli leapt to his feet as he saw them.

"It's eaten a handful of grass," he announced excitedly. "And now I've given it some straw."

The horse's head was completely buried in a bundle of straw.

"Why, you fool, you might have stifled it," cried Osmandja as he hastily swept away the straw. "Now let's get going. Durmush, you're strong, you take its head. You, Mustuk, the tail."

The horse had sunk into the mire. Its neck was thin and elongated. Its coat, once iron-grey, was now of a dirty white colour with large reddish-brown blemishes and with the skin laid bare in spots. Only a few hairs were sticking out on its short stubby tail. It had no mane at all and its ears were only two pieces of raw flesh. Its yellow listless eyes were almost entirely clogged with crusts of pus.

"Come on, all together. One, two, one, two!" shouted Osmandja.

They managed to heave the horse to its feet.

"Now hold it tightly as we go along!"

The horse's trembling legs went limp. They tightened their grip and almost carried it as they dragged it along.

"Alas, poor Küheylan!" said Osmandja. "To think I should see you in this state! Do you remember, Ali, when Küheylan first came to you? How he galloped like the wind?"

Ali nodded sadly, slightly comforted.

The sun had just risen when they entered the forest and laid Küheylan by the fire right before Meryemdje. The sick horse was instantly surrounded by a silent crowd that stood there reverent as though in the presence of a corpse or a saint. Old Halil was looking on sorrowfully.

When they had brought Meryemdje into the forest the night before he had gone wild. "Unbind this rope and set me free this minute, you son of a whore," he had shouted to the Muhtar. "Just wait till we get down to the Chukurova and I tell the Party leader how you treated me at my age. You'll see the nape of your own neck first before you ever see the Muhtar's chair again, you mongrel. Being a Muhtar was your poor father's business, not yours! Come here and let me spit right into your eyes, you wild hog sired by an ass. . . . You wretch, you miscreant. . . . Unbind my hands!" The Muhtar had backed away hastily with his hands over his ears and had signalled to the watchman to set the old man free. Old Halil's voice had then risen to a shriek as he relentlessly poured imprecations on the Muhtar and his family. The Muhtar could do nothing to stop him. He had accused the old man falsely. But what bothered him was that not one of the villagers had come forward to say: "Hush, Uncle Halil, for shame. After all, he's the Muhtar. He thought you were guilty." On the contrary, they were all pleased. And so Old Halil had railed on until it was nearly midnight. In the end a relative of the Muhtar's had raised his head from his bed and had enjoined him to be careful. Old Halil had shut up immediately, wondering how he could have been so reckless.

He now sidled up furtively to Ali, his tiny eyes full of tears.

"My Ali," he whispered, "my brave one, don't think it was my fault. The confounded beast was very old. How was I to know it could not carry us? Please forgive me."

Ali patted his back.

Old Halil's throat tightened and he turned away. "His father was like him, may he rest in peace. Ibrahim would have died for me if I'd asked him to. . . ." He was weeping as he squatted down against a tree away from the crowd. "Allah," he exclaimed suddenly, "you just don't do things right. If you did would you have killed Long Ali's poor horse and left that accursed Meryemdje alive? Forgive me, Allah, it's a sin to say this, but you do sometimes put the cart before the horse!"

There was a commotion as the Muhtar pushed his way through the crowd, shouting angrily. He stopped short at the sight of the horse and lowered his voice.

"Where's Yemen Agha?" he said, looking around.

A thin voice like that of a girl's answered him. "I'm here, Muhtar Bey."

"Have you taken a look at this horse?"

"I haven't, my lord."

"Well, come here and tell us whether it will live or die."

Yemen Agha stepped forward and examined the horse at great length.

"This horse's death is near," he said, "and a pity it is, for it's a pure-blood Arab." He shook his head as he stroked the horse's neck.

"You've all heard him, haven't you?" said the Muhtar. "Yemen Agha is never wrong. When he says a horse will die, it will die even if it's up and trotting and not sick like this one. He knows his business. So come on, all of you, let's get going.

If we're late the other villages will occupy all the good fields and I won't be responsible then. Come on, look sharp!"

Those standing about the horse did not move.

"Tell them to get a move on," the Muhtar said to the watchman.

The watchman started to call out in a loud voice: "Hey, village-folk, attend to my words and don't say you haven't heard. . . ."

Slowly the villagers turned away and only a small group was left by the horse.

"Ali! Long Ali!" the Muhtar shouted. "If this horse doesn't die to-day, it'll die to-morrow. Come with us. He who strays from the flock is devoured by the wolves, the saying goes. I've pardoned you, so come and don't disturb the order of the village just because of a moribund horse." He knew these were the very words that would strengthen Ali's determination to stay. In order to exasperate him still more, he turned to Old Halil. "And you, drivelling old dotard," he snarled, "get going too. You've managed to save your skin this time, but I've got my eye on you. Yemen Agha, you too, forward march. Your family's far off on the road by now."

Old Halil spat on the ground. "Curse your mother, your wife, your forefathers and all your breed, and may your father's bones dance out of their grave!"

Yemen Agha pulled himself together. "Yes, my lord, you're quite right. Quite right!" He hastened away.

"Ali, brother, it's no use," said Tashbash, "you don't die with the dead. That Yemen Agha knows his business. The horse is done for. As for the Muhtar, he's hugging himself at the idea that you'll be left behind. Come, let's finish the horse and go all together just to take the wind out of his sails. Look at him, just look how he keeps turning back to gloat on us."

"The horse'll die for sure," Osmandja urged him. "Come, don't stay and give that enemy of ours an occasion to rejoice."

Old Halil had moved on, still vituperating at the Muhtar and stopping only to cast back anxious glances at the horse, Meryemdje and Ali. He could not make up his mind to leave them. And if I do stay, he thought, what good will it do? I can't breathe life into their horse, can I? He walked on listlessly.

Tashbash, Lone Duran, Osmandja and Veli were still doing their best to persuade Ali. They all repeated ten times over that he would drive the Muhtar off his head with joy if he stayed behind. It was no use. Ali was unshakable. They gave up and moved off silently, their heads hanging as though departing from beside a death-bed.

Only Veli remained. "I'm staying with you, cousin," he said.

"You go too," shouted Ali angrily, "your wife is ill. Whether the horse dies or lives . . . it's only a matter of a couple of days to wait."

Veli hesitated. He was unnerved by Ali's strange look.

"Go, Veli," repeated Ali peremptorily, "off with you."

Veli left him reluctantly.

Meryemdje, Elif and the children were sitting in silence, their eyes fixed intently on the horse. Ali came and sat beside them. They did not speak or look at each other.

The chinking of cans and the crowing of cocks faded into the distance. The branches of the trees crackled and the falling leaves rustled on the ground.

The horse's mouth rested on the earth and was covered with mud. Ali rose suddenly and disappeared among the trees. Soon afterwards he was back with an armful of green grass which he threw down at the foot of a tree. There was a saucepan on the fire with the remains of the morning's cracked-wheat soup.

"One of you spoon this up," he said, "it's a pity to throw it away."

The boy came forward with a huge wooden spoon and scooped up the soup in the twinkling of an eye. Ali turned to his wife. Elif guessed what he wanted. She took the saucepan to the spring, washed it clean and brought it back filled with water. Ali put it over the fire.

The horse's head was now sinking into the ground.

Ali tested the water with his little finger. It was tepid. He took the saucepan off the fire and carried it to the horse. Then he tore off a piece of cloth from the bedding, dipped it into the water and wiped the horse's eyes. Elif took the rag from her husband and washed the mud off its running nose, while Ali brought the fresh grass and laid it near the horse. He sat down, cradled the horse's head and gently pressed the grass into its mouth. The horse remained motionless with its mouth open and teeth bared. Ali removed the grass and put in a fresh handful. Again and again. . . . At last he laid the horse's head down. Painful twinges were shooting through his left leg as he got up. Elif was crouching behind a tree-trunk quietly weeping. Meryemdje was curled up with her chin on her knees and her hands covering her face. The children, their eyes wide as saucers, were looking on dazedly.

Noon passed and it was already afternoon when suddenly the horse shook its tail two or three times. Ali's heart leaped with joy.

"Mother, Mother! Elif! Look, it's wagging its tail."

Meryemdje looked up dully, then she took her head in her hands again. The children glanced at each other and smiled. They ventured up to the horse.

"It's moving," said Hasan, "look, Ummahan, how beautifully it's wagging its tail. And what a beautiful tail it has too." He leaned over the horse and stroked its ear.

Ummahan laid a timid finger on the horse's ear. "It's moving its ear too," she said.

The children went on fondling the horse, casting apprehensive glances at their parents.

"Get away from the horse, you brats," cried Elif angrily as

she strode out from the trees. "Here we are worrying ourselves sick, and you two playing with the horse!"

The children withdrew guiltily to their grandmother's side.

A cloud cast its shadow over them. Far off a turtle-dove was cooing. A shrike settled on a bough, so near they could have caught it. Then it flew off.

Elif was gathering wood and piling up the dying fire. She filled the saucepan with water, placed it over the fire and threw the bulgur-wheat into it. Then she sat down and waited. When the *pilaff* was cooked she removed the saucepan from the fire, and taking a small chunk of butter from the firkin she tossed it into the skillet. The butter sizzled, giving out a rank smell, and she poured it on to the *pilaff*. She spread out a cloth quickly.

"Come and eat," she said wearily.

Ali sat down cross-legged with the children beside him. Elif went to Meryemdje and touched her shoulder.

"Come along, Mother, and have a bite."

"I'm not hungry, my beautiful girl," replied Meryemdje, "you go and eat. It's poison you should give me now!"

She was hungry, and when Elif did not insist, she felt like hurling a stone at her. She started mumbling furiously to herself.

The sun set and the western sky turned red. The evening star hung like a mirror in the sky. Ali had lit four fires around the horse so that the place was bright as day. He carried faggots and kept on feeding the fires.

The horse's nose and mouth exuded a continuous flow of mucous.

The children had laid their heads on their mother's lap and were fast asleep. Meryemdje sat huddled in the same position.

The howling of jackals, perhaps a hundred of them, rose from the depths of the forest. Then came the faint, untimely crowing of cocks. Who knows, perhaps these cocks belonged to another village trekking down to the Chukurova. . . . The night was vibrant with the humming of cicadas. Ali lifted up his face to the star-studded sky, gripped by the strange feeling that the stars were cold, so small and brittle did they seem.

It was almost day when suddenly the horse's forelegs stretched out rigidly, quivering slightly. Then the quivering stopped. Ali quickly lifted its head. The horse had stopped breathing.

"Ah, I'm undone!" he cried and collapsed to the ground.

Elif, who had been dozing, jumped up with a cry. Started out of their sleep, the children began to whimper. Meryemdje flung herself on to the horse.

"Dead! My Ibrahim's keepsake dead!" she moaned. "What shall I do now without you?"

The jackals howled to the rising sun. The fires died out.

Meryemdje grasped Elif's arm. "Listen, my girl, I'll never speak again to those who have killed my Ibrahim's relic. Now the horse must be skinned, so that its hide should bring in something at least."

Ali flared up. "With what shall I skin it, Mother? And anyway how could I carry the raw hide in addition to all this load?"

"My daughter, it's you I'm talking to," said Meryemdje, "there's a sharp knife in the bulgur sack. As for carrying the hide, I'll take it on my back myself. Have you understood, my daughter?"

Ali fell silent. He knew that if he did not obey, his mother would not budge. Elif brought him the knife. Stropping it on his large leather belt, he stared sadly at the horse. Then he set to skinning it, while Elif and Meryemdje turned their backs. The children watched his movements with huge grieving eyes, and Hasan tried to help his father. Overhead, vultures were whirling slowly.

"Elif get me some salt,' said Ali when he was through. He spread the skin out and sprinkled it with salt. "Now bring some ash."

They scattered ash over the skin, which they left to dry in the sun for an hour or two. Then Ali folded the skin up and flung it on to his back atop the bedding and the tin cans. He gave the rest of their belongings to Elif.

"Who'll ever want to buy the skin of this old horse," he muttered bitterly as he helped his mother to her feet.

They had not walked a hundred yards when the vultures swooped down on the horse. Ali looked back. The carcass was invisible under the great flailing wings.

They passed by a white-barked plane-tree, its branches sagging with age, and came to the road.

"If we keep up this pace," Ali said to his wife, "we'll catch up with them at the Lower Andurun."

Elif made no answer.

"Only five or six days, and before they know it we'll be with them. Isn't that so?"

Elif did not seem to hear.

"They're rejoicing now, the trouble-mongers, because we've been left behind, because our horse is dead! They don't want . . ."

He looked at Elif intently. She avoided his gaze. He felt the hide weighing on his back, heavy as lead, and stinking with a putrid unbearable stench.

"We have to catch up with them," he shouted in a sudden burst of rage, "we must join them before they reach the Lower Andurun. We must, we must. If we don't, then my children will go hungry and naked this year. If I'm not able to pay back my debts, Adil Effendi will make short work of me. If I don't catch up with them, woman, the villagers will be victimised by the Muhtar and Batty Bekir. We must catch up, do you hear? We must, woman, we must! It's sink or swim for us now."

Elif had never seen Ali in such a passion. She wanted to say something, but she was entirely at a loss. He was running ahead of them now, while she panted in his wake. Her load was heavy and she kept looking back worriedly at her mother-in-law, who was walking more and more slowly and unsteadily. The children had adapted their pace to their grandmother's flagging gait and were skipping beside her. Meryemdje kept carping at them, venting her pent-up resentment. Hasan suddenly ran to Elif.

"Mother!" he cried.

"Can't you stay near your grandmother, you little pest," she shouted. "Wait right here for her."

"I'm hungry," the boy snivelled. "I'm so hungry that . . ."

"Eat poison!" cried Elif.

The boy stood rooted there, frightened at his mother's outburst.

Meryemdje's body ached all over and was drenched in sweat. Every two steps she stopped and jerked her mouth up gaspingly like a bird drinking water. Her eyes had disappeared in their sockets and straggling strands of hennaed hair plastered her face and neck that were parched like a sun-cured hide.

Elif turned back and went up to her. "Are you all right, dear Mother?" she asked, taking her arm.

"If you can call this all right, I'm all right, my good daughter," sighed Meryemdje, "as you see . . ."

"Do you think you can walk on?" asked Elif, eyeing her apprehensively.

"Of course I can walk," shouted Meryemdje as if a red-hot iron had been driven into her flesh, "I can walk so fast that the ground will go rolling past me."

She pushed Elif away and drawing herself up she took a few steps alone. She swayed and would have fallen had not Elif sprung forward and caught her.

"I'm not yet broken to the road. The first one or two days a person feels awkward, but you soon get to be like an old trooper. Wait a moment, my daughter. Let me get my breath and you'll see how I can walk! Like a girl of fifteen. . . . Ah, if only our horse were alive! My beautiful grey horse. . . . Would I have been wasting away like this?" There were tears in her eyes. "I will never forgive that husband of yours, not even at the crack of doom. I hope he'll burn in hell for all eternity!" She was ashamed of her tears and curbed down the sobs that rose to her throat choking her. After a while she wiped her eyes and smiled wanly. "Come, my daughter, let's go. If you have to listen to a foolish old woman . . ." She held on tightly to Elif. "See how beautifully I'm walking now? It's because you're beside me, my lovely girl."

Ali was rushing on and would soon plunge out of sight into a narrow gorge. Elif knew her husband. Pushing on blindly towards his goal, he could go without food or drink for days, completely oblivious to everything and everyone.

"Ali, Ali!" she called at the top of her voice.

"Let him go, the son of a whore. Let him go to the pit of hell!"

"Mother, he's mad. He'll forget all about us." She put down her load. "Mother and you, children, sit here beside the pack until I come back."

She started running. Her red kerchief slipped about her neck and her hair streamed out. When she overtook him at last at the bottom of the hill she was almost swooning with exhaustion.

"Your mother's in a desperate state," she gasped, "you've got to stop here. Light a fire while I go and get her."

He threw off his old broken-peaked cap and wiped his brow with a wide circling gesture, shaking the drops of sweat off his fingers. Then he propped the pack against a rock and spread out the hide on the grass. A green fly flashed down like lightning to settle on it, buzzing off almost immediately. Soon three green flies were crawling over the hide. He lit the fire and sat down beside it. Every muscle of his body was twitching with pain. He waited, building up the falling fire again and again.

"Where can they be, those pests," he grumbled. "The sun's almost setting. At this rate we'll never get to the Chukurova. And we must. . . . Where are they, where?"

Clenching his teeth, he ran up to the top of the ridge. There, in the distance, he caught a glimpse of his wife and children. He pressed on, fear gripping his heart. As he drew nearer he realised that Elif was carrying Meryemdje on her back. He bounded forward and lifted her on to his own.

The cold had set in with the oncoming of dusk. It was going to be a freezing night, and they would have to keep the fire burning till morning. Elif put some bulgur-wheat to cook and the others waited in silence. When she placed the soot-blackened saucepan in their midst, they all swung their spoons hungrily.

Meryemdje chewed a spoonful or two and shuffled away. Ali was smitten to the heart.

"Mother, I'm sorry. Please forgive me. It's just that the old man nagged me for three months, pleading. . . . How could I refuse him? He was my father's friend."

Meryemdje turned to a thick mastic-oozing pine-tree.

"Tree," she said, "it's you I'm talking to and not anyone else. Old Halil cut my horse's life down. You're a very old tree, you've seen many years. Old Halil was no friend of my Ibrahim's. Worse than an enemy to him, that's what he was. Oh lofty tree, there are certain things one can't talk about, even to one's own son. My Ibrahim, whom everyone took for a thief, never even stole a pin. Do you hear me, tree? People won't believe this, but you must believe me, tree. You are great and your branches stretch up to the sun. Light pours upon you. Why did Ibrahim always shoulder the blame for all these thefts? Let me tell you something, tree on which the dawn sheds its first rays, my Ibrahim died because of that poison-green-eyed Halil. And now he's killed my horse, and my own son has been his accomplice. So I'll never forgive this son of mine, not even at the day of judgment. And I will not speak to him again until I die. You are my witness, tree."

Her muttering had become unintelligible. Ali lifted her up in his arms.

"You must sleep, Mother dear," he said, "it's late."

He laid her beside the children who had already gone to sleep under a hanging pine branch. Then he went to his bedding which

Elif had spread under another pine. She crept in beside him and they fell asleep at once.

Meryemdje tossed and turned. Did you have to come to this, Meryemdje? To be carried on other people's backs? Her mind churned on relentlessly. Only death is fitting for you now. Towards dawn she dozed off.

The sun was high when she awoke. Ali and Elif had been waiting patiently since early dawn and now brought some bulgur-wheat for her. She was hungry. Washing her face quickly, she ate the food. Then she addressed her tree again.

"Hearken to me, tree! Praise Allah, I won't be needing anyone's help. I can walk on my own two legs. Don't let anyone fear he'll have to carry Meryemdje on his back."

She took her grandchildren by the hand and started off.

Ali said nothing. He shouldered his pack. The hide had dried a little but it still weighed heavily. Elif picked up her load too.

Towards noon they reached the Karaduman slope, a long steep ascent, over two miles to the top. They stopped for a short rest and then tackled the slope, Ali and Elif leading the way.

Half-way up, Ali slumped to the ground, his eyes starting from their sockets. Down the hill he could see his mother and the children creeping up like struggling ants. Elif was ahead of him. The stifling noon-heat had descended upon the valley.

Meryemdje stumbled and fell. She tried to get up but fell again helplessly. To stop now would be to admit her own weakness. She started crawling up on all fours.

"Children," she said, "it's much easier to climb up this way. You do it too."

Ali reached the top, puffing like a bellows. He stretched himself on the ground, utterly exhausted and did not move for a while.

"Curse you, man," Elif's voice roused him. She was pointing at the three figures that were crawling up, their hands grappling at the small sharp stones strewing the path. "This slope will be the death of her. . . ."

He hurried back. "Mother," he cried, shaken at the sight of his mother's bleeding hands and legs, "my poor mother! Even your own son is failing you."

Meryemdje was struggling as he pulled her on to his back.

"Slope, slope," she screamed, "I'll climb you even if I have to die in the end. Tell this renegade on whom I wasted my milk to put me down. Let him put me down!"

She kept on thrashing at his body all the way up.

The valley appeared to them now a dark, fathomless abyss. Ali had taken his head in his hands. Suddenly his face lighted up for the first time since the death of the horse.

"I've found a way," he cried out joyfully. "Elif, help me hoist this up and give me some of the things you're carrying. Mother is to stay here with the children and I'll come back for her later." He leaned towards her ear. "I'll throw away this hide somewhere on the road," he whispered, "my load will be lighter then. Don't stir from here, will you, children? What do you say, Mother?" He plunged ahead.

Ali and Elif walked on briskly till mid-afternoon. At the Knotted Spring, Ali put down his burden under a huge walnut tree. It was a holy tree and its branches, spreading out vault-like, were hung with votive rags. Pausing only to wash his face at the spring, he fell to the road at once and reached his mother at sunset. He saw that she had walked on a little, but how far could she go, poor thing? He forced himself to put on a show of light-heartedness and vigour before her.

"Mother dear," he cried cheerfully. "Why did you walk at all? It's not necessary. You'll see how I'll carry you like the wind now."

He knelt down beside her. Meryemdje's face was like a stone.

"Listen, my beautiful mother, I've carried the load way down to the Knotted Spring and left it under the Holy Walnut. Haven't I been quick?"

She was staring at the ground as if she had not heard him.

He drew her on to his back and strained to his feet. Meryemdje had been a large-set woman in her youth and her bones were heavy.

Happy to see their father his old self again, the children were skipping on ahead of them.

Meryemdje had made no resistance this time, but her resentment had increased and the more Ali tried to soothe her, the angrier she grew.

"We'll soon catch up with the village, you'll see," he said brightly. "Won't they be surprised? What are you fretting about, Mother? Who knows how old Küheylan was? You yourself said it was in its prime when it came to us, and I still a child then. Yemen Agha told me a horse doesn't live longer. 'Son,' he said, 'this one's over twenty.'" He was gasping for breath and his words tumbled out in spurts, but he dared not slow down. "When a horse is over twenty, it's as good as dead. I know why you're cross, my beautiful mother. It's because I let Old Halil ride along with you."

Meryemdje's rancour was growing apace.

Cross! Cross indeed, you son of a whore. So cross that as sure as my name's Meryemdje, I'll never forgive you, not till my bones grind against each other in their grave. When I think of the sleepless, freezing winter nights I sat up rocking your cradle, of the pains I wasted on you! You'll go straight to flaming hell, Long Ali, and with a demon's yoke shackled round your neck too. Haven't you heard what the imams say about a mother's claims? Yes, you're in forhell fire, my fine Ali.

"It would have died anyway, even if Old Halil had not ridden it. And the old man looked at me so . . . I couldn't turn him down."

Looked at you! I wish he'd looked on his own corpse

instead. Spare your efforts, my Long Ali. I shan't speak to you to my dying day.

"Who could have resisted? To see an aged man so sorely pressed . . . Didn't you notice how ill he looked? I had to put him on the horse, my beautiful mother. How could I do anything else?"

He waited expectantly, but there was no sound or movement. She might have been dead but for the warm pressure on his back.

Save your breath, I shall never forgive you. I've called down Allah's curse on you. A sin against one's mother can never be atoned, and nothing you can do will make me change my mind. The heart is like glass, Long Ali. Once broken it can't be mended. You can carry me on your back, not just to the Chukurova plain, but all the way to Mecca and Medina, you can take me to the Haj on your back if you like, your back can become one big wound, your feet can swell to bursting, but the wound in my heart will keep raw for ever. You've killed my horse, my Ibrahim's relic. You've made me the laughing-stock of the village.

"What have I done to you that you won't relent, Mother? Why do you want to throw the blame on a harmless decrepit old man?"

Harmless? They say the swallow's a harmless bird, but you go and ask the Yemen folk what the swallow does to their coffee! I could tell you a thing or two about harmless fellow. A whole life long he made your father cough blood.

"Take it easy, Mother dear. I'll carry you like the wind. I'm strong enough, thank God."

Ali's pace was gradually slackening and this irked him.

The stars were shining and the night wind carried the bitter scent of dry thyme. He felt the sweat streaming down his body. If he could only stop and rest a while. The cold autumn wind cut through him like a knife. This was not a mountain wind.

The Wind from the Plain

It blew from the distant grassless steppes. If he stopped to rest, he would be numbed to death and that would be the end of him. His back was sore and his mother's grip had tightened painfully on his neck. The soles of his feet were burning. But there was still that smell of thyme . . . the distant rustling of the trees, the gurgling of a stream. . . .

On turning into an uphill path he gave up and lowered his mother to the ground.

"You're cold, Mother, with your back exposed to the icy wind. I'll light you a fire so you can warm yourself before we set off again."

If I had my horse, I wouldn't be cold, I wouldn't be left on the roads at night. You've destroyed me, you've sealed my doom. What life is there left in me anyway? At the slightest puff it'll die out. Come on, blow on me and finish me, you monster!

"Children, gather us some wood. Your grandmother's cold."

The sweat was cooling on his back and he walked about until the children had brought some brushwood. He struck a match. The dry wood caught fire at once.

Meryemdje looked at the children tenderly.

How much more I'd love you, my darlings, if you weren't Long Ali's children! How can I call you my grandchildren, you, the offspring of my arch-enemy? He may light as many fires as he wishes. Ah, Long Ali, whatever you do, in the next world I'll drag you myself into the presence of Allah by the scruff of your neck, and I'll say, throw him into the deepest part of hell.

"The night has overtaken us on the road this time, Mother. But I won't let it happen again." As the sweat dried on him, his body grew limp and he felt his weariness more intensely. It seemed to him he would never be able to stand on his feet again.

The moon was haloed. Crepitating sounds came from the forest. In the bitter cold the earth was cracking like an underbaked jug. The children huddled together close to the fire.

"Father," said the boy, "you feel the cold more when you stop. When you walk you burn all over."

Ali felt riveted to the ground. "Mother, are you warmer now, my beautiful mother? Before coming to get you I told Elif: 'Woman,' I said, 'we'll be cold when we come. While you're waiting, cook us some *tarhana*[1] soup, so that it'll be piping hot when we arrive.' "

It's no use. Even if you find bird's milk for me, not just *tarhana* soup, but bird's milk, I won't drink it. My heart will remain twisted against you for ever. A broken, shattered heart....

"Mother dear, why don't you say something, why don't you speak to me? I know your heart is mourning for Küheylan, but one can't die with the dead. With Allah's help we'll gather plenty of cotton this year, and I'll buy you a donkey, a sturdy Cyprus donkey."

Speak to you! After what you've done to me I'd rather be struck dumb, and my dying wish will be that you should not attend my funeral and carry my bier with those who love me.

"See, Mother, how the children have grown? This year they'll be able to pick more cotton. Isn't that so Hasan?"

"I'll pick cotton, and how, Granny dear! I'll start before dawn. And Ummahan too."

"At midnight, Granny," Ummahan piped out in her small voice. "I'll steal a little cotton too in the dark from the other heaps, like Köstüoglu's daughter."

Ali added a few twigs to the dying fire. He was overcome by a warm drowsiness.

"The donkey will be yours, Mother, yours alone. If you like you'll let the whole village ride it, and if not you won't let a soul come near it, not even the flying bird or the buzzing fly."

---

[1] Wheat mixed with yogurt and dried in the sun. This is stored in sacks to be cooked in soups for the winter.

Meryemdje was leaning forward, her white-kerchiefed head almost touching the fire.

"As sure as my name is Ali, I'll buy you this donkey next year. I'll get it by hook or by crook, even if I have to beg Adil Effendi to lend me the money."

You can't! Let alone your own debts, your father's ten-year debts are still standing in Adil Effendi's yellow book.

The children were slumbering. It was past midnight. A mule's bell tinkled once in the distance. There was no other sound in the night. The moon had dropped low in the sky. It must be right above the Chukurova, thought Ali. Elif would be anxious. He shouldn't have left her there, a young woman alone on the mountain. If only the children had been with her. Suppose someone should see her, attack her. . . . Her name would be soiled for ever.

"Come, let's go, Mother. We're rested now."

He pushed himself up with his large, long-fingered hands and swung for a while on the weight of his arms and legs. Then he forced himself to his feet.

"Come on, children," he said.

Startled out of their sleep, the children sprang up dazedly.

He crouched before Meryemdje, but was unable to raise her at the first try. He tried again. The third time, he stood up, but only barely avoided pitching over. Meryemdje seemed to him to weigh as much as a lead ingot. He felt a sudden fear rise in him. That's bad, he thought, fear paralyses a man. Suppose I fall right here in a faint and can't get up any more. . . . We'll see who'll do the talking and who'll be silent then.

He covered a good distance without uttering a word.

For the first time Meryemdje felt a gnawing hunger. She longed for the *tarhana* soup Elif had cooked, and pictured it piping hot with the smoke curling above the gleaming tinned basin. She kept her numb hands tightly locked about Ali, for she knew that if she let go she would never be able to close her fingers again.

The moon had gone down and in the darkness Ali struck his foot painfully against a stone. He bumped Meryemdje down and took off his sandal.

Not a sound escaped Meryemdje's lips as her body struck the ground. She lay sprawling, her eyes closed and her ears throbbing. The children stood by, staring fearfully at the shivering shadow that was their grandmother.

He ran his fingers over the injured toe and rubbed it. Then he drew on the hard sandal over his foot and tied up the laces hastily. Making a huge effort, he was off again, almost running now, with his mother bouncing up and down on his back.

A white blur lingered in the sky where the moon had set.

His feet were smarting, the pain shooting into his heart. But it would not do to stop now. It would soon be dawn. The first streaks of light could already be discerned beyond the distant mountains. And Elif all alone there in the wilds. . . . Women are so timorous, worse than children. A man's heart goes out to them, to these strange, beautiful and faithful creatures. Why hadn't he left the children with Elif? Nothing could have happened to his mother. Anyway, old women are tougher than young ones. A hundred dreadful possibilities assailed him.

"Mother," he said at last in a broken voice, "do you think Elif will be frightened all by herself in the dead of night? Do you think anything might happen to her?"

Meryemdje, whose body and thoughts, fancies and dreams were immersed in a deep numbness, was suddenly lashed into anger.

Frightened! Huh, huh! She'll be terrorised. All alone there. . . . Anything may happen, Long Ali, anything! These mountains are infested with wild beasts and bandits. Is it now that you come to your senses, Long Ali? Damn you, I hope she'll meet with just what you're dreading, and then I'll dance and make

merry right in the centre of the village. 'Hey, listen, neighbours!'
I'll say. 'Just listen to the disgrace that's befallen Long Ali, and
all through his own foolishness.' Yes, I'll dance my legs off with
glee. I'll jingle like a marriage bell.

"She won't be frightened, will she, Mother? Of course not!
Why should she be frightened?"

That's what you think! Why, she'll be frightened out of
her wits. Besides the runagates roaming in these wilds, the savage
beasts, the fierce monsters and the dead who haunt the mountains
wrapped in their white shrouds, besides the roaring tiger with
bared fangs, there's the Holy Walnut Tree that can cast a crippling
spell on a man. Not frightened! Don't you know of the jinn who
prowl the land, in the shape of rocks in a row, who scour the
skies, who can change themselves into a shepherd's haversack on
the road, the better to deceive a man and to pin him powerless
to the ground? You're not reckoning with these invisible beings
are you? You'll soon see what mischief they can wreak on you.
And you, without your mother's blessing, with her curse upon
you. . . . You've heard tell of the invisible ones, but you won't
believe in them. What can a godless infidel believe in anyway,
when he's skinned his mother's horse before her very eyes? . . .
But when you find your woman with her mouth all twisted, in
the spell of the Holy Walnut, then we'll see what you believe in!
But, as sure as I'm Meryemdje, if some foul thing happens to my
daughter-in-law because of you, then I know what I'll do to
you. . . . Oh dear, I'm freezing! Oh, how cold it is! He doesn't
feel it, with me on his back warding off the wind. If I had somebody warming my back like this, I could walk a whole night and
more. Oh, save me, Allah! Take me down safe and sound to the
Chukurova. . . . How can a man be so foolhardy as to settle
under the Holy Tree for the night? It was Sergeant Mustan,
God rest his soul, who had told her about it. He had a long
white beard that gleamed like a doe's fur. Surely he is sitting
with the saints now. . . .

85

"One night," he had recounted, "one dark, pitch-black night, I was riding past the Holy Walnut Tree. Its spreading branches swished like the flow of dark waters. All at once, I heard a snap. I looked about me and behold, a ball of light was rising from the earth towards the tree, setting its branches aglow, bathing the whole tree in glory. I stopped there, frozen, muttering prayer after prayer. Soon the huge walnut, with its trunk, its branches, its leaves, was like a tree of light carved into the black night. Then it started to swell and swell, till it touched the distant mountains, illuminating them. The whole world was as bright as day, and the darkness of the night was put to rout. Have you ever seen an enormous tree of light, as large as the world, engraved into the darkness? Oh, almighty Allah, praised be your infinite wisdom! A gigantic tree of light, spreading out to where the sun rises, to where the stars should be, but I swear there was not a single star to be seen. And it was still growing, a tree that was now a flood of light streaming into the sky! A sight that dazzled my eyes as I remained awestruck, unable to move until the dawn broke. My horse, that sacred animal, stood still, its ears pricked. Then, as the dawn touched the mountain tops, the tree grew smaller and smaller, shedding off its light gradually until it reached the ground again. When the sun rose, the Holy Tree stood before me, the same as ever, with its green leaves and cleft trunk. As for me, I sped straight off to the Imam of Karatopak."

"It's almost dawn, Mother," said Ali.

Does a man in his right senses ever put up for the night under the Holy Walnut, which is a tree only in the day-time and turns into a world of light at night? A tree that sometimes vanishes into the night and is no longer to be seen. . . . No trace of it for months on end. And then, one day, behold, it's there in its old place. How can a man go and camp under such a tree?

Mother, are you cold? If you like I can give you my coat to wear. I'm all in a sweat anyway."

The devil take you and your coat, Long Ali. If the tree has killed my daughter-in-law . . .

"How could I have taken the load so far? I'll be more careful next time. I just thought it would be a good thing if we could halt under the Holy Tree for the night."

A good thing indeed! What if we find Elif struck unconscious there?

Ali could only barely drag himself along. He stopped every once in a while on the pretence of saying something.

"Old Halil told me . . ."

Confound Old Halil, and you too.

". . . that there's going to be such a cotton crop in the Chukurova this year, enough and to spare for everyone, and that we'll each earn at least a hundred liras. He knows that because the whirling thistles were very large this year and they whirled more quickly than ever. It's a sign that the cotton will be plentiful this year."

What's it to you, my son? The others will pick all the cotton and be back in the village before you've even reached the plain. People will jeer at you and you'll only be getting what you deserve. My heart feels no pity for you. Serve you right if you're tired! I only wish it were light so I could enjoy the sight of your face in the wretched state you're in!

"He says the crop's going to be so plentiful that more than half of the cotton will remain unpicked and we'll only have to gather up the surplus."

That was just to wheedle you into letting him ride the horse, my poor simple child. What am I saying? No, no, that Long Ali's not my son. Rather the son of a sow.

What have I done that she should be so hostile, thought Ali, his heart rankling.

He came to a standstill.

" Are you tired, Hasan?" he asked weakly, unable to find any other pretext for stopping.

"I don't tire ever! I can walk and walk. . . . Ummahan's tired."

"He's lying," cried the girl, "I'm not tired at all."

It was growing light now. He was seized with sudden panic to see how far they still had to go. Clenching his teeth, he took a few dragging steps, but his trembling legs were giving way. Quickly he put his mother down. The world spun about him as he threw himself blindly at the foot of a tree. Tugging desperately at his collar, he tore it open and bared his breast. Beads of sweat stood out on his dark face and his eyes had narrowed into slits. He leant against the tree, panting for sheer life.

The sun appeared and sat on the crest of a mountain. Then it rose in the sky. Meryemdje felt her numbness thawing. She rose gingerly and, venturing a step or two, found that she was able to walk. She looked down at her prostrate son, cursing him with all her might to crush the aching that was welling up in her. But the more she looked, the more her anger melted into pity. She had to go. Snapping a branch off a tree, she trimmed it into a stick. Then, casting a furtive glance at her son, she turned her back on him quickly.

She heard the children pattering after her.

"Come, my darlings, your grandmother's companions, my lovely Ummahan, my brave Hasan. If only you weren't the children of that infidel! How could he kill my horse? Better I should have borne a black stone instead of him! Allah plague him, *inshallah*!"

"*Inshallah*, Granny, *inshallah*," echoed Ummahan soothingly, "it was a pity about the horse."

Hasan gave her a push. "Eat poison," he scolded her. "Why Granny," he went on, "Father said he was going to buy you a donkey to replace your horse."

Meryemdje brandished her stick at him. "Shut up, you son of a whore. Shut up, you ill-omened contrary brat. Who wants his donkey? Let him drop dead instead. May his legs break on the road, that infidel!"

Hasan lapsed into a sullen silence.

When Ali caught up with them towards noon, they were still walking steadily, but Meryemdje was ready to drop. Ali crouched down and she almost threw herself on to his back.

He pointed to the trees before them.

"Look, Mother, isn't the Knotted Spring over there? Isn't that tall slender tree top the Holy Walnut?"

Curse you and curse your Holy Walnut. It's no use, Long Ali. I know that in the end you'll skin me as you skinned my horse.

She lifted her head and caught sight of Elif in the distance. For a moment she forgot all her anger.

He sees the tree and he doesn't see my beautiful girl! Ah, what a good, pure woman you are, my Elif! But you have one fault. You shouldn't have got yourself married to this wicked man."

Ali suddenly started and cried out with joy. "Mother, Mother, look! See? Elif's coming."

Chapter 7

Ali lowered his mother on to a log at the foot of the walnut tree, while Elif hurried to the saucepan of *tarhana* soup she had kept by the fire since the evening before and placed it on the cloth. Then she went first to Meryemdje and made her sit down before the soup.

"Come, Ali," she called.

He was swaying on his feet dazedly. Without even a glance at the soup, he reeled towards the pack. Quickly he drew out the goat-hair cloth, threw it down in the sun and curled up on it. Elif slipped a small dirty cushion under his head. He was asleep the instant his head touched the cushion. She covered him with a blanket and stood beside him gazing compassionately at his drawn and emaciated face, on which the hairs of his unshaven beard stuck out like the quills of a hedgehog.

"He's very tired, Mother," she said as she sat down beside Meryemdje. "In two days his face has grown as small as a child's."

Meryemdje laid down her spoon and slapped her knee. "May he burn in hell!" she cried. "Let the worst befall him. The worse he is, the more I'll rejoice."

"But, Mother! Aren't you sorry for him?"

Meryemdje was impervious. "I'm not sorry," she said, "not sorry at all. A witless head makes weary feet. Why did he have to let Old Halil ride our horse and kill it? Just so people should say, what a good chap this Ali is!" She held up her hands to the sky. "Allah," she pleaded, "may woe betide this Long Ali. You've left him stranded miserably on these mountains with all his family. Now bring upon him a greater scourge, my great Allah, my beautiful black-eyed Allah."

"Don't say such things, Mother," said Elif. "How could he know it would turn out this way?"

"Shut up!" shouted Meryemdje. "Don't you side with him too! Let him crawl in the dust, *inshallah*, and not be in time for the cotton this year. That'll bring him back to his senses. Let Adil Effendi strangle the life out of him!" She rose and hobbled away towards the bushes behind the tree. "I'll have a little doze here. Wake me up when you set out."

"All right, my good mother," said Elif sadly. She folded up the cloth and put it away. "You sleep too, children," she called.

Ummahan was already nodding. Elif lifted her up and eased her down beside her father.

"Tuck in beside your father too," she said to Hasan.

Her eyes were heavy. She had sat up for them all night, full of misgivings. Now that they were all fast asleep, it would not do if she slept too. Someone passing on the road below might see them and steal something from the pack.

She crouched down by the fire, her legs drawn up and her chin on her knees, lost in thought. In all the ten years since she had joined this household, she had never seen Meryemdje in such a mood. Never had she known her to be as angry with anyone as she now was with her son. At every mention of the horse Meryemdje trembled with fury, foaming at the mouth as though struck by an evil spirit. If somebody she knew had died, say one of the children, it would not have rankled so. After all, had she been left behind or obliged to walk? Here was her son who was bearing her on his back and would go on like this all the way down to the Chukurova, but instead of being grateful or pitying him, her anger and spite grew apace. And how she had loved him, lavished her affections upon this Ali, the only child left to her of the eight she had borne! She still loved and fondled him as if he were a two-year-old baby. Should Ali happen to go somewhere, should he be a little late, she would eat herself up with worry. Once there had been a hailstorm. Meryemdje had been seized with frenzy at the idea that a hailstone might have hit him on the head and she had stirred up the whole village. In the end, Ali had been found in a house at the other end of the village and she had fainted with relief. And here she was suddenly nursing virulent feelings of revenge against this same Ali and all for a moribund horse that would have died next year if not now. Allah forgive us, isn't it a sin to think it possible for any creature to live on even a moment beyond its appointed time? That's exactly what the Hodja of Karatopak had said. Well then, what did she want, this woman? Hadn't she heard the words of the Hodja? What did she mean by cursing Ali? Why, one wouldn't curse one's enemy like this, let alone one's own son.

She slumbered. The sun was at its zenith. Noon passed. The fire burnt out, but she did not notice, half-asleep as if dreaming awake.

She raised her head as she heard a rumbling noise. Another group of villagers was approaching along the road below, some mounted on horses and donkeys, the rest on foot, some sick or lame, others merry. A baby was crying. Babies always cry on these roads. Joy welled up inside her, why, she did not know. She went and stood on the edge of the road, watching as they filed past. No one looked at her. When the last of the caravan had gone by a sudden heavy gloom and bitterness overcame her. She turned and sat down again by the dead fire.

Maybe they had a horse or a donkey the old woman could ride, she thought. I should have woken up Ali. There may be some hope still, who knows. . . . They can't have gone far.

Ali was sleeping like a baby, the only sign of breath being the indrawn movement of his jutting upper lip. She hesitated, then touched his arm gently.

"Ali!" she said.

He did not stir.

"Ali, wake up! It's already afternoon."

He drew his right leg up to his belly, as he always did on waking up, and rubbed his eyes with his fists.

"What's the matter?" he mumbled.

"The sun's low in the sky, Ali. If we're to walk at all to-day, we must be going. If we decide to stay here for the night . . ."

"We'll stay!"

The boughs of the great walnut tree sighed faintly over them. The sky was invisible.

"A village has just passed," Elif whispered into his ear. "I don't know which village, but . . . I thought of something. . . .

"Let it go," said Ali.

"You can still hear them," continued Elif. "They'll probably camp a little farther off, at Topaktash. They wouldn't stop here. They're afraid of the Holy Walnut."

Ali smiled. "Everyone is. Only you and I aren't afraid. The fools! Is there anything to be feared from good spirits?"

"I had an idea . . ." Elif blurted out. "I said to myself . . ."

Ali laughed, but his lips were strained. "Look here, woman," he said bitterly, "have you lost your mind? Is it ever possible to find a mount at this time of the year, when all the mountain villages are trekking along on the roads? If you looked, you must have seen how many people were being carried on other people's backs. The sick and the maimed . . . the old and weak . . ." He lay on his back, his face hopeless and angry. "We must spend the night here and recover our strength."

"Let me get a meal ready then," said Elif. She set about gathering brushwood to build up the fire.

He felt as if he were going through a nightmare in broad daylight. In a daze he caught a blurred glimpse of Hasan relieving himself over a clump of bushes. Get away, you little whelp, does one ever do such a thing under the Holy Walnut? It can strike you with its spell, by Allah it can! People forget that trees have souls too and can hurt a man that offends them, leaving him maimed for life. But if you do them no harm, then these holy trees can bring you luck. Who knows, this lofty, all-powerful tree may be good to us. Ah, if only I could muster some strength, I'd make my *namaz* prayers now, complete with ablutions and five genuflexions. . . . These holy trees have a liking for the *namaz*. If only that mother of mine would have the wisdom to pray now. But no! She does it for months on end in the village, and now, here, under this holy tree, she doesn't even pray once. Should I tell her? But then, even if she had intended to, she wouldn't do it. . . . I'll wake up at dawn and pray till the sun rises. I must come into the presence of Allah, after having cleansed my heart of all envy and hate, I must not think of Batty Bekir and the Muhtar, I must wipe out of my mind the image of Batty Bekir's wife. . . .

Try as he might, he had never been able to shed the evil thoughts that plagued his mind, not even during the *namaz*, so that his prayers had always been of no avail. One dark night when his father was still alive—he could not remember how old he was and yet all the sounds of that dark night, the shouting, the game and the cursing rang in his memory—the village children had been playing hide-and-seek, fifteen, twenty children chasing one another, tumbling over one another. . . . Whipped into a frenzy by the chase and the tussle, Ali had been tracked down by three children where he had hidden in a stack of hay. He had been afraid in the dark and he had held an open penknife in his hand. Suddenly the children had heard him move and had swooped upon him. A scream, and he had felt his knife sinking into someone's neck. Then he had slipped away before anyone could recognise him. It was Memet, the orphan, who had been the victim. For months afterwards Ali had not been able to look him in the face. The orphan had a deep scar that ran from his chin down his neck. A year later he had died of malaria in a stable.

If only this orphan had not existed. If only I could forget. . . .

And once also, he and some other children had been stoning

94

tortoises and Ali had broken the shell of one of them. Its back
had been laid bare, bathed in red blood. This image too he could
not drive away. The tortoise had made a small moaning sound.

I shall rise before dawn, wiping off the orphan and the
tortoise from my mind so as to be clear and bright as day in
Allah's presence. Perhaps the tree will do us a good turn.

He half-opened his eyes and saw the red glow of the fire and
his mother sitting on the other side. He lifted his head and
suddenly, without being aware of it, he spoke in a dead voice.

"Mother," he said, "I'll rise before dawn to-morrow and make
the *namaz* under this Holy Tree."

Huh, go ahead! We'll see! You can pray for a whole month,
day and night, but do you think Allah will ever help a son who's
broken his mother's heart, killed her horse, left her without a leg
to stand on?

"And after we get to the Chukurova I'll start making the
namaz regularly, five times a day."

So you think your prayers will find grace with Allah?
You killed my horse with your own hands. Just to spite me you
let that ill-omened Halil ride it. And on top of all this, he struck
at me, the old pimp. He gave me such a kick in the ribs, I thought
my lungs had been torn out. Another kick like that and I'd have
thrown up all my lungs piece by piece. No, Ali, my heart will
never forgive you and I don't think my beautiful black-eyed
Allah will forgive you either.

Ali turned to his wife joyfully. "Woman," he cried, "from
now on I'm going to make my *namaz* prayers regularly, five times
a day. May my head be severed from my body if I ever miss a
single *namaz*."

Elif smiled indulgently. "You'll do well, man. My father
never skipped a single prayer and that's why he never came to
any harm. Is there anything like the *namaz*?"

"I'll learn all the prayers from Father," said Hasan, "and I'll
make the *namaz* too."

"Children don't make the *namaz*," said Ummahan scornfully.
Hasan considered this a while. "Well then, I'll grow up and afterwards . . ."

That's right, that's right, Meryemdje's mind churned on, you all make the *namaz* together and go to Paradise. Even he who killed his mother's horse! Such a palace, all red and green, they have prepared for him there! They're all waiting for Ali Agha to arrive! Yes, make the *namaz*, all of you, and the hens in your yard too, and your dog and your cat. . . . Yes, kill me right here and make the *namaz* and go straight to Paradise. They'll welcome you all the better and invite you to sit in the Prophet's own circle. Here they come, these people, they'll say, who after killing their mother's horse, murdered her too. They deserve to be placed among the Forty Saints!

Elif took the bulgur *pilaff* off the fire. She melted some fat in the skillet and the smell of rank burning butter filled the air. The *pilaff* sizzled as she poured the melted fat over it.

Ali felt ravenously hungry. He sat down by the cloth, waiting impatiently.

"Ah, woman," he said, "an onion would be just the thing now. . . ."

"They're at the very bottom of the sack," said Elif as she placed the saucepan before him. "Not within easy reach."

"I just had a sudden craving. . . ."

The sack was propped up against the trunk of the walnut tree. She rolled up her sleeve and plunged her arm deep into it, raking the bottom. Finally, breathless and sweating, she managed to draw out a single onion.

"Here you are, man," she cried triumphantly as she dropped down near her husband. Meryemdje and the children were already eating.

Ali had just split the onion with a single blow of his fist when he heard footsteps behind him.

"*Selamunalaykum!* May Allah give you plenty."

He turned round, a little taken aback.

"*Aleykum selam*. Many thanks for your good wishes, brother."

The man flung down the *heybeh*[1] of goat's hair which he was carrying and squatted before the fire.

"Won't you partake of our meal, brother?"

"Enjoy your bread!" said the man. "I'm very tired and I don't feel like eating."

Ali half rose. "Come, brother, come," he insisted, "there's plenty for all of us. You haven't fallen on a destitute household, praise Allah!"

The man hoisted himself up. He was very tall with broad shoulders and an eagle's nose. He sat down beside them and rolled some *pilaff* into a wafer. Ali handed him a chunk of the onion.

"There's nothing like onions," said the man, "onions and salt, these are the best of foods. I wouldn't call a meal a meal without onions."

"Pray tell us your name," said Ali.

"I'm from the village of Yanukoglan and they call me Blunt Osman. I'm going down to the cotton, as you are too, I suppose. Where do you hail from?"

Ali told him.

"Did you leave the rest of the village behind?" asked Osman.

"No, they're ahead of us."

He was about to explain when Meryemdje interrupted him and started enumerating their mishaps with such vehemence that Ali was amazed. "Ah, my brother, have you a child?" was the leitmotif that interlaced her story. "Ah, my brother, bring up your child as a comfort for your old age, the saying goes. Well, here you are! Bring up your child so that he may be a torment to you." She was roused. The horse's death, the cold, how she had

[1] A double-bag of goat-hair in which Anatolian peasants carry their belongings.

frozen, the kick Old Halil had given her, all came pouring out in a quick torrent. When she had finished, she felt as tired as though she had been carrying heavy stones on her back all day long. "And so here I am now, helpless on these high mountains, all alone among the wild beasts and the jinn. . . ."

Ali hung his head with shame. As soon as the meal was over he drew Osman aside. "You don't believe her, do you, brother?" he asked. "Would a man ever kill his own horse in order to abandon his mother in the mountains? And would he then carry her on his back for days on end?"

"Of course not, brother," Osman smiled. "Don't I know these old folk? They get to be so very touchy."

They went back to the fire and sat down side by side.

Ali had taken a liking to the wayfarer. He had a smile that came from the depths of his heart. A spark of hope stirred in him. Then he noticed Osman's brand-new coat, made of the best smuggled material. It was not a coat that could be worn by just anyone. The spark of hope died out. He lifted his gaze above the coat. The black eyes were filled with sadness and there was a softness about the full red lips. Warmth and frankness emanated from the dark-complexioned face. Ali's hopes were rekindled. One can ask anything of such a man, he thought. Then his eyes fell on the silver watch-chain and all his hopes were dashed. He gazed into the fire thoughtfully. Some time passed before he could raise his head again and meet Osman's large black eyes, bright and cheerful and kind. What if he does have a chain, thought Ali. His sandals are of raw hide, worn and torn. I'll ask him, he decided. I'm sure he'll accept with pleasure.

Just then Osman put his hand into his pocket and drew out his tobacco case. It was a beautiful oakwood case inlaid with ivory in the shape of hares, birds and snakes. On the back of the case was a large ivory flower. He opened the case and expertly rolled a cigarette which he placed before his host. Ali was not used to smoking. His hand hovered over the cigarette. Then he picked it up and, drawing a brand from the fire, he lit it, puffing and blowing with the awkwardness of the amateur smoker.

Curse this poverty, thought Elif as she followed his self-conscious movements. It's a yoke shackled round a man's neck that he can't break and throw away, that drags him on wherever it chooses. Alas, my Ali, that you should never have had the chance to smoke like other men, in a leisurely manner, leaning against a tree. Alas. . . . Her eyes filled with tears.

Ali's gaze lingered on the ivory-inlaid case. Damn you, he thought, you've shattered all my hopes. Go your way and may your road be clear. You're different from us. I can't ask anything of you.

He smiled. Osman gave an answering smile as he finished rolling his own cigarette and, leaning back on his left elbow, began puffing away contentedly.

Ali longed to do the same, but he felt cowed as if in the presence of an agha or a bey.

"Brother," he said at last diffidently, "if it is not disrespectful to ask, why are you travelling all by yourself? Have your villagers left you behind too?"

"I've left them behind," replied Osman, his cigarette dangling from his smiling mouth.

"Why did you do that?" asked Ali bewildered.

"I got angry at them," replied Osman without changing his expression. "They made me angry, so I turned my back on them."

Good for you, wayfarer, Meryemdje exulted. Praised be your words of wisdom. So they offended you, did they? Then don't you ever speak to them again. How handsome you are, wayfarer! You're like an Arab steed. Beautiful Allah, keep him from the evil eye. *Mashallah, mashallah!*

Ali bowed his head. This must be a very important man, who could quarrel thus with a whole village.

"What did they do to make you so angry, my Agha?"

"I get like this, and when I do, I never look a person in the face again. I'll never set foot in that village as long as I live."

"But why?" Ali insisted.

"I got angry," repeated Osman obstinately, "but they'll be sorry. They'll come and whine at my door like dogs, but they'll never win me over again."

"Good for you, my son," Meryemdje broke in vehemently, "let them rue the day. Don't ever turn your face towards that village again!"

Osman was relaxed and smiling. "I won't, Mother," he assured her as he rose. He took up his *heybeh* and slung it over his shoulder. "Good health to you all," he said. "It's getting dark already, and for me the best time to walk is at night. The mountains smell so good that you'd think Paradise had set on earth. Well, good health!"

He moved away with long strides.

"God speed you, my brave lad!" cried Meryemdje, "don't ever go back to those infidels!"

Ali gazed after him until he disappeared. Then he looked at Elif. "Should I have asked him?"

"I wish you had. Maybe he would have carried part of our load."

"Did you notice his watch-chain?"

"Yes."

"There was that tobacco case too . . ." sighed Ali. "I couldn't bring myself to ask."

Darkness had fallen. The children were asleep, curled up by the fire.

"What would you say if we toasted some bread on the fire? We're not really hungry after that late bulgur *pilaff*."

Elif took a folded slice of wafer-bread from the bread container, while Ali raked some embers from the fire and spread them over a wide surface. He unfolded the wafer-bread and laid it over the embers, turning it over almost instantly. Then he cast it into a roll.

"This would call for a little cheese. . . ."

"We've got plenty," said Elif joyfully, "all the *ayran* I could lay my hands on this summer I made into cheese."

Ali woke the children up. He then made a second roll with cheese in it and offered it to Meryemdje. She ignored him. Ali realised that she would take nothing from him so he gave the roll to Hasan who in his turn handed it on to his grandmother. Meryemdje started munching slowly with her toothless gums.

"What are you thinking about, man?" asked Elif as she bit into her roll.

Ali was laughing happily. "I was thinking what characters there are in this world. Look at that man now. Breaking away from his village and setting off on the roads all by himself!"

Elif laughed too. The children burst into laughter. Only Meryemdje did not laugh.

Laugh away, laugh! Why didn't you laugh when he was here? What's so funny about his getting angry? That's what I call a man, not those creatures who conspire with old pimps to kill their mother's horse. Laugh away!

"We've slept all day," said Ali, "but still it would be better if we went to bed right away. To-morrow I must rise before dawn and make the *namaz*. Elif, let's lay the bed at the foot of the Holy Tree so our heads should rest on its roots."

Spare your efforts. My black-eyed Allah won't be deceived by your blandishments.

Their fire burnt till morning for they had thrown a huge log in the centre of it.

Chapter 8

When Meryemdje woke up she saw Ali in deep prayer, his back to the stately walnut tree. Mercy on us, good folk, was her first thought, this lad doesn't know any prayers at all and there he is, trying to deceive Allah!

Ali turned his head once to the right and once to the left in the final ritual salaam. Then he heaved himself up half-heartedly. The sun would soon be rising. Streaks of dancing light glimmered on the tree-studded crag that hung like a cloud of smoke high above them. He stood there feeling dull and numb. The *namaz* had swept away all images of the tortoises, of the orphan Memet and of the other thing, but the effort to cleanse his mind had worn him out. He glanced at Meryemdje and it seemed to him that she was laughing up her sleeve. No, she was laughing outright, as though she knew all about the tortoises bathed in blood with their bulging eyes, the amber-yellow wound of the orphan Memet and also that other thing. Anger began to well up in him again. He frowned and peered at her face which was half hidden by the shadows. Ever since he could remember, whenever he got angry, as angry as could be, he only had to look at his mother's face and his anger would disappear immediately. Now, for the first time, this was not so. He felt disconcerted and alarmed.

"Mother," he said as he walked a few steps towards her, "you stay here under this blessed tree. I'll be back to get you long before noon."

Meryemdje made no answer.

He turned to Elif, who was binding the bedding and their other belongings into large packs. "Have you finished?"

She nodded. Ali loaded the pack on to his back and struck out towards the road. The boughs of the lofty walnut murmured like a vast forest in the morning breeze.

Meryemdje faced Elif defiantly. "Thank God," she cried, "that my legs can still bear me. That husband of yours need have no fear. I can walk down to the Chukurova better than he can, indeed like a horse at the *jereed* games. How many times haven't I trodden these same paths. Why, if you look carefully, you'll see my footprints on this very road. But when it comes to climbing hills . . . that's what breaks my back. I never liked them anyway." She picked up a long stick. "Do what you like, I'm off and you'll see if I can't walk." She looked at her grandchildren. "Come with your grandmother, my bright-eyed darlings. Ah, if only you weren't the children of that infidel! I'd have given my soul for you then."

The leaves of the camel thistles bordering the road were covered with dust. From that point onward the road was narrow and stony and wound through squat trees and brush.

Elif had read the anger on her husband's face and she sensed that something was about to break out between mother and son. Up to now, may the Devil not hear of it, there had never been the slightest argument between them, nor between Elif and her mother-in-law. Meryemdje had never given rise to a quarrel. She had always acted with great wisdom and pliancy.

"Mother, please stay here and wait for your son. You can't possibly walk."

Meryemdje's face darkened and her lips trembled.

"I? I, not walk?" she screamed, striking the ground with her stick. "I'm off, do you hear, and all by myself too. And I don't want you either, you bastards of a no-good father."

Elif stopped short. Her face changed as she looked after Meryemdje. Then she went to take up her pack.

103

Meryemdje was now walking so quickly that Elif could barely keep up with her. The children had fallen behind.

"Granny's very angry with Father," said Hasan to his sister, "she hasn't opened her mouth once to answer anything he says to her."

"She won't ever," declared Ummahan. "Father's killed her horse, Grandfather's old relic."

"Father didn't kill her horse," protested Hasan. "Old Halil killed it, but now he's run away, Granny's taking it out on Father."

Ummahan tossed her head crossly as she spurted on to join her mother.

Infused with a vigour that surprised her, Meryemdje was walking at a brisk and tireless pace, just as in her youth. She was so elated that the death of the horse, her grievances against her son, seemed nothing to her now, as if those dark days had been as merry as a wedding. What had the poor lad done after all, she asked herself. He had only been merciful. There's a vast ocean of mercy in him. His heart always aches for the stricken. And didn't I see how that poison-eyed one stuck to him like black gum-mastic? It's my fault. I never spoke to the lad seriously. When I tell him all the things that Halil did to my Ibrahim, Ali's mouth will drop open with astonishment. He'll understand then why that husband of mine, who wouldn't have hurt a fly, was known as the greatest robber in the Chukurova. My fine, kind-hearted child, my darling, how could your mother ever be angry with you? And for three whole days I've made you spit blood! You took me on your beautiful back and carried me all the way up these slopes, and I was cruel to you, may my two eyes fall out of their sockets! For three days now you've been waiting for a kind word from me and I haven't moved these lips of mine, may they shrivel away! O, almighty Allah, I take back everything I've said against my fine-hearted Ali. He's a grown man now, but never in all these years has he had a hard word for me.

I've become old, and in my anger I say whatever comes to my head. Don't you pay any attention, my black-eyed Allah. I'm just a witless, crazy old woman. Forgive me. My Ali's a good lad, help him, my gracious Allah. He made the *namaz* for you too. . . .

She was wrapped in a dream of gladness, a whirlwind of light, filled with sensations that were vague and far like a song, a scent, a colour. A pure blue on the far-distant shores of the Mediterranean, and above that blue the flowing of a snowy whiteness. Her husband, young and slim and tall, with his sunburnt face, his large grey-blue eyes and his glossy hair tumbling over his forehead, his friendly laugh after a man's heart, sweet as that of a child laughing in its sleep. So dear . . . Alas, curse that Yemen desert. . . . It was on a night of wedding festivities. Someone had taken her hand in the dark and pressed it, and a thrill had raced through her veins. She had known that instant that it was Ibrahim and she had melted with joy and pleasure.

On the higher side of the road was a single tall pine-tree, its boughs spread open like the wings of a great bird poised for flight. She looked lovingly at the tree that she had seen standing there for perhaps thirty years now, its branches and leaves always the same, always as though about to fly off. And who knows, thought Meryemdje, there is life in trees just as in human beings. Why not indeed, since saints inhabit them?

The cold had broken and the sun was warmer now. Meryemdje was sweating ever so slightly. Just as in my youth, she rejoiced. It's good to sweat. I haven't sweated like this in a long time. She glanced back at Elif and the children who were lagging behind her.

By the grace of Allah, even my young and healthy daughter-in-law can't keep up with me! It wasn't in vain that I prayed to the Holy Walnut. If Allah grants strength to my knees, I said, next year I'll kill a cock at the foot of your trunk and then without eating a morsel I'll hand it out to passing wayfarers. Yes, I owe you this, O Holy Tree, though you deserve not one, but two cocks. Just look at the way my legs are going! Were it in my power, I'd offer you a huge camel, just as the Circassians sacrifice horses. Yes, a male camel with two humps.

She passed the lone walnut tree, beyond which the forest started again.

There flows a stream called the Savrun with tall poplars on its banks, and the fish in its depths can be seen as clear as on the surface. And there is the mill at Süleymanli that smells of warm flour when you pass near it. Then, just before the plane-trees begin, the big meadow of mauve-flowering marjoram spreads out like an embroidered *kilim*. Once when Hasan was still alive, Jabbar's son, Pale Hasan, whose mother was such a pleasant-tongued woman, we were passing along this meadow. Such a fragrance filled the whole world that the stones and the earth, the trees and the stream, everything smelled sweet of fresh marjoram. Then Hasan stopped suddenly and said—he was so handsome was Hasan, beautiful among all men, so that looking on his countenance you would have thought: surely he is as beautiful as our Lord Joseph was—"Uncles, we must pause and spend one night here in the mauve-flowering of this meadow. Let the cotton picking wait for one day, what matter." His voice was like magic. No one uttered a word. They all went and laid down their loads under the plane-trees.

On the sixth day of the journey, at midday, one reaches the marjoram meadow, but the villagers no longer stop there at night any more. They never did after that one time. Who knows why . . . Hasan is dead. . . . How lovely are the poplars of the Chukurova, each one adorned like a bride. How they sway at the slightest breeze. And the Chukurova like a green garden stretching out endlessly.

What's that? My God, are my knees failing me?

The forest, the red rocks with lizards on them. . . . A weasel cleaving the road like lightning. . . . The flashing of stubble in a harvested field. . . . There is nothing as sturdy as stubble, nothing that sparkles so, filling itself with the whole light of the sun to gush forth again in coruscations.

She turned back towards the Holy Walnut, whose crest was barely visible, and gave herself up to prayer, remaining like that, her hands held palms open to the sky, until overtaken by Elif.

"How fast you're walking, good Mother! I tried and tried, but I couldn't catch up with you."

Meryemdje's hands dropped to her sides. "Well, you've caught up now, my daughter," she said despondently. She felt so exhausted that it was as though she no longer had any body, feet or arms. She took two steps forward. "You've caught up, as you see," she repeated and her voice was so bitter and hopeless that Elif's eyes filled with tears. Meryemdje's face frightened her. It had taken on the ashen hue of sick people nearing death. She hurriedly put down her load.

"Sit down, Mother," she said, "my loyal, good Mother, there's no one like you."

Meryemdje sank to the ground, her head drooping. She took a deep breath.

"I'm coming round," she murmured, as she saw the frightened faces of Elif and the children, "it's all right now. You get like this when you walk very fast even if you're young. What are you standing and staring at me for?"

"My own good Mother," Elif blurted out, "I'm just looking. . . . You're better, thank God!"

Meryemdje bowed her head. "You've caught up, you see," she repeated in a moan.

Elif was relieved to see that the colour had returned to her face, but she hesitated, not knowing how Meryemdje would react to what she was going to say.

"Mother," she began at last in a small voice. "My lady Mother, please don't stir from here. We have to catch up with Ali. Otherwise he won't be able to leave the load and come and get you. You wait right here. I'll send him back quickly."

She hurried away. The children followed. When Meryemdje raised her head to reply, they were already far in the distance. Her heart jumped as if scalding water had been poured over her.

"You've caught up indeed, you bitch of a daughter-in-law. You've even passed me, wife of a cuckold," she groaned. "I should have called down Allah's curse on myself before I ever took you as a bride for that Long Ali, may he be struck blind. Still, you're not as bad as he is. But the children . . . just look at those little pigs whelped by a bitch. They too. . . . Yes, you've caught up indeed, and left me too, all alone in this wilderness."

Suddenly, with unexpected quickness, she sprang up, her eyes bulging from their sockets, and let out a scream.

"Ali!" The echo resounded from the distant rocky slopes. "Aliii!" Then she dropped down exhausted, beating on the ground with her fists. A thought flashed through her head striking her like a thunderbolt. Those people have laid a trap for me. Foul play! Woe on me! Scatter earth over my head! If it weren't a trap, would they have taken the children from me and gone off? Help, oh help!

The fear grew apace and rooted itself in her mind. Foul play. . . . On these mountains . . . with the wild beasts . . . and the Holy Walnut. . . . At the memory of the holy tree a light broke out within her and all her fears melted away. She lifted her head in the direction of the tree and started to pray quickly.

But her relief was short-lived. Here she was on this solitary mountain, alone with only a tree. The feeling of forlorn helplessness overcame her. Desolate, quite quite desolate. . . . An emptied world. . . . Even its bees and flies, its ants and birds, its snakes and lizards, its little worms and insects seemed to have gone. Only a tree and Meryemdje were left in this world.

And of what use is a tree to a human being? It has no hands and feet to drive away attackers. It has no gun, no knife. It has no village, or house, or family, or food. No medicine or fire.

The Wind from the Plain

Just a long lonely tree jutting out gauntly into the sky. What help can one expect from a poor tree?

The overwhelming terror of being treacherously abandoned in the mountains spread within her like a powerful poison.

How pleasantly they smiled at me! How innocent was Ali's face, like that of an angel. But the children could not look me in the eyes. What do children know of deceit? What do they know of double-dealing? That's only for grown-ups who play every devilish trick on you and then smile to your face, who embrace you when they are plotting to kill you. What can children know? My Hasan and my Ummahan were ready to burst into tears at a word. Especially my brave Hasan who was turning and turning about me, trying to whisper something into my ear, but he didn't have a chance. Poor little thing, how he walked, his head hanging as if to say: I won't stir from Granny's side, let the wild beasts devour me too. Yes, he did say it, but those godless wretches didn't care. They kept talking in whispers. They were careful not to let the children come near me. I should have understood. But is there any sense left in me since the death of my horse?

She rose slowly, staring towards the hill over which they had disappeared. She looked to right and left and up at the lofty crags. Then she fixed her eyes on the crest of the Holy Walnut Tree.

How many days is it from here to the Chukurova, she wondered. She counted in her mind all the stops on the road. The ascents, the dark forests, the black streams barring the way, the graveyards beside the road, the Tiger's Crag . . . People have heard huge tigers with fangs of flame roaring on this crag. They say that these tigers snap a man's head right off his body. And then there's the Forsaken Graveyard, long and dark and terrifying, its gravestones aslant and untended. . . .

Who cares if they've deserted me! I'll go down to the plain and knock at the house of an Agha. Lady, I'll say to his wife, it's like this, and I'll explain everything. Tears will come to her eyes. This world is full of charitable souls. You can sit here in a corner for ever, good Mother, she'll say. We have plenty of bread and food, and you can look after the children now and then. And I'll say to her: I've had children too and see what they've done to me! But still, maybe you know better. I'll tend your children with more loving care than I did for my own.

Then the news will reach Ali that I am in the Chukurova staying with the Agha. He'll come and beg and weep and do everything to talk me over. And I . . . but the Lady will come. She'll give Ali a fine dressing down, and to me she'll say, I hold you in higher esteem than my own mother. Don't go with this wretched man who threw you into the jaws of death, who left you stranded with a Holy Tree.

From afar came a muted roaring. It was as if a hive of bees were swarming in her head.

She started walking, picturing the Lady with her white head-kerchief, her black eyes, her sweet smile. Many long years had elapsed since she had last seen her. It was after the cotton picking. The Lady had said she needed somebody to do a little sewing and Meryemdje had offered to work for her. Afterwards the Lady had given her one of her cotton dresses. What a lovely Lady she was! Since that day the Lady's kind smile had lived on in her thoughts.

One can reach the Chukurova anyway, even though starving and thirsting. I'll go by the high road. It's longer but maybe I'll come upon some villagers. There should be many now trekking on the high road. They'll see me and ask what's befallen me and when I tell them the women will all weep. They'll sit me on a nice horse with a Circassian saddle and I'll say to them: Good people, have no fear because you're late for the cotton. I never forget a kindness. Once we reach the Chukurova, I'll find you such a field to pick that in one day you'll gather a week's cotton and earn bags of money. I may be a weak and decrepit old woman, but it's to me the Lady gave her red cotton frock that was brand-new. It's still in my trunk as fresh and unfaded as the day she gave it to me. A keepsake. . . . If only I'd taken it with me. I'd have shown it to her. How pleased she would have been to see that I still have it!

Suddenly she came to a standstill. The image of the Forsaken Graveyard passed before her eyes, the graveyard winding in a long endless rush of darkness, its stones rolling and tumbling over each other. . . . The dead! The bones of the dead! Oh, the Forsaken Graveyard! It takes a whole morning to walk from one end of it to the other. Near the road is a huge long grave with its stone aslant and a leafless worm-eaten oak over it. No living soul can pass all by himself near the Graveyard without being paralysed with terror. One can pass by the dark waters, the Tiger's Crag, the Jinn's Cave, but one cannot even approach the Forsaken Graveyard.

She turned back towards the village, as if fleeing from the Graveyard. The Chukurova, the Lady, the travelling village, the horse she was to ride, everything had faded away. If only this graveyard did not exist. If only . . . She pressed on, not daring to look back.

I'll go to the village. There's some bulgur left at the bottom of the bulgur sack. I'll take out the grain from the pit and grind it in the hand-mill. What does it matter if it's only roughly ground? Can't one eat it? I'll pass it through the mill twice, then it'll be softer. . . .

An uninhabited village, without a soul. . . . One cries for a soul, but . . . Alone there for two months, a body can lose her mind. Not a sound, nothing. . . . What could the empty village be like? Desolate. . . . Only the buzzing of flies. . . . And if a strong north wind should blow, its roar would burst over the village like cannon. And what if all the whirling thistles should drift in and fill the village?

She sank down on the side of the road, the loneliness growing upon her. The skies were widening in all their blue immensity, the mountains flattening out, the trees and houses vanishing and the emptiness echoing and re-echoing. Only the silvery thistles are whirling round slowly in this desolation. Not even a breath of wind. . . . Nothing stirs. . . .

She shivered and shrank in fear. She rose again and turned towards the Chukurova.

But weren't the dogs still in the village? And the cats too? And there was a starling that came to build its nest in a corner of the house. Jet-black with white specks, but changing in the sun to green and to other colours. Its young kept falling off. She would take them in the palm of her hand, the soft little things, and without hurting them would carry them back to the nest. At times the sky would be dark with flights of starlings and then the village lads would make a feast. Although a small bird, it has a tender flesh. Five starlings make a really good meal. The village would resound with the crack of shotguns and the mountains and plains would fill with grey smoke. Before every house a fire would be lit and the sizzling of fat and the appetising odour of burning fresh meat would fill the village. The starlings pass and fly off, but for a fortnight after they have gone, the smell of roasted starling permeates the village, lingering in every house, in the pots and pans, the clothes, the beds, the walls, even in the skin itself.

Once she had found a wounded starling. She had picked it up and held it against her breast, feeling the quick frightened beating of its heart. Its eyes were like the eyes of a wounded gazelle, the disconsolate black eyes of a beautiful girl who has not found happiness. Yes, just like that! She had brought it home and chewed a little wheat with which she had dressed the wound. Outside, the whole village smelled of starlings, of the smoke rising from thousands of starlings being roasted over the red embers in every hearth. "I won't give you up to the fire or to the hunters," she had murmured, slipping her fingers under the bird's warm wings. "Eat, drink, and when your wound is healed you'll fly off to your home again."

The Wind from the Plain

There was one person, only one, who did not hunt at starling time. His eyes were like those of the wounded starling and he always laughed, always, even when he was weeping. Spellbound Ahmet, my child where are you now?

Spellbound Ahmet's face is white as if frozen. He is tall and willowy. The village has never seen and never will see a man as handsome, as sweet-spoken as he, who has never hurt anyone nor ever will. On the lofty mountains, way back among the oak trees, is the realm of the King of the Peris, who dwells in a palace all of crystal. It is from that crystal palace that the sun rises each morning. One day the daughter of the Peri King sees Ahmet, who is chopping wood in the oak-grove and she is struck dumb on the spot. She burns with such a passion for him that smoke rises from the top of her head. That minute she appears to Ahmet in the guise of a beautiful human maiden. As soon as he sees her Ahmet becomes enamoured too. So the maiden takes Ahmet to her father's palace and there they are secretly wed. In the course of time the Peri King discovers that his daughter is married to a human being and he flies into a formidable rage, Allah protect us! And in his fury he strikes Ahmet and cripples him with the blow. He would have killed him but for the Peri maiden who throws herself at her father's feet, crying: "Don't kill my Ahmet before you kill me! What if he is a human being? I adore human beings. Just give me a cave hereabouts and allow me to live there with my loved one." The Peri maiden's mother, her other sisters all plead for her, and obtain permission for the two lovers to live in a cave far away from the palace. "More than anything else in this world, I love the smell of human beings," the Peri maiden always says to Ahmet (and it's true, for Ahmet repeated this himself to his own mother). "Ever since I was a child, whenever a breeze happened to blow from your village, I would be crazed, out of my mind, especially in the spring-time when all the trees and plants are in full blossom."

"In full blossom," Meryemdje sighed aloud.

When the villagers go down to the Chukurova leaving the village quite empty, Ahmet descends from the mountain, bringing along with him his wife and children and his sisters-in-law and all those other Peris who also like the smell of the human being and wish to live in the village.

If I arrive at the village now, I'll find Ahmet as sure as if I'd put him there myself.

She turned back and started walking very fast.

When Ahmet sees me, he'll be surprised at first, then he will laugh softly in the way small children do and he'll say: "Don't hide, women, don't run away, children. Have no fear, Peri-folk. Mother Meryemdje here knows how to keep a secret." And I will say: "Come here, my lovely girl, come. You've shown how wise you are, for if you weren't the wisest of Peris you wouldn't have chosen the most handsome, the sweetest-laughing of human beings. Don't be afraid of me. Aren't the Peris part of the Islam community too? Aren't they made like human beings? You run about and play. I'll sing lullabies to your children and put them to sleep. My voice may not be as sweet as a Peri's—who knows how sweet a Peri's voice is—and yet my lullabies used to hush a crying child like a charm. But it's so long since I've sung babies to sleep. After Ali, after Hasan . . . I must love a child and then only can my voice be soothing to it. I will love your children. You'll teach me the Peri language, my daughter, and I'll sing to the children, half in the human language, half in the Peri language. And when the villagers return from the Chukurova, you'll make me invisible like you and take me to your cave. They say, my daughter, that in your father's palace are forty chambers, all of them locked, and in each of these chambers is a golden fount of spring water. They say that he who drinks of this water will never die. Have you made Ahmet drink of it? You should, my daughter, even though your father be a harsh king. They say he hides the keys in his hair. You must find a way to get hold of them, my daughter, while your father is asleep, for if you survive your husband you'll be as miserable as I am. To live on after your husband, bereft and all alone, is like living on in a desolate world without people. Steal the keys while he is asleep, quickly, quickly. . . . Let my Ahmet drink of the spring. Let him not die. They say that only Köroglu's white horse has drunk of the spring of life and will never die. That accursed Old Halil tells how, each year, his white horse is sold at the Aleppo market for one gold coin. It is brought to the market-place before dawn and tied to a post, a horse so thin, so emaciated, that all its bones jut out and it totters on its feet. But the very first person to arrive at the market who sees the horse takes it away, for into whichever house it is sold it brings abundance and good luck that year and no evil fortune ever befalls that household again. That is why there are many who wait up all night, all the year round on every market day, so as to be the first to see the white horse and own it for a year. You must find a way, my daughter, of unlocking one of the forty chambers and of making your husband drink of this water that bestows immortality. A Peri who is so in love with the odour of the human body should do this, my daughter."

You'll look after me, won't you, my Ahmet? You'll be my soul's comrade. Isn't it you who, at cotton time, brings the whirling thistle to Old Halil's door and tells him the cotton is ripe? Let that infidel Long Ali abandon his mother on the high mountains, a prey to the wild beasts and birds. What does it matter since you're there, Ahmet, my child? Let him go and perish ignominiously in hell. . . .

It is said that the Peris have no bridge to their nose. Do your children have noses like that too? Well, it doesn't matter. It's not a great defect, really. What if their noses are slightly flattened out? Don't worry about that at all, Ahmet, my child.

Would Ahmet come to meet her when he learnt that she was trudging up towards the village? Would he bring his wife along? A sudden misgiving gripped her and her feet dragged to a standstill as if heavy lead weights had been clapped on to them.

What if he did not come to meet her? What if, according to the Peri custom, he did not show his wife and children to her?

It was past noon. The sun had sunk westward. For the first time she looked back with some hope. There was no one to be seen. She slumped to the ground, her body aching as if beaten to pulp.

"Allah, take away my soul!" she cried in fear and anguish.

The forest was turning purple. She saw a squirrel on the summit of a tree, its eyes rolling like that of a humming-bird. A ladybird came and settled on her hand.

"This means luck," she rejoiced, "it brings me good tidings from the Peris, from my Ahmet." She petted the ladybird with her chapped fingers. "Little insect," she said, "please tell me. What news do you bring from my Ahmet? How is his wife, little insect?"

She wanted to take the tiny insect between her lips and kiss it again and again. Her body felt light as a feather now.

"It's my Ahmet who's sent you, is it not, so as to meet Mother Meryemdje? That's why you've come to me, is it not, little insect? You may be the fairies' insect, but you're still a baby for sure. How small you are! Lulla-lulla-lullaby. Sleep, pretty insect. I'll give you your due reward for good tidings. . . ."

The ladybird rested on her finger, and as she sang she swayed her finger to the melody as if rocking a cradle.

"Sleep, little one, sleep! Lulla-lulla-lullaby. . . ."

She rose gingerly, holding out her forefinger cautiously for fear the insect would fly off.

"Wait," she said, "pretty insect, clever little insect, soldier of the Peri King. I know you bring me greetings from my Ahmet. Let people scoff at me if they wish. If a Peri maiden can be wife to a human being, why shouldn't a ladybird be a harbinger?"

Her eyes were fixed on the speckled, red insect. Once or twice it opened its wings and attempted to fly, then it folded them back again.

Here on these mountains are greyish ball-shaped thistle plants that are called fairy's nests. They grow close to the soil like mushrooms. In these thistle balls shelter myriads of ladybirds.

"Poor little one," Meryemdje crooned. "Who knows how far you've fared. Your wings cannot bear you any longer and your body must be racked with pain, who knows. . . ."

She drew out a corner of her headcloth, picked up the insect delicately, and placed it in the kerchief, which she carefully tied into a loose knot.

"You lie there, little one. . . . You've come from very, very far. After you've had a good rest, I'll put you on a flower. Now your wings must be bruised and aching. . . ." She smiled. "Stay there," she said, "stay, little one, and when I find a beautiful flower . . ."

She was walking joyfully towards the village.

Chapter 9

It was past midday by the time Elif caught up with Ali. His thin face was dark and drawn, his eyes clouded and troubled.

There are faces that always hide their feelings, and then comes a moment when they break down and their sluices burst open. The floodgates of Ali's face had collapsed. Weariness, sorrow and bitterness were frozen so indelibly on his features as to be almost tangible.

Elif's heart ached as she looked at him, bent double under his pack, his feet dragging him on laboriously.

"Haven't you gone too far again?" she said. "It's past noon."

"What if it is?" he cried violently. "The others will be reaching the cotton in no time." The sweat was streaming down his face. He stopped a moment and wiped his brow. "At this rate we'll be there only after all the cotton's been picked and we won't get a duck's egg. Walk, walk, woman. The children aren't tired, are they?"

"Do I ever get tired?" cried Hasan, with a whoop as he pranced about before his father.

"Mother's under the Walnut Tree, isn't she?"

"No. She started off, almost flying at first. Then she tired and I made her sit down on the roadside. What can she do, poor thing? She tries her best not to be a burden to you, but . . ."

They reached the outskirts of a forest that spread far into the distance, black as a raincloud. They were now on the brink of the

Taurus woodlands, where it is cold as ice even in the height of summer.

"Shall we camp here, Elif?"

"All right, but let's hope we don't freeze here this night. At least there's plenty of wood. I'll have a good fire blazing by the time you come."

Ali eased the pack down, took a deep breath and stretched himself. His bones cracked. There was a burning pain in his feet. He lifted his left leg and saw that the sole of his sandal was torn. Small sharp stones had slipped in and cut his foot.

"I know my mother, Elif," he said, "she just can't bear to be disabled. It kills her to have to be carried by me. Her quarrel is not against me but against old age. The horse, too, is just an excuse. If it had simply died, I mean, without Old Halil riding it, and I had to carry her as I'm doing now, she would have been just as angry."

"Mother's a strange woman," mused Elif. "Doesn't everyone grow old and impotent?"

"She just can't get used to old age," said Ali. "If you don't humour her, she'll kill herself. Don't you see how she hennaes her hair even now, every single day?"

Elif smiled.

"Why," added Ali, smiling too, "she's almost ready to dress her hair in curls like a bride." He sat down and leant against a tree.

Hasan had been gathering wood and stacking it under a fir-tree. He had also found a fairy's nest which is even better than resinwood for lighting fires. He struck a match and was about to set fire to the fairy's nest when Ali shouted at him.

"Hey you, did you shake that? Don't you know it's a nest, full of ladybirds? Throw it away and use resinwood."

Hasan waved the thistle ball in the air. Myriads of ladybirds began to drop out of it. Seeing that there was no end to the downpour of insects, he hurled the plant into the distance. Then he broke a piece of resinwood off the bark of a pine-tree and lit it.

Ali shrank from setting out again, but the longer he sat the more he felt the pain in his body. He jumped to his feet with sudden decision as if shocked out of sleep.

"I'm going," he said, as he started off on the road.

Elif ran after him and handed him a roll of wafer-bread. "You must be dying of hunger. Eat this," she said, "I've put some cheese into it too."

He took the roll without looking at her and hurried on. She stood still for a long while, gazing after him. "What can he do, poor man," she sighed, "it's no use. The cotton picking will be over long before we get there. Perhaps it would be better if we stayed down in the Chukurova this winter. . . ."

She went to sit by the fire. The children were chattering away, but she did not hear them.

"Mother lass," said Hasan, "won't Granny be frightened all alone there on the mountain?"

"Of course not," Ummahan broke in, "if she were frightened, we wouldn't have left her."

"Shut up," cried Hasan, "I'm not talking to you. Mother, won't she be frightened?"

Elif's head was on her knees. Hasan nudged her. "Hey, Mother, won't she be frightened? Mother! I'm asking you!"

"She's not frightened, she's not frightened!" Ummahan repeated.

"Mother," insisted Hasan, "I'm talking to you. Won't Granny be frightened?" He shook her fiercely.

Elif lifted her head. Her eyes were glazed. "She won't," she replied listlessly and laid her head down again.

Hasan was cross. "Hah! Not frightened! She'll be scared out of her wits."

"No, she won't," Ummahan shouted defiantly.

At that he pounced on her, tugging at her hair. Elif raised her head again. "What do you want, you shameless brats?" she said wearily. "Don't we have enough worries as it is?"

They stopped short, abashed and downcast, cowed by their mother's lifeless voice.

As Ali walked, he kept muttering to himself: "If not to-morrow, then the day after. If not to-morrow . . . They'll be starting on the cotton. And if the crop is good, everyone will be back with a stack of money. Oh, my black fortune! How will I ever get there in time if I have to cover every stretch of the journey three times? No one's going to wait for me. As for Adil Effendi, there's no question of Moslem fellowship with him. He'll unhinge the door of my house and take it away. He'll carry off even the burnt plough in the field, even the flour and bulgur we still have in our sacks. . . . If not to-morrow, then the day after. . . . And is there any mercy to be expected from the Muhtar? He'll put us in the first batch of taxpayers, he hates us so. . . . If not to-morrow, then the day after. . . ."

He hurried on, his steps falling into the refrain of these words. If not to-morrow . . . An insistent lament kept recurring within him and rising to the tip of his tongue, but he held it down, the heart-rending dirge for Osman, that drives a grown man to sit on the ground and sob his heart out. On returning from a long journey, Osman, a cousin of his, had perished in a snowstorm that had overtaken him in the Meryemchil pass, and it was only in the spring that his body had been found under the melting snows. Old Sultandja it was who sang this elegy so beautifully. She sang and wept, and always, always, she would try to stop any villager who was planning to set out alone on a journey.

> Cold is my dear son now, so cold
> What evil hand did touch him
> Lord almighty, why didst hurt him
> Among four daughters my one and only.

The Wind from the Plain

The flag[1] will never fly over your door
Nor *sinsin*[2] fires be lit for you
You will not press a hennaed hand[3]
My virgin son, my blighted one.

The keening swelled within him against his will, like something gliding slowly up from the depths of a pool. It surged to the surface and he found himself singing the sad mournful dirge to the lonely road. His eyes filled with tears. If not to-morrow, then the day after. . . . He could see no way out.

It was late afternoon when he suddenly saw the Holy Walnut soaring above him. He looked around eagerly, but she was not there. Then he remembered what Elif had told him. She was somewhere back on the road, he thought. Do I ever look about me when I walk? She didn't speak to me, but I can't blame her. It's all my fault. What business did I have to put Old Halil on the horse? Perhaps it wouldn't have died. . . . She's perfectly right to be angry. . . . But still, she must have seen me as I passed her by. Couldn't she have given some sign, a cough at least? Allah, stifle the cough out of her and let me be delivered from her clutches. No, no, I didn't mean that, Allah. . . . But after all, why did she let me walk on, tired as I am? Is it human to make me suffer like this? Maybe she's fallen asleep somewhere among these bushes. . . .

He started to shout, straining his lungs, and his voice echoed from hill to hill.

"Mother! Mo-ther! Answer me! I've come to fetch you. You needn't speak to me, lady Mother, just make a sound. Speak to the trees, to the rocks, to the earth, but say something. Don't torment me dear Mother. I know I've mucked things up and killed your horse. Forgive me. Answer me, Mother. Mo-ther!"

[1] A marriage ritual in Anatolian villages.
[2] Ritual dance around a fire, survival of an ancient worship.
[3] The bride's nails are tinctured with henna.

There was not the slightest sign of life. Convinced that she was not there, he slowly retraced his steps. Every now and then, he stopped to shout.

"Mother, Mo-ther!" His voice was broken. "Just call out once, Mother, just once. Not to me, to the earth. Just say, earth, I'm here. Say it, beautiful Mother."

He reached the camping place after midnight. From afar he saw the fire burning under a tree and as he drew nearer, he caught sight of Elif, her head resting on her knees.

"Mother's come, hasn't she, Elif?" he cried out anxiously.

She sprang to her feet and ran towards him.

He grasped her hands. "When did she come?"

Elif swallowed hard.

"Why don't you speak? Isn't she here?"

"No," she replied faintly, "have you missed her?"

He let himself fall to the ground like a corpse. They were silent for a long time. Then Ali raised his head.

"Where can she be now in the dead of night?"

Elif did not answer. She was weeping quietly.

"Drink some soup," she said at last, "and let's start back to look for her."

She pushed the saucepan towards him and gave him a wooden spoon, but it was all Ali could do not to drop it. He swallowed a few spoonfuls, then laid the spoon aside.

"Come," he said in a voice like a moan, "let's go."

"I hope the children don't wake up. . . ."

"We'll be back before daylight."

Again they set out towards the Holy Walnut. From the distant forest came the barely audible murmur of the wind. Now and again, whiffs of pine, fir, wormwood and mint wafted over to them. A jackal howled in the distance.

Ali was musing, half asleep, half awake. If only it would rain now, he thought. Such a rain that would flood the whole of the Chukurova plain. . . . It was long ago in the days of his childhood. The sea had stretched before him, unbounded, almost purple. There was a beach, and one morning the sun had risen, beating down upon the sands and turning the sea to molten gold. A short golden turmoil, and then, as the sun mounted in the sky, the sea had become the sea once more, with its white, foaming waves. Such a strange vast water is this thing they call the sea, rolling beyond the edge of the earth.

Yes, it should rain as it rained that year, when the wattle huts had been swept away by the torrents. Where the cotton field ended, a forest of poplars spread out into the distance, ten times more vast than the pine and cedar forest of the Taurus. Looking on that forest, one thought: There are three things in this Chukurova. A smooth, level plain, so flat that if you put an egg at one end, you can see it from the other end. Then a vast sea, that turns to purple, to orange, constantly changing into various colours, mighty, unfathomable, having no beginning and no end. And then, there is this poplar forest. They say that a large river flows beyond it, with villages, dams, fields and orange groves as far as the eye can see. But, from the Taurus range way back up to the sea, the world is just one immense poplar forest, haunted by serpents and tortoises, hyenas and long-tailed foxes, demon-eyed jackals and all kinds of unknown, unseen creatures, such as fairies and jinn.

Yes, it must rain, taut-drawn cords of rain that would come lashing down, uprooting the trees and sweeping them along with all the huts. The mighty waters should roll on like grey earth. Yes, it should rain slime, not water. Just as it had been that time, when the waters had set in motion a whole forest with all its creatures and driven it right up to the shores of the Mediterranean, so it must be now.

All the cotton pickers had taken refuge on a mound, some distance from the sea. The day was about to break. Drenched to the bone, we were huddling close to each other, waiting for the morning. The rain never abated one whit, not even for the wink of an eye. Frozen and shivering under the relentless downpour, we were fast losing hope. If the rain did not let up, we were doomed to freeze to death on this mound, for the whole area around us was flooded. The rain came down in sheets between us and the dawning day, between us and the sea, the kind of rain you would wish upon your enemy. Such a rain should rain now. . . .

And then, what did we see? From afar over the plain, a poplar forest was gliding towards the sea, its every tree erect, standing firm, not even tilted. We looked on as the forest neared the sea. People can say what they like, but Old Halil is a wise man. "Look, people," he said, "look on this wondrous mystery, this miracle Allah has laid before our eyes. What else can you call this rain that uproots Djingiloglu's great poplar forest? Not just uproots it, but bears it along with all its earth too!"

And as the eastern glow lit up the flooded Chukurova plain the villagers forgot their plight and riveted their gaze on the advancing forest. It reached the sea and, for a moment, stood poised there on the shore. Then the foremost trees abruptly toppled over into the sea. Row after row of long-ranging, upright trees drifted to the shore and crashed down into the sea, in an incessant flow that lasted till nightfall. And still the rain poured on.

In Ali's mind, in his heart, a leafy poplar wood was streaming down to the seaside, hovering there for a moment to hurtle deafeningly into the waters.

The rains had lasted for a whole week and all the while the forest had come gliding down to plunge into the sea. If we had not been rescued, it would have been a frozen death for us on that mound. . . .

He tripped against a stone and almost fell headlong, but he managed to regain his balance. Elif ran up and took his arm. From the rocky slopes, an owl hooted three times. And then a turtle-dove cooed, calling out "Yusufchuk. . . ."

At last Ali spoke. His voice was as soft as velvet. "Do you

recall that rain, when the poplar forest had rushed like a torrent into the sea? Wasn't your village down in the Chukurova too that year?"

"How can I ever forget it, man?" cried Elif. "May Allah never bring such days upon us again. Our villagers had wandered about desperately under the rain for three days before we managed to find refuge somewhere. And all the time it was one long dark night."

"Now, this very moment," went on Ali, "or even to-morrow, it should rain over the Chukurova, a fiercer rain than at that time, so that for a week or ten days the labourers should not be able to work in the fields. And by that time we'd reach the Chukurova. . . . I remember as if it were only yesterday. After the rain had stopped we'd gone into the cotton field, and what should we see? All the cotton had spilled on to the muddy ground. The plantation owner had not been able to hold back his tears. In the midst of all the labourers, before everyone, he had sobbed like a child. 'Oh, almighty Allah, how could you have done this to me? If this is your justice, then I deny it.' As for us, we fell to gathering the soiled cotton, and when cotton has got caked with earth it weighs heavier. So that year we made twice as much money as in other years. Now, Elif, a cloud should overcast the vast Chukurova plain, a gleaming, oily, black rain-cloud. A wind should arise, lightning should flash and peals of thunder rend the sky. That would give us time to reach the cotton. Then we'd be able to pay back Adil Effendi and still keep a pile of money for ourselves."

"It was the same with us," said Elif, "the cotton weighed heavy as lead. The plantation owner paid us only half of what we'd gathered, but still we earned twice as much as usual. But more than half the villagers were taken ill and never recovered. Back in the village, that winter, they died, one by one, one by one. . . ."

"So it was in our village too," said Ali, "but still, now or to-morrow morning, a cloud should lower over the plain, an icy wind should blow, churning up whirls of dust, and it should rain twice as hard, three times as hard as that year. The sky should be rent. . . ."

"For mercy's sake, man," cried Elif, frightened at his violence, "let the winds blow your words away! Forget about that rain. We'll get down anyway in time to pick some cotton. We are in Allah's hands. Whatever our lot may be. . . ."

"The sky should burst with thunder. They say that thunder scares both sheep and tigers. It should thunder so as to strike fear into a tiger's heart, like the roll of a big drum, a thousand drums, two thousand, beating all at once." He knew Elif was terrified and he himself was not without misgivings, but he could not help it. He took relish in this repetition. It roused in him a voluptuous sensation and galvanised his weary body. "You know the two great rivers of the Chukurova, the Seyhan and the Jeyhan? Well, a hundred thousand such rivers should be lifted up into the sky and let loose all at once over the cotton fields—such a rain that the waters should swamp all the Chukurova, just like the mighty flood in the time of our Lord Noah."

"Stop it, man, for pity's sake," Elif cried, "think of all those poor children. . . . We've got children too."

"I don't care," thundered Ali vindictively, "what are other people's children to me? If it doesn't rain this year, I won't be able to pick any cotton at all. Come what may, it must rain. The Deluge again. Oh, my beloved Allah, grant me a good hard rain and I'll offer a sacrifice to you, a fat tufted red cock. Please, almighty Allah, make it rain as if the roof of the sky had been pierced through."

Elif was on the verge of tears, though she knew that Ali was speaking not from the heart but out of a crushing despair.

"Like the poplar forest rain," he hammered on, "hey, my all-powerful Allah. . . ."

"Perhaps she's fallen on the roadside and can't cry out for help. Let's listen, we may hear her. Let's call out to her," Elif suggested desperately to make him stop.

"Mother, Mo-ther," shouted Ali at the top of his voice. "Damn her, no sound, nothing. Where can she have gone to?" He caught Elif's arm. "If she's played a trick on me this night, I swear to God I'll make her pay for it. There won't be any mother or father business for me then!"

Elif was struck dumb. It was the first time she had heard Ali speak like this of his mother.

"Night and day she's been eating me alive because of that horse, boring into me, tearing me to pieces. And now she makes me walk this same road ten times over. . . ." He was panting with anger.

"Don't, Ali," pleaded Elif. "She's your mother. It's a mortal sin before Allah. . . ."

"I don't care if I'm thrown into the very heart of hell to roast there for ever," thundered Ali. "If she's played a trick on me, then may I be damned if I don't abandon her here in the Taurus among the wild beasts and monsters. . . . I don't care if I'm led into the presence of Allah, naked and ready for hell, between two demons. I don't care if I don't rise again at the resurrection. Do you hear me? If she's a mother, let her act like a mother!"

"Ali!" cried Elif. "What if she's lying dead there under that tree? What will you say then? Don't speak like this. You'll regret it a thousand times."

At the word "dead", Ali's anger dropped. He felt his whole body grow limp and an overwhelming drowsiness took hold of him. . . .

The first snow had fallen that year. It was cold outside. They had thrown a huge log into the fire-place, and the log had burned to glowing crystal-red embers. But Ali was still freezing. His mother had bared her breast and had held his head to her bosom, and soon Ali's trembling had ceased. A pleasant, warm human breath, a mother's breath, had suffused him. Then there were those times when he was sick. . . . And during his service in the army she had never let him go without money, not even for a day. Meryemdje was not like other mothers. She was valiant, mettlesome. When she embraced you, her kiss was like a thousand kisses. There was not another mother like her. But how obstinate she was, how mulishly stubborn. . . . He heaved a sigh.

"Don't worry so, Ali," Elif comforted him. "If we can't pick cotton, we'll just stay down in the plain this year. You'll work in the fields breaking up the earth. I've heard that there's a lot of money in that too."

Ali flared up again. "Yes, and become the laughing-stock of all those rascally villagers."

After this outburst he lapsed into a brooding silence. Elif talked on soothingly, offering a thousand sources of hope. But he was not listening. . . .

How warm is the earth of the Chukurova, black and glistening, and soft too, as cotton. Who knows what they do to make it so fine, like flour, so that you sink into it right up to the ankles. At dawn the earth is swathed in a dream-like mist. The light seems to glow not from the sun, but from the earth itself. There is nothing like it here in these mountains. . . .

Batty Bekir's wife has round swinging hips. She is rather short, but her coquettish ways arrest a man. The shadows of her long lashes fall over her cheeks that are tinged with the hues of a ripening apple. A man can't resist the gaze of her coal-black eyes. Stop and look back, and you'll find yourself riveted to the ground, trembling before her like a leaf. What does the proverb say? "Oh to sleep in the cool shade of the rocks were it not for the big serpent, oh to love a pretty maid were it not for her fickleness!" Batty Bekir won't believe it. But then he wouldn't even if he saw it happening with his own two eyes. That a youth should come of age and not have an affair with Batty Bekir's wife! That would be unheard of. It's been so these past ten years, as if it were a writ in the Holy Book. A lad first goes to bed with Döndülü Lass. Then he gets married, he has children and a family, and still he raves about Döndülü Lass. But she will almost never go to bed with a married man. Ballads have been sung about her, even under the very nose of Batty Bekir. Once he was so ill-advised as to ask, "Who's this Döndülü that everyone is singing about?" And one of the men had answered, "She was a grandmother of mine, such a beautiful woman that people composed songs for her." Ah but he knows, he knows everything, only he chooses to shut his eyes, this Batty Bekir. He's that kind of a man. . . .

It should be on a warm night, when the west wind blows gently, the wind that wafts small white clouds from over the sea. It should be towards dawn, when the night is cool, when the morning star seems to take wing in a scintillating whirl. How good it should be then to take Döndülü Lass and lay her down on the soft yielding soil of the cotton field, feeling her warm hips sink into the earth. The ecstasy of it would make his head swim and his body light and airy, and he would want it to go on for ever. Such a woman can only be met with once in a lifetime.

Elif was walking on his right and, as he lurched sideways, his arm brushed hers. Poor thing, he thought, she has aged in the past two years. Nothing's left now of her charms and lures.

"For pity's sake, Ali," Elif said, "why don't you call out to her?"

The dark shadow of the Holy Tree loomed in the night. They kept on calling out in turns until they came to the tree. Day was dawning. They collapsed at the foot of the tree and leaned against its trunk. Ali looked into Elif's pale face on which the sweat stood out in beads. "What can have happened to her?"

"If she had heard us, she would have answered."

"I'm not sure. . . ."

"She would never make us run up and down like this in the

dead of night," said Elif. "There isn't any village around here, is there?"

"No," Ali sighed.

On a bush nearby a single leaf quivered in the morning breeze. Way off a white covey of pigeons took wing, tossed about in the air like a ball of foam and fluttered down on to the rocks. Ali had always loved pigeons, loved to watch their snowy flocks spread out into the sky and close in again. At any other time, his thoughts would have followed the pigeons for a while, travelling with them over stream-banks, into warm fields and orange groves, wherever there was anything pleasant and lovely under the blue of the sky.

Elif was looking at him intently, a question in her eyes. He lowered his gaze. When he looked up again he saw that she was crying.

"So you think something's happened to her?" he whispered.

She rose. "Let's walk back to the camping place and search all about the road in the light of day. The children . . ."

"The children will be all right," said Ali sharply.

Each of them covered one side of the road, searching behind every bush and tree, into every ditch and hollow.

When they came to the camping place the children ran up to meet them. They had guessed that their parents had gone to look for their grandmother and, without feeling any fear, they had waited for them patiently.

Ali flung himself on to a stone, his arms dangling down his sides. His face was a sickly yellow and his eyes were screwed up and tiny in the sun. The children and Elif stared at him, alarmed. They had never seen him so broken down. He looked at Elif, silently asking for the thousandth time the same sinister question. Her eyes answered "yes" again.

"I've killed my mother," he burst out suddenly, "I deserve to be torn to pieces and my carcass thrown to the dogs. How will I ever face the villagers again? Until I die I will always be known as Ali-who-killed-his-mother. I've committed a terrible crime, Elif. If we could find her body at least, and bury it properly . . ."

"Mother," said Hasan, hanging on to his mother's arm, "is Granny dead?"

"No, silly," said Elif, "why should she be dead? She's just lost. We can't find her."

Hasan assumed an air of great importance and laid his right hand on his temple, the way his father would do when he had something serious to say. "I know," he said, "where she's gone. I was walking right behind her and she was muttering things, and I heard her."

"He's lying," said Ummahan, pouting, "I was walking near him and I didn't hear a thing."

"Well, I didn't really hear her, but I knew from her lips, from her face."

"Well, say it," shouted Elif impatiently, "what did you hear?"

"I didn't hear," insisted Hasan, his hand on his temple again, "but I understood. Granny's gone back to the village."

Ali sprang to his feet. "I knew she'd do this to me. I knew it!"

"It's a lie," cried Ummahan, "Hasan always lies like this." No one paid any attention to her. She was piqued. "Would Granny ever go back to the village? This Hasan does nothing but tell lies all day long."

"You stay here," said Ali as he rushed off, "I'll catch up with her and bring her back."

It was late afternoon when he passed the Holy Walnut. The tree, heavy and murmuring, sat in its place firm as a mountain. One of its branches was overhung with blue beads of every shape, large and small, ranging from dark to light blue, talisman beads that people had tied there over the years. He did not see the tree, only the bead-adorned branch abided in his mind.

"Allah, you for whom this branch has been decked with

beads," he pleaded, "don't you see what an evil plight I'm in? The villagers will be starting on the cotton any time, and here I am left behind with all my family." He boiled over with rage. "What does she want of me, this woman? Isn't it enough that I should have to walk the same stretch of road three times? Does she have to make me walk it ten times?"

He was quivering all over and his anger swelled as there was still no sign of his mother. The sun was near to setting, sinking fast behind the high mountain range before him. The shadows lengthened. He stopped short.

I ought to abandon you and go back. I ought to let you go right up to that deserted village and to perish there. . . .

Suddenly the heat of a summer's day and, on the flat ground before their house, his mother's corpse. The sun, like the Chukurova sun, stewing . . . thousands of green flies swarming over the corpse, crawling into the nose and buzzing out of the mouth, into the mouth and out of the nose. . . . The villagers, just back from the Chukurova, their packs still unloaded, clustering about the corpse, staring with terrible eyes at Ali. . . . And the murmured reproof: "Alas, accursed be such a son. Better a woman should give birth to a stone!"

I don't care what they say. After what you've done to me, I ought to turn back. If it weren't for you, I'd be down in the Chukurova in five or six days.

But his feet moved on.

Just let me find you and you'll see what I'll do to you. You'll rue the day you were born.

"You'll rue the day," he shouted with venom.

He had just turned a bend bordered with squat trees when he made out a shadow in the distance. His heart jumped. Was it his mother or only a rock? He spurted forward.

She was sitting huddled on the wayside, her head on her knees.

"Mother!" he shouted, amazed at the joy he felt.

Meryemdje lifted her head. He dropped down and put his arm around her shoulders, laughing helplessly.

"Were you going back to the village, Mother lass? If Hasan hadn't told us, I'd never have found you and I had such a scare. . . . How in the world did you get it into your head to do such a thing? How could you live in that deserted village alone for so many weeks? You'd die for certain. Come, my good Mother, get on to my back and let us go. Our camping place isn't far. We'll be there before midnight. Come!"

Meryemdje rose to her feet heavily. She rested her hand on a nearby rock.

"Rock, rock, it's you I'm talking to and no one else. I'll go to my village and die there rather than be a load on other people and deprive their children of their bread. Rock, it's you I'm talking to, you who haven't suckled raw milk like the son of man. I'll go and lay my head on the threshold of my house and die there in my father's birthplace."

Then she limped off painstakingly in the direction of the village.

Dusk had fallen. Ali stood staring for a moment. Then he ran up, squatted before her and with a quick movement hoisted her on to his back.

Meryemdje had no choice. She had been expecting this for some time with a mixture of resignation and hope.

The pity of it all! That he should have to carry an old woman like me on his back. My poor lamb if I'd known you'd come after me such a long, long way, would I have stirred from my place? Would I have you wearying yourself out on these roads, my brave one, when the others are picking the cotton by now? . . .

Chapter 10

The first rays of the sun would soon be lighting up the slopes of the mountain opposite, which seemed to be drawing a deep breath and stretching itself as it awaited the warm bright day. With its yellow, red, greenish-blue, mauve-circled, luminous-winged wild bees, its long-legged ants crowding about the entrances of their holes, its eagles, one eye already open, nestling in their eyries, its cloud-white mountain-doves huddling together in a single hollow, its savage hawks and falcons, its thousands of ladybirds filling the ball-shaped thistles that are called fairies' nests, its mountain goats and timorous jackals, its foxes, their long red tails tossing like flames, its soft purple bears lying full-length in their winter sleep over the withered yellow leaves, its springing sad deer, their languid eyes like those of a love-lorn girl, its worms, its large and small birds, with all its creatures above the earth and beneath it, the mountain lay, with bared breast and open mouth, waiting for the warm sun to strike its flanks.

Now, on the peaks, in the valleys, over the roads, there would be an awakening, a stirring, a tumult, a frightening activity, as the mountain, its stones, its earth and trees, all rose from their sleep.

The sun first lighted the space of a threshing floor on the mountain slope. Then the light crept down into the valley. Two ants at the entrance to their nest groped at each other lengthily with their feelers before crawling off in opposite directions. The sun then touched Ali's forehead and he woke up, but for a while he could not gather his thoughts and remember where he found himself. Then his eyes rested on the peak of the mountain and a heavy pain settled within him like salt water. He rose and laid out his bedding, wet from the night dew, to dry in the sun. A pungent odour of sweat rose from it and was dissolved in the air.

His aching feet could scarcely bear his weight as he limped through the fir-trees. He rested his left shoulder against a rock and relieved himself. Still leaning, he tied up the cord of his shalvar trousers. Then he sat down heavily on a stone.

Elif had risen before dawn to put the *tarhana* soup on the fire. After having waited a while for Ali to return, she went after him through the trees and roused him from his half-sleep.

"Your mother's still asleep. She's completely worn out, poor thing. Her face seems to have shrunk to the size of a child. How are your feet?"

"That salt water did them no good at all. The pain's just the same, as if they had been flayed."

"If only you hadn't let her walk so long! If only you'd taken her on your back!"

"I couldn't do otherwise. She'll walk till she hasn't an ounce of strength left in her. Nothing can stop her. It's me you should be thinking of, woman. Our children will starve this year. Adil Effendi will make me pass through the eye of a needle. Think of me . . . I'll never reach the cotton fields in time this year. Never!"

He plucked the dried stalk of an autumn asphodel and broke off its end. A tiny bee buzzed out in a flash of blue. Then he slit the stalk in two. It was filled with honey which he started lapping up with his tongue. He broke another stalk, then another and another. The honey had a strange acrid taste that went to his head. It carried the smell of new, green herbs. Drunk with sleep and honey, it seemed to Ali that all the scents of the mountain were flowing through his veins.

Elif was staring at him. "For heaven's sake, man! Why,

you've become a complete baby," she cried. "Come and drink your soup instead of picking at stalks like a child."

Ali paid no attention. Once, when his uncle was still alive, they had gone searching for honey together. His uncle knew every nook and cranny in these mountains and by noon they had finally come upon a plane-tree that was perhaps a thousand years old. Its trunk and even its long branches were hollow. Ali's uncle had lit a rag, placing it in a hole in the tree's trunk and had then kindled a fire that had filled the forest with suffocating smoke. About half an hour later a hive of bees had burst out of the tree swarming off into the forest in a vast cloud. "The tree's full to the brim with honey," his uncle had rejoiced, "the whole village could eat of it for a year and there'd still be more. Take out your bread, son," he had added and, cutting off a chunk of honey-comb, he had handed it to Ali. Ali had become drunk. A maddening wind had blown through his head like humming bees and he had felt in his blood the scent of all the world's flowers of cedars, firs and pine-trees, and the intoxicating smell of the earth fresh with rain.

Ali broke off another stem and slit it open eagerly. It was again full of honey, which he started licking again. What a pity, he thought, a man should be able to eat a pound of this and forget the pain in his feet, forget everything.

"You're out of your mind, man," cried Elif, snatching the stem from his hands and throwing it down. She had begun to be afraid of Ali. On the edge of his lips was a vague white line, like that of a madman who tries to laugh but cannot and whose face is somehow frozen. "Come and drink your soup!"

Ali was smiling. Only madmen smiled in this manner, all expression wiped away from their eyes.

"What is it, Ali?" murmured Elif. "My darling, my brave one, what is the matter with you?"

Ali gathered his wits. "Elif, we'll never make it at this rate. What can I do, tell me? What the hell can I do? Adil Effendi will

have me thrown into prison for my debts." He looked towards
the spot where his mother was sleeping. "And it's all because of
that old sow, may she die like a dog, the old whore, and leave
me free. If it weren't for her, we two and the children would
have reached the Chukurova long ago."

Elif seized her husband's arm and shook him. "Hush," she
whispered, "she's awake. If she hears you . . ."

"Let her hear," shouted Ali, "I hope she dies on the spot!
Why should my children starve because of her?"

Elif clapped her hand tight over his mouth. "For God's sake,
Ali, if she hears you she'll kill herself."

"I hope she kills herself," snarled Ali from under her hand.
"I'll be so glad that I'll celebrate it and in two days, not more,
I'll be down in the cotton fields."

"We'll get there anyway. Don't be afraid. When one door
closes, Allah always opens another."

"I don't care what He does," growled Ali.

Elif was horrified. "Say you're sorry," she cried, "say it
quickly! It's a sin!"

"I won't," shouted Ali at the top of his voice. "Let Allah not
open any door and let that house of His crumble in ruins over
His head. Let it be wrecked! Wrecked! If He has eyes, He can
see me and if He has ears He can hear me. I won't repent."

Elif sank to the ground, her hands covering her face.
Ummahan and Hasan had been standing at a slight distance,
trembling at their father's anger. When Ummahan saw her
mother was crying she ran up and, throwing herself down
beside her, started weeping too.

Meryemdje had been making her way towards the fire when
she heard her son's words. Her ears buzzed and her head swam
as she dropped down where she stood. Gathering herself into
a ball, she remained crouched there, still as the earth, not even
stirring a finger.

At the sight of Elif and Ummahan sobbing their hearts out,

Ali's anger subsided. He had released his pent-up feelings and was now hovering around Elif, not knowing what to do, how to console her. He laid his hand on her shoulder.

"Get up, Elif," he murmured in a weary voice, "I didn't mean anything really. Come, let's go and drink our soup. Get up, we must be on the road again. Look how high the sun is already."

Elif and Ummahan's shoulders continued to heave.

"Shut up," shouted Ali to his daughter, "shut up, you daughter of a dog!"

Ummahan's sobbing stopped as quickly as it had begun.

"Elif," pleaded Ali, "please don't cry. Please!" He smiled bitterly. "There, I'm sorry. You see? I'm saying I'm sorry to Allah." He took her hand and pulled her to her feet.

"You've killed her," murmured Elif, wiping her eyes, "she'll never recover from this. Poor Mother!" She walked to the fire and looked at Meryemdje. "My beautiful mother, you must excuse him, he's your son. He was so blind with anger he didn't know what he was saying. Would a man in his right senses speak of Allah like that?"

Ali looked guiltily at his mother as Elif helped her to her feet and led her to the fire. She then laid the food before Meryemdje and handed her a spoon. They all sat down to eat their soup. Throughout the meal Ali could not bring himself to look his mother in the face, but Meryemdje's eyes, wide-open and bewildered, were fixed on her son as though she could not recognise him. Was this Ali? Scenes of long ago rose before her eyes. She could not weep or speak and something was choking within her. A baby as small as your hand . . . Ali . . .

You can't remember those days, can you, Long Ali? she murmured to herself. I've seen no good from you, Long Ali, and, *inshallah*, you too will see no good from your children! When you suffer this same bitterness, Long Ali, you'll see how a bad word from your child is worse than a bullet, yes, worse than a bullet that pierces right through your heart.

She rose and said aloud, "I pray to Allah that your children will make you suffer as you've made me suffer, Long Ali."

She ran limpingly into the bushes to conceal her tears.

"See what you've done, man," cried Elif angrily.

Ali drew a deep breath. "Shall I kill myself, kill myself right here?" His eyes fixed on Elif's, he was gnawing his forefinger, almost biting into it. Then he tore at a patch in his jacket and threw it down, shouting: "Shall I kill myself? Kill myself?"

She was astounded at her husband's uncontrolled fury. "For heaven's sake, Ali, don't. Not before the children," she whispered.

Ali went into the bushes after his mother and found her in tears, leaning against a sapling. He came up to her silently, took her hand and kissed it. Then he came back.

"Go and get her, Elif," he ordered, "it's late, terribly late! What shall I do about these feet of mine? I can hardly walk a step."

Elif took Meryemdje by the arm and led her out of the bushes.

"I'll never be able to walk in this state. See how swollen and red my feet are?" His eyes were bloodshot, but there was no trace of anger left in him. "I've thought of something, Elif. . . ."

"What is it?"

"We have that sack, you know, and if we cut it in two we could tie each piece around my feet."

Elif found the gunny sack, which Ali cut into four pieces with his knife. He wrapped one piece around his right leg and tied it up with some hemp rope. It was just like a broken leg set in plaster. He carefully did the same to his left leg and then rose. It felt strange but at least it was soft.

"Get going, Elif," he ordered, "you too, children. Mother, stay here beside this warm fire and I'll be back early in the afternoon to fetch you. For God's sake, don't attempt to go back to the village again."

Meryemdje pretended not to hear. She grasped her stick and made for the road, where she paused.

"Allah, may none of your creatures ever have to be carried on other people's backs," she prayed, lifting her hands to the sky. Then she passed her hands over her face in the ritual gesture and added: "Amen, amen!"

Ali hastened after her. "Don't be obstinate, my beautiful mother, stay here. You'll never be able to keep up with us. See, you can't even stand on your feet."

"Who says I can't stand," shrieked Meryemdje. "My daughter, it's you I'm talking to. Mind your own business. Just walk on and leave me. I'll go down to the Chukurova all by myself."

Ali took her arm. "Mother, don't make things difficult for me. A little farther off I want to branch off the road into a short cut which is hard to climb but will save us a great deal of time. You'll never find your way and we'll lose each other. Please wait here!"

Meryemdje propped her stick against her waist and again lifted her hands to the sky. "Allah, my beautiful, black-eyed Allah, see to it that nobody should be reduced to being carried on another's back, not even a mother by her son!" She looked at Elif. "Walk on, my golden-hearted girl. I'll follow you slowly. I wouldn't want your children to go hungry this winter because of me. . . ."

Realising that his mother had not missed a word of his former outburst, Ali became angry again. "Stay," he shouted, "or go anywhere you please. I won't have my children starve because of you. Come on," he cried to the others, "get going." Elif started towards Meryemdje, but he seized her arm and thrust her forward. "Get going! I've had enough of her tricks these past days."

Elif was really frightened, and the wide-eyed children were darting uneasy glances now at their grandmother, now at their father. He herded them before him and Meryemdje was left there leaning on her staff.

He was pressing forward at a running pace, his bandaged feet rolling like rubber balls. Soon his figure was only a spinning blur to Elif and the children.

From the trees and bushes, from the dark forest that covered the flank of the mountain, from the grey earth decked with short brilliant mountain flowers, a white vapour arose like a cloud and drifted away.

"Poor Mother," sighed Elif, "you who brim over with the love of a thousand hearts, you who would give your life for us, how could this happen to you?"

Her eyes filled with tears. Yes, she should go back and entreat her forgiveness, kiss her hands and feet, and stroke her hair, and bring laughter into her eyes again.

Just as she was about to turn back, Hasan spoke up.

"Father's gone," he said, crestfallen. "He's gone and deserted us."

"He's very angry," said Ummahan. "As if he's going to kill someone. . . ."

"Let him go," said Elif resentfully. "He'll walk and walk. . . ." She hesitated, knowing how he could speed on, oblivious of everything, until he collapsed, utterly spent. They are both as obstinate as mules, she thought. They won't give up. They'll carry this business on to the bitter end.

Her head throbbing, she started to run, straining every nerve to overcome the faintness in her legs. By noon, her body was drenched in sweat, her hair, her clothes, all dripping wet. The sweat streamed down her flaming face, burning her eyes. Her heart was thumping and her breath came short and broken through her parched open mouth. Her legs could hardly bear her along now, and she stumbled at every other step. It was well into the afternoon before she spied Ali, a tiny dot moving down a slope. She shouted after him with all her strength, but he did not hear, or if he did, he paid no attention. She hurled herself down the slope. The wind blowing on her face revived her a little, but when she reached Ali, her eyes clouded over and she slumped down at his feet.

Ali looked down at her unseeingly, his face frozen into a deathly pallor as though all the blood had ebbed away.

"Water," she moaned.

The pack slipped from his back. His hand drew out the water bowl. His feet moved towards the spring bubbling under the fir-tree. The water filled the bowl. In a trance, he saw Elif extend her lips and drink.

After she had recovered a little, she leaned forward on her elbow.

"Come and sit near me, Ali," she said and patted the earth with her hand. "Right here." He sat down mechanically. "If I hadn't overtaken you," continued Elif, "you would have walked right down to the Chukurova. Look, the sacking has fallen off your feet."

Ali looked down. His feet were bare, fluttering like newly-born birds. For the first time in his life they seemed pitiful to him.

"I never noticed it," he said, shaking his head.

Elif went to the spring. She held her head under the water, then washed her face, hands and feet.

"You come too, Ali," she called.

A stabbing pain shot up furiously into the very core of his heart. It came from the sole of his right foot where the sharp little stones of the road had lacerated the flesh into a red wound.

"Where did you leave the children?" he asked as he hobbled to the spring.

"They're on the road," replied Elif.

And my mother, he thought, but the words froze on his lips as he recalled how he had treated her that morning. "Something strange has come over me these days, woman," he said. "What can be the matter with me? The things I've done!"

Elif's eyes were glued to the ground. She could not look him in the face. For a while they remained sitting there, one on each side of the spring. Then Ali rose and drew out of the pack the two other pieces of gunny sack. He took one of his two pairs of woollen socks and put them on. Then he wrapped the rags of sacking around them and bound them fast.

Elif went with him this time, for Meryemdje had to be mollified.

An hour or so later they met the children, who were frolicking on the road. Hasan had peeled a chunk of *yalabuk* from a pine-trunk and Ummahan was chasing him to snatch it from his hand.

"We've left the load near the spring, a little way off," Elif told them, "go and find it. Light a fire and put some water to boil. Don't be afraid if we're late. The jinn and other sprites never dare approach a fire, and even if they do they never hurt little children. And the fire also frightens away the bears and wolves. If you keep that fire going, no one will come near you."

"Whoops!" cried Hasan, "I'll light such a huge fire. . . . As large as a threshing floor."

"Not that big," said Elif, "or you'll set the forest afire."

"Mother, come back quickly," pleaded Ummahan, "I'm dying of hunger."

"That's not true," Hasan interrupted her, "she's not really hungry."

"Go to hell," cried Ummahan, fetching him a blow on the back.

"Go to hell yourself," retorted Hasan. "Just wait till Mother's gone. I'll squash your nose till it's as flat as a jinn's and then the jinn will think you're one of them and carry you away."

"Mother," shrieked Ummahan, "look how your son's carrying on!"

"Stop it, Hasan, will you," cried Elif as she walked off, "what do you want with the girl?"

They walked on side by side, their shadows wavering like tracery over the grey earth. An agonising bitterness had laid its crust on Ali's features. One of his sunken cheeks was twitching fitfully and his face was aflame, as though feverish. He was walking at an increasingly slower pace, with a drunken roll, his feet catching into each other. Elif touched his arm.

"Let's rest a little. There's still quite a while before evening."

"We can't," he said with muffled anger, for he had no strength left in him even for violence. "They'll be starting on the cotton to-morrow, if they've not done so to-day. I can't risk going hungry and naked this winter, woman. Come on!"

He took a firmer hold on himself and managed to steady his tottering gait and shake off his air of sleep-walking.

A lump rose in Elif's throat as all the love in her heart went out to him. A big child, she thought, my unlucky one, my darling, my soul, how I wish I could carry you on my back and put you down right on the soft earth of the cotton field. She thought of the Chukurova with the blue haze enveloping its earth and stones, its white cotton plants and its teeming multitudes. . . . Such a blue, oh my God . . . She recalled her first sight of the sea. . . . A blue that seeps into you. You feel it over your face, in your hair, so that you can never wash it off. The briny blue of dreams. . . .

"Ah!" The sigh rose from the very depths of her being. "How tired I am. . . ."

The words had escaped her somehow and she regretted them immediately. How could she look Ali in the face now? Even she was making things difficult for him.

Ali stopped dead, his eyes bulging from their sockets. "Why did you have to come after me? Go away. Go back to the children. Go, go! You're every one of you a load on my shoulders. Find her now if you can, that accursed woman. If she's gone back to the village again, I swear by Allah I won't run after her this time. Let her die like a dog on the road and I'll gather up her bones when we return from the Chukurova, her bones picked white by the bald vultures. They'll swoop down as they did over the horse and make short work of her." His lips were foaming and had turned purple. "Yes, they'll make short work of her, *inshallah*!"

Elif stood still, all the blood drained from her downcast face.

Ali raved on until, spent by his outburst, he realised that he had gone too far.

"Elif," he said with an effort, softly, almost inaudibly, "don't get tired tagging along with me. Go and wait with the children. I'll find her. Don't be afraid, I'll go after her even if she has turned back to the village again." He longed to push on, to be flying over the road, but he sank to the ground, exhausted. "Come and sit here too, Elif. Only for a moment. Don't worry. If we can't be in time for the cotton, then there's no help for it. It's our fate this year. And there's always the Holy Saint Hizir, isn't there, to help those in distress?" He tried to laugh, but only a painful smile flitted over his lips like lightning. Suddenly he sprang to his feet again and lunged towards the road. "It won't do. I must be there before they start. Yes, just as they're about to enter the cotton field, I'll be there with my can and basket!"

How amazed the villagers would be. He's a swift-winged bird, this Long Ali, they'd say. Look at his long legs, just like a stork's.

"Just as they're about to pluck the cotton out of the first boll they shall turn around and see me there. We must get there without fail, Elif, we can't afford to rest."

He quickened his pace. It was as though he had never known fatigue, as though he had only just set out.

Chapter 11

She stood stock-still where they had left her in the middle of the road. Slowly her anger wore out and in its stead an overwhelming fear gripped her.

But wasn't Elif slowing down? There, she's stopped now, my golden-hearted Elif. She's turning back to me, my lovely black-eyed girl. She'll never abandon me, even if that godless Long Ali does.

Her confidence returning, anger stirred within her again. When he was a baby, a mere lump of raw flesh as big as a hand, why didn't I do like Durmush's mad wife, throttle him and throw that lump of flesh into the graveyard? His muck is still under my nails. Oh, my sleepless nights! Oh, to think of all the pains I wasted on him! What's that? She's walking away! You too, daughter of a bitch? And it was I who took you as a wife to that dog and paid two hundred green banknotes for you! If only I could strangle you too, together with that son of a whore! Ah Long Ali, when you were a soldier and people said there would be a war, how I rent my hair, how I cried out aloud with a fire in my heart, how I wept every day until your return! If I'd only known you'd do this to me, I would have tied bells to my skirts instead, and danced and made merry!

Terror filled her and she started shouting without knowing it. She ran screaming after them until they disappeared down the valley. Then all her strength ebbed away and she rolled to the ground, her body shaken with convulsions. Darkness encompassed her. She saw death and emptiness closing in on her.

Clawing at the ground, she dragged herself up in a desperate effort to break free from this darkness, this nothingness, and wheeled about this way and that. Was there no village around here? No one going down to the Chukurova for the cotton? Had their village been the last to go, delayed because of that accursed Old Halil?

Wolves were swooping down in packs, ravenous wolves with huge fangs. Each one of them pounced on her, tearing at her flesh until there was nothing but a white carcass left. In an unending, onrushing pack, the wolves came galloping, flying, teeming like ants. . . .

"Ali!" she shrieked, "Ali, my child, run! Help! The wolves . . ."

Her screams had the power to drive away the wolves. She kept on shouting, spinning around blindly all the while, till it was evening and her voice broke. Then, enormous, rapacious-beaked vultures, with dark unending wings, were swarming in thousands in the maddening dusk. She fell in a heap face to face with death.

A fresh wind blew down from the mountain tops and the stars were bright in the sky. "But I'm still breathing," she said, "thank heavens, I'm not dead yet." Joy spread within her, the joy of relief at suddenly finding again what one had lost. Staggering to her feet she searched in the undergrowth and found herself a stick to replace the one she had lost. Her throat ached, but she kept up a confident mutter.

My Hasan's as valiant as a lion. He's taken after his grandfather. There's not the slightest likeness between him and that infidel Ali. His eyes, too, are just like his grandfather's, frank and obstinate. When a man's obstinate, then he's a good man. No evil can come from him. At the most he can only harm himself. Hasan will throw himself down on the road. If you don't bring my granny along, he'll say, then I won't go either. I won't budge. They'll try to drag him along, the infidels, but he'll give them the slip and escape into the mountains. He'll never give in.

Her thoughts dwelt on Hasan lovingly, exultantly. That girl? She's all right, but she's taken after her mother somewhat. She felt a pinch of hunger and with it a sudden pang of uneasiness. What if they trussed Hasan up hand and foot?

Now a fear more terrible than before was setting in, a dark, heavy, almost palpable fear. She broke into a run, calling out Hasan's name in a hoarse voice. She ran until she could run no longer. There were no wolves now, no shadowy long-winged vultures filling the darkness of the sky. But the devastating fear of death, spreading like thick murky water, made her crouch into a small trembling heap, shrinking smaller and smaller until her bones cracked. She drew her legs up tightly to her breast and hid her head between her knees. There was not the faintest sound around her, not even the humming of the night, not even the howling of a jackal or the twitter of a bird, only a cold emptiness that sent jolting tremors through her body.

She turned stiffly southward, in the direction of the Holy Kaaba, and lifted her quavering hands for the prayer. But not a single one of the few prayers she had managed to learn came to her mind. Allah, my beautiful Allah, I beseech thee my black-eyed one, make me remember just one prayer so I should not pass unclean into the other world. . . .

Allah appeared before her eyes, a luminous-haired venerable ancient, his beard ablaze with light, and a prayer flashed across her mind. She pattered it out hurriedly, losing herself in its monotone as she swayed from side to side. The emptiness around her was complete now. Alone with her prayer, fear and death and everything else quite wiped out, she mumbled it over and over again hypnotically.

The first glimmer of dawn found her still huddled there. It was then that she heard the sound of far-off voices. First a man's deep tones rose from beyond the mountain and faded away.

A woman's voice echoed the call. Then everything was buried in silence. When the voices sounded again, her heart leapt and the prayer froze in her parched mouth. She ached to fling herself towards the voices, to fly there like a bird, but she was petrified, rooted to her place, and try as she would she could not even utter a sound.

As the voices came closer, the warm gladness of deliverance, of coming to life again, flowed slowly into her heart. Now she could hear them quite clearly. "Mother! Where are you? Call out to us. Make a sound so we can find you."

And then it was Elif. "Mother darling, please call out!"

My sweet girl, thought Meryemdje, have you really been looking for me all this time? I must get to the road. If they pass me by, that'll be the end of me indeed.

She struggled hard but she could not stir.

As Elif and Ali neared the bushes that hid Meryemdje, they were arrested by a drawn-out moaning. They strained their ears, but there was not the slightest sound of life again. Ali took a few weary steps, then he stopped. His head was throbbing and numb with lack of sleep.

"Are you sure we heard something, Elif?" he asked.

"It seemed like your mother's voice. Let's search this brushwood."

"You go and look," said Ali as he let himself drop to the ground.

Elif penetrated into the thicket. The morning dew had fallen and she was soon wet through as she moved among the close-growing underbrush. The sun was just rising when she sighted the tiny heaped-up shadow on the narrow track.

"Mother," she sobbed as she ran up and threw herself at her feet, "we've killed you. We are murderers."

Meryemdje tried to say something, but only a hoarse rasp broke from her throat.

Elif lost her head. She turned about frantically, not knowing what she should do. For a moment she attempted to take Meryemdje on her back, but gave it up in despair. Distractedly she picked up a stone, placed it by another, then stooped to pick up one more. In a flash, the matches in her pocket came to her mind, and like lightning she was at the brushwood. In less than no time she had a fire burning before Meryemdje.

A round, crisp sun had dawned. The earth, the thicket steamed, cleaving to the rising sun. A column of ants, newly awakened, came crawling along the path with groping feelers, but was sidetracked by the fire. As the sun grew warmer, the forest became alive with the twittering of birds.

"We're murderers," Elif repeated as she set about rubbing Meryemdje's limbs, "your murderers, beautiful Mother. . . ."

"Water," Meryemdje croaked, "a little water, my lovely girl."

Elif went mad with joy. "At once, at once, beautiful Mother!" she cried as she kissed her hands and face again and again. Then she let go of her abruptly. "Ali," she shouted, "Mother's spoken. She's all right!"

But where was she to find a spring? How would she bring the water to Meryemdje even if she did find one? The thought plunged her into sudden despair.

"Where can I find some water?" she kept muttering to herself as she looked about her helplessly.

The old woman's eyes were upon her, loving and grateful. "If only I'd given birth to you, my flower, instead of to that godless renegade," she said in a faint voice, "what a good thing it would have been!"

"Mother," Elif interrupted her excitedly, "there's a small spring a little farther off. I remember. Only a small trickle, but . . . I could carry you there."

"I'll walk. I can do it. I wouldn't want my precious girl to carry me on her back." She tried to heave herself up. Again and again she struggled, but in vain. On the edge of the shrivelled lips there flitted a wan smile. Then the lips, the smile, the whole face were submerged in grief. "So I'm really old, really worn out now. . . . I might as well be dead." The plaint, low-murmured and slow, was the despairing cry of death, of one left quite alone in a deserted alien world.

Elif turned away to hide her tears. "Curse this old age. It shouldn't exist. People should die while they're still sound of wind and limb."

She propped Meryemdje up on her feet. "You're not old yet, my good mother, the best of mothers! Goodness never ages."

Holding her arm, she drew her along slowly towards the spot where she had left Ali. He was fast asleep in the middle of the road, so oblivious of his surroundings that he looked as though he were not of this world but of the fairy-realm of Spellbound Ahmet. You could have cut off one of his chapped yellow hands clenched like the claws of a bird or one of his legs tightly drawn up to his belly or his suffering feet like babes in swaddling bands, and he would not have felt a thing.

Water, thought Elif. Water . . . she's dying of thirst. If only we'd brought a bowl with us. Never had she seen Meryemdje's face like this, not even in the year of the big famine. The eyes in the shrunken, shrivelled face were bleary, like the dusty wrinkled surface of a muddy sheet of water. She resolved to carry her to the spring herself, for she knew that Ali would never wake up. She squatted down and drew her on to her back. Bracing her right leg forward and leaning over it, she strained up in a desperate effort. A stabbing pain shot through her ribs, but she was on her feet.

In her mind the spring had seemed far away. She rejoiced when soon after she came upon the thin streak of water bubbling forth over white pebbles at the foot of a fir-tree. The water, the earth, the branches of the fir-tree, the whole place was scented with resin. First she washed Meryemdje's face. Then she cupped some water in her hands and held them up to her. But Meryemdje, thrusting forward stiffly, bumped her chin against Elif's hands.

Her gaze lingered on the spilled water and she smiled bitterly. Then she looked at Elif. Her eyes seemed tó speak. Elif understood. She dragged her to the edge of the spring and held her head close to the water. At last Meryemdje was able to slake her thirst.

"Drink slowly. Not too much at once, darling Mother," she cautioned her, pulling her back again. "Have some food now."

She took the food pouch that was tied to her waist and laid it open before Meryemdje. The old woman's eyes filled. "Ah," she murmured, "you should never have been the wife of that infidel."

She took some bread and made a roll with the goat's cheese. She started munching slowly with her toothless gums, dipping her hand every now and then into the spring at her right to cup water in her palm.

"May the great Allah turn everything you touch to gold, my daughter. If it weren't for you, he would have abandoned me."

"Don't say that, Mother," said Elif. "Didn't you see what a state he's in?"

"I've seen him," cried Meryemdje, flaring up with unexpected violence, "and I hope he gets even worse. But for you he'd strangle me on the spot and throw my body to the wild beasts. You must never leave me!"

"Don't say that, Mother! Don't," Elif repeated. "How could your own son ever wish you evil!" She rose hastily. "You lie down here and rest a little. I'll go to him. If he should wake and not see us . . ."

"Go! Go to the pith of hell! Go to the side of that Long infidel!" She raised her hands to the sky. "Allah, my black-eyed one, hear me. Make me see the dead face of that Long Ali. . . ."

"Say you never meant that, Mother," cried Elif, a deathly pallor settling on her face. "Say it, please say it! He's your only son. How can you cast your curse on him?" She rushed off blindly.

151

Meryemdje went on cursing until Elif was out of sight. Then her hands dropped to her sides.

"Allah, my white-bearded, bright-faced one, take my soul away quickly and save me from this Long Ali. My sky-eyed one, I'm just a spent old woman, standing at your door, begging for deliverance. . . ."

Her throat tightened. Casting a furtive glance around to make sure she was quite alone, she burst into a flood of tears. It had been a long time, twenty years perhaps, since she had wept like this.

"Oh, my silver-bearded, black-eyed Allah, I'm a calamity that you've brought on Ali's head. Oh, my sky-eyed one, help my Ali!" She could not dispel the vision of her son curled up on the road, his feet like two swaddled babes. "I've forgiven him. I wasn't in my right mind when I cursed him so. I've told you before and I know you never forget, you mustn't heed what I say when I'm angry. Help my Ali by taking my soul away. You who know every single little thing, you who hear even the call of the ant from under the earth, make my Ali be in time for the cotton. If you do, I'll bring a huge red cock from the Chukurova and sacrifice it to you under the Holy Walnut on our way back. I'll kill it for you only and may it turn into baneful poison if I so much as touch a morsel. You sway the world and the heavens above, and even the roots of the trees from deep under the earth cry out unto you. Hearken to my prayer."

She murmured on for a long while. Then she lay down and fell asleep.

It was late afternoon when Ali opened his eyes. Elif was dozing beside him, her head resting on her knees. He shook himself into wakefulness. Every part of his body ached as if it had been pounded in a mortar.

"Where did you go off to?" he asked. His mouth tasted like poison.

"I found her and carried her to the spring."

A wave of relief swept over him. Then his face fell. What! Was he to haul that cumbersome load on to his back again? His mother loomed before his eyes like a mountain, a huge massive mountain. He felt a sinking, a sickening, inside him.

"You've found her, eh?" he muttered. "Quick then. We must be getting on. We've lost one day, but we've still four left before they start on the cotton and we should make it if that accursed woman doesn't run away to the village again."

"Yes, let's hurry, Ali." Elif could no longer hold in the anguish in her heart. "The children . . . alone and hungry . . . they must be scared to death. My Hasan . . . my Ummahan . . ."

He leapt to his feet, a mad, haggard look on his face, his clenched fist beating the air frenziedly.

"If anything's happened to my children I'll strangle the life out of her," he cried savagely as he swung into the trees, cursing under his breath, but all the while haunted by the image of his mother, her neck bruised purple, her sunken face chalky and her open mouth buzzing with green flies. When he came upon her where she was sitting huddled up, a small, pitiful bundle of dirty rags, he was overcome by remorse. He wanted to throw himself at her neck and smother her with kisses, but he stood quite still, unable to utter a word, his arms two lifeless boughs dangling from his shoulders. His back ached like a festering wound and he shrank away as if someone was about to plunge a dagger into this wound.

Elif was standing by. She looked at him oddly, her face a welter of harried urgency, her gaze holding his unflinchingly. All sense of time was lost.

He shuddered as he imagined the terrifying weight of his mother on his back, on his smarting feet. And the long interminable road! Is there ever an end to roads? Would he ever see the end of this one? How was it that for years now he had trudged out this same road so easily? Oh, for the company of the villagers! What with the talking and merry-making and squabbling, the road ends in no time and one feels neither the pain in one's back nor the ache in one's feet.

As if Meryemdje had read her son's mind, she raised herself to her feet.

"My daughter, find me a stick and let's get going. Think of the children, poor mites, all alone and hungry."

And all because of you, accursed woman, thought Ali, seething again, his breath coming more quickly.

"All alone and hungry . . ." Elif repeated, sighing. She wrenched a branch off a tree, lopped off its twigs and leaves and handed it to Meryemdje, gladdened to see that her face was its normal colour again.

Leaning on the stick, Meryemdje moved forward with tentative steps. Elif followed her.

Ali stared after them. They were walking steadily and quite quickly too. He took heart as he fell to the road in their wake. Ah, if only they could keep it up, they would soon reach the Chukurova. They might even catch up with the villagers on the road. How wonderful that would be! This time, with Tashbash at his side, he would know how to defy the Muhtar and find the right words to move the villagers. He would talk of the rights of the orphan and the widow, of the destitute and the poor. He would show them that their labour was branded with blood. He would persuade them to raise money and give the Muhtar the bribe he usually got from the Agha. There's plenty of good sense in these villagers. Once you show village folk on which side their bread is buttered, you can leave the rest to them.

He basked in these sunny hopes until the road grew steeper. There Meryemdje gave way. She stumbled and fell.

Lashed into rage, Ali rushed up, seized her by the arms and flung her on to his back, bumping her down and locking his hands firmly under her body. By the time he had climbed the slope he was drenched in sweat. His neck was stretched taut under the strangling yoke of his mother's arms. Now and then he would toss her up higher on his back so as to loosen her grasp and be free to breathe. But after a while she would sag down again.

The sun had set and it was nearly dusk. A moisture-laden, scented wind blew from the south.

It would be some time before moonrise.

Chapter 12

Not a soul passed on the road which every year at this time would be thronged with villagers wending down to the Chukurova.

Perhaps Old Halil had blundered and had roused the villagers long before the cotton was ripe. They would be forced to wait, then, their eyes fixed anxiously on the unblown cotton plants, just as it had been that time long ago when Old Halil had been sick. Such ill fortune would befall neighbouring villages very often. They would kick their heels there watching the cotton bolls burst open one by one, counting them, five to-day, twenty the next, more and more each day until at last early one morning they would open their eyes upon a snow-white world.

Ali had rubbed some fat over his swollen feet and now lay flat on his back in the sun. Close by, water gushed forth from a little spring and farther off stood a hulking pine-tree with resin oozing down its burnt bark. The grass was almost all withered on the grey earth. Old Meryemdje was crouching motionless on the other side of the spring, never so much as casting a glance at Ali, while Elif, her back against a lone medlar tree, was delousing the children's clothes. The sun shone as in the spring and not a breath of wind stirred in the leaves. They had now reached the warmer flank of the Taurus mountains that faced the Mediterranean. The children, stark naked, sat on the ground, forlorn and silent, chewing some gum-mastic they had found in the forest.

A faint drone was heard in the skies. They all lifted their heads except Meryemdje, who did not stir. The children jumped shrieking to their feet. Ali sat up and Elif moved up to him still holding the children's clothes. His eyes were searching the sky. She looked up too, awe and wonder on her face. Finally, even Meryemdje raised her head.

High up, three jets were cruising across the blue leaving in their wake shimmering silvery streaks that cleft the sky. They glided on out of sight and soon after their sound died away.

Ali smiled as he looked at the awed faces around him.

"These are called airies," he told them. "One of them can hold a hundred men, a thousand, two thousand, a whole army. Each of these soldiers is given a bomb which he throws over the villages of the infidels. Under this shower of bombs the infidels are killed in masses and not one of their houses is left standing. You've seen for yourself how they vanish in the sky in the twinkling of an eye. When I was a soldier, my sergeant told me, 'Come on, Ali, you try riding on one of these.' 'For pity's sake, my sergeant,' I said, 'don't make me! I'm sure to fall.' He laughed. 'Why, you fool,' he said, 'they call these airies. They're a gift of Allah, so how could a fellow ever fall off?' 'Perhaps not,' I said, 'but I'd never dare.' You should have seen how the sergeant laughed then. 'Ali,' he said, 'to think I took you for such a brave fellow. And here you are quite lily-livered.' 'Look, Sergeant,' I said, 'bravery's all right when you've got your two feet on the ground, but when you're up in the skies like a bird, of what good is bravery to you?'"

Elif sat down quietly beside her husband. The children nestled up to her. Ali was talking on, pleased and oblivious now of the unending roads, of his mother's hapless condition, of the cotton, of Adil Effendi, of the unscrupulous Muhtar. It was not the first time he was telling the tale of the aeroplane and the sergeant. The villagers had all heard it several times, but they never tired of it.

"If a man's really brave, then he's brave on earth, in the skies, on the high seas. . . . 'Don't insist, my sergeant,' I said, 'I can't do it. I can't trust my soul to the wings of a bird.' 'What about those fellows who fly them?' he said. 'Haven't they got souls too?' Elif, do you remember the flat country where we picked cotton one year? And how a train used to pass through the middle of the field? The place was called Misis. Well, the Government has now made that flat land into a nest for these airies. Each morning, like bees radiating out to the flowers, they fly from their nest, a thousand, two thousand—count them if you can—and take to the sky, cloud-like."

He lifted his head. The three silvery streaks still lingered, wavering far up in the sky.

"See, woman, how they trace paths for themselves, not to lose their way when they return. If you could only come close to one, your jaw would drop. Each wing is of a different colour, purple, yellow, green. . . . Praised be their Creator, how they flash with light and colour! And do you know, woman, they also fly by night, hung with red, orange and green lamps. What a sight in the night as they fly all together studding the sky like many-coloured stars. Ah, if only you could see that place called Indjirlik where they come from. The German says, good for the Turkish nation, they're a brave, clever, democratic people. Why, these Turks have more airies than us Germans who've been making them for so many years. With all the airies they have now, the German says, there's no defeating the Turkish nation. No one will ever dare make war on the Turks any more. Thanks to democracy, the Turks need have no cares at all. A nation which turns out a hundred airies a day can never be beaten. My sergeant used to say the same thing. From now on the women will not be widowed any longer nor the children orphaned. And do you know? These airies go right up to the edge of the sun and see the villages there. My sergeant would say—he was a fine, brave fellow—there's nothing doing on this earth any longer, we must travel to the stars now. . . . If only you could have seen these airies returning to their nests like bees to their hive. My sergeant would tell me, Ali, what are you gaping at these for, he'd say, are these airies? Wait till you see the giant ones, as large as that mountain there. You can pack three villages into one of them and carry them way down to Adana with all the people and cattle and horses and donkeys."

He wanted to tell them so much more, but words failed him. How could he describe what he felt? At last he said: "In the dark of the night they shine so, woman, that you'd think a mountain of light and colour were moving through the skies. As Allah is my witness, it is so!"

Elif bent her head over the clothes again. She was thinking that the villagers must have reached the Chukurova long ago. The children drew away from her. Gazing up again and again at the sky, they walked over to the clump of bushes farther off. There was a long silence before Ali spoke again.

"Woman," he said, as he flexed his limbs, his blood stirring in the warm autumn sunshine, "look at this." He held out a tuft of grass he had just plucked. "See? It's still fresh. One day I watched Old Halil to find out his secret and I saw him picking grass and examining the roots. When they're dry, it's a sign that the cotton's ripe in the Chukurova. That's what he watches for in the whirling thistle." He threw the grass before Elif. "You see?" he said. "Not only the roots, but the grass itself is still fresh. Even if our villagers get there to-day, they'll just have to wait until the cotton opens. Isn't that so, woman?" he shouted triumphantly.

"Yes, indeed," said Elif soothingly.

"Well then, they still have four days of walking. And ten days or so of waiting for the cotton to ripen. That's fourteen days. Why, in a fortnight we could walk not only down to the Chukurova plain, but right across Anatolia to the Dardanelles! What surprises me . . ." He laughed. "Well this just shows again that only Allah is infallible. Old Halil's reckonings went amiss this year. Look at this grass. It'll be a month before it dries." He lay back, humming a gay little tune. A flock of birds flapped past noisily overhead. The sun was beating down hard now. He sat up again, his face sweating. "Mine's an ass's head indeed, woman," he said, "I must have been out of my mind to rush on like this during the past days." Elif's black eyes were fixed huge and unblinking on her husband's face. "Fie, Allah forgive me for being such a fool. To think I never noticed that, save for one misguided village, we haven't met a single soul. How I can see them all cooling their heels before the unopened cotton! Salaam to you, I'll say and roar with laughter. You've still five days to wait. I knew that all along and that's why I took it easy on the road. So you thought you were being clever leaving me behind, eh, my fine friends? Then I'll take my pipe and rouse the very mountains into a merry dance, just like this."

He drew his pipe out of his waistband and blew a merry tune, tripping up and down all the while without feeling the pain in his feet at all. The children came bounding from behind the bushes. Elif's eyes grew wider. Meryemdje raised her head at the sound of the flute.

Play on, play on, Long Ali, she said to herself. How suitable to play the pipe after bringing Meryemdje down to this!

"Woman," Ali now shouted joyfully, "I'm famished. Is this a time for lice? Cook us a good soup and let's fill our bellies." He ran up to his mother, seized her hand and kissed it. "My good Mother, it's my ass's head that's brought all these troubles upon us. Why, the cotton won't open yet for . . ." He began to count on his fingers. "Eleven, twelve, thirteen, fourteen . . . fourteen days! Allah be praised, we're not late at all." He circled about her, kissing her hands again and again in a hurricane of joy.

Ah, my son, Meryemdje mused, how could you have let yourself be fooled by that old driveller, that worthless infidel. Ah, Ali, you're good and guileless, but . . .

"Elif!" Ali called out, "add plenty of fat to the soup to-day.

It'll do Mother good. She's worn to a shadow, poor thing." He lay down in the sun again, his legs outstretched.

The children skipped merrily off into the trees. Hasan set about breaking off wild cherry-tree shoots and whittling them into rods.

"Down in the Chukurova I can get ten water-melons for one of these rods," he boasted happily.

Ummahan puckered her lips in disbelief.

"I can even get twenty," insisted Hasan. "They give anything for cherry rods in the Chukurova, because they have no trees at all there in the plain."

Ummahan laughed scornfully.

"Laugh on! If you think I'll give you a single one of my water-melons . . ." said Hasan. "However much you beg me and go whining to Father . . ." He broke into a mock show of a whimpering Ummahan, with himself condescendingly handing her some water-melon. Then she was snatching at the imaginary slice and gobbling it up greedily.

Ummahan only shrugged her shoulders and started pulling faces at him.

"I'll buy a sling as well, and bag a nice juicy hoopoe." He smacked his lips. "I'll light a fire and salt the bird and roast it so the fat drips, and then I'll eat it while you look on with your mouth watering. You'll run snivelling to Father . . ."

Ummahan interrupted him with a peal of laughter. To mask his vexation he fussed about with the cherry shoots which he measured, cut and pruned with a great show of diligence. Ummahan was prancing before him, aping his every movement. From the corner of his eye he cast angry glances at her. At last he raised his head.

"Wench," he said stiffly, "stop plaguing me and go away. Can't you see I'm busy?"

Ummahan retired to a safe distance, but persisted in her teasing.

"Wench," said Hasan, "be careful or I'll crush you like an ant. Leave me in peace. Just look at her! Look at that mouth, those eyes! What a sight! Stop it, or I'll give you a good thrashing. Don't drive me mad."

Suddenly Ummahan cut her antics short. "You're just a crazy fool," she burst out, "we can hardly get along as it is. Our horse is dead and Granny can't walk, and Father's feet are all swollen. And you, stupid, you're making cherry rods!"

Hasan was taken aback.

"I'll carry them myself on my own back," he said with studied aloofness.

"If you want to carry anything, why don't you take some of the load off Father's back?"

"He wouldn't give it to me."

"Wouldn't give it to him! Have you asked?"

"Wench, go away from here," Hasan flared up, "go f—— yourself."

Ummahan stuck out her tongue. He snatched up a stone and hurled it at her, but she had already made her escape.

"Bitch," he shouted, as he shot off in hot pursuit in and out of the trees, "you'll become a whore just like Batty Bekir's wife."

Ummahan turned in her tracks and faced him threateningly. "I'll become what? Say it. Say it again if you dare!"

Hasan was unnerved. "I was only joking," he pleaded, "don't tell Father. I'll give you three water-melons. And I'll shoot down the fattest hoopoe just for you."

Ummahan's large black eyes were unsmiling. "Don't you ever say that again," she admonished him. "If Father hears you, he'll tear your limbs apart. Anyway, he's worried sick."

They went back to the cherry rods. Hasan took up his cutting and trimming again, while Ummahan looked on until they heard their mother calling.

The meal was ready and their grandmother and father were dipping their spoons into the soup. They sat down quickly.

"Be careful," warned Elif. "It's very hot. You'll burn your-selves."

They began to eat slowly, blowing over each spoonful. Elif had put plenty of butter into the soup and had added fried onions sprinkled with red pepper. The burnt onion had an even more appetising odour in the pure mountain air. As soon as the soup had cooled a little, they gulped it down so fast that the saucepan was soon drained empty.

"My belly's swollen," complained Hasan as he slapped it resoundingly, "it's like a drum."

"Mine's like a drum too," chimed in Ummahan proudly.

Meryemdje smiled as she looked at the children rapping their naked bellies. Her smile was balm pouring into Ali's heart.

"Wasn't it a tasty soup, Mother?" he said. "Good for you, Elif." Then he went on, "What a stroke of luck it's been for us that Old Halil reckoned amiss this year. If he hadn't, we'd have been lost, undone, ruined. Adil Effendi . . ."

"Allah be praised," Elif interrupted him hastily, "don't I always tell you that if one door closes Allah always opens another?"

"Allah be praised," echoed Ali.

Meryemdje held up her hands to the sky. "Thank you, my beautiful Allah, my black-eyed one. My words are for you alone. Praised be your name."

Hasan and Ummahan laughed with glee as they too joined in the general thanksgiving.

"We'll camp here near this spring for two days," said Ali, "and recover our strength. What difference does it make if we wait here or down in the Chukurova cotton field, where we'll only champ the bit and be devoured by mosquitoes. Isn't it better if we stay here, Mother?"

"I'm telling you, my daughter, it's better, much better."

Hasan jumped to his feet. "I'll go and peel some *yalabuk* from the pine-trees.

Elif was clearing up the remnants of the meal. "Don't you get your fingers cut or I'll kill you," she warned him, as she went to put the dirty saucepan under the spring. "As for me, I'll boil the children's clothes in the cauldron to-morrow. I've been delousing them all morning, but there's no end to the lice."

Ali felt a dreadful itching all over his body. "Mercy, woman," he cried. "Why, here I am covered with lice myself and I didn't even notice it." He started scratching himself with frenzy.

"We'll all have a good wash to-morrow," said Elif, "my hair's so dirty it's as stiff as a broom."

"And perhaps Mother would mix me some of that ointment of forest gums and herbs that she alone knows how to brew. Why, that ointment would heal a bullet wound, not just a swollen foot!"

"I'm telling you, my daughter," Meryemdje said as she wobbled to her feet, "five days to heal a big fat bullet wound. Only five days with my ointment." She called to the children, "Quick, get me some pine gum and a handful of beech gum and also a sprig of thyme. . . . But no, wait. I must go myself."

She moved off haltingly towards the trees. Somewhere deep down in her there still lurked that fear like a thick, murky water. Then she heard Ali singing.

"You can well sing, my Long Ali," she mumbled, "now you've had this piece of luck. I'd have liked to see what you'd have done if that old spook hadn't sped the villagers down too early. What with your swollen feet and all, you'd have got there only when the others had finished picking all the cotton, and you'd have been quick to throw the blame on me then. Well, Allah has been merciful to you and now I'll make you such an ointment that by to-morrow morning your feet will be as new as on the day you were born. Eh, sing on, my Long Ali, sing on! As for me, my knees are breaking, my soul is heavy-laden. Ah, help me, my black-eyed one!"

She started to pray and the words of the prayer mingled with Ali's warm voice in the distance.

"Thank you, my black-eyed one. You've willed this. Thanks to you the cotton is not ripe yet. Thank you, thank you! And now let that Long Ali see what an ointment I can make. Let him not call me a mother if he likes. Let him curse me. . . ."

Chapter 13

The inner side of the pine bark is lined with a white, paper-thin pellicle. When a piece of the bark is stripped from the tree, this pellicle can be peeled off and eaten. It is the *yalabuk*, and the cedar and the fir as well as the pine-tree have it. As you start chewing it, all the flavour of a vast forest rises within you, with its running waters and murmuring breezes, its aroma of wild flowers, thyme, mint, marjoram and resin.

Many years ago, in a forest of the Taurus on the foothills facing the Chukurova, perhaps not far from this very spot, Ali had peeled off a slice of *yalabuk*. He still carries within him that fragrance of forest, rosemary and wild roses, of orchis and worm-wood, of heather and yellow everlastings and sage, of rotting leaves and earth. The taste of that slice of *yalabuk* is like honey on his palate and mingles with a green rustling that flows in his blood, making his head reel, intoxicating him. He hears the sighing forest and is born afresh, blown by fragrant starry winds into a young new world.

It was early. The sun had risen only the height of a poplar tree and a haze hung over the wooded slopes below. Still half asleep, he sat up. His blanket was sprinkled with the dew that had dropped from the pine branches overhead. He rubbed his eyes with his fists. Then he bent over his feet and slowly, apprehensively, unwound the bandage. He stood up on the pallet. To his surprise his feet did not hurt at all. He stepped to the ground and still he felt no pain. The swelling had fallen.

Elif stood by watching as he walked to the spring and washed his feet. He had been unable to walk for the past three days.

"Elif," he shouted joyfully, "Mother's ointment has worked wonders, bless her hands. Just look at me walking!" He stamped his feet and took a few steps. "As solid as rocks! By Allah, I could load that mountain on to my back and go galloping down like an Arab horse." He kneeled before Meryemdje and clasped her hands. She lifted her wizened face in which the eyes had sunk still deeper. Her pinched nose quivered.

"No more quarrels, eh, dear Mother? You've forgiven me, haven't you? We've still fourteen days . . ." He broke off and suddenly let go of his mother's hands. His brow was clouding over.

The children came running to him. "Father," cried Hasan, "you promised to cut some *yalabuk* from the forest when your feet got well. Shall we do it now?"

How good it would be to eat some *yalabuk* now, to feel the maddening forest winds and tempests in his head, in his blood, the gushing of the forest within him, a life-giving radiance, soothing his weary body.

"Father, I ate some. It tastes so sweet that . . ." The child's voice tailed away as he saw that there was no trace of joy left in his father.

A dark flush was spreading over Ali's face. All at once he whirled round.

"I'm ruined, woman, I'm lost. Quick! Hurry!" His eyes starting from their sockets, he rushed about gathering up their things. "For heaven's sake, woman, hurry. Let's pack up quickly. Come on, children, you too."

Elif was stunned at the sudden change in Ali.

"Hurry, hurry. We mustn't waste time!"

She caught him by the sleeve. "Wait. What's taken hold of you? Have you gone out of your mind?"

"We can't wait," shouted Ali. "The children this winter . . . And Adil Effendi . . ." Elif's wide questioning stare arrested him. "We must hurry," he continued lamely, "the autumn rains will soon be upon us. Is there a worse calamity than the autumn rain? If the rains come upon us in these mountains, we're lost. We'll all catch our death. Allah protect us! We must be quick. Quick, before the rains come. . . ."

Meryemdje slowly rose to her feet. She lifted her eyes to the sky. Not the smallest cloud marred the calm, boundless blue.

What's the matter with this whelp? she wondered. What's he up to now? So it seems we must be on the road again. Still, she comforted herself, I feel all right now after this three days' rest. Thanks to my black-eyed one, I don't need to ride on anybody's back any more. And my feet haven't swollen either like other people's. Allah be praised. A bite of *yalabuk* would have restored me to my old self, but that renegade won't go and cut some, on purpose, just because he knows I love it so. Well, let him not go. Eh, Long Ali, I can bide my time.

She picked up her stick. "I'll be hobbling along as best I can, my lovely girl. You'll catch up with me no doubt."

She set off at a brisk pace, her back less stooped than usual.

Ali was the first to overtake her. "Why exert yourself so, Mother? I'll be back to get you by noon," he said. "Hurry, Elif, quickly, children. We mustn't be caught in the rain. Mother, if it rains, take shelter under a big tree. The minute clouds show up, I'll race back to you. Come on," he shouted to the others as he bounded past her, "walk!"

Elif and the children hurried after him down the valley and soon after Mereyemdje lost sight of them. This time she felt alive and sprightly. The hills, the stones, the road laughed up at her. There was no pain in her back, no weakness in her knees. She hummed a gay tune, matching her pace to its rhythm.

Well, Long Ali, who did you take Meryemdje for? Did you think she wouldn't be able to walk? Go on, leave me if you like, alone on this solitary mountain, and take your wife and children with you. Good for you, my legs! So long as you keep steady like this, I won't be in need of those murderers who've killed my horse, my husband's own heirloom.

She came to the stream that flowed at the bottom of the valley and sat down on the bank to rest a while. The noontide heat was beating down. She bent over to drink and dabbed water over her face and hair. The world was bathed in light. A rock in the distance twinkled out fitful sparks. She looked up and saw Ali lumbering up the hill. It was a steep slope, covered with small, slippery stones.

If only there were no slopes on these roads, no mountains, no impassable streams to cross, no rains, no snowstorms. If only all roads were as flat as those of the Chukurova, if only all the year were like the day of Hidirellez, the feast of spring. . . .

She tore her eyes away from the hill. I shouldn't look at this accursed unhallowed slope again, she thought as she rose and started up the hill. She had not gone far when she slipped and pitched forward on her hands.

"May your hearth be destroyed, infernal slope fathered by a hog," she cursed. A new boldness filled her now, the boldness of defiance. "I'll climb you, slope," she shouted. The sound of her own voice heartened her. "Yes, I'll climb you, slope," she shouted again, "right up to your very summit."

But the top of the slope seemed so very distant. . . .

"I vow I won't look at your summit again, slope. Let Allah turn me into an infidel if I do, and cast me into his hell to burn for ever more. There now! It's a bargain!"

"It's a bargain," she repeated over and over again. The words stimulated her. "If I climb you, slope, I'll kill a fine red-crested speckled cock under that bright holy tree and not eat a single morsel. It's a bargain. . . . And give the meat to poor hungry children, not to big fat ones. It's a bargain. . . ."

She trudged on, panting out these words until she was gasping for breath. Her knees shook and she could hardly keep on her feet. But what if the end was near, only a few steps away?

How could she find out without breaking her vow? Furtively, as if she might be found out, she cast a quick peep upwards. There was still half of the way to go.

Her courage failed her and she crumpled to the ground. The stones were burning hot. Not a breath of wind relieved that noonday heat. In the distance, way off on the yellowing plateau, fields of thistles sparkled under the sun. That must be my Slim Memed's country, she thought, as the sweat grew cold on her flagging pain-racked body. Those are surely the thistle fields he used to plough. Should I go there and take refuge on Goodwife Hürü's hearth, where that Long Ali would never find me? You're a brave loyal woman, I'd say to her. Had it not been for you, Memed would never have become Slim Memed, the outlaw.

Her eyes dwelt a while on the plateau, old memories flitting through her mind. She remembered one Hidirellez feast day in the spring. . . . The village decked with flowers. . . . The great fire they had lit. . . . The merry-making, the songs, the dances. . . . The *saz*-players and drummers had come all the way from the distant province of Horasan.

She made a move to rise and felt all the bones in her body cracking. But this slope must be climbed, she thought. I mustn't have that Long Ali gloating over me. I'll go to Goodwife Hürü on the way back. Yes, I'll go to her and say, ah sister, that Slim Memed, how he must have loved his mother to have left no stone unturned until he avenged her. But look at this monster of a son I have. And Goodwife Hürü will grab Long Ali by the collar and her eyes will burn him like flames. He'll be looking for a hole to hide himself in, but she'll spit right into his face and say, There, I hope you remember this all your life.

It was high noon and Ali would soon be back. He'd be only too glad to find her here, nailed to the ground like a corpse, helpless, pitiable. If only his feet swelled twice as much as before and he didn't come! Make an ointment for him again? Allah forbid!

"Help me, Allah," she cried, "you who rescued Joseph from the well, help me now!"

She began to crawl forward on her hands and feet. Yes, if she had to die, it must be at the top of the slope. What a gallant woman, this Meryemdje, everyone would say, as valiant as Slim Memed's Mother Hürü, and even more. She would not be a burden even to her own son while she still had a breath of life left in her. . . .

"Allah, please hold back this Long Ali," she cried aloud, "break his shins. Delay him please, my holy, white-bearded one! Do this for me, great creator of the earth and skies."

She tried again and again, her body soaked in sweat, and at last she was on her feet, moving again, her heart pounding as if bursting out of her breast.

Perhaps she was nearing the top. But that vow . . . crazy Meryemdje, why did you have to bind yourself so? What difference would it make if you looked or not? The slope was there, wasn't it, and had to be climbed.

She peeped up again out of the corner of her eye. There was just a little way to go.

I didn't look really. It's just that my eyes couldn't help seeing it because I'm so near now. But that rock planted there like a mountain on the road! Who could have brought the unholy thing and dumped it in such a place? Don't they have anything better to do than play with rocks, those mighty creators of the earth and heavens? Oh dear, oh dear, there I am blaspheming now. . . .

"Allah," she cried, as she extended her arms to the sun-drenched sky, "forgive me my sins. And please delay this Ali. From the seventh story of seven-storeyed heaven you hold sway over the earth and waters. You can make him be late."

With a desperate effort she spurted forward and clambered past the rock. She had reached the top at last. In a blur, she saw a long road unfolding through an expanse of level land and winding away into distant wooded mountains. Then she surrendered herself completely and sank to the ground.

After a while she heard a voice. Ali was standing beside her.

What was he saying now, this Long Ali? Hadn't she scaled the slope right to its very summit, when he'd thought she would die on the way? She had no need for the whelp. While she still had a drop of blood left in her, she would drag herself on the ground rather than be carried on his back. Her name would become a legend among all peoples, among the Russians, among the French. . . . An old woman of eighty, or was it ninety, refuses to be carried by her ungrateful son and walks all the way down to the Chukurova, going up a slope as steep as a minaret too! Long live such mothers, people will say. Let that Long Ali stand by and hear that!

Ali talked on until he realised that his mother was not listening, or perhaps was in no mind to answer. He let himself drop down beside her. A pain shot through his spine, or so it seemed to him. But it was only his back quivering, dreading the impending human contact. Her silence was a relief, but, as time went by, a heavy disquieting darkness spread in him as before some imminent calamity. The Chukurova was still such a long way off. . . .

He rose and looked down at his mother. Was this Meryemdje, the large, full-blooded, vigorous woman? What would the villagers say when they saw her? They'd be sure to blame him. Well, who cared what they said? . . .

"Mother," he murmured at last reluctantly, "climb on to my back. We must be there before sundown."

At the word "back", a strange, nauseating panic seized him at the throat. Sick to death, he crouched down before her.

"Get up!" The words whistled through his clenched teeth like a bullet.

Meryemdje tore at a tuft of grass and rose slowly to her feet.

"Fresh green grass, it's you I'm talking to and no one else, you, the soul of the earth, the eyes of the soil. Fresh green grass, if you so much as cast a glance down this slope, your head will whirl. Won't a woman who has conquered this slope be able to walk on that flat road? Let no one be afraid. Let them rejoice. I've no intention of getting on to anyone's back. I'm walking on by myself. Fare you well, fresh green grass!"

She went up to a clump of bushes and endeavoured to break off a branch. Ali hurried after her. He chopped off one of the longest branches with his knife and whittled it deftly.

"Here you are, Mother," he said.

Meryemdje drew herself up, gazing at him steadily, her eyes boring into his. Should she accept the stick or not? She wavered a while and then took it.

The sun was setting when they reached the forest.

"Come, Mother, let me carry you a little," Ali offered with ill grace. "Elif's by the Kechigöz spring. Not far. Do you remember, Mother, how we had roasted a lamb there once?"

Do I remember? How could I forget, Long Ali? I had barbecued a whole leg for you alone, and how you had glutted upon it! And you have the impudence to remind me of those days?

She was tired out, but she wanted Ali down on his knees entreating her. Ali, who had been dreading to hear the words "come, carry me" was relieved at her silence and did not insist.

At evenfall a breeze arose from the south. The forest smelled of warm melting gum, of the blending of a thousand flowers.

She was scarcely able to drag herself along, but she gritted her teeth. Allah, make me get there quickly, she pleaded. Don't let me fall. Hold firm, my knees, there's only a little more to go. Don't fail me now!

Ali plodded on beside her unaware of her inner struggle. "Well, there's nothing to be said against Old Halil," he said. "But for him, we'd all have gone hungry and naked this winter. After the cotton picking, I'll spend some of the money I've earned to buy five packets of cigarettes for him. Won't he be surprised! That's for your pains, I'll say, because you made the villagers set out too early. Why, you wizard, I'll say, how could you know my horse would die on the way? He'll laugh heartily and I'll say, take them, they're your due. May all your worries drift away like smoke."

Suddenly Meryemdje boiled over with rage.

"Forest, it's you I'm talking to, may he smoke poison!" she shouted as she collapsed to the ground. She was choking. "Water," she gasped. "Quick, a little water!" She could hear the children's voices in the distance. "Water, my little ones!"

Ali filled his cupped hands from a stream nearby. "Drink," he said. "Come on, drink!"

Elif and the children came running up. She grasped Meryemdje's hands. She could hear the loud beat of the old woman's heart.

"Let him smoke the very root of the poisonous hemlock, that old hog," Meryemdje burst out again as soon as she had recovered a little. " The deadliest of distilled green hemlock. Let him smoke five packets, not one . . . five packets of potent poison, soon-speeding as the snake-bite that fells a man down before he can run from the sunshine into the shade. . . ."

Chapter 14

Before he can run from the sunshine into the shade. . . .

Lies, all lies from first to last! Doesn't a body know the heart and soul of the husband she has lived with for forty long years? He wasn't that kind of a man. People were wrong about him. Ibrahim, this confounded Ali's father Ibrahim, wouldn't have hurt an ant. Such a gentle, retiring soul he was, he could scarcely bring himself to look up at a man. He may have been sparing of words, but his pleasant laughter had the softness of cotton in bloom. He was not one for crowds and festivities. Still waters run deep, folks would say about him. Lies again. As Allah's my witness, it was only bashfulness.

It's that ghoul, that Old Halil, who made a thief of him. Yes, it's that wily snake-in-the-grass, that canting pig, that sinister fiend whose murder is sanctioned by all the four Holy Books, who for years and years made life a hell for my poor Ibrahim. Not a soul knows this, no one but Allah and this grief-scared, broken-hearted Meryemdje.

That year, the year of want and famine, when all the village was reduced to grinding gum-tree burrs in the mill for makeshift bread and had to forage for herbs and wild artichokes in the mountains, on a hot summer day, the news spread like a bush fire that Halil had escaped from the Yemen army and was back. The villagers rushed out to see him, all old men, women and children, for almost every male fit to wield the plough had gone to the wars.

Halil had lost all human aspect. His skin was parched and

black and clung fast to his bones. His green eyes had sunk into their sockets.

"So there's the famine?" he asked. "What! No bread? The earth dried to cracking, eh? Flames darting from the ground? The children wasted by the fever? Everybody's caught the mange? The women tilling the land, are they? Tilling the land's not a woman's job, eh? You just thank your stars! There's farther faring and worse. . . . Way off, beyond those mountains, lies a fiery sea of sand. Once trapped in it, there's no escape. And if one does break away . . . Well, look at me! Isn't it exactly seven years since we went away? Yes, seven long years. How many were we? I can't remember. All the men of a whole village. I'm the only one left, I and Ibrahim. Go and get him, if he's still alive. Where? By the Kechigöz spring. It's there he gave up. We couldn't travel on the road for fear they'd catch us and send us back to the Yemen. We were famished, at the end of our tether. But I set my teeth. If I have to die, I said, let it be on my own hearth. For pity's sake, friends, there are no gendarmes here, are there? Don't let the Headman find out I'm here. He's sure to send me back. The Yemen's hard. No human being should ever be forced to go there. I'll kill myself, or kill him, rather than go back. What? Köroghlu's son Osman? Did you say Duran? Who? Kizginoghlu? Battal? You mean Slim Battal? Wait till I come to myself and I'll tell you all about the Yemen. You'll see. I can hardly stand on my feet. Did you say there was a famine? Can't you rake up something for me to eat? I feel strange after living on wild mountain plants for so long. But a bite of black bread? What, not even a few ears of wheat or corn, just one or two kernels? For three months I've been on the road. And Ibrahim too. Strange . . . he was all right until we came to the spring. Then he just crumpled over. Ibrahim, I said, you've got to hold out. There's such a little way to go. I can't, he said, I'm done for. You go on and get help from the village. Don't worry about me now. Even if I die, it'll be on my own native mountains and not in that desert, that flaming hell. Maybe he's not dead yet. Isn't there a single man in the village who could go and bring him back?"

"Not one," they replied.

"Well then, let the women go. Goodwives, you've tilled the soil and reaped the crop these many years. You must go and fetch Ibrahim before he perishes there by the Kechigöz spring. Where's his wife? Where's Meryemdje?"

"She went to him the minute she heard," they told him.

"Who? Güdük Ahmet? Wait, wait, in Allah's name. Don't you see I'm more dead than alive? I'll tell you all about the Yemen later."

Wives whose husbands were still serving in the Yemen army, mothers whose sons had not returned, children who had never seen their fathers, all rallied to scrape together a plate of hot food for Halil, the fugitive from the Yemen, swirling about him all the while in a whirlwind of lamentation.

Ibrahim had lost consciousness by the time Meryemdje found him. She could not recognise him. Was this her tall, willowy Ibrahim, this drift of dry bones and dirty rags? She took him on to her back and carried him up to the village. Only three months later did he regain full consciousness, three whole months it was before he could laugh again, his own sweet, fresh laughter. Meryemdje was happy as a queen. "He's come back to me," she would repeat exultingly. "I lost him, but I've found him again."

In the years that followed, no pains were spared to conceal Ibrahim and Halil from the military police. All the villagers were on tenterhooks, trembling over the safety of their two men, their only survivors from the wars. As for the Headman, if he had so much as made a move to denounce them, the villagers would have made short work of him. He might have been the Sultan himself for all they cared.

Halil endlessly told and retold his tales of the Yemen, and the villagers wept, were amazed and laughed in turn. The Bald

Minstrel would sing all the Yemen ballads he knew, and compose new ones too. Contentment reigned in the whole village, although most households were bereft of husbands and fathers. Since Halil's arrival life and animation had returned to the village. Before that the Bald Minstrel never sang or played his *saz*. He would sit on his door step the whole day long, brooding and sullen, and woe betide who should approach him. Now, the villagers could at least sob their hearts out unrestrainedly.

Meryemdje alone was displeased. Something in Halil's talk vexed her and wounded her pride. True, he always praised her husband, but still she smelled a rat in all this business. Ibrahim himself never opened his mouth, but merely laughed as softly and pleasantly as usual at whatever Halil said.

"Yes, poison that will fell him down before he can run from the sunshine into the shade. . . ."

The stark deserts of the Yemen, the soldiers who fell dying of thirst, those who went mad, howling "water, water, water," tearing over the boundless wastes, lost for ever beyond the horizon, the sand-storms, the sickness, the hunger, the Arabs who gutted the routed Turkish soldiers, the villagers knew it all, just as if they had been there and seen it and lived through it. As for the escape of the two survivors, everyone knew every detail of it by heart.

"That afternoon the sea of sand heaved again. In the desert first a few lowering clouds appear. Then these clouds merge, and a black shroud is spread out between the sky and the earth. Oh, what a fearful sight, the world going suddenly dark in broad daylight! A wind springs up, churning the sands, sweeping mountains of sand from here to there. A body feels as though he had fallen into a boiling cauldron.

"We were being marched from one town to another, a week's journey afoot across the desert. Not a drop of water was left in our flasks. Our tongues clung to our palates. Yellow Durdu's son came up to me. He was swaying on his feet. 'I'm dying,' he said,

'I can't take another step.' What could I do? 'Get on to my back,' I said, 'you can't walk in this state.' We trudged on like this well into the afternoon. The body on my back grew heavier. It was then that the sands heaved again and the storm broke out, catching us all unawares. Waves of sand lashed about us, here, there, everywhere. The body fell off my back. I groped in the dark of the driving sands, and searched and searched, but the dead man was nowhere to be found. The storm let up and still there was no trace of the body. Who knows under what sand-hill the poor fellow lay buried? Güdükoghlu also died on the way that day. We plodded on, and all the while comrades were dropping in batches. We had to leave them behind. At last we came to a place, just a droplet of green, where water flowed. Later the Arabs fell upon us, hacking and butchering. When we reached our bivouac at last only a hundred and thirty men were left out of three hundred."

That night Meryemdje plied Ibrahim with questions. "Didn't you tell me that it was you who had taken Yellow Durdu's son on your back and then lost him in the sand-storm? Now Halil says he carried him and we've become the laughing stock of the village. Who's the one that's lying? Why didn't you say a word?"

But Ibrahim never answered, never opened his mouth.

"We had been fourteen from our village. But now we were only six. Ibrahim came to me. 'Friend,' he said, 'there's no other way out for us but to escape from here. If we manage to save our skins, all right. If not . . . It's death for us here anyway.' 'Friend,' I said, 'isn't this called treason? Treason to the fatherland?' 'Who cares?' he replied. 'What has the fatherland given us but death?' 'But if they catch us,' I said, 'they'll shoot us, and if we're found in the village, we'll be court-martialled.' Ah, but this Ibrahim you see here is a brave, fearless man. 'We must risk that,' he said. 'Think of going back to our country!' 'All right,' I said at last, 'but what about the others? Will they agree?' So we went and asked them. 'Suppose we do escape,' said one, 'suppose no one catches us on the way, no one slashes our guts out, can we ever reach our country? Do you realise how far we are? Why, it's a six-month road to the Taurus mountains for sure! It's impossible.' There was no word of assent or dissent from the other villagers. I talked to them and Ibrahim talked to them, we talked for two whole days, but they would not be persuaded. So one dark night we rose stealthily and crept away. We walked on in the sands till it was dawn. And when the sun rose we burrowed in the sand so no one should see us. 'Ibrahim,' I said then, 'it's a monstrous thing we're doing, leaving our comrades there and running away. How shall we face their mothers, their fathers, their children, their sweethearts, once we're back in the village? Shall we say that we abandoned them to their fate in the Yemen desert? That we only sought to save our precious lives? What shall we tell them, Ibrahim?' You know Ibrahim. He has a mouth, but no tongue. 'Let's go back,' I suggested. 'You go,' said Ibrahim, 'and bring them along if you can. I can't walk this stretch of desert all over again. I'll wait here.' So I went back and pleaded with them all night. 'Think, my friends,' I said, 'you've served seven years and you've still seven years to wait before you're released. Think of the smell of the pines in the Taurus, of the icy mountain springs, of the fragrant *yalabuk*. Is that not worth risking death for?' But they were immovable. 'Then I'm going, friends,' I said, 'I wash my hands of you.'

"I found Ibrahim as I had left him, buried to the neck in sand. He had not stirred. 'Come on, Ibrahim,' I said, 'let's go.' He sprang out of his bed of sand and we set off. We had only covered a short distance when I turned to him again. 'We can't do this, Ibrahim,' I said. 'Well, what shall we do then?' he asked. 'I must go to them once more,' I said. 'I'm sure we can make good our escape. Let them not remain behind in the desolation of the Yemen, poor fellows. I can't help thinking of their weeping children and mothers.' 'If they wouldn't come the first time,' said

Ibrahim, 'then they'll never come. Let's go before we're caught.'
'I know you're right, Ibrahim,' I said, 'but we must do our
human duty. We mustn't return with shame on our faces.'
Ibrahim buried himself into the sands again. 'Go then,' he said
angrily. 'And find a little water.' I went back again. I fell at their
feet, begging them. They would not listen to me. I found two
flasks of water and returned to Ibrahim once more. 'Damn them
all, Ibrahim,' I said, 'they're hopeless. Let's be on our way.'
But a worm was eating my heart. You're saving your own skin,
Halil, a voice kept saying, but you're leaving your friends, your
fellow-villagers, in the blazing sands of the Yemen desert, leaving
them to die. You must go back and do your best to bring them
to their senses. I was afraid of Ibrahim, afraid that this time he
would go off by himself without me. But how could I leave my
friends? That would be treason indeed. I braced myself and
spoke to Ibrahim. He was furious. 'Go to hell,' he said, 'I can't
dally with you any longer. It's clear you don't feel up to the
escape either. Go back and stay with them.' Yes, you wouldn't
believe it just looking at him like that, but Ibrahim is as brave
and fearless as a lion. He set off alone. And I went back to our
friends. I implored them. I kissed their feet. In vain. I walked
for a whole day and a whole night in the boiling heat, on the
red-hot desert sand and overtook Ibrahim. He was sitting under
a date-tree. 'Are you convinced now?' he said. 'Yes,' I said, 'they
haven't got the spunk of a sparrow. They're terrified of being
gutted by the Arabs, of being seized by the gendarmes at home
and turned over to the Government. . . . Still, I haven't the heart
to do this.' Well, my friends, I went back to them five times again,
yes five times, until one night the guards were on me, almost
killed me, but I managed to give them the slip. 'It's no use, they'll
never come, Ibrahim,' I said, 'the sands of the Yemen are dragging
them down. Their fate is to die here. Let's hurry.' "

That night Meryemdje went into a fury. "Which of you is
lying, I'd like to know? Didn't you tell me that it was you who

had gone back five times to bring the villagers over? Didn't you say that if it weren't for Halil you'd never have come away without them? Who's the liar here?"

Ibrahim never answered, never opened his mouth. . . .

"That Halil? Let the plague seize him! Cigarettes for him? The root of the baneful hemlock. . . . Let him smoke poison that will fell him, swift as a snake-bite, before he can run from the sunshine into the shade."

It was a time of want, of misery, of hunger, in the village. One day Halil came to Ibrahim.

"Look here, Ibrahim, what with the famine and the women doing all the jobs, it seems there's nothing left for us to do but loll around. I've heard of something. Down in the foothills, not far from Kozan, a certain Aslan Agha has earned renown for his gang of horse-thieves. Wherever there is a fine horse on this land of the Osmanli, Aslan Agha sets one of his gang after it. The horses stolen in one part of the country he sells in another, trafficking them from Anatolia to Arabia or Kurdistan, from Smyrna to Trebizond, from Kars to Aleppo, from Aleppo to Kayseri. Now, you and I, we know the land of Aleppo well. What do you say? Shall we go and join Aslan Agha's gang?"

Ibrahim made no answer.

"All right then, friend," Halil decided, "we'll be off to-morrow morning. Let Meryemdje pack us some food for the journey. Just think, you'll be rid of that harridan! Why man, Meryemdje's worse than the Yemen! She'll whittle you to death, you whom even the Yemen could not kill!"

A few days later the two friends turned up at the village of Aslan Agha. The Agha's gang was made up entirely of army deserters and of Yemen fugitives. Halil and Ibrahim were enrolled on the spot and were promptly dispatched to the Long Plateau, along with a master-thief. They were to carry off horses from the Circassian tribes that lived there.

From that day on, for years, Halil and Ibrahim stole horses

from the Long Plateau and sold them in Aleppo. All the money they got was handed over to the Agha to the last penny and the Agha gave them a yearly pay. But what a pay! A mere pittance. Still they were not worse off than the others. Why then did all these men remain in the gang? All were gallows-birds, outlaws who found in the gang some kind of backing, of protection against the world. And Aslan Agha never let his men down.

One day they fell into the hands of the Circassians, who gave them a sound thrashing and, thinking them dead, left them on the mountain. A peasant found them and brought them back to the village. They were bedridden for three months. This was their longest stay at home during the years of horse-thieving. Usually they would turn up once every six months for a few days only and then pack off without leaving a bean. "Are you Halil's slave?" Meryemdje would rail at him. Her jeremiads would rend the air and rouse the whole village. But Ibrahim never opened his mouth. He followed in Halil's wake as if nothing untoward had happened.

Another time, after the proclamation of the Republic and when Aslan Agha's power was on the wane, Halil and Ibrahim were apprehended by the gendarmes at night on the Gavur Mountains as they were making for Aleppo with a herd of stolen horses. Halil, as well as Kurd Dursun and Circassian Idris who had been with them, were sentenced to two-year prison terms and thrown into the Adana jail. To everyone's surprise Ibrahim got off scot-free, although Halil had laid all the blame on him at the trial and he himself had not uttered a single word in his own defence.

People thought that after this Ibrahim would go back to his village and keep his nose out of such shady dealings.

But he did not go back, not even once, not even to see his wife and child. He remained in Adana, and with an axe slung over his shoulder went from door to door offering to chop fuel wood. Every visiting day he would be at the prison with a basket

185

of vegetables, flour and butter, which he would hand over to Halil together with a little pocket money, smiling happily all the time.

"Go to the village," Halil would urge him, "go and see how our families are faring. It'll be a good while before I'm out. This huge town of Adana will be the death of you."

Each time, Halil would be sure he had talked Ibrahim into going home, but when, on the next visiting day, he would see him there at the prison gate, he was glad.

Ibrahim slept in a damp grimy *han* that stank of horse urine. He subsisted on scraps and spent all his earnings on his friend. This, along with what he received from Aslan Agha, enabled Halil to live in clover.

Then Ibrahim caught a fever that made him tremble like an aspen leaf, but still he would not abandon his friend in his prison-hole.

A week or so before Halil's release Ibrahim came and planted himself before the prison. He waited there, night and day, in the dust and the heat, his eyes glued to the prison gate. At last Halil came out and Ibrahim went almost mad with joy as he hugged him.

"To the mountains," said Halil.

Ibrahim thought he meant the Long Plateau.

"Halil, brother," he ventured timidly, "it's so long since we've been home and seen our families. How about going to the village first?"

Halil laughed. "We're done with Aslan Agha, and besides he's finished now. And the Yemen wars are over too. We're going back to the village and we'll do whatever work the others are doing."

The villagers gave them a hearty welcome. Wherever Halil went he brought life and excitement with him. Now the village was regaled with tales of Aslan Agha's horse-thieves, of the Long Plateau and of the Aleppo road.

"This Ibrahim!" As usual, it was Halil who spoke, while

Ibrahim listened, smiling. "There's not another thief like him in the whole world. He'd steal the kohl off a woman's eyes! Way up there on the Long Plateau there lives a Circassian Bey who used to own a famous pure-bred, as swift and handsome as Köroghlu's white horse. For years Aslan Agha had sent forth his men, hundreds of them, to capture it, but none had succeeded. Each night the Circassian Bey snapped double fetters on his horse and locked it up in an iron-gated stable with two men to stand watch. Well, you see this Ibrahim here? He was the one to steal that horse at last."

That night in bed Meryemdje flared up again. "One of you is lying all the time. Didn't you tell me that it was Halil and his men who had stolen the Circassian Bey's horse?"

Ibrahim was silent.

"Ah, this Ibrahim," Halil marvelled. "He knows exactly how many stones there are on the Aleppo road, how many ants in their ant-holes, how they eat and make love, what's worth filching from them. This Ibrahim here can waggle the world on his little finger, with no one any the wiser. He can drive a herd of three hundred horses through the Adana market in broad daylight without a soul seeing him. Does he change himself into a jinn or a *sheitan*? What a man! Ask me! I would give my life for him. But accidents will always happen. It's an accident that befell Ibrahim. The gendarmes came upon us by surprise one night. We all got off except Ibrahim, who was our leader. They gave him two years. The others all went their way. But would I leave my soul's comrade to rot in the Adana prison? I bought an axe and started chopping wood for people. I didn't eat, I didn't drink, whatever I earned I gave to Ibrahim. The other prisoners would say: 'Why Ibrahim, it's not a friend you have there, it's a real brother and more.' Isn't that so, Ibrahim?"

Ibrahim nodded in agreement. He was happy.

"A week before his release I was at the prison gate, waiting for him in the rain, in the dust, as if somebody had tied me there with a forty-ply rope. When he came out he looked at me and said: 'Good for you, Halil. You've been the friend in need.' Isn't that so, Ibrahim?"

Ibrahim nodded again, smiling.

"You're a big liar," Meryemdje shouted at him, "didn't you just tell me it was you who had waited? I'll never believe a single word you utter again, no, not even if you say 'there is no god but Allah.' "

Ibrahim meekly bowed his head.

Cotton growing was now a booming business in the Chukurova plain and for the past two or three years the villagers had gone down for the picking, young and old, with all their livestock, even their dogs and cats, not leaving a single soul behind. Halil and Ibrahim would also go, but not at the same time as the others. They went either long before or long after, heading for the cotton plantations in far-off Yüreghir or even in the Tarsus plain. And there Ibrahim would steal cotton, or so Halil would maintain. They would load the cotton on to large wooden-wheeled ox-carts and sell it on the Adana market, making lapfuls of money which they invariably spent in Adana, returning empty-handed to the village. This lasted until two years before Ibrahim's death.

That night Halil had stuffed a large jute sack full of cotton, and they were cautiously wading through a water-filled ditch on the side of the field, making away with their booty. In the morning, at a safe distance from the cotton field, they intended loading it on to a passing cart and then disposing of it in the town. It had seemed a perfect field to plunder, with the cotton all ready-picked and stacked in mounds and not a soul about. But as fate would have it, half an hour later the cotton-owner together with a group of villagers had sprung upon them. The punishment for cotton thieving in the Chukurova is very heavy. The culprit is not handed over to the police or anything like that. A rope is tied around his neck and with the stolen cotton still on his back he is dragged around from village to village to be exhibited in each of the village squares. There everybody, old and young, women, men and children, turns out to spit in his face.

How they gloated over Halil's capture! This was an exceptional thief indeed who could run with such a heavy load, and although large and brawny he was no longer young. Accompanying him was his friend, a meek, mild man, obviously innocent. There and then a rope was slipped around Halil's neck and he was hauled forward to the nearest village. Confound them, what a hell of a lot of spittle these Chukurova fellows can muster! Halil's face, his eyes, were streaming with saliva. Even his clothes were soaked. They tugged him on to the next village, and then to the next. . . . His knees were failing him and once he fell, the load on his back almost crushing him. But still they pulled him onward. For four days the peasants of fifteen villages spat in his face. Halil was more dead than alive when they let go of him at last.

As soon as they were out of the last village Halil grasped Ibrahim's hand. "No more cotton thieving for us, friend," he said, "Allah forbid! It's a dirty job, the devil take it! Never, never, never more, my friend."

"Never more," echoed Ibrahim.

Winter was setting in when they returned to the village. The whirling thistles had all disappeared, rotted on the ground or been swept away by the winds.

"Ibrahim has sworn never to go cotton thieving again," announced Halil, "how could he do otherwise, when they caught him with a sack of cotton weighing more than a hundred kilos, tied a rope around his neck and paraded him from village to village, where everyone spat in his face! Allah, how they spat! They almost drowned him. Why, for a whole week fifty villagers with their dogs, their cattle, their donkeys, all spat on Ibrahim's face. Allah keep us from such a scourge!"

This time Meryemdje was crowing. "So the whole population of fifty villages spat in Halil's face? For a whole week, eh? Serve him right! Did they do anything to you?"

Ibrahim was silent again.

Yes, everyone knew Ibrahim for a master-thief and Halil for a timorous inoffensive fellow. . . .

"And he didn't die. To think he's still alive, that beady-eyed monster! Cigarettes? Rather the root of the poisonous hemlock for him. . . . Before he can run from the sunshine into the shade. . . ."

Chapter 15

The first streaks of dawn were lighting up the eastern sky and Elif was waiting with sickness in her heart for her husband to wake up. The soles of her feet were smarting. With a twig she started picking out the earth and small stones that had got stuck in the torn flesh. Now and then she cast a glance at Ali. His face was drawn and bitter as poison, even in sleep. His neck had thinned and lengthened and his eyes too had changed. They were enormous now. Under an oak tree farther away, Meryemdje lay in a lifeless heap between Ummahan and Hasan.

The children are worn out too, she thought. What if they're taken ill? And Meryemdje battered to exhaustion. . . . She's trying hard, but what if she breaks down altogether? And before us there's that Süleymanli slope, steep, towering, more than a full morning's climb. Once this slope is scaled the Chukurova is as good as reached, hardly a day's walk, and downhill too. But how can we weather such a slope, weary as we are? What if we're stalled, helpless, at the foot of the slope? And ever since Ali branched into this short cut, we haven't come across a single soul. What if something happens to us, and not a body about to give us a drop of water? Ali has forgotten all about this slope. If it crosses his mind, he'll kill himself. I must be careful not to breathe a word. . . .

A warm smell of earth drifted up to her, the fresh smell that seeps out of the soil after a passing shower, that same smell that sometimes rises from the Chukurova earth at daybreak. The sun appeared and the wet, withered grass glistened. A patch of sunlight fell on Ali's forehead. Elif was seized with fear. He would wake up now, frantic, shouting that the rains were upon them and would dash off like a madman in the direction of the Chukurova. She shifted so as to cast her shadow upon him.

There was a flurry of rustling in the crags on her right. A bird of prey had plunged upon a covey of pigeons, stirring up a panic of flapping wings. The pigeons billowed frantically in the air while the struggle lasted. Then the bird of prey snapped up a pigeon and was gone. The rest of the covey fluttered wearily out of sight.

Just then Ali bounded to his feet. He staggered dazedly for a moment, casting wild looks about him. Then he rushed to the spring and threw a little water over his face.

"Quick, woman, get ready," he cried. "No, no. You stay here. No leaving Mother behind this time. I'll carry her first and then come back. Is she up?"

"Hush," whispered Elif, "she's asleep."

"Damn her sleep! She's mucked up my hearth, my children will go hungry this winter because of her, and there she goes sleeping! Let her wake up!" he shouted.

Elif was clinging to his arm. "Hush," she pleaded, "the poor woman has been awake moaning all night. You told me she'd walked all day yesterday. She's exhausted. She only just fell asleep, a little before dawn broke. For pity's sake, hush, Ali!"

"Hush! What hush? She's destroyed me, that woman, and on top of that am I to dally here and watch over her for days on end while she sleeps? I'll go and grab her by the feet. . . ."

He snatched his arm from Elif's grasp and strode over to where Meryemdje was lying, but at the sight of her shrunken, shrivelled face, as small as a sparrow's, half buried in the mattress, his arms fell to his sides and a lump wedged in his throat. He turned away and slumped on to a rock. His head fell to his breast.

The sun was now quite high in the sky and it was getting

192

warm. Such a blaze had settled over the yellow grass, you would think this was the Chukurova. The earth was cracked also, just like the earth of the Chukurova. The spreading, unbroken flatness of the Chukurova plain rose before his eyes, a boundless level white world, and, stuck on this whiteness, the labourers, ant-like, all picking cotton feverishly. . . .

"I'm ruined, my hearth is burnt to ashes," he groaned aloud.

So little was left for the Chukurova now, a three-day walk, perhaps four at the most. The others still had four days to go and, as they always stopped for a couple of days at Sögütlü to wait for that cuckolded son of a bitch, Batty Bekir, that gave him six days. Six days! He had to make it.

"Elif," he called to his wife, who was trying to steady the saucepan over the fire, "come here. You must rouse that confounded woman. We've still got six days left. The villagers . . ." He leapt to his feet. "Wake her up! Go on! What are you standing there goggling at me for? I'll show you how to rouse her." He swung angrily towards his mother. "Just watch!"

But no sooner had he bent over her than he recoiled again before that shrunken and shrivelled face and her sleep helpless as a child's. He rushed back shouting, "Wake her, wake her, wake her!"

Elif neither stirred nor spoke. She stood there petrified, staring at him with widening eyes.

"What's the matter with you? Wake her up. . . . God damn you too. You're all banded together, all of you, to skin me, to finish me!"

He threw himself towards Meryemdje, but stopped once more. Just then the children sat up, rubbing their eyes. He caught hold of them by their arms and shook them out of bed. "Accursed brats," he ranted, "you too . . ."

Bewildered, they broke into tears, while Ali went on shouting in a terrible voice that rang from the craggy slopes.

"She'll never wake up," he said at last as he dropped back on to the stone. "Elif, take a look. See if she's breathing. Maybe something's happened to her."

Elif moved stiffly. She bent over Meryemdje and listened, while Ali looked on expectantly.

"She's breathing peacefully," she murmured, turning back to her husband.

It was as if a knife had been plunged into his flesh. "We're done for, Elif," he groaned, "we might as well be dead!"

The soup was ready. They sat and drank it, setting aside Meryemdje's portion. Noon passed and still Meryemdje slept on. Ali shuttled to and fro, writhing like a madman and bellowing curses at the top of his voice.

"Woman," he said finally, choking with exasperation, "if she doesn't wake up I'll just leave her and . . ." He stopped. "Oh, my ass's head!" he said wearily. "Why didn't I think of it before?" Some of the tenseness left his face. "Let the woman sleep here, while we go on to the next stopping place. I'll come back later. Pack up the load."

Elif clung to him. "Don't Ali! Don't, I beg you. She'll die of fear when she wakes up. She'll think we've deserted her. We can't do this!"

He flung her aside. "Pack, I said, pack!" His eyes wild, he rushed about in a whirl, snatching up their things.

Elif burst into sobs. "Wake up, my unlucky mother," she cried as she knelt down and passed her fingers tenderly over Meryemdje's forehead. "Wake up, my forsaken one, look, we're leaving you! Look, we want your death! We're praying for your death so we should be rid of you. Wake up!" She pulled her up by the shoulders and shook her gently. "Wake up, dear Mother. We have to go."

Meryemdje opened her eyes.

"Mother darling, it's far into the afternoon and time we were going."

"Afternoon?" Meryemdje whispered. She looked at the sun. "Afternoon?" she muttered again. She tried to rise. Elif helped her walk into the bushes where she relieved herself.

"Mother," Elif called to her happily, "I found we still had some cheese and I kept it for you. There's a red onion too. I'd set some soup aside, but Hasan drank it all up."

Meryemdje washed her face at the spring, then sat down and started munching slowly. After a while she rose and, without a word to anyone, made for the road.

Ali looked after her, his spirits rising. "Woman, you stay here. I'll be back by midnight," he called as he ran up and squatted before Meryemdje. "Get on my back, Mother."

Drawing her stick aside, Meryemdje slowly passed him by and went her way with never a backward glance, leaving him crouched there almost bursting with relief.

"Mother of mothers!" he cried as he caught up with her again. "Is there anyone like you? You're as good as an angel in heaven, and to think I never knew your worth! To think I killed your horse when it was still young and vigorous and could have lived another ten years! My noble mother, how I've wronged you. And all because of that ill-omened Old Halil!"

Meryemdje moved her head almost imperceptibly and cast a quick glance at her son.

Aha, Long Ali! So you've come to your senses at last? You wouldn't take your mother's word, you wouldn't listen to your elders. Didn't I tell you what an evil-eyed vile wretch he is? One look of his is enough to drain the vast Mediterranean lake and turn it into parched sands. If he so much as passes through the Taurus forest, it goes up in flames. When he steps into the city of Adana, he brings an earthquake upon it. So you've come round to what I said, eh?

Ali realised that his mother was now less hostile and he felt gladdened. "From now on, I'll never give that Old Halil even a twig again. Had I herds and herds of horses grazing on the

Chukurova earth beside the white Mediterranean, I would not let him ride a single one of them. Had I loftfuls of wheat lying in wait, flocks and flocks of milk-yielding sheep, bee-hives oozing over with honey, piles and piles of glittering gold, and even if Old Halil's eyes should pop out of their sockets with hunger, I wouldn't give him the tiniest scrap. Never again!"

Meryemdje pulled up, her head held high, her eyes fixed on some distant point before her. "Stick," she began after a pause, "long-suffering stick in my hand, it's you I'm talking to and no one else. Babies' cradles are made of you, and the plough in the fields and the yoke of the oxen, and always you carry the scent of the mountains in you. With the autumn you wither and turn bare, but when the spring comes you sprout forth the greenest of leaves. But for you, how could I have covered all this long, long road? Allah keep me from depending on other people's backs while I've got you, you the support, the faithful companion of the old and helpless. How can I ever repay you, my faithful stick? I ought to deck you out in festoons and spangles and hang you up right in the centre of the house. So listen well, now, stick, to what I have to tell you. Somebody's just come to his senses, but a bit late in the day. He's trying to lock the stable door after the horse has been stolen, after the heart, that crystal palace, has been broken to shivers. Hey, my stick, have you heard me?"

"I have, Mother, I have," cried Ali, "you're quite right. Forgive me, I didn't know what I was doing."

Meryemdje rapped her stick twice. "Hey, beautiful stick, king of sticks, you've really seen daylight at last. But where is the builder that can put together this shattered crystal palace? And even if someone could, wouldn't there be a crack left somewhere? Do you hear me, stick?"

"I hear you, Mother," said Ali, "and now don't be obstinate. Come, let me carry you."

"My young sapling," said Meryemdje in her mocking, tired voice, "I'd rather trudge on with you till I die than be carried on anybody's back. And death is not so far away either. It has drawn nearer, nearer, it's right here where I can see it now. Oh, my black-eyed Allah, watch over me."

The sun was setting when Meryemdje slowed to a stop, concentrating every ounce of her energy on keeping upright on her trembling legs. She was leaning helplessly on her stick, waiting for Ali to say, "Come, let me carry you."

"That Old Halil? That devil-worshipper? That thieving renegade whose murder is sanctioned by all the four Holy Books? Ah my long-suffering stick, I'm telling you . . . because of him . . . this crystal palace . . . he . . ."

Ali closed his eyes and squatted before her. He drew her swiftly on to his back and pressed forward at a running pace.

The sun set. They did not stop or speak until they came to a spot where the trees boomed like a stormy sea and became dark with distance like black waters. Here the night smelled of pine-resin and cedar, and the air was like silk. Ali heard the gurgle of a spring. He walked towards the sound and lowered his mother on to the soft knee-high grass. The crushed grass gave out a fragrant smell.

"Mother, the weather's warmer now because we're drawing near the Chukurova, but I can light a fire for you if you're cold. You won't be afraid of the dark, will you?"

He waited, swaying on his feet, not daring to sit down, for he knew that if he did he would never be able to rise and walk again. He waited, for it would not be fitting to leave without a word from his mother.

"Forest," Meryemdje began at last, "happy forest, a hundred thousand trees in company, immovable, inseparable, thundering all together, shedding your leaves together and flowering again together, bathed in the same rain, facing the same dawn . . . listen to me well, thank your stars that you're not human. Spring flowing beside me . . ."

Meryemdje was now in her stride, and once started, heaven

knew when she would stop talking. Ali sidled away cautiously towards the road.

"Pure-watered stream, sparkling under the sun, flittering over lofty mountains delving into the earth to bubble out again into the light, thank your stars you're not a human being. You, dear little star above me. Whose star are you, I wonder? Where is your owner? On what plain, on what mountain? Maybe asleep now in his warm bed, without a care in the world. Maybe awake, suffering under a thousand burdens, writhing in pain. I know that when he dies you will plunge down from the skies and die too. But you have no troubles, you don't need bread or water like your owner. You fade by day and light up by night, and all you have to do is to shine. Give thanks to heaven that you're not human.

"Black earth beneath me, you the beginning and the end of all things, they hurt you, wear you out. . . . They do all kinds of impossible things to you, and yet you never bear malice, you let all creatures find comfort and shelter in you. The waters gnaw at you, the lightning strikes you, but be thankful still that you're not human. . . .

"I'm telling you all, I'm not afraid any more, not of the slightest thing, not even of the cold and of death."

She looked about for Ali and a pang of loneliness shot through her. "He's gone," she muttered. "Well, let him go. . . . Yes, give thanks." she added. "Bless your stars."

She lay back. A few remote stars twinkled in between the branches.

In this world every living creature has a star for himself. Even the ants and fishes and bees, yes, every creature. How else could the sky be teeming so with stars, a granary of stars? Old Halil too has a star, may it be struck down! And my horse had one too, my noble Küheylan, and now it has fallen who knows where, into what ocean, on to what black earth? That star right above me may be mine, who knows? It twinkles so feebly. . . .

When its owner's future is dark, then his star dims away. It sways in the sky as though hanging on a loose thread, because it it is about to sink.

She sat up shivering. A star shot down in a long trail of light and was lost.

Meryemdje sighed. "Who knows what poor creature has died just now? . . ."

Ah, this deceitful world. . . . And yet she had not had her fill of it. She lay back and slept.

Dawn was breaking when Ali sighted the smoking fire and Elif hunched up beside it. She lifted her head at the sound of his footsteps.

"Haven't you slept at all?" asked Ali.

She shook her head drowsily.

In the twilight of dawn, Elif appeared to Ali as lovely as when she had been a young girl. Something began to pulse in him, a pleasant warm flowing, a freshness, a lustiness in his body.

He took her in his arms and kissed her, holding her closer, his weariness melting away in a rush of green freshness, a newborn vigour. He tightened his arms about her and her bones cracked. Choking with emotion, he lifted her up and made for the bushes, away from the sleeping children.

The sun was up the height of a minaret when they came out of the bushes. They plunged into the Kechigöz spring and washed themselves. Then they lay down under a pine tree and fell asleep at once.

Meryemdje started up in a sweat. The sun was high and beating down upon her. As she gazed around and slowly realised where she was, she stiffened and her hair began to creep. He had left her in the very centre of the Forsaken Graveyard! All night long she had slept in the midst of the dead! Terror-stricken, she hurled herself blindly towards the road, her feet thrashing against the bushes and briers. On the road she redoubled her speed, her terror growing apace, but when she came to the single long grave that stretched along the roadside with the leafless oak tree looming above it, she could not take another step. She flung herself face down on the ground.

"Allah, Allah, my black-eyed one, help me! Save me!"

She crouched there trembling, praying to Allah, averting her eyes from the grave. Then with a desperate effort she dragged herself up and rushed on.

What a long, unending graveyard it was! She tripped and fell again and again, and when at last she could rise no more, she crawled on, her face caked in dust and sweat, her hands and knees bleeding, her dress all torn. She moved with the heaviness of a big tortoise.

It was only towards midday that she dared look back. At last there were no more gravestones about her, no more black oaks tied with votive rags. The graveyard was far behind her, out of sight. She managed to reach the roadside, where she threw herself into the shade of a single pine tree. Her throat and mouth were parched dry and, as her wounds cooled, the pain increased, shooting into her heart.

I'm dying, she thought, I'm really dying now. Help me, my black-eyed one. Help Ali find my body, so it should not be torn to pieces by the wild beasts. Grant me a grave and a burial shroud, oh my black-eyed one!

Elif was cooking the *tarhana* soup over the fire while Ali lay stretched out staring before him unseeingly. His head was emptied of all thought. The children sat silently by the spring, their huge, sad eyes gazing listlessly out of their sallow faces. There was in them that tired wariness of the very old.

Elif poured a little butter into the skillet. "Come and eat," she called.

Ali did not stir. The children moved up, hunger written on their faces.

"Come on, Ali," Elif called again. Her voice was tender and full of love.

"Bring the food over here," ordered Ali.

Without a word she gathered up the cloth and food and set them down again before him.

"I'm dead beat," he said at last. "I've lost all hope of ever reaching the Chukurova. I can't keep this up, I know."

Elif's face changed. She stiffened. Anger and a kind of revolt waxed hard within her.

"You stop worrying," she said sharply, "you've done a wonderful job, carrying Mother and the load for so long. Now it's my turn. What is there left anyway? I'll carry Mother and the load too. If it weren't . . ." She checked herself in time. If it weren't for the Süleymanli slope, she had been about to say.

She thrust her spoon angrily into the soup and drank.

Ali felt a sob choking at his throat. How he wished he could let himself go now before his wife, before his children, and cry to his heart's content. But he kept on munching steadily, unable to swallow the morsel in his mouth. His trembling hand went to Elif's slowly, caressingly.

When they had finished Elif rose and packed the load.

"I'll carry it again for the time being," said Ali, drawing close to her. "I can still hold on. When I really can't go on you'll take it."

She knew that it was useless to argue. He was already squatting before the pack. She pushed it on to his back and supported it as he heaved himself up. The motley embroidered *kilim* which they always wrapped about the pack was dusty. She brushed it mechanically, thinking how difficult it had been for Ali to get to his feet this time. Still, they were almost there now. Ah, that accursed Süleymanli slope. . . .

"Did you take her very far?" she asked. "It's so late, she'll be dying of hunger."

"She's at the Forsaken Graveyard," he replied.

His voice was weak and low. The rags of sacking on his feet were torn and hung down, sweeping the road.

The children no longer ran or played or laughed, but dragged on dully behind them. Ummahan's eyes were sore with crusted mucus and Hasan's nose was running. Every now and then he sniffled violently, drawing up the long green rivulet that hung down to his mouth.

Chapter 16

The village had been camping at Sögütlü for days now, waiting. This was the last stopping place. Down below them lay the Chukurova soil, with its trees and mounds and running waters all swathed in a sunny mist.

Never before, as far back as anyone could remember, had they camped here for more than one day. Usually they arrived at night and left early the next morning, making straight down for the Chukurova cotton fields to start work at once.

The days came and went, and restlessness spread among the villagers. What sense was there in idling away up here when everyone was already picking away for all they were worth down in the Chukurova, not a day's journey away? Murmurs of protest began to rise here and there. But the Muhtar was not disturbed. "Let them prattle away to their heart's content," he said, "we're not without our plan either."

Finally Tashbash was stung into action. He took Lone Duran along with him and went to tackle the Muhtar.

"This can't go on, my friend," he began, "do you intend going down after all the cotton's been picked and done with?"

The Muhtar held his temper in check. "Tashbash Mehmet Effendi, my friend," he said in a mocking tone, "we are the Muhtar of this village, and this by the grace of Allah and of our Government and also of our Party. These villagers are more to us than our mother, our wife, our very soul. And we are always ready to prevent them from straying into wicked ways at the instigation of certain rascally mischief-makers. Yes, we will save them from those fiendish claws! Why do I make the villagers wait here? I know why, and I take full responsibility. You go on and side with the doddering old idiot who brought the whirling thistle so late that . . . Listen to me, Tashbash Mehmet Effendi. I know you've got many relatives and supporters in these parts and that even some of my relatives are for you. But beware of treasonable acts! See what happened to Long Ali, left to himself with his dying horse on the high mountain stretches. My father's father was Muhtar of this village, and so was his father's father. I didn't become Muhtar through any vote of yours, my friend. The job of Muhtar is a divine trust of Allah to our family. For time out of mind my ancestors have played host to all the gendarmes and commissioners and governors and majors that have come to visit this village, and never once have we brought low its lofty honour, never once have the villagers had cause to be ashamed of us. And now that the Government has brought this Democracy to us, you all, with big families, you put on kingly airs and come swaggering into our presence asking questions. If this goes on I won't be your Muhtar any more. At the very next election I'll refuse the nomination. And to top it all, you assemble a big congress at Lone Duran's house as if he were a general, and there you speak ill of me. Do you know what it means to hold a meeting without permission from the Government? Haven't you heard about the law against meetings and demonstrations? This is a weighty crime you've committed and it can take you all to the gallows. Do you know that?"

"Nobody can prove anything at all about our meeting."

"I can!" shouted the Muhtar. "I would too, but I've no wish to see half the village swinging at the end of a rope because of the likes of you!"

"Go ahead, do your dirty work!" Tashbash taunted him. "We'll see if the Government will hang us."

"Ah, but I've got a heart here!" cried the Muhtar, smiting his breast. "A heart that beats like the smith's anvil, that weeps blood when evil befalls a fellow villager! Even the stone that strikes a snivelling village child's little fingernail pierces this heart of mine like a dagger. I'm not like you, Tashbash Effendi. I wouldn't go and denounce you and have the whole village dangling on the gallows." He thumped his breast again and shouted: "It's a heart I've got here, my friend, pure as a jewel, a heart that burns even at the death of my arch-enemy's horse. In—deed! What did you think we were, Tashbash Effendi?"

"Don't go railing at me and calling me Effendi as if I were a townsman," retorted Tashbash calmly. "I'm not an Effendi and I haven't come here to quarrel with you either. What I'm saying is this: the other villages have been picking cotton for a good ten days now. So what are we waiting here for?"

The Muhtar lowered his tone and laid his hand on Tashbash's shoulder. "In that case, you may rest at ease, Mehmet, my brother. The Muhtar always does what's best for his beloved villagers. But this year we're late because of that rascally Old Halil, and as soon as we get down I shall deliver him into the just and equitable claws of the law for having given the signal too late, which is a crime of false witness, and thus having caused damages and injury to a whole village. And heavy indeed is the punishment for this. So you see, my friend, the only reason for our long wait here is that we set out too late to begin with. If we'd been in time as every year, Bekir Agha would have found a field for us and been back to meet us here with the good news before we'd had time to settle for the night. But now, because we're late, poor Bekir Agha's got to move heaven and earth to secure a field. But he'll find one, never fear, and the minute he does he'll be back. That is all I have to say. What I've done is for the good of you all, but if you don't like it, well, just don't vote for me at the next election, that's all. We'll see if you'll find a better man, a man that'll serve and further your interest more than I've done."

"That means we're going to wait some more, then?" said Tashbash.

"What else can we do?" replied the Muhtar. "That old pig's been our ruin. Never again! I'll never believe a word of his again!"

Tashbash took his yellow beads out of his pocket and turned away disgustedly. Lone Duran, who had not spoken a word, followed him, his head hanging.

The villagers had been standing around, not missing a word of what was being said, and for a moment their anger was turned against Old Halil, who was so ashamed he dared not look anyone in the face.

He was guilty, yes, he admitted it. Even if they tore him to pieces and threw his carcass to the dogs, he could not blame them. But he had never meant to do them wrong. It was only that he was so old, so utterly spent. . . .

Trembling with fear and shame, he crept into a clump of bushes and remained hidden there till nightfall. When it was quite dark he emerged stealthily from the bushes and made straight for Tashbash.

"My gallant Tashbash," he cried, clutching tremblingly at his hand, "I've come to you for help. Save me from these villagers. Ah, I remember your father, Tashbash Hüsein Agha! You could pick him out among a whole army, the tallest and handsomest of the brave. 'Halil,' he used to tell me, 'you're my blood brother. If I die before you, I shall tell my son Mehmet to consider you henceforth as a father in my place.' Yes, that's what your father always said. Didn't he say the same to you when he died? May a plenteous light fall upon his grave. He always had such a large harvest he could not cope with it alone and would call on me for help. And in the twinkling of an eye I would reap his crop for him. 'Halil,' he would say to me, 'you've got the strength of our Lord Ali.'[1] And here I am now, tottering on the brink of the grave. Help me, my brave Tashbash. Did you know your grand-

---

[1] Fourth caliph, son-in-law of the Prophet Mohammed and revered as a prophet himself by the Shüte sects of which there are some in Turkey.

father? When he went walking by you'd have thought he was
a grand vizier with nine egrets. . . . I can't lie to you, my son.
I did delay bringing the whirling thistle to the Muhtar. But only
because I was terrified of the road. . . . And now there'll be no
cotton for the villagers to pick. They'll starve to death because
of me!"

Tashbash was laughing. "Don't be afraid, Uncle Halil," he
whispered, leaning towards his ear. "You're not to blame at all.
Would that infidel ever have waited for your whirling thistle if
he hadn't got something up his sleeve? Doesn't he know when
cotton picking time is come?"

"He doesn't," said Old Halil heatedly, "nobody knows cotton
picking time but me. It's my fault the villagers are late."

"Why, Uncle Halil, have you gone mad?" cried Tashbash.
"If he hadn't done it on purpose to be late, what would he be
making us cool our heels here for? He knows cotton picking
time better than anyone else."

"No, he doesn't," insisted Old Halil obstinately, "he doesn't
even know where his wife's thing is. Who is he anyway? Just
Silly Hidir's son, still only a young whipper-snapper!"

"Now, be reasonable and listen to me, Uncle Halil," said
Tashbash, "I have this from a very reliable source, no less than
the Muhtar's younger wife! And she told it to my wife. They're
cousins, you know. She overheard Sefer talking to Batty Bekir.
'I don't like the look of these villagers this year,' he was saying.
'If they get down early, before the other villages, when field
hands are badly needed, then they'll attempt to choose a field of
their own, and we two will go empty-handed. Village folk are
like sheep, just let one of them pull in one direction and all the
rest will go following after and there's nothing the shepherd
can do about it. The only thing now is to delay them up here
until all the fields are taken. Then they'll have no alternative but
to work in the colonel's plantation. So you're to go down before
the rest of us and make the usual deal. Don't return until you're

sure there isn't a single unoccupied field.' Do you see now, Uncle Halil? Do you understand why he's making us waste our time here? You should know Sefer, Uncle Halil, you should know what a twister he is. . . ." He paused. They were both silent for a moment. Then he said: "You mustn't tell this to anyone, Uncle Halil. But you may be sure I won't let him get away with it. If not this year, then next year. . . . These villagers! They're afraid of him. Behind his back they're all for me, but the minute they come face to face with him, they don't dare open their mouths. He rants about his position in the Party, he threatens them with the gallows, with general mobilisation, and they believe it! I can't get it into their heads that those times are over, that one man can't do anything by himself. Why, Uncle Halil, even you are afraid of him!"

Old Halil only heaved a deep sigh. "Ah, my good Tashbash, he'll set the villagers upon me to tear me to pieces, and I can't blame them. It's because of me they're late." He grabbed Tashbash by the elbows. "Look, I'm asking you not to lie, not to go about spreading the tale that Sefer knows when the cotton's ripe. I'm the only one who knows because the whirling thistle never deceives me. Can you save me from the fury of these villagers without disgracing me, without having me branded as an ignorant old dotard? Can you find a way of telling them I did it, and still save my skin? Ah, what a cunning schemer he is, that Muhtar! Now, he's set his wife loose to try and convince you he knows all about cotton time. He wants to take even that away from me. Do you see the ruse now, poor innocent son of my old friend Tashbash?"

Tashbash gave up. "There you are!" he muttered bitterly. "Even you, a man who has been to the Yemen, who has seen life! I can't root this stupid fear out of you. I'm telling you, Muhtars can't have people hanged at their slightest whim any longer. And how can you believe one single man could proclaim a general mobilisation? Send you to the Yemen? Why, the

Yemen wars have been over and done with for years now!
There's no earthly reason for you to be afraid, Uncle Halil."

Old Halil was at the end of his tether. "I'm guilty," he
moaned, "terribly guilty. I've ruined the whole village. They'll
tear me to pieces."

Tashbash patted his shoulder compassionately. "Uncle Halil,"
he repeated with the hopeless sadness of one who knows he can
never be understood, "would he ever depend upon your thistle?
It's just that it suited his plans to wait."

Old Halil sat up and shoved Tashbash away with unexpected
vigour. "I don't know about all that," he snapped. "I know he
always waits for my thistle, and what's more he said as much in
the presence of the whole village!" He was riding his high horse
now, with no trace of his former pleading and chastened look.
"Are you trying to say that I'm an old dotard and my word not
worth a straw? Who's this Sefer that he would not wait for my
thistle? I think nothing of him as I thought nothing of his father
before him. What would he know of cotton time? What do any
of you know? Ungrateful wretches! Who is it that's taken you
down to the Chukurova these many years without ever being
a day late or a day too early?" He stood up in a huff. "Go on,
then," he growled as a parting shot at Tashbash, "tear me to
pieces, kill me, eat me!"

He made straight for his pallet. Without even taking off his
shalvar trousers or his shoes he lay down quickly and drew the
blanket over his head, deaf to the surprised inquiries of his son
and daughter-in-law.

"That mangy Tashbash," he rumbled on to himself, "wants
to make the villagers believe that yesterday's child Sefer knows
about cotton time. Just try to convince them of that, man, just
try! Why not even a child would believe you. Yes, you dirty-
bottomed Tashbash, ask any one-year-old baby in its cradle who
it is knows about the cotton and see what it'll answer. 'Why,
Old Halil of course,' it'll say, and laugh in your face besides!

And the powerful Muhtar of a huge village knows it so well that he's proclaimed it in front of everyone. Who would believe you, Tashbash, my fine cock? Who are you, beside our Muhtar? Why, your head could never even aspire to be where his feet tread!"

A new hope was dawning in him. He lay there, tense and waiting, until it was well after midnight, with not a soul astir and only the breathing and snoring breaking the stillness about him. Then he crept out of his bed and crawled along on all fours, straightening up only when he was a good distance away from the others.

The best thing now is to go to the Muhtar right away and beg his forgiveness. Ah, my valiant one, I'll say, there isn't your like in all the land of Marash, in the whole Sandjak[1] of Kayseri, no, neither in valour, nor sagacity, nor learning. I've sinned, yes, but you who see into the very heart of all your villagers, you know I had no evil purpose, you must know it was only because I was so sore-pressed. Here I come, in the dead of night, helpless, aged, to throw myself at your mercy. That mucky Tashbash with his talk. . . . He said . . . What would that mangy cur know? You know who is noble and who is base in this village, you, the crowning jewel of the Ottoman and of the Democrat, you, whose fame has travelled far and wide, into the Yemen and the land of the Franks, you, with the countenance of a pasha, indeed of the Sultan himself, you, the apple of the eye of the Democrat! Didn't that fat chap say so, the one who came to visit the village with all those gold rings on his fingers? Didn't he say you were the right arm of the Democrat? And I say so! Right arm? Why, you're the body and soul of the Party! How could I have vilified you, cursed your father's bones? May this tongue of mine be blistered. But now I know who's somebody in this village. I may have one foot in the grave, but from now on I'll be a yoked slave at your door, ready to die for you at a word. As for that mangy Tashbash, putting on airs before you, just because he

[1] Former provincial division of the Ottoman Empire.

happens to have a handful of dirty-faced relatives to support him, don't let him weigh on your mind. I'm behind you now. You'll never catch me voting anything but Democrat now. Never, never for that Ismet Pasha.[1] And I'll tackle the villagers too. Neighbours, I'll say, listen to me, an old man who's seen life, who knows the world. Don't you ever stray from the guidance of your Muhtar, from the path of the Democrat which is the way of Allah. Don't you follow in the wake of that Ismet Pasha, for it's he who brought to ruin this land of the Osmanli, who gave away our provinces to the giaours as if they were his father's own property! It's pashas like him who drove our people to the Yemen wars, it's because of them the bones of our countrymen rotted away there in the desert, as I tell you I've seen with these very eyes. And the top leader of all those pashas was Ismet Pasha. He lured our nation into the Greek War too and caused all that bloodshed and misery. And people have the face to come and say that this Ismet is against war! Against war! Then why did he ever go and become a general, eh? Mark my words, had it been in his power he wouldn't have left a single man alive on this land except for himself. Sapping the flower of our manhood! But praise the Lord for sending us the Democrat to save our nation. That is why we must all vote for the Democrat. Yes, indeed my Muhtar, the villagers will all fall in with me. They have a great respect for my white beard. So now get me out of this mess and I promise you never, never again to let the villagers be late for the cotton.

With slow, timorous steps he tiptoed towards the tree under which the Muhtar had set his camp. The donkey stood there tied to the tree, its head drooping to the ground. Old Halil held his breath as he groped his way slowly around the tree and stood

[1] Ismet Inonu, actual Premier of Turkey, one of the most important generals of the War of Independence, Prime Minister to Ataturk's Government and, after Ataturk's death, second president of the Turkish Republic for a period of twelve years. Putting an end to the one-party system in Turkey, he allowed the formation of other parties in order to introduce democracy into the country. He was defeated at the 1950 elections and then led the opposition for ten years.

at last over the Muhtar who lay sleeping peacefully between his two wives. His younger wife's luxuriant hair was strewn over the pillow, covering half his face.

Old Halil forced out a cough in a timid attempt to wake the Muhtar, but it was such a small, faint cough he might just as well have made no sound at all. A quivering spread over his body and he began to lose his nerve.

If only you were like other people, he thought, kind-hearted and merciful. If only my words had the power to melt your heart as they do everyone else's. . . .

He tried to cough again, but his throat tangled in a knot. What if he were to open his eyes this moment and catch him standing there, he, Halil, who had cursed his father's bones, who had brought ruin on the villagers, this very same Halil right here, near him, at his mercy? What if he should call the watchman and have him trussed up on the spot and bundled off straight to the Democrat, without even giving him a chance to say a single word?

The Muhtar turned in his bed. My God, he's waking up! He's waking up, damn him! What shall I do?

He crouched down behind the tree and waited, cowering, his eyes glued to the bed. Then, with slow, cautious movements, he slithered off into the dark safety of the bushes, where he slumped flat down on the ground, his heart beating with loud thumps against his ribs.

Oh, my God, it'll soon be dawn! Oh, my God, what shall I do?

He began to creep down into the gully, bending low so as not to be seen. The gully was covered with pebble-stones and what a noise they made in the night! He pressed on, farther and farther away. Suddenly, a pain gripped his bowels. He wanted to relieve himself, but his bowels were paralysed. It's fear that's doing this to me, he thought. Yes, it does that to a fellow. Why, just imagine if he'd woken up! A sorry figure he would have made me cut there in the middle of the night! Allah be praised for bringing me to my senses and saving me from such a scandal. When he managed to relieve himself at last, a bracing gladness filled his body. He washed himself at the little stream that trickled in the gully. Now he felt even better.

He started up the opposite slope of the gully and limped on painfully until the east began to pale. Then he put his ear to the ground and listened. Yes, the village was far away now. He was out of danger. Filled with a youthful glee at having made good his escape, he sat down on a stone and watched the rising sun strike into the gully and set alight the narrow rivulet. It was going to be a hot day.

But his face was turning pale now, and the fresh youthful glee he had felt a little while back was melting away. Instead, the hopeless emptiness of being utterly alone in the whole wide world came crushing down upon him.

Far from the other villagers, away from every human soul, without a morsel of bread to put in his mouth, where was he to go now, what was he to do with this decrepit, mouldering body of his?

Chapter 17

Tashbash was awake at the crack of dawn. He asked his wife to give him the shalvar trousers with festooned pockets which he wore only on festive occasions, while he rummaged in the bundle for a clean, untorn shirt and his one pair of embroidered woollen stockings. Then he brushed his sandals until they were spotless and, for the first time on the journey, he washed his face with soap. After that, he spent a good while trying to straighten out the battered rim of his cap. He did not neglect even his prayer-*tespih*, polishing the beads with a rag until they were shining bright. If only he could have had a shave too. But there was no time now. Holding a small mirror, he twirled his moustache into proper shape and frowned at his reflection as he tried to give his face a stern, resolute expression. Satisfied at last that he now looked imposing enough, he called out to Lone Duran.

"Hey, Duran! Go and tell Osmandja and the Bald Minstrel and Nimble Mustafa to come. Don't forget Pale Ismail and Shirtless. Get Home-Leave Memet and Zaladja Woman, and also Shitty Hasan. . . . And Mangy Mahmut, Barefoot Mustafa, Dusty Poyraz.. . . . Get anyone who's got some mettle in him."

Soon quite a crowd was assembled in the gully. The deep silence was broken only by the rattle of Tashbash's prayer beads. At last he rose and faced the crowd. "I'm sick and tired of the lot of you," he proclaimed.

There was an uproar of protesting voices. Tashbash went on counting his beads until they were quiet again. "Yes, I've had enough of you. Time and again you've sworn on the honour of your wives that you'll stand by me, but when it comes to action you let that Sefer draw you over to his side with only a couple of words, blockheads that you are. Now, why do you think he's making us dawdle here, when we're late enough as it is? And laying the blame on poor Old Halil too. . . ."

"The old man's gone," somebody interrupted him, proud of being the one to break the news. "He was so terrified he fled into the mountains. His daughter-in-law woke up some time ago and found his bed empty. God knows where he's gone to."

"There you are!" cried Tashbash bitterly. "He's driven a poor old man to roam in the wilds, to his death perhaps. Now listen to me and I'll tell you all about this scheming Sefer." Without pausing to take a breath he poured out all he had revealed to Old Halil the night before. "Do you doubt me now?" he asked. "Do you doubt that he and Batty Bekir have hatched up this plot together?"

They all hung their heads without a word.

"Neighbours," Tashbash concluded in cutting tones, "to-morrow I'm off to the Chukurova with my family. We'll find some place to pick cotton. God knows it's much too late now, but still I'm going to take my chance. This just can't go on. This man's been dipping his bread into our blood these many years. . . . Those of you who wish to come with me are welcome, and those who don't . . . well, I wish them well."

For a while no one spoke or stirred. Then all of a sudden there was a coming to life, an indistinct muttering. Tashbash stood quite still, clicking his beads and lighting one cigarette after another. His keen, anxious eyes scanned the crowd.

At last Pale Ismail stepped up to him. "I'm for you, my friend," he declared. "Up to now I've always supported the Muhtar, but this time you're clearly in the right."

After this everyone began to speak at once.

"We're going, whatever the Muhtar says. He can have us all hanged if he likes."

"It's more than flesh and blood can bear."

"Why, the cotton picking's as good as over!"

"Hah! And we're supposed to make some money after this."

"But the curse of all the villagers will be upon him. He won't prosper either."

"The blood-sucking crook!"

"He never even puts a hand to the cotton. How is it he always makes so much more money than we do?"

"Our blood-toil!"

"Preying on us these many years."

"May his days be blighted!"

"May the blizzard overtake him wherever he goes!"

"Now, look here, neighbours, don't go cursing him so. He's not a bad man, except for this one weakness of his."

"Ah, he knows how to pull strings with the Government all right! But he's got eyes for nothing but his own pocket."

"May Allah so afflict him with sores that even mangy curs won't go near him. . . ."

Still showering curses on the Muhtar they started back for the camp in small groups, firmly decided to leave for the Chukurova on the following morning.

Such sudden reversals, such outpourings of maledictions, were not new to Tashbash. But this time, with Pale Ismail unexpectedly supporting him, he nourished a gleam of hope. But even if not one single villager were to come with him, he still intended to defy the Muhtar and leave alone. He even toyed with the idea of settling in another village for good. That would be a heavy blot on his own village. Yes, but on himself too. . . . Who knows what strangers might think? They would look on him askance, thinking no doubt that he was a shady character, cast out from his native village. Well, come what might, his mind was made up.

The news of Pale Ismail's defection reached the Muhtar in less than no time. He flew into a mad rage.

"Why, you scoundrel, who was it rescued your daughter from the hands of her ravishers? To say nothing of what our gendarmes would have done to her. . . . Why, man, they'd have dragged her from village to village and all the male population of the Taurus would have had her. Hah, but for me she'd have ended up in the Adana brothels ɔr dead, her body cast at the foot of some rock. A girl, abducted into the mountains, kept there for five months on end, passing from one man to another! She could very well have remained there for five years too. Lucky for you she came back with just that one bastard in her. If I hadn't acted in time you'd have found yourself with five bastards on your hands, not one, and a collection of fathers to boot! So you too, eh, Pale Ismail? I'll have you dragged here and trampled underfoot. I'll have your beard plucked out hair by hair until you bellow like an ox. . . ." He was foaming.

"Watchman," he roared.

But when the watchman was there, standing at attention, the swift thought came to him that anger is a poor counsellor. He recalled his father the Headman Hidir's warning words: "He who rises with anger will sit down with loss. And truly in dealing with people, art and suppleness are stronger than anger, which like caustic vinegar corrodes its own container. Anger," the Headman would say, "is the luxury of the powerful, of the lords of the land, of the Government, not that of Muhtars." How right he was. . . .

He changed his mind about sending for the Pale Ismail. "Watchman," he said.

"At your service, my Agha."

"Put on wings and fly like the wind straight down to the colonel's plantation, where you'll find Bekir Agha. Tell him the game's up. He's to come back in double quick time, and no matter if there are still some unrented cotton fields. Let him borrow a horse from the colonel's son and be here before morning, this very night! Quick, march!"

Shame on you, Pale Ismail! Ah, there was no trusting anybody in this world. What would become of his credit with the Chukurova aghas if even one single villager happened to stray from the fold? Everyone knew him as the beloved father, the undisputed authority in his village. How could he face the colonel's son, who was such an important Democrat too? But, why, with all this power, didn't the fellow get a better plantation for himself? The villagers would never have objected to working in a plentiful cotton field. Ah, yes, but where would he, the Muhtar, be then? There's to be no extra money for him then. . . . What a mess! Ah, confound this Tashbash! And that Long Ali? Just like his father, that rascally, thieving Ibrahim who plundered the whole of the Chukurova, that wolf in sheep's clothing, that traitorous Yemen deserter. It's Long Ali who's brought all these troubles on me, may he remain stranded in the mountains, *inshallah*! Would these poor innocent villagers ever have thought all this up by themselves?

No, this was not a matter he could settle by his usual method of calling a meeting and haranguing the villagers. He had to think of some other way. He chewed at his hand furiously. Yes, he had to cow the villagers into submission somehow. Should he have the gendarmes beat them up? No, that would never do. Ismet Pasha's partisans would be only too delighted to make use of this in order to further their own designs. And once you've got mixed up with politics, there's no telling where you'll find yourself next.

"Just look at those faces," he ruminated angrily, "every one of them sore as a boil. Ah, you should have fallen into my hands some other time. Then I would have called you to account for these faces!"

Village folk are like this, he thought. When their blood is up no amount of browbeating will avail. They take the bit between their teeth and are ready to sell their lives dearly. Take a single twig and you can easily break it, but two hundred twigs all in a bunch, never. And here they are, all bunched together, unbreakable. . . . The thing to do now is to tackle them one by one and bend them your way, yes one by one. That's the trick! And to be soft, for sweet talk can lure the serpent out of its hole. What is it Fahri Bey, the Democrat leader, always says? To govern, he says, is to act as suits the occasion. In certain situations be a murderer, a bandit, a monster, and in others an angel, a saint, a man of religion like the Hodja of Karatopak. This precious secret way to power is not easily accessible to any ordinary creature. . . .

"Woman," he called out to his second and younger wife, "get me some bread and treacle, and warm up the preserved meat. I need to fill my belly satisfactorily. And truly, I must don the war apparel of our Lord Ali and like him ride out into the fight with naked sword, for our enemies have laid a siege about us. A tough battle lies ahead. Alas for the vanquished! Alas, my beauty, alas!"

It was the first time in her life that he had ever spoken to her in this tender confiding manner. Her eyes sparkled and two dimples appeared on her cheeks.

"Why do you stand there so surprised, Sultan? Do be a little quick. I've got pressing and important business to attend to. Perhaps you'd better toast the bread. I've heard that eating toasted or even burnt bread brings luck. Isn't that so, my beauty?"

The spark of love that had been kindled by his tone grew into an unknown, rapturous sensation, as though a magic spell were being cast over her body. She hesitated to move, fearing to break this spell. As in a dream she extended her hand to the skillet and slowly melted the treacle and butter over the fire. Then she sliced some bread into the mixture.

"Ah, that smells good," said the Muhtar, "you're a wonderful cook, Sultan."

His voice had never been like that, not even at those times when he used to make love to her. Was this unwonted pleasantness a sign of renewed love? She came forward eagerly with the food and sat down before him, willing him to talk on so that she should feel for ever this unaccustomed voluptuousness in her body. Ah, if only this had happened at night. Her dimples deepened.

He finished his meal and walked off with ponderous steps and thoughtful mien. Her eyes followed him worshipfully.

The first thing to do now, he was thinking, is to find Old Halil and win his heart in the presence of all the others. Village folk are so simple, like children. They'll be pleased at my lenience.

But how was he to find that old goat, who was a past master when it came to covering his tracks? He summoned Old Halil's son and addressed him in the ringing tones of a public crier so that everyone should hear.

"You must set out right away and look for your father. Tell him the Village Council and the Muhtar have pardoned him, and so have all the villagers. Only Allah is infallible. He mustn't be afraid. I give him my word no one's going to hurt him."

Old Halil's son was touched to tears. "Thank you, my Agha," he cried, "I'll go and find him right away."

"The poor thing must be quite exhausted by now," added the Muhtar, modulating his voice into as soft and friendly a tone as he could. "Take two young men with you and let them carry him by turns. On no account must you let him walk."

The villagers were standing about in straggling groups, trying to figure out what could lie beneath their Muhtar's new paternal attitude. They felt something was afoot and waited, on their guard.

Out of the corner of his eye the Muhtar was taking their measure. He sensed their distrust and knew very well that his every move was being watched. Then his eyes fell on the little girl. She was in a filthy state, the discharge from her nose trickling down right into her mouth. What a disgusting creature, he thought. Allah curse such parents! This peasant race will never learn civilisation.

She was Yellow Mustafa's daughter. For years and years Yellow Mustafa had prayed for a child and in the end Allah had granted him this! Well, no one can meddle in Allah's business and secret ways. . . . At first Yellow Mustafa had been struck dumb at the news that the child was a girl. But in no time he was raving about the child. Certainly no man ever rejoiced half that much at the birth of a mere girl. What's a girl worth anyway? As easily gone as the dirt on your hands, gone to tend a stranger's hearth. But a boy! Ah, is there anything like a son? The most ardent flame of your hearth, keeping it alive and burning to the end of your days.

The idea struck him like lightning. He picked up the little girl, tossed her in the air with a whoop and settled her on his shoulder. Then he made straight for Yellow Mustafa. The little girl's dirty dress and hair were bedizened with amulets, a head of garlic, a scorpion made of beads, some chicken excrement knotted into a talismanic rag, a few wish-bones such as the jaw-bone of the black serpent and the long beak of the plover-bird, a whole assortment of coloured buttons, a few seashells. . . . He plumped the child down before her mother and forced himself to plant two resounding kisses on her cheeks. He wanted to vomit, but thank goodness it was over.

"Why, this girl's a beauty! A real houri from Paradise! Just wait till she grows up, just wait and see how she'll set all hearts aburning. Yellow Mustafa's going to have quite a job on his hands with all those village youths, I can tell you. Who would have thought such a perfect beauty could ever have sprung from our Yellow Mustafa? It's the grace of Allah. . . . She must have taken after her mother's family, that's for sure."

Yellow Mustafa stood there delighted, his mouth spreading in a huge grin from ear to ear. You want to get something out of me again, you rascal, he was thinking. Why else would you deign to take my girl into your arms? You would never have bestowed a look on her, you the great Muhtar Agha! Still, he could not help being flattered by the Muhtar's attentions.

"Please sit down, Muhtar Agha," he said.

The Muhtar only smiled as sweetly as he could and took leave, considering that this much was more than enough for the likes of Yellow Mustafa. He drew out his handkerchief and stealthily wiped his mouth.

He strode on chatting with everyone he came across, and petting and kissing the little children.

Ah, the infidel, the villagers thought, he's courting us well and proper now. Just look at him! You would think he was an angel come down directly from heaven.

After more than two hours of this he returned to his camping place, where he conferred a warm smile on his older wife, a thing he had not done in years. He even held her hand for a minute, but only after making sure his younger wife was busy putting the baby into its cradle. Then he played with the baby for a while, another thing he rarely did.

He waited until the villagers had dispersed a little. Then he bent his steps in the direction of Pale Ismail, who lost his head at the sight of him. His confusion was such that he could not proffer even the customary invitation to sit down.

The Muhtar did not wait for any invitation. He slumped down on a heap of bedding.

"What's the matter, Ismail Agha?" he began. "Why this cross face? Have we killed your father or something? I just thought I would drop along and tell you not to worry about the cotton. Batty Bekir's rented us such a field, why, a man could pick fifty kilos of cotton a day and become as prosperous as our Lord Abraham. Ah, these peasants don't know the meaning of patience, they don't know that patience brings roses. No, they let themselves be led into temptation by the very first rascal they come across."

The Wind from the Plain

Pale Ismail was still too flustered to lift his head or say a word. The Muhtar turned towards Ismail's daughter, who was standing farther away with her mother and her two brothers.

"Come here, my lovely girl," he called, "it's for you only I come here. Otherwise I'd rather have my head cut off than consort with Ismail Agha, even though he be my first cousin. There now, sit down and listen to me. Those ravishers of yours won't easily evade my vengeance. Months and even years may elapse, but I forget nothing. Their punishment will be as heavy as their crime. So you thought I'd forgotten all about it, hadn't you? Yes, yes, I know that in your heart you were reproaching me. But there is a right time for everything and now the time to deal with this scandal has come. Come up a little closer to me, my girl. If your father thinks I've come to beg of him, he's much mistaken. I beg of no creature, but only of the great Allah because he is the creator of all things seen and unseen, because he has peopled this earth of ours and looks down upon us poor mortals from the highest of seven-storeyed heaven. As for your father, he can follow whoever he pleases. What do I care?"

The girl was sitting on the ground before him, her eyes pinned to the ground.

"Yes, my girl. Do you think I could ever get a wink of sleep again if they went unpunished? The honour of our whole village is in question, and I am responsible for it. What does your father care? He would swallow any dirt, but I'll not stand for it. No one shall boast of carrying off a girl from Muhtar Sefer's village, of keeping her in the mountains for five months and of getting off scot-free. Why, think! The next thing we know, all the young men of the Taurus will be swooping down on us and bearing off all our women one by one. They won't leave a single virgin girl in the village, to say nothing of our women, Allah forbid! No, this is a matter of life and death, and that's why I've come. You must tell me the whole story again, down to the minutest detail, and I will draw out a petition to the high authorities of the

Chukurova. Everything you say, even the smallest detail, I will put into this petition so that everyone who reads it shall be moved to tears, so that all those town people shall sob their hearts out! And then, burning with horror, they will seize those infidel ravishers, and all the rest of their village too, and throw the whole lot of them into the steep-walled prison of Kozan, never to see the light of day again! Hah, what does that bloodless father of yours care if they carry you off into the mountains, and kill you even? If he had an ounce of blood in him, would he ever let down his own kinsman and join forces with his kinsman's enemies? Hah, if he had blood in him, my daughter, he would keep out of such plots and concern himself with killing your ravishers. Now, you start telling me your story, my girl. I'll make him ashamed of what he's done to me."

The girl's face was ablaze. Her head drooped still more. That inescapable torture was about to start again. She could not bring herself to speak.

The Muhtar insisted again and again. Then he lost patience. "All right, don't speak," he roared, "you're just like your father, not a drop of blood in any one of you. If you don't tell me exactly how it happened, how do you expect me to plead your cause with the Chukurova Democrats?"

All of a sudden the girl's mother pounced upon her daughter and shook her. "Why don't you speak, you little fool?" she cried, her voice resounding all over the camp. "What harm is there in pouring forth one's troubles? Go on, tell your Uncle Sefer everything." It was like this each time the Muhtar would try to make the girl tell her story. "Who else but your Uncle Sefer can go to the Democrat and have those infidels convicted? If your father had been a man he would have taken a gun and killed all your ravishers. Yes, and gone to prison for it too, what of it? I would have looked after him splendidly while he served his term and been proud of it too, not hanging my head in shame as I am doing now! Go on, tell your Uncle Sefer everything exactly as you did last time, so he can have them clapped into prison, now that we've got this great Democrat Government that never takes bribes and always upholds our rights."

"That's right," cried Sefer, "tell me all just as you did that day when I wept and trembled. Ah, this memory of mine is like a sieve. If I hadn't forgotten the details, I would never have stopped here for a minute. I would have gone to the Chukurova bigwigs this instant."

The girl lifted her head and looked at him with wet, pleading eyes. Then, hopelessly, she turned her gaze on her brothers. The two young men slipped away.

"Well, what are you waiting for?" cried her mother impatiently. "You're not ashamed, are you? What can you do, it's happened and there's no changing the facts."

"And you lost the child too," said the Muhtar, his voice even softer and warmer than before. "It was born dead, eh? Ah, the poor luckless mite!"

The girl nodded.

"Ah the pity of it! How my heart bleeds for poor fatherless babies, for poor stillborn babies. Ah, ah!"

At this the mother seized the girl's arm as though she would wrench it off. "Why don't you speak, curse you? Here's this great man come right up to your feet, and you keep him waiting!"

Pale Ismail's face was changing from minute to minute, and he kept shaking his right hand in a gesture of exasperated anger. But he knew there was nothing he could do. He let himself drop to the ground and remained squatting there without saying a word.

The girl looked desperately first at the Muhtar and then at her parents. Her face was sweating. She wiped it with her head kerchief.

"It's like this," she blurted out, "I was in the field. Father had gone to get Uncle Ökkesh to winnow the grain. He was late. . . ." The words came pouring out in disconnected sentences. "As I waited for him, I swept the threshing floor. You know

Bald Osman from that village? Well, it was his son, Ibrahim. . . .
He kept coming to our village and passing before our door,
and last year his village was picking the field next to ours in the
Chukurova. It was then he spoke to me. 'Look,' he said, 'my
father's rich. Will you have me?' But I didn't answer at all.
As I was sweeping the threshing floor, two men suddenly sprang
out from the clump of medlars. One of them was that infidel
Ibrahim. Without a word they pinioned my arms and carried me
away. I couldn't make out where they were taking me. Night
had fallen. . . ."

She choked and came to a stop. Her mother nudged her. The
Muhtar's face was tense and his eyes gleamed.

"They brought me to a huge dark cave. Ibrahim tried to come
near me, but I shouted and fought."

A slight tremor passed over the Muhtar.

"And then? You must tell me this part without skipping a
thing. Don't be ashamed. There's only your father and mother,
and I'm like a father to you. More than a father. Go on. This is
what they call defloration. In the law of the Democrat, the punishment for this is very heavy. Go on, don't stop!"

"His companion joined us. I fought against them till dawn.
Then Ibrahim produced his knife and before I knew it he had
ripped through my dress, torn off all my clothes and thrown them
into the fire they had lit at the entrance of the cave."

The Muhtar quivered. "This is important. By Allah, it's a
great crime before the law to burn a girl's clothes, leaving her
naked as the day she was born. Go on, go on. Quick!"

Some of her shame and nervousness had gone now. "I ran
to the depths of the cave and crouched there. They laughed
at me."

The Muhtar grated his teeth. "Laughed, did they, the devils?"

"They laughed and then Ibrahim said: 'We're off. Try and go
back to the village, mother-naked as you are.' They went out of
the cave. I thought they'd really gone, so I crept out and started

running away. Then I saw them. They were hiding behind a bush and splitting their sides with laughter. I ran more quickly, but they caught me and brought me back to the cave. Ibrahim said to his friend: 'She's ashamed of you, that's why she's making such a fuss. You go to the village and bring back some food.' We were left alone. He turned to me and his eyes were like a madman's. 'I'll make a woman of you, by God,' he swore. He spread his coat on the ground. And I . . ."

She choked again. The Muhtar rose and sat down quickly. "And you lay down?" he said, his voice strangling.

"I was afraid of his eyes. He forced me to lie down."

"Didn't you struggle?"

"Yes, I did. I begged him to go and ask my parents if he wanted me. But he never listened. He was like one possessed."

"Didn't you bite him? You didn't just give up without a fight, did you?"

She bowed her head. Her face had gone pale.

"Well, speak, speak!"

His frenzied voice frightened her.

"I went limp and couldn't move any more."

"What do you mean, you couldn't move?"

"I closed my eyes and I know I screamed."

"Ha, this is important! This is what we need."

"Afterwards he sat down beside me breathing hard. . . ."

"Not that part," shouted the Muhtar, "it's when you lay down together that's important before the law. That's the main point."

She lifted her eyes in amazement.

"Well?" insisted the Muhtar. "You went limp and he lay down on you, is that it? Didn't you even cover up your breasts with your hands?"

The girl was silent. Her mother gave her another shove.

"What's the matter, you fool? You're not ashamed now? A body's got no cause to be ashamed of the Government. Your

227

Uncle Sefer's our Government. You must tell him everything."

The girl's eyes pleaded for mercy. Her mother pushed her again.

"He came upon me," she said almost in a whisper. "His breath seemed to burn all over my body. It scorched me so, I just couldn't stir. Then the pain. I cried and he left me. . . . And when I opened my eyes, he was sitting beside me, panting."

"Was he naked too?" asked the Muhtar, his mouth dry.

She lowered her eyes. "Yes."

"Stark-naked?"

"Yes."

The Muhtar was beside himself. He made her retell the whole scene over and over again.

"Was he in a sweat? Yes? His whole body? And you? Your body too must have been streaming with sweat. . . ."

After a while the Muhtar's sensual excitation seemed to abate. He settled down on the bedding and drew his right leg under him.

"I didn't know all this, or I must have forgotten. They ought to be hanged for this."

"And that isn't all, my Agha," cried the mother, "come on, my girl. Tell him what they did to you afterwards."

Pale Ismail was hunched up in a frozen heap. He seemed deaf to what was going on.

"Yes, my daughter," said the Muhtar more calmly, "tell me what happened next."

"I was still lying like that, unable to move, when his friend came into the cave. And then Ibrahim ran away. He left us . . ."

"You've forgotten something," the Muhtar interrupted her. "Last time you said Ibrahim lay on you a second time before the other one returned, and it was after this second time that you could not stir a limb. Did you lie then? Be careful! If you make your deposition first this way and then that, they'll think you're not telling the truth and those blackguards will get off free."

"Yes, it was as you say," she whispered. "After that second time, he ran away, the devil, leaving me half dead. And then his friend lay upon me. I cried and pleaded with him. 'Don't do this to me,' I said, 'I'm his woman now.' But he had no pity. He would not listen to my prayer. They kept me in that cave for a month. They brought some bedding and food. A whole month . . . both of them . . . and no way of escaping. They took turns at night to keep guard."

"And his friend was stark-naked too?" The Muhtar's mouth was drying up again.

"Yes."

"And then?"

"This month passed, and one day four more young men appeared. They gave me a dress and took me to a little hut in the forest of Alakömech. There they took my dress away. A few days later five others came and carried me away to a deserted sheep-pen. There they beat me and made me dance naked for them. Afterwards they passed me on to the young men of Chitil village. It was when two young men had a fight over me that the gendarmes came. But this time it was the gendarmes. . . . They kept me in their post until one day Ibrahim appeared and told the gendarmes I was his wife. He took me back to the cave. He wept and was so filled with remorse that he looked after me very well. He brought me food and butter and even honey. And in a month I was well and strong again. But he still wouldn't bring me any clothes. And one morning I looked up and there you were, Uncle Sefer. I threw myself at your feet, do you remember?"

"And what did I do when I saw you there, lying stark-naked at my feet?" The Muhtar had assumed an expression of infinite grief.

The girl looked at him with grateful eyes. "You took off your coat and threw it over me."

"And then?"

"You kept guard over me, gun in hand, and no one could come near me any more. Then you brought me home."

"And when you were naked, did I do anything to you? Did I so much as touch you?"

"Oh no," said the girl, her eyes full of tears.

"What would have become of you if I hadn't rescued you? And you with child too?"

"I would have died," she said. "Anyway, I was freezing."

The Muhtar rose. Pale Ismail was watching him, his face devoid of all expression.

"You've heard the girl tell you how I rescued her and brought her back to you," said the Muhtar. "And now I'm going to take such a revenge on her ravishers that the whole world will be agape with wonder. They'll say: 'That's how a Muhtar should be, a father to his villagers, faithful to the interests of his friends and relatives.' Now, go and throw your lot in with a band of strangers! Go and abandon your own cousin!"

He strode away before Pale Ismail could put in a word. He could hear Pale Ismail's wife shouting at the top of her voice: "You can go off with Tashbash if you like. I'm staying right here with Sefer Agha and so are my children. Look, he's going to avenge us, which is more than you could ever do. They can cut my head off, but after what he's done for us, I'll never desert him, not while I've got a drop of blood left in me."

A great many of the villagers heard her too, and that was more than enough for the Muhtar.

He now decided to see Mangy Mahmut, who always set camp some distance away from the rest of the villagers.

"Hey, Mahmut!" he called. "I've come to visit you."

Mahmut jumped up, filled with exultation. The great Muhtar was coming to see him! He rushed to greet him half-way.

"Welcome, Agha, welcome!"

"Well, Mahmut, my child, how are you to-day? Did you go to Tashbash's meeting too?"

Mahmut flushed. "Oh no! God forbid!" he protested. "I'm for my Muhtar always! Ready to die for him! So is my wife, and so are my children." He was scratching away furiously at his body all the while.

He's all right, thought the Muhtar. Still, he'll be quite safe if I go and talk to his family a little. Show poor folk a smiling face and you give them the world. These poor folk are so good and simple, but woe betide if they should get anything into their hands. When the lice on their bodies are less starved, then they become stiff-necked and insolent. They should always be poor and destitute in order to remain good and clean and innocent like children. And that's why Allah does nothing to better their condition. So that they shouldn't be spoilt.

Mangy Mahmut's wife was all in a dither. The Muhtar had deigned to come to them, and here she was without even an old mat for him to sit on. She fluttered around him helplessly.

"I won't sit down, sister," said the Muhtar, "I just thought I'd drop in and see how our Mahmut's getting along. Do you still have that sickness?"

She closed her eyes and nodded.

"I've heard that the children have caught it too."

She nodded again. Her clothes were tattered and her large feet were cracked and black with dirt. The children were naked as the day they were born.

"The only way out is for Mahmut to be conscripted, as he should have been long ago if that accursed father of his hadn't made him out younger in his birth certificate. This winter, on our way back to the village, I'll go and beg the District Commander to take him. Once a soldier, Mahmut, they'll put you in a hospital and pour drugs over you and make a newborn man of you. You know about Mistik and Clumsy Veli, don't you? One had the mange ten years, the other a whole fifteen years. Why, who hasn't had the mange in this village? Well, I saw that at this rate they would just never get well, so I sent them off into the army and they returned to the village bursting with health. Yes, this mange sickness can't be cured anywhere but in the army. So you try and do a good job with the cotton picking now, and if Allah grants me life till then, I'll make a soldier of you this winter. And when you come out on leave, you'll go to your commander and explain to him how it is with your wife and children. He'll give you a huge bottle of that medicine which you'll rub over them and they'll get well too. Yes, I'm going to do you this good turn. Isn't it a good six years you've been like this?"

"A long time," laughed Mahmut, more and more pleased. He drew nearer to the Muhtar. "God forbid, Uncle! Would I ever take sides against you? If you make a soldier of me this year, I'll be your slave."

"I will, I will," promised the Muhtar as he walked away.

Now he had to tackle Zaladja Woman, the hardest stone in the fortress. She was a woman of independent spirit who cared for nobody and would tolerate no interference in her affairs. And she had money and land too. Zaladja had been married only a month when her husband had gone off to the wars and never returned. Although very young at the time, she had never married again. She had tilled her own field, reaped her own harvest, looked after her cows and sold the butter without even keeping an ounce for herself. As a result, she was the richest inhabitant of the village. People even said that she had a treasure buried somewhere. But her cousins and nephews had long despaired of ever getting anything out of her. She would carry off everything she had into the grave.

She had been a good friend of the Muhtar's, until only a week ago when suddenly, inexplicably, she had joined the Tashbash forces. Since anyone in the village could remember, Zaladja Woman had been plagued with dreams. And these dreams she would relate to everyone who would listen, asking them what the meaning could be. The Muhtar, sensing a good opportunity there, had bought a book of dreams and, with the help of the public letter-writer in the town, had managed to memorise a good part of this thick book. After this, Zaladja had fallen into the habit of coming to him and he would interpret her dreams. Each time she would bring him some eggs, or butter, or money, and each time the Muhtar would find a favourable explanation to her dream. This was a great subject of gossip among the villagers who were of the opinion that this crazy woman was spending all her money on the Muhtar.

She was washing some things in a large basin as he approached and did not lift her head or make any sign of greeting although the Muhtar knew she had seen him from a distance. He squatted down before her, but she still paid no attention.

"Well, Zaladja," he said, "what's the matter? Why don't you have a greeting for us?"

Zaladja gave him a cold stare and went on with her washing.

The Muhtar laughed with forced heartiness. "I know what it is! These villagers have been stuffing you up with a whole lot of nonsense about me, telling you I'm trying to embezzle your money, to fleece you of all your possessions. Isn't that so? But you, how can you believe that, my lady sister, when you know very well that I gave ten gold pieces for that dream-book, to say nothing of the two I gave to the public letter-writer? This I did only for you, thinking, ah, it won't do to let this woman's lovely dreams go to waste, their meaning lost for ever. And it's a book that came all the way from the Holy Kaaba, a book blessed by our Holy Prophet himself. Ah, there are many dream-books, but only those touched by the hand of our Holy Prophet have any potency. Yes, I know, you bring me some eggs and butter and a few coins, but haven't I saved your life countless times by reading your dreams? What would have happened to you the day of the earthquake? And that time we had the floods? If it hadn't been for my interpretation of the signs in your dreams, you would have died with those others. Twelve gold pieces!

Have I been able to get even that much out of you in all these years? As the great Allah above is my witness, did I ever make use of the book to interpret anyone else's dreams? And you look at me as if I'd tried to rob you of your treasure! Well, that's as you wish, sister. I won't meddle with your dreams any more. There are plenty of villagers in these parts who long to know the meaning of their dreams. I can go to them and earn pots of money."

Zaladja's hands stopped, suspended over the basin. The Muhtar pressed his advantage. "And when I use the book for other people, it will lose its virginity. It'll never be of any good to you again. But since you want it this way . . ."

"Go and do what you like," said Zaladja coldly.

"Ah, now I see! You don't dream any more these days, that's it! Ah, poor book, loyal for fifteen long years! You're cast aside now because she has no use for you. Forty gold pieces I was offered for you and I refused to sell you! Just so one of my villagers should find help in times of stress. But now I'll have to sell you, poor book." He took the book from under his arm and gazed at it pityingly. "Ah, poor book, one day they'll start having dreams again and you won't be here. They'll beat their breast with stones, but it'll be too late, the bird will have flown from its cage." He pressed the book to his heart reverentially. "Tell me, sister, have you really stopped having dreams?"

There was a heavy silence. Zaladja had left her washing. The Muhtar noticed the hesitation on her face. He smiled.

"No," he said, "I don't believe it. You'd never stop dreaming. However, it's your business. I'm going to sell the book."

Zaladja circled the basin and came over to him slowly. "Why do you want to sell the book? It's not as if it were a burden to you?"

"Why should I keep it if it's going to be of no use at all?"

It was clear that Zaladja was bursting to talk. She must be full to the brim with a full week's unexplained dreams.

"Well, all right," said the Muhtar, "I'll just interpret one more dream for you."

Zaladja gulped. "Well, last night, I had this dream," she said quickly and stopped.

"May it augur well for you, sister," the Muhtar encouraged her.

"I was on top of a mountain, a steep rocky mountain. . . ."

"Ah, sister," he interrupted her, "I knew you always had dreams! You just let yourself be ensnared by those lying tongues. Now, before you go on, bring me a little salt and then I shall be able to interpret the dream properly."

Zaladja took a pinch of salt from a bag and the Muhtar threw it into his mouth. He always said it brought bad luck to interpret dreams without first receiving something for it. Anything would do, money, butter, bulgur. He had to have something so that the truth would manifest itself.

"There, on top of the mountain," Zaladja went on, with the ease born of long habit, "I saw a single, huge flower, spread wide open. A deer climbed up and lay down under the flower. Suddenly a young man sprang up from beside the deer and advanced towards me. He took my hand, but I could not look him in the face. Then he vanished. And the deer gazed up at me. Its eyes were like those of a human being. But a serpent slipped out from under a rock and swallowed up the deer. I screamed in fear. Don't scream, the serpent said. He spread a soft bed for me. Lie down, he said. I lay down and the serpent crept up upon me. I felt I was strangling and I woke up in a sweat. . . ."

She stopped and looked anxiously at the Muhtar.

"Is that all?" asked the Muhtar, astonished.

"There's a lot more. But you tell me this now."

The Muhtar lifted the book up piously with both hands and swayed from side to side a few times.

"To see a mountain in a dream, to set up station on a mountain, is a presage of forthcoming great fortune through the patronage of a powerful person, a Democrat or a Muhtar. The mountain in your dream was the sacred hill of Arafat near Mecca and that is a sign of drawing nearer to Allah, a benediction. It means Allah will love you most particularly. And now we come to the deer, a sacred animal. Let us see what the book has to say about it and what meaning we can extract therefrom!"

Zaladja was listening with rapt attention. The Muhtar lowered his voice and began again in a sing-song tone, almost like an incantation.

"To see a musk-deer is a sign that a woman is as beautiful as the houris of Paradise. No matter how old she is, Allah will make her appear beautiful in the eyes of all men. The death of a deer is a sign that a woman will be loved passionately by a noble youth, that their bodies will be joined in unforgettable ecstasy, and all this in broad daylight. To eat the meat of the deer is a sign of much property coming to you from a rich, eighteen-year-old husband whose love for you will burn like an ardent flame. Ah, this is good, Zaladja! Yes, it just shows that one should never despair of Allah's merciful bounty.

"To see a serpent swallow this large deer means that you will gather a lot of cotton this year and that, if you hide the money you get for it under a stone, it will multiply. To see the serpent coming upon you, making a bed for you, is a sign that you have been abusing some friend who loves you. It is a sign that if you speak ill of him once more you will die. Beware never to malign him again! To wake up in a sweat is a sign that you are hostile to a good Moslem, but that you will be sorry for the wrong you have done him, and will turn to better ways. To see a dragon means to fall into the wake of a bad man, and what you saw was a dragon, there's no mistake about that. It is a sign that this man is a harmful trouble-monger, an enemy of the villagers, that he will cause them much damage and misery. But all these signs lead in the end to a great blessing, a plenteous light. That the serpent should be red, and yours was red on one side but you didn't notice it, is a sign that this noble youth, who burns with love for you, is having intercourse with you day and night without your knowing it."

He was sweating. He lifted the book to his lips, then put it into his pocket and rose. Zaladja rose too.

"But this isn't all," she said, "I only told you one of my dreams."

"No more reading dreams for me," said the Muhtar, "I'm selling the book. I just thought I ought to do you one last good turn."

Zaladja's happy face clouded over at the prospect of losing the only thing she loved in the world.

"Don't sell it please, Sefer Agha. Ah, how could I have let myself be taken in by your enemies? And all these days when I didn't come to you, I was like a mad woman. I didn't know which way to turn. Here, on my breast, something was burning me, strangling me. Now I feel a load has come off me. Don't give our book to strangers. What will I do then? May my two eyes drop down in front of me if I ever listen to your enemies again!"

The Muhtar had never expected to win her over so quickly. "All right, then, I won't. Have no fear," he reassured her, "I just said that because I was angry. I wouldn't sell this book even if I were given a thousand gold pieces for it. A book written by Hadji Kamil the Egyptian, that he brought over here himself all the way from Arabia . . . sell such a book? How could we ever find the like of it again? But don't you go and fall for the provocations of such scoundrels again or I won't answer for anything. I'll explain the rest of your dreams to you when we get down to the Chukurova. Now, go to the villagers and tell them how you saw that Tashbash will bring misery upon them, for the dragon in your dream is no other than he. And the deer is the village. He aims at swallowing the village. Do you understand now? You must proclaim this to the villagers, so that they should see the truth too. And don't worry, the book remains ours."

He walked away, muttering gleefully to himself, "Eh, Tashbash, my poor child, I pity you now, I really do! So you thought you would cross swords with me, eh? If I leave a single man behind you, except for that filthy Lone Duran, my name's not Sefer!"

He went back to his place and called to a young man from a neighbouring encampment. "Quick, go and fetch that Köstüoglu and bring him to me."

As soon as Köstüoglu came into sight the Muhtar bounded to his feet and flung up his right arm, pointing the two forefingers like arrows straight into his eyes.

"You!" he stormed, "you worthless bastard! I ought to pierce your eyes with these two fingers. How was it you managed to go without shoes all through your army service? Thanks to whom? Why don't you speak, you traitor? If I hadn't sent a petition to the Government, explaining how you'd never worn shoes in your life, saying that our village folk just aren't used to shoes, where would you have been, I'm asking you, you ungrateful wretch? Be off with you, I don't want another word out of you."

Köstüoglu, that huge man, seemed to have shrunk to half his size. He slunk off without daring to say a word.

"Now, go and get me Home-Leave Memet," the Muhtar ordered the young man.

The villagers were filled with misgivings. Mangy Mahmut, Pale Ismail, Zaladja Woman and Köstüoglu had been put out of action. And now it would be the turn of Home-Leave Memet. Tashbash was seething as he looked on helplessly. There's no getting the better of this rascal, he was thinking. He has laid his shoulder to the wheel with a vengeance. There's a touch of devilry in the fellow. . . . Not a man he cannot win over in a couple of words.

Home-Leave Memet's face was sullen as he planted himself before the Muhtar.

"What do you want, Muhtar Effendi?" he asked dourly.

The Muhtar changed his tactics on the instant. He smiled and invited him to sit down. Home-Leave remained standing, undecided.

"Come on, sit down," insisted the Muhtar, "we're not going to eat you, my son. Look, we're going down to the Chukurova. Perhaps I can do something for you and save you from this curse, this never-ending army service of yours."

Home-Leave dropped down weakly with the laboured breathing of the tubercular. He was all yellow skin and bones.

"Why didn't you think of that before?" he asked in the same dour tone.

"Ah, but then our Party wasn't as powerful as it is now! Why, it was only a poor political party with nothing at all really. It's only recently that we've strengthened our position, you should know that, my son. This time when we get down, I can speak to the big people of the Chukurova. 'Look here,' I'll say, 'this lad's situation is unbearable. Either have him discharged as infirm or else put him in an army hospital and cure him. Is it fair to let him suffer like this? Even his nickname now is Home-Leave Memet.' Yes, I'll insist they do something. How many months have you left to serve?"

"Five."

"That's plenty."

"I'll have to go back. They'll put me in the hospital for a couple of days, and then, as usual, they'll send me packing to the village."

"Tst, tst!" the Muhtar ejaculated pityingly. "This time we must do something about it, and this is why I've called you. To-morrow we go down. Now, the very day after we start on the cotton, come to me and I'll take you to Adana myself and plead your cause with the great. Don't forget."

"I won't!" said Home-Leave Memet as dourly as ever.

Dusk was falling, but the Muhtar resolved to pursue his present successful tactics all through the night. Let that Tashbash see how a party-man could work.

Shirtless was a murderer and a former outlaw, but you could more easily cut his head off than make him budge an inch from his given word. And he feared no man, nothing. It was true they were distantly related, but of what use was a relative who could be so difficult to deal with? Still Shirtless had to be won over, for he controlled at least thirty men in the village, and if he followed Tashbash this would open a large breach in the village's cotton picking force. It would never do to talk to him in broad daylight. He was quite capable of making a laughing stock of him before all the villagers and of sending him packing without any more ado. Yes, it would be better to wait till dark, with no witnesses around.

He felt disquieted.

These peasants haven't got an ounce of decency in them, he thought. You can slave for them and go to all lengths to protect their interests, they won't turn a hair. Indeed, they'll be ready to pounce on you like hungry wolves the minute they discover the slightest fissure in your flank. It's all the Government's fault. It's the Government that has spoilt them, giving them the right to vote and what not. Think of it! These peasants electing a Government! Hah, just look at this Government formed by Mangy Mahmut! Much it cares about Mangy Mahmut! But at election time, you can hardly approach them, they're so arrogant. You've actually got to beg for their votes. No, really this Government has no idea of what it is doing. Granting these peasants the right to vote! Why, they're not even capable of counting half a dozen goats and herding them properly! Ah, all this nonsense is the invention of that Ismet Pasha. If he hadn't brought this democracy business upon our heads, would the likes of Tashbash ever have had the cheek to stand up to a Muhtar? Eh Ismet, but you've fallen into your own trap. Look at all these barefooted ragamuffins you gave the right to vote to. Do they give you a single of their votes now? Ah Ismet, you may have become a great pasha and even a president of the Republic, but if there's one grain of sense in that head of yours, I'm ready to shave off this moustache of mine! Would a man in his right senses take the knotted rope he holds in his hands and tie it about his own legs? Hah, you'll see the nape of your neck first before you ever see the Presidency again! I, for one, will die rather than side with you again. A man who lets the presidency slip out of his fingers, just by trusting himself to the vote of a handful of barefooted peasants, is surely incapable of ruling a great nation. No, my friend, I don't call that clever! You may be considered as an astute politician, your fame may have spread even to the Land of the Franks, but if you ask me, you're simply no good at all, my friend! I'll never forgive you as long as I live. Because of you, I almost lost my post of Muhtar. If I hadn't passed over to that new Democrat Party in double quick time, it would have been all over with me. Ah Ismet, why didn't you consult your faithful muhtars before deciding to change our comfortable one-party system? Look at the result now! Oh yes, I know you're sorry for what you've done, but it's too late. The bird has flown out of your hand and you can exert yourself as much as you like you'll never catch it again. Ah Ismet, ah, you're much to blame! You deserve what you got, but you've done us a great deal of harm too.

He lay on his bed, fully dressed, his eyes fixed on the starry sky, still ruminating on the incomprehensible behaviour of Ismet Pasha. In the end, he decided it must be ascribed to old age. Yes, obviously old age had impaired Ismet Pasha's mind!

Everyone was asleep now. The camp-fires flickered slowly as they died down. From the darkness floated the whine of a baby

and the faint weary voice of its mother trying to soothe it to
sleep with a lullaby.

It went against the grain to plead with this Shirtless fellow,
but he had no choice. He got up muttering, ah, this Ismet Pasha,
ah, and washed his face with water from a pail before tiptoeing
off.

Shirtless was asleep, his pillow propped against a bush. The
Muhtar knelt down and touched his shoulder. At the touch
Shirtless sprang to a sitting position in his bed and started
groping about. He was looking for his gun, an old habit left
over from his days of banditry.

"Brother," said the Muhtar apprehensively, "it's me, Muhtar
Sefer. I'm sorry I had to wake you up."

Shirtless was still fumbling among the bedding and under
the pillow. The Muhtar clutched his hands.

"For God's sake, Shirtless, it's only me, Sefer! Do come to
your senses. I've got something very important to say to you."

Shirtless remained motionless for a moment, then drew his
hands away.

"What are you doing here in the dead of night?" he asked
stiffly.

The Muhtar grasped his hands again. "I've come to throw
myself at your feet and beg for your help. Yours is a great and
noble ancestry. There's no counting the number of people
they've killed, the number of heads they've cut off. Not one of
your ancestors ever died in his bed. Not one, except your women,
that did not die from a glorious bullet! That is why I always
bow down in homage before your noble family. And if I may be
entitled to a little pride, if I may consider myself that much a
man, it's because I have the honour of being related ever so
distantly to this noble Shirtless race. Yes indeed, brother! I know
that it is in the great tradition of your house never to turn away
anyone who seeks shelter with you, were he your deadliest
enemy. That is why I've come to you, I, the Muhtar of this

village, the head of the Democrats, the son of the Headman Hidir. Yes, I've come to find sanctuary with you." He held the other's hands to his breast. "You're my only hope, you, the flaming torch of the ever-merciful Shirtless tribe. I've come to beg you not to abandon me now that all the villagers have gone over to his side. Won't you help me?"

He paused, but there was no answer.

"Well, what do you say, brother? Can't you protect a fellow who's deserted by all, who throws himself into your arms? The Shirtless race was ever the champion of the forsaken, the downtrodden. Is it that you can't maintain this tradition any longer?"

"True," uttered Shirtless weightily. He lapsed into silence. The Muhtar waited for him to speak again.

"You have spoken very truly about the Shirtless race, and you can go now and sleep without a care, for the Shirtless household will protect you. You've acted wisely in coming to me. You knew that this household would not turn you away with empty hands. Never have we done this to anyone who came to us for help. But you are wrong and Tashbash is right. You are robbing the villagers of their livelihood by obliging them to work in arid cotton fields. Don't you ever do such a thing again!"

"I won't, I won't! As Allah's my witness, I won't," said the Muhtar as he rose. "Thank you, Shirtless. May your hearth ever burn brightly."

He walked away briskly. A heavy load had been lifted off him.

And now he must see to Ökkesh Dagkurdu. . . . Of mild disposition, extremely pious, perhaps the only man in the village never to miss a single one of his *namaz* prayers, Ökkesh's only aspiration in life was to make the Hadj to Mecca. Although getting on in years, he always picked more cotton than the others, but he never spent a penny of the money he earned, not even to buy the barest necessities for his family. This had been going on for years, but still he had not managed to scrape together enough money for his pilgrimage.

"You, Ökkesh Dagkurdu, are a holy man, a devout Moslem. You have travelled a straight, clean road all through your long life. You have wronged no man and even in your youth you never once lay with asses or other forbidden creatures. You shall leave this world as pure and innocent as when you were born into it. And when you appear before Allah at the Day of Judgment, He will say: 'O my servant Ökkesh Dagkurdu, there is not one single sin I have to call you to account for. I have prepared for you in my Paradise a palace as glittering with light as the train station at Adana. Go and settle there to live in pleasure and comfort for all eternity.' He will give you your wife too and forty houris to serve you, each a peerless beauty, and all virgin, mind you, and also forty male-slaves, ready to minister to your every want. And the river of Paradise will flow as wine, and stretching all about you as far as the eye can see will be gardens and orchards with ripe fruit waiting to be picked. All day long you will feast on fruit and honey and bird's milk and other delicacies. You will eat but you will have no dirty, evil-smelling excretions like us human beings. What you eat will be exuded as sweat. And when I say sweat, I don't mean the kind of sweat you have when you're gathering cotton. Oh no! A gentle sweat will seep from your pores unawares, smelling sweet, now of ambergris, now of roses, now of marjoram, now of fresh pine, in fact of whatever scent you happen to desire at the moment. Goose-meat, fat ducks, quails will materialise before you, already roasted and golden brown. And the Saintly Tailor Idris will fashion garments of pure silk for you, without ever using scissors or thread, and their colours will be as vivid as the flowers of the Long Plateau. You will be able to change every day without any trouble at all. It'll be enough for you to wish you had other clothes on and, before you can bat an eye, you'll find yourself dressed in new clothes.

"The birds of Paradise will shed their softest feathers for your bed. Yes, your bed will be all of bird's feathers. That is why it is meritorious for a man to lie on a hard bed during his earthly sojourn. You know this well. As for us, our eyes are blind and our ears deaf, and we let ourselves be snared by the Devil. We are led into temptation by our rude earthly substance. There, in your palace, it will be neither hot nor cold, but pleasantly warm as in the early spring when a warm sun stirs the blood. For that reason, it is meritorious to go naked in this world, to brace the body against the biting cold and the burning heat. No one knows this but you. All these foolish villagers think only of their present life, whilst you alone toil for your palace in Paradise. And they even scoff at you for this!

"Yes, it is true the colonel's plantation is arid, unproductive, yielding only half as much as other fields. This is bad for the other villagers, for Tashbash, for me, for us who seek an easy field and big earnings. But you, you seek a hard field and rightful earnings. If you were to earn your money easily, then the walls of your palace would begin to collapse. You have to work harder than all the others to earn your Hadj money, so that Allah may set you apart. Do you know what I've been aiming at all these years? I've been trying to protect the one man of our village who ever showed a desire to make the pilgrimage from having his pure eyes dazed by our tainted earthly goods. And you, instead, fall into the wake of that Tashbash, you pull down your palace with your own hands, you level it with the earth.

"That last time I levied the village tax and you didn't pay up, why did I take your bedding away? So that you should lie on the hard ground. Why did I take your food? So that you should go hungry. Why did I make you sell your cow for the road tax? So that your earthly possessions should not lead you astray. Do you realise now all I've done to foster your holy aims? No you don't, you're a poor human being after all. Your heart is rich and pure, but your head is empty and there are many things you don't know.

"Now listen to me. Our Holy Book orders us to obey Allah and to set up no rival god against him. Who is Allah—may He forgive me? He is our all-powerful Lord whom we cannot disobey. Who is Allah's representative on earth? Our Government, our Democrat Party! And who are the representatives of the Government and of the Party in the town? The Governor and Tevfik Effendi. And who represents the Governor and Tevfik Effendi in this village? The Muhtar! And who is the Muhtar? I am. So think hard now. What does it mean to go against me? No, I won't give you the answer to this. You'll have to figure it out all by yourself. Then you will see that what you're doing is to destroy at one fillip this palace you've been slaving for these many years, this wonderful palace in Paradise which no other man could have built in a lifetime. No you can't do that, my friend! Is Tashbash more valuable to you than your palace in Paradise?

"Well, I'm going now. You think this over. You had better spend this night in prayer. You have to persuade Allah you didn't realise what you were doing so He should forgive you. Keep well and Allah help you. Praised be the beautiful name of Mohammed!"

He was pleased with himself. He had spoken well, finding just the words that would touch Ökkesh's heart to the core. "Allah, Allah! Only you can save me!" Ökkesh had kept mumbling tremulously over and over again. . . .

"Look here, Durduman, what's the idea of dragging these villagers along with you when you know very well there isn't a single empty field left by this time except the one I've got for you? You'll all be left without jobs, like fish out of water, and I for one will wash my hands of you. Even you won't be able to pay your debts to Adil Effendi. No, you've no right to do this to our uncomplaining, long-suffering people. Next year you can

246

do whatever you like. But if you persist this year . . . well, I warn you, it'll go ill for you. You'll be breaking the law."

"Oh, get off it, Uncle! What's this got to do with the law?"

"Because this is called swindling and it's written down in the law, clause for clause! You can't know because you're not a Muhtar. But I . . . I advise you to shut your mouth and not incite the villagers to what amounts to plain rebellion. You haven't got a good name in town as it is. They say you hold our religion in contempt and if I repeat to the villagers what the gendarmes have told me they'll make short work of you. You're a brave and clever man, yes, but you've got a record with the police, mind that. You think I don't know about your subversive propaganda? I'm just biding my time. But I'll catch you one day by the scruff of the neck, never fear, and that'll put your nose out of joint. And the Government knows everything too, yes, and all about your inseparable friend the blacksmith, that stranger. I warn you, be careful. If I haven't acted up to now, it's just that I couldn't bring myself to smear the honour of the village. I couldn't confess we had such a renegade among us. So you'd better mend your ways and keep straight. You're not to go with Tashbash to-morrow."

"Why not? You're the one who's to blame, cheating the villagers like that. Look at the miserable straits you've brought them to. . . ."

"Now, listen, Durduman, I give you my word. Next year we'll get together and find a really good cotton field for our village. Anyway, I'm sick of the colonel's son. He's a dirty, lying fellow. And I promise to protect you too. He's a clean lad, I'll say. He wouldn't have any connection with such subversive elements."

"I'll sleep upon this, Uncle. To-morrow we'll see."

"Well, do as you like. Only bear in mind that it is a serious crime to incite the people to sedition."

Osmandja was awake and waiting for him.

"Welcome, Agha," he called from a distance. "What an honour for our household! I've been all agog waiting for you since this evening. Why does my turn come so late? I'm always first on your list for the village tax. . . ."

"Excuse me, Osmandja. I just thought you would turn from the wrong path more quickly than the others. After all, our grandmothers were sisters and you're a true Democrat, the delegate of our Party," said the Muhtar as he sank down beside Osmandja on to the bed.

"I've heard you haranguing the villagers. You've no right to mix our Party up in this. Village business is one thing and Party business another. If you go on plotting with Batty Bekir, I'm afraid that at the next election all the villagers will vote for Ismet Pasha."

The Muhtar rose agitatedly then sat down again.

"You're right. I'll do what you say and have nothing to do with Bekir any more. But you must promise me not to go away with Tashbash. Look, I've given you my word, a word stronger than steel. This year you'll be delegate again. That's another promise. All right?"

"I'll think it over."

"Now, Osmandja, what kind of a delegate, what kind of a party comrade are you? A party means that wherever the feet of one member go, the heads of all the other members follow! Don't you remember what our leader said? That this was the first condition of democracy?"

Osmandja drew his legs under him.

"If you break off with Bekir, then I promise," he said. "And no changing your mind afterwards!"

"It's our word we've given you, my friend," said the Muhtar. "Our head may go, but our word remains ever firm. Don't you worry."

He was terribly sleepy and his throat ached from so much talking. But there would be no rest in a warm bed for him this

248

night. He knew that most of the villagers had woken up and were sitting in their beds, attentive to his every move, not missing a word of what he said. He hoped they had not overheard his talk with Shirtless. That would be the end of him indeed. But now they were awake, he had to show them. . . . He paused for a while, then walked over swiftly to one of the beds and stood over it. This was the bed of Slick Ali.

"Get up, you son of a dog," he roared. "Slinking around from house to house, calling me names. . . ." He grabbed his arm and jerked him up. "Who do you think you are, you shameless brat? Have you forgotten that your father entrusted you to me when he died? So you're going with Tashbash to-morrow, eh, Ali Pasha Effendi?" He dealt him a stinging box on the ears. The cracking sound travelled far into the night.

"Oh, never, Uncle," protested Ali, clutching at the Muhtar's hands. "Allah forbid! I've never had anything to do with him."

"I can't prevent those ungrateful villagers who forget my bounties from dragging themselves wretchedly from plantation to plantation hunting for work. But you, I'm responsible for you. It's I who must answer to Adil Effendi for your debts. Now go back to sleep and don't you ever get mixed up in such affairs again. I know it's not your fault, my poor child. A thousand curses on those who turn your heads, who lead you to destruction and then strut about twirling their moustache and clinking their yellow beads!"

He felt really tired out now. Going to his bed, he lay down to rest a little. His head was whirling. But he could not give up now. Those villagers whom he had not visited would feel slighted. They were awake, expectant. Yes, he had to talk to them all, one by one, and last of all, at daybreak, he would go to The Bald Minstrel.

It was past midnight when he rose and set out again. He carried his plan out to the letter and when he had finished he felt exultant.

He knew that the seeds he had sown during the night would sprout and bloom with the morning sun. He had even, for a while, toyed with the idea of going to Tashbash, but he could not bring himself to swallow his pride to that extent.

The Bald Minstrel was dressed already and sitting with his back against a tree. Without a word, the Muhtar sat down facing him.

After a while, he ventured to speak. "Hey, you cranes!" he said.

"Hey, you tufted cranes!" replied The Bald Minstrel.

"Hey, my minstrel, who was the joy of my father's house, charming the very nightingales with your song!"

These words always pleased The Bald Minstrel particularly.

"You, the glory of our village, you, whose honeyed songs move the wild creatures of the woods to speech and melt the hard mountains and rocks, whose voice soars up to the piebald dawn on this beautiful morning Allah is giving us! Battered and foot-sore, the son of the old Headman Hidir has come to you, begging for the relief of your song. He is overwhelmed, besieged by enemies, abandoned. Sing to him so he should be strengthened and forget the persecution of his enemies."

The sky whitened in the east, lighting up The Bald Minstrel's wasted, wizened face with its sparse white beard. He was a very old man, no one knew how old. He himself did not know his age, and in the memory of all the villagers he had always been as he was now.

"Greetings to the nascent sun, to the winging bird!"

He drew his *saz* from its cloth cover and caressed it trem-blingly. Then he started to strum the strings first slowly, then more and more forcefully. Overhead the boughs swayed gently in the morning breeze.

The children were the first to appear, then the women came and formed a big circle around the minstrel and the Muhtar. Then the men drew up to the minstrel and squatted on the ground pressing against each other. A donkey brayed and everyone laughed. Then a hush fell over the crowd. It was not often that The Bald Minstrel was roused to play in this way.

His was a family of musicians. His grandfather and his grandfather's grandfather, his uncle, his brothers had all been minstrels, and each one went by the name of The Bald Minstrel. They claimed descent from those great folk-bards of old, Karadjaoglan and Yunus Emre. There was not a single person in these parts, man or woman, who did not cherish in his heart a reminiscence of The Bald Minstrel singing on this or that occasion, as he would cherish the memory of a sweet dream, of his mother's lullabies, of the dear words of his beloved, or of the days of festival and *bayram*.

The Bald Minstrel looked upon the gathering with a pleased face. "Greetings to you all, who have come here in the twilight of this beautiful dawn! Greetings to the wakening earth, to the rustling grass, to the bud breaking open at dawn, to the humming insect, to the sparkling murmuring streams! Hey, you tufted cranes!"

A ripple of laughter passed over the crowd. "Greetings to the minstrel," came the response, "greetings to the strings of his *saz*. Hey, you tufted cranes!"

"To the children and babes in arms, to the white cotton of the Chukurova, greetings!"

"Greetings!" they repeated, thoroughly delighted.

"To our father-bards Karadjaoglan and Yunus and Dadaloglu, to the past glory of the Turcoman, greetings. . . ."

The minstrel was silent for a long while as the last echoes of the answering greetings died out. Then he called out once more: "Heheey, you tufted cranes!" And he began, his voice at first frail and hoarse, then gradually gaining strength and warmth.

"A pair of nightingales have lighted on the hawthorn. Green are their heads and red their feet. . . . In the dark night, three woes assail me, fast joined together, parting, misery and death. . . .

See how the Chukurova plain wears its festive livery. . . . My sorrow and my joy vie with each other. . . . O ye mountains decked with purple violets and blue marjoram and white clouds. . . . On the face of the sky a stork, a stork, its leg like a gold-red stalk. Since death is the end of all things, my dear, you shall sway from your sacred path, but shall never forsake your love. . . . Oh leave me be, poverty, and cling not to my waist like a sash. . . . Azrael looms before me asking for my soul. Ah, is there strength enough in me to give even that? . . . Oh grant me ten brothers with spirit unflinching, and together we will drive these lords from their mansions. . . . Hey, you lords of the Chukurova. . . . Pain and woe and trouble. . . . Grieve not, my soul, oh grieve you not, for a day dawns behind every hill. . . . Hey, you tufted cranes. . . ."

It was as though the echoes of a great festivity filled the whole world. The Bald Minstrel had worked himself into such an ecstasy that it was soon impossible to make out what he was saying. Then, abruptly, without warning, the music broke off as though at the stroke of a sword. And at the same moment the edge of the sun rose into sight. The crowd remained silent, watching the minstrel who had cast away his instrument and whose arms hung limply to his sides now. It had always been like this with him, even in his younger years. At last he rose and the crowd broke up. There was a happy smile on everyone's face and some were humming bits of songs.

The Muhtar put his hand on the minstrel's shoulder. "Thank you for your beautiful songs and blessed be your beautiful voice which is just like that of our Lord David. Greetings to the sacred house of The Bald Minstrel!"

As he turned away, he saw Old Halil's son and the two young men. "What!" he shouted. "Haven't you found him?"

They shook their heads.

"There you are!" he began in a loud wail. "That's what happens when you upset the order of a village! And truly, poor decrepit old men are made to think the villagers will kill them and are driven into the wild mountains to perish there. And truly, their bodies cannot be found, and they are devoured by green flies and birds of prey. Ah, even a decent burial attended by friends and relatives is denied them! No one to recite the Koran over them. . . . If certain people had not set themselves up against authority and disturbed the order of the village, would this poor old man have sought refuge in the wilds? Alas, my wise, all-knowing Uncle Halil, you are made one with the black earth! I'll find your body and bury it in a large grave with a big stone such as they set up only for great men, and on it I'll put an inscription: 'Here lies Old Uncle Halil, victim of village anarchy. Allah rest his soul!' Alas my poor father's faithful comrade, who's to weep for you if not I? They've killed you. . . ." He soon had all the women weeping.

Just then Tashbash's voice was heard.

"Come on. I'm setting out. Those who're coming with me, get ready!"

The Muhtar interrupted his lamentations and cocked his ears. There was a deep silence in the camp, except around Tashbash's place where people were coming and going and two donkeys stood loaded and ready to depart. Suddenly the Muhtar took his head in his hands.

"Alas that I should live to see such a day!" he moaned loudly. "Ah, poor Uncle Halil, they've murdered you and now they're going. Look how they flee, those who called you Uncle in your lifetime and tried to wheedle you over to their side. Ah, if you were still alive, Uncle Halil, you would have understood now who's an enemy and who's a friend in this village. Ah, poor Uncle Halil, ah. . . ."

He was interrupted by a villager with the news that Batty Bekir and the Watchman were coming up the slope. The Muhtar's mournful face lit up. A few minutes later Batty Bekir was before him.

"There's not a single unrented field left, except the colonel's plantation to serve you, Sefer Agha. I would never have come back otherwise."

"Tashbash's gang is up in arms again. They're leaving us."

"All the worse for them. This year there's such a crop on the colonel's plantation, Allah be praised! Fluffy, shining cotton. . . ."

"Watchman!" the Muhtar cried out excitedly. "Call out a proclamation at once. Give the news that this year the colonel's crop is better than ever, while all the other plantations have dried up. Tell everyone to get ready for we're going down immediately. And say that the lamb who strays from the fold falls into the jaws of the wolf. Go. Quickly!"

Tashbash, Lone Duran, Veli and a few others had already left the camp and were threading their way down a path. But the disappearance of Old Halil had shaken their resolution and they walked on dispiritedly, wondering whether it was right to leave the others when one of them had just died or was lost.

The Muhtar could not tear his eyes from the little group that was moving away. He was thinking bitterly that for the first time a breach would be made in the old tradition of the village. His father, the Headman Hidir, would never have allowed this to happen. He would have done something about it, saying that it was never the villagers' fault if he went astray, it was always the Muhtar's fault. And that is what people would think and say now, make no mistake. No, he must swallow his pride, there was no help for it. Anyway, great men, great leaders, had no pride. They had to bring themselves to the level of the people in order to be loved and respected.

He rushed up to Shirtless. "Agha," he said, in a loud voice so that all should hear, "you're the only man of noble extraction in our village, not an ignorant villager like us. Your great mercy, your conscience, cannot allow you to stand by and see some misguided fellow villagers run to their ruin in the Chukurova. Come with me and let's make them turn back. Come, my friend!"

He grasped Shirtless by the arm and dragged him along.

"Tashbash," cried the Muhtar, panting, as they caught up with the group, "wait! We have a few words to say to you."

They had all stopped, but Tashbash's back remained turned to the Muhtar.

"You see, he won't even look me in the face. He's bent on making himself miserable. I wouldn't care if it weren't for his dear children, for his sensible, honest, beautiful wife. And truly, Tashbash, we have lost one villager because of this business. We have driven Old Halil into the wilds. Our heart is on fire, it is torn to shreds. It wouldn't be right to turn your back on the villagers on this day of mourning. Look at me, my friend." As Tashbash did not turn, he went up to him, but recoiled before the other's burning gaze. "Shirtless Agha," he said, "tell him that I'm holding out the hand of friendship. Tell him there isn't a single empty field left in the Chukurova. Tell him he can't do this, he can't go and join another village, he can't trample the honour of our village under his feet, he can't have the whole world know there is dissidence among us and that because of this dissidence the oldest man in the village has taken to the hills and is lost, dead. Tell him, Shirtless, that next year I'll follow him, word of honour! Even if he takes us to the Mediterranean Sea and says this isn't the sea, this is a cotton field, I'll take my villagers just where he wants. But this year he mustn't break up the unity of our village!"

Shirtless took Tashbash's arm. "Memet, my friend," he said, "don't do this. It's not a good thing to damage the order of a village. Look, I broke all the rules and see what I've come to. Neither wife, nor family, nor anything, left, only my own life, and that I only just managed to save. Next year, I'll stand by you to the last if he breaks his promise. And you know that I always keep my word."

Tashbash was white as chalk. He put the yellow prayer beads

back into his pocket and looked at Lone Duran with misty eyes. Duran hung his head.

The Muhtar knew that he held victory at last, but it would not be wise to press it further.

"You wait for us here. There's no need for you to come back. I'll go and speed the villagers. Look, Memet, brother, let's forget all that's happened between us. I like you. You're the bravest, most reliable man in this village. For me you're more than a brother."

"I like Tashbash too," said Shirtless, "he's got sense. Any other man would have been obstinate. But not he. He's got oceans of good sense. And, as our fathers said, better to have a thousand clever foes, than one mad friend."

A great tumult, interspersed with merry voices, came from the camp where the villagers were hurriedly packing up. Some of them had even set out by this time.

They were still talking to Tashbash, who had not once opened his mouth, when a youth came up to them. His clothes were torn and muddy and he held a stick in his hand.

"The cattle are down in the colonel's plantation, Muhtar Agha. There's some good grazing there this year. The cattle will be fattened."

The Muhtar patted the youth on the shoulder. "Good for you, my lad," he said. "Ah, what wonderful people these villagers of mine are! So quick in the uptake! Why, a man could go even to Hell with such people and turn Hell into a garden of pleasure!"

They left Tashbash and returned to the camp. The Muhtar mounted his newly-curried shining black donkey and rode off. He soon passed Tashbash, who was still standing in the same spot wrapped in thought, and reached the head of the descending column.

Down below, the Chukurova earth was hidden in a whirl of dust. A bitter smell floated up from the burdock shrubs.

Chapter 18

This remote pomegranate garden lies abandoned on the flanks of the Taurus mountains. Down below is the plain, with yellow-eyed jonquils and blue-flowering marjoram, aromatic lemon and orange groves, sparkling fields of white cotton and golden wheat, busy tractors glowing star-like in the night, rumbling trucks and harvesting machines gorging and disgorging the crops, noisy factories and incredibly large towns with teeming populations: the white-clouded Chukurova soil at last, hot, dusty, sweltering.

It is a very old garden, spreading out far and wide. Some say it dates from the time of the Christians. The pomegranate trees are thick and gnarled, most of them half seared, with their bark cracking open and their boughs crooked and intertwisted. The ground is strewn with stones swept there over the years by the floods.

At blossom-time the whole expanse of earth and sky, the moss-grown springs, the shining mountain streams, the forest of the Taurus, the Chukurova plain below, all appear as though swathed in a reddish haze, and the garden hums with the noise of myriads of bees that have left their hives and combs in the mountain and the plain to suck the flowers of the deserted garden. Then, each red flower swarms with hundreds of bees, big and small, shining downy bees of every hue and colour. Their buzzing can be heard from way off as you approach the garden.

Although situated at a cross-roads, it is an unfrequented place, for the roads that meet here are merely small paths used by villagers going down or returning from the Chukurova. The solitude, filled solely with the humming of thousands of bees and the flash of their wings among the red blooms of flowers, is intensified even more by the neglect into which the garden has fallen.

This deserted garden is the unrestricted abode of the black serpent who loves red flowers and whose mating season happens to be at blossom time, when even the ground is red.

The world was drenched in sunlight and a reddish vapour simmered over the pomegranate garden. A black serpent slipped out from beneath a white rock and started on a slow meandering course in and out of the green grass. Now and again, it lifted its head as though searching for something. The bees hummed on, the flowers smelled bitterly and a tiny white cloud floated down from over the Taurus. The serpent slithered up on to a stone and paused there, waiting, almost crying out. Then it slid down and rolled itself around the trunk of a tree.

It is a sin to kill the black serpent, for unless you step on its tail it will never attack you.

After a while the serpent left the tree and slid towards a sandy patch where it stopped again. It was gathering itself into a coil, when a faint rustling caught its attention and it turned. From among a clump of tall blue flowers another serpent had appeared and was gliding towards a granite rock. The new serpent seemed blacker than the first one and even longer, perhaps two fathoms long. They moved towards each other and together crawled on to the rock, at the same time gradually intertwining the lower parts of their bodies. Without separating, they slid off the rock again. The little white cloud was now passing over the garden and, for an instant, cast its shadow over the flowers.

Couch grass is like the skin of the earth. It clings to the earth like a thin tegument and never grows. The two serpents undulated on until they came to the couch grass patch. There, their bodies interlocked as though welded and their tails quivered with sensual delight.

It seemed to her that the red of the flowers, the green of the couch grass, the blue of the sky, even the white of the passing cloud, all quivered in unison with the serpents. Her breath choking her, she would close her eyes, then open them again, fascinated by the amorous convolutions of the black serpents. She could not have been more than seventeen years old then.

Many tales are told of love between serpents and humans. There is the one about the serpent who had fallen in love with a young girl and had pursued her for years. It would creep into her bed at night, lay its head on her pillow and sleep with her. It would even make love to her without her being aware of it. At first the girl was frightened out of her wits each time she woke to find the serpent lying on her. Then she got used to it and came to like the black serpent who would always vanish at dawn. But one day the serpent tarried too long and the girl's brothers slew it. And the girl wept and went mad with grief at her loss.

They were moving more and more quickly, clinging and falling apart, the one chasing the other, catching it, embracing it, leaving it again. This lasted till midday, with the serpents now pursuing each other around the garden at flying speed, now curling up into black coils, now lying panting on the ground. At last they came back to the patch of couch grass and stood upright on their coiled tails, facing each other, the upper part of their bodies interlocked, their tongues flickering out of their open mouths. Then they dropped down. This they did again and again and each time they rose higher into the air, until at last they seemed to be standing on the tips of their tails. She noticed that their colour was changing and turning to red. Their heads were like glowing coals and the red was spreading slowly down their bodies.

The bees buzzed on, swooping about the pomegranate

flowers. Bee-eaters flashed by. A blue-glinting bird settled on a rock. It caught sight of the rising and falling serpents, cocked an eye sideways, then streaked up into the air.

Now their bodies were all ablaze, down almost to their tails. They tossed and twisted like flames that are fanned high and low by the blowing wind. They were as red as the pomegranate flowers, and perhaps that is why the black serpent makes love in the pomegranate garden at blossom time. Perhaps it feels safer there.

It was far in the afternoon when they fell to the ground one last time and did not rise again, but remained sprawling over each other utterly exhausted, their bodies still vibrating. Then one of the serpents flowed slowly into the clump of flowers. The other followed it.

She had watched them disappear, with wide eyes, craning her neck after them. Her mouth and throat were parched. How long ago it seemed. . . .

Elif was tired. She had lost all hope. The serpents and the bees, the wolves and the birds . . . she mused. All these creatures . . . Allah has afflicted us worst of all.

Still wrapped in a dream of the past, she opened her eyes. The only sign of life was a thin smoke rising from a distant hill. Ali had lowered the pack and was resting against it. Meryemdje was sitting on the other side of the pack, a motionless shadow.

She turned back, but the children had dropped far behind. She stopped and waited until they came into view, walking with tired shaky steps. Elif felt a pain that made her head whirl. They're exhausted, the poor things. A whole month won't be enough for them to recover. This madman, pressing on like this, covering a five-day stretch in two days . . . he's killed the children. Damn him and his mother and his horse. . . . Damn everything! She took a few steps towards them.

"There's only a little left now, my little ones, very little. Look, there's your father."

The hand that was pointing fell to her side suddenly. Was that not the Süleymanli slope before them?

Five days down to two, we've done that. But the Süleymanli slope . . . no, we can't make it. If only we could be in the deserted garden now, with the bees and the serpents. . . .

The children's faces were thin and dark and their eyes seemed to fill their whole face.

She looked up again. The slope was there, wrapped in a mist, gliding up to the clouded sky. No, they could never climb it. On their return from the cotton, the villagers would find them there, sick or dead. And Meryemdje who had such a loathing of solitude and strange places . . . would they leave her body here? I'll take her, she thought. I'll carry her body back to the village. I'll never leave her to rot in this wilderness.

She looked about her. The valley was overspread with pebbles from the stream that flowed low at this time of the year. Tamarisk trees were rooted in the soft sandy banks. A scent of heather wafted over to her.

"My little ones," she murmured softly. "My own darlings. . . ." Then she saw the cherry shoots that Hasan had trussed on to his back. "Why, my child, you still have those sticks? You can hardly walk as it is. Throw these things away."

She untied the faggot and cast it off. Hasan looked at her dumbly. Elif averted her gaze. "Come on, let's go to your father."

They walked on, but Hasan could not take his eyes off the cherry shoots. At every step he stopped and looked from the cherry shoots to his mother. Elif felt herself choking. She rushed back, picked up the cherry shoots and hurried back. Hasan's tired face lighted up with joy.

Ali opened his eyes as they approached, but he did not stir, not even when Elif took his hand. It was cold as ice.

"Are you all right, Ali?" she asked anxiously.

He did not answer.

"You're not ill?"

"No."

"What is it?"

"The slope . . . that Süleymanli slope! I had forgotten all about it. After all we've gone through, we're stuck here for good, finished, done for!"

A sudden revolt blazed in her. "We've climbed it before," she cried fiercely, "and we'll do it again this time. You're tired, Ali. To-morrow morning, the slope won't seem so terrible to you."

Ali was not listening. "What will we do this winter?" he kept on muttering. "Adil Effendi . . . curse him, damn the infidel. . . ."

"We'll climb it, you'll see," Elif shouted. She left him and went to gather firewood from the banks of the stream. "We'll make it. To-morrow's another day and you'll see how to-morrow evening we'll be at the abandoned garden."

She lit the fire quickly, filled the saucepan at the stream and placed it over the fire. When the bulgur *pilaff* was ready, she poured a liberal amount of fat over it. Then she drew out a huge red onion from the food sack. Laying the food before Ali, she went up to Meryemdje. "Come, Mother dear," she said. "I've cooked the *pilaff* with fat to-day. You haven't eaten in two days. Come!"

Meryemdje's eyes remained closed. Since the incident of the Forsaken Graveyard, she had not opened her mouth to utter a single word or to eat a morsel of food. Everyone was her enemy now, Ali, Elif, the children, the flying bird, the whole world. She was convinced that Ali had brought her there to the Forsaken Graveyard because he had not found some other way of killing her, and that Elif and the children were all a party to this plot. She had refused to be carried, and for a long time she had hobbled on with the aid of her stick, tumbling down and crawling to her feet again, until in the end she had fainted away. Ali had taken her for dead. He had recited a prayer or two that he happened to know and was shedding tears and wondering how and where to bury her when suddenly Meryemdje had opened her eyes and fixed them on him inquiringly. Taken unawares, his unavowed hopes dashed, Ali had flown into a hard rage. He had hauled her forcibly on to his back and had walked on for a whole night and a whole day without pausing to rest or to look back for the others. Elif had been obliged to load the whole of their belongings on to her back and to follow him. But at the sight of the steep Süleymanli slope he had given up, overcome with despair. Dropping his mother and before he too should drop from weariness, he had rushed back up the road mindless of the piercing pain in his wounded feet from which the rags of sacking had long ago fallen off. He had met Elif, and taking the load from her he had returned to the foot of the slope so quickly that Elif and the children had been left far behind.

Now, the steaming *pilaff* set before him, a piece of bread in his hand, he waited with increasing irritation while Elif pleaded with Meryemdje.

"Please, Mother, just a morsel or two. There's an onion too, red as the pomegranate flower. Please. . . ." She began to cry.

Ali was enraged. "Come here, Elif," he shouted.

She came over and sat with them. They all stared at the steaming food. Suddenly Elif's face brightened. "I'll set some aside in the copper bowl," she whispered into Ali's ear, "and place it beside her. Even if she doesn't eat now, maybe she'll eat during the night."

"She'll eat it, don't worry!" The words came whistling through his clenched teeth. "It's poison she should eat!" He broke the onion fiercely with his fist.

Elif took a piece of it and put it over Meryemdje's portion. They began to gulp down the *pilaff* with quick, hungry motions. After a few mouthfuls, Hasan felt better.

"I didn't get tired at all," he declared, thumping his breast. "Not like Ummahan. Why, I could walk twice as long!"

"Liar!" cried Ummahan, "what a liar! Was it I who whined all the time that I was dying?"

"Yes, it was! You looked at your foot and started whimpering. . . ."

"But that was only because a thorn pricked me. . . ."

"Hah, a thorn! You were tottering on your legs! But me, I never get tired."

"My brave one, my lion," said Elif, "does he ever get tired?"

Ali smiled bitterly.

"But he did," protested Ummahan, "he whined and blubbered so. . . ."

"That's enough, girl," Elif scolded her.

"Elif," said Ali, "my feet are in a terrible state. Isn't there any of Mother's ointment left?"

"Why yes," she said happily, "but there's no sacking at all. Still, we'll find something."

She rose and gathered up the food implements. Then she spread out the bedding. "Mother," she said, as she helped Meryemdje to her bed, "look, I'm putting your food here. There's some onion on the *pilaff.* Eat just when you feel like it."

An angel, thought Meryemdje, an angel, that's what you are. It's that infidel who leads you astray. . . .

Elif found the ointment which she had stored in a hollow fragment of pine bark. She applied it to Ali's wounds and bound up his feet with some old rags.

It was no longer as cold as in the mountains and they did not have to feed the fire during the night. The children lay down one on each side of Meryemdje. Hasan was still muttering to himself. "Does a man ever get tired? Look at my father, he's not tired, and neither am I . . . hurray. . . ."

Meryemdje waited for the others to fall asleep. Then she

slipped out of her bed and groped about for the plate of food. How good the onion and *pilaff* smelled!

Elif was the first to wake. It was not quite light yet. She lit the fire and, although it was warm now, she held her hands above it absent-mindedly. It had become a habit.

She was thinking of the slope. There it was, stretching up more and more clearly in the growing light, a polished clay-coloured acclivity, with purple streaks and patches of green and red and light blue. The road was just a narrow path that twisted up like a pale stripe and seemed to lose itself in the distant blue of the sky.

She could not take her eyes away from it, glinting faintly now in the early sunlight. No, it was impossible. This was really the end for them. Ali could never carry his mother up such a steep path. And Meryemdje was not in a state to take another step. Who knows, perhaps even now . . . Elif rushed over to her. She saw the empty bowl and turned back, relieved. To be so near, and yet . . . If it weren't for this slope . . . There were ripe pomegranates in the garden now, and also golden figs, there for the plucking. And the black serpents that turned red at mating-time, did they still twine together so tightly and then drop to the ground, fainting with love? If only the great Halladji Mansur[1] would come to earth now instead of at Doomsday, and blow over the slope with his charmed breath! He'd blow and blow and the hill would flatten out and soon the Chukurova plain would appear in the distance with its white cotton fields. . . .

She was disconcerted to see Ali before her. Rising quickly, she forced a smile. He was looking at the distant peak of the hill over which the heat haze was already settling. They both stood silently, staring at the hill. Ali's face was bitter.

[1] An early tenth-century Moslem mystic who was executed for saying "I am God." According to popular belief, he will return at Doomsday with the task of flattening out the earth to make easier the emergence of the myriads of human beings.

"No," he moaned at last, "we can't make it. To think we've gone through fire and earth to get here, and now . . . Aaah!"

Elif rallied instantly. Her huge eyes flashed. "It's not worse than what we've already gone through. Of course we'll make it!"

Ali glanced despairingly at Meryemdje, who was sitting drawn up in a small heap near the bed. The children were crouching beside her, motionless, waiting. The thing to do now would be to leave everything and rush down to the Chukurova, join the cotton pickers and work, work. . . . Work like five men, like ten men. Night and day. . . .

"Elif!" he exclaimed. "I know what. You'll wait for me here until cotton picking is over, while I go down and gather some cotton at least. I could even borrow a horse or a donkey and come back to fetch you."

"No," Elif said. "Look, Mother's much better to-day. She ate everything I put for her last night. We'll hold her, each by one arm, and . . ."

Ali shook his head. "We can't!"

"Yes, we can. And after we've taken her up, we'll come back for the pack."

"But the children? They're more dead than alive. Just look at them."

"Well, they'll have to be carried too if they can't walk. I'll carry them."

Ali hesitated.

"Look, Elif," he said softly, "it'll be difficult. Now, if you remained here while I . . ."

Elif flared up. Ali had never seen her so angry. She shouted and her voice echoed from the hills. "Yes, leave me here with two children and an old woman, at the mercy of wild beasts and evil-doers! Here in this valley, to be carried away by the floods if it rains!"

He was crushed. She took the pot of *tarhana* soup from the

fire and laid the cloth. Filling the copper bowl again, she brought it over to Meryemdje as she had done the night before.

"Take this, Mother," she said. "I've crushed some good strong garlic into it and sprinkled it with red pepper. We must get over the Süleymanli slope to-day."

Meryemdje remained still, her head bowed, while Elif waited expectantly with the bowl in her hand. Suddenly she cast a sidelong glance at them and took the bowl from Elif.

After they had all eaten Ali and Elif started packing again. A sultry heat, worse than the heat of the Chukurova plain, had now set in and the valley swarmed with myriads of tiny flies that stuck maddeningly to their faces, penetrating even into their ears and nose.

"You go to her and see if she can walk a little," whispered Ali.

Elif took Meryemdje's hands in hers. "Well, Mother, here we are at the Süleymanli slope. It's a steep climb, as you know. But with Ali on one side supporting you and me on the other . . . do you think you could walk a little?"

Without any warning, Meryemdje uttered a cry and collapsed in a faint.

Elif lost her head. "Ali," she cried, "quick! She's dying. Water! Quick, say some prayers, Ali. Ummahan, get some water!"

Ummahan ran to the stream. Standing beside his mother, Ali started mumbling out prayers at top speed, as if afraid of missing something. The few prayers he knew were soon exhausted and he began all over again, hurriedly repeating each line ten times over.

Elif wetted her headkerchief in the water Ummahan had brought and gently patted Meryemdje's face. After a while Meryemdje opened her eyes and stared at Ali. "I'm dying," she moaned, "I'm dying, children. A little water!"

Ummahan ran to the stream again. Ali smiled, a bitter rancorous smile. He bit his knuckles as he stood watching his mother drink and sit up again. Suddenly, unable to hold himself in any longer, he began to cry. Stuffing his handkerchief into his mouth, he stumbled away towards the stream. There, hidden by the tamarisks, he threw himself on the sand and sobbed unrestrainedly.

"Mother," cried Elif, "thank God you're better. You gave us such a fright. Now, Mother, you must try. . . . With Ali on one side and me on the other. . . ."

There was a mocking crafty glint in Meryemdje's eyes as she listened. So, she thought, you want to make me walk up this steep hill so I should die, eh? Well, I won't climb this hill or any other hill, my girl! You can carry me up if you want to, that's all. You've been praying night and day for my death, I know. That's why you left me right in the middle of the Forsaken Graveyard. And now you're going to fling me on to this Süleymanli slope in the hope I'll die half-way, eh?

"You're still as strong as steel, Mother. The old earth, that's what you are. How else could you have weathered all this. . . ? Why, you've walked all this way as briskly as if you were fifteen years old."

Don't try to wheedle me. I won't stir. I've been a fool to have walked all this time. You've got to carry me, that's all. And if you try to kill me . . . well, Allah is on my side. He won't help any murderers. Didn't I see how that Long Ali's eyes gleamed when I fainted? Don't I know what he wants? Why, he was almost frisking with joy as he recited those prayers. Do you think I didn't notice? And when he saw I was all right . . . She closed her eyes and fell back again. This time Elif remained quite calm. She had detected Meryemdje's stratagem.

"Mother," she said firmly, "we're going to support you up this hill to-day. The only thing I ask of you is to help us a little by moving your legs."

"I'm dying! Water!"

"Die!" Elif cursed under her breath.

"Yes, die! " echoed Hasan.

Ummahan stared at them aghast. "Let her die and be delivered," she murmured as she went to the stream again.

A flock of birds rose from the tamarisks. Ali had wept until he could weep no more. He staggered up, but his feet were quite numb now. Instead of that burning pain he now felt at every step a sickening twinge, grinding into his heart as if two hands were twitching it this way and that. The new pain was worse than anything else.

"Elif, come here," he shouted, "something's wrong with me. Every time I put my foot down I want to vomit. If you could take some cotton out of a pillow . . ."

Elif was soon back with a few tufts of cotton, while Ali untied the rags. His feet were all livid raw flesh. He applied the cotton and bound the rags over it. Then he tried to take a few steps but the same sickness came over him again. He sank down, holding his head in his hands.

"Ali," Elif spurred him, "look at the weather. I'm sure it's going to rain, and here in this valley . . . We must go."

Ali looked up. A few dark clouds were gathering in the north. He bounded to his feet, forgetting everything.

"Rain!" he shouted. "Mother, rain's coming! We must get to the top or we'll be flooded down here. Elif, let's carry the load up out of the valley at least."

They lifted the pack together and hauled it to a large rock some distance up the slope.

"It'll be all right here. And the children can wait here too."

The sun was now blazing down upon them. The gravelled earth of the path was as hot as though it had come out of an oven.

"Mother," said Ali, "you know I would have carried you up if I could. Children, you wait for us near the pack."

Elif had already propped Meryemdje up and was trying to make her walk, but Meryemdje's feet dragged as if she had no bones left in them. Ali grabbed her other arm and they started

269

heaving her up. The black clouds had given him strength and hope. He no longer wanted to vomit. His feet and legs still ached unbearably, but he was pleased. He did not care if his whole body were riddled with bullets so long as he did not feel that sickening twinge in his heart.

Meryemdje hung on to their shoulders like a dead weight, more and more heavily. And the heavier she grew, the more Ali pulled, almost dragging Elif on too. Her shoulder was racked and she could not breathe, but she knew it would be useless to say anything to Ali. It was his nature. His eyes were bulging out and even the whites were not white any more, but a strange colour, neither black nor red. His skin was strained like tanned leather.

Suddenly Meryemdje slipped out of his hands. Elif lost her balance and they both tumbled down, one over the other. Ali had fallen too and was breathing heavily. Meryemdje was the first to straighten up. She took Elif's hand and pulled her up too. Ali stared at her, grinding his teeth. "Why don't you die?" he muttered. "Die!"

The sun was at its noonday height, torrefying them.

"It's the heat that comes before rain," murmured Ali, his eye on the black clouds. "Ah, bring the rain, Allah, with thunder and lightning. The rain that sweeps everything away, every-thing. . . ."

Meryemdje pointed to the stick Elif had been helping herself up with and which had dropped farther off. Her legs trembling, Elif brought it to her. Stick in hand, Meryemdje hesitated and looked up at the slope. The stone-strewn path sparkled under the sun, like the stubbled fields of the Chukurova.

You've got to do it, Meryemdje. You've got to climb this slope and show that Long Ali, who's sprawling there panting like a bellows, who left you in the middle of the Forsaken Graveyard so you should die. Come on, my brave legs, let's show him.

Ali could not believe his eyes. There was his mother making slow but sure progress up the slope. Why, he thought in a sudden wave of joy, at this rate the woman will even be able to pick cotton! His face changed and he even smiled as his eyes met Elif's. She pointed down to the children who were clambering up, holding to each other. Hasan was bent under the faggot of cherry shoots. This enraged Ali.

"Throw them away, you little whelp," he shouted, "as if our own load weren't enough. . . . And cherry shoots to boot!"

He snatched the faggot off Hasan's back and threw it into the distance. Hasan remained motionless and silent. Ummahan began to cry.

"Mother seems to be doing quite well," said Elif. "Suppose we go down and get the load?"

Going downhill was even more difficult than uphill. They kept slipping and falling on the steep gravelly path. The rock where they had left the load was burning hot. They could not sit and rest. They were thirsty. Down below, the stream flowed like molten silver. They could not go down and drink. They divided up the load between them and started up again.

It was the first time that Ali had carried such a light load. He felt elated. The slope was not so steep after all. . . . His mother, bent in two, was still dragging herself up and a little way behind Hasan, the cherry shoots on his back again, had taken Ummahan by the arm and was walking steadily. Soon afterwards he had passed them, staring unseeingly before him, and was hurrying up the path, slipping, falling, rising, never slackening for a minute. When at last he came to the great gum tree at the top of the hill, the sun was sinking into the valley. The west wind blew refreshingly over his tense body. His eyes were smarting with sweat. He threw off the load and plunged back down the slope.

"Quick!" Elif gasped as she came up to him. "Mother's fallen down there and now she's trying to crawl up on all fours.

271

I told her to wait for you, but she only struggled the harder. Hurry, Ali!"

His knees bleeding and his hands scratched from slipping and stumbling, he finally reached Meryemdje. Her hands, face and hair were caked in mud from the dust and the sweat. Ali drew her up quickly and squatting before her raised her on to his back. He managed to carry her up a little way, but his foot slipped and he pitched forward, rolling down the path. He picked himself up immediately, but this time he had not the courage to take her on his back again. He seized her arm and thrust the stick into her free hand. "Only a little more, Mother darling. Just a little!"

The children gazed with empty eyes as they plodded on past them. Then Hasan remembered the cherry shoots. He crouched behind Ummahan, trying to hide from his father.

"Don't worry," said the girl. "He won't see. He's wrapped in his own troubles."

The sun was setting when mother and son reached the top. Elif had lit a fire under the great gum tree and was cooking some soup. The west glowed red, and down below the Chukurova land could be seen swelling under a mantled haze.

Elif looked at Ali. "The children?"

"They're coming. . . ."

Chapter 19

It was after midnigl t when the first peal of thunder came rolling over the northern steppe. Hard upon it a cold chilling wind sprang up, carrying the smell of earth and rotting bark and water.

Ali lay in his bed, kept awake by the pain that racked his feet and body. The great gum tree was only faintly discernible. In the south one or two stars glimmered faintly. Then they were wiped out and the boughs above him faded into the darkness, as impenetrable now as a black wall. The rain he had so much prayed for was coming now with a vengeance. He felt a mixture of gladness and fear.

"Elif," he said, shaking her.

She turned in the bed. "Huh?"

"Do you hear what's coming? It's not rain, it's a cataract! Ah, if we'd made a little effort we would have been in the Chukurova now, and not caught in this rain. . . ."

Elif leapt out of the bed.

"And by the looks of it," Ali went on, "it won't stop for a whole week. The autumn rains of the Chukurova are worse than anything. Praise Allah, woman, we're saved now. This rain will give us time to rest and recover, and to gather some cotton as well."

Lightning flashed and the wind blew more fiercely. The boughs of the gum tree cracked as though they would break. A strong blast swept the blankets up and the children awoke in a fright. Ummahan began to cry. Meryemdje had risen from her bed at the first gust and was huddled up at the foot of the gum tree.

At each flash the white road leading down to the Chukurova and the distant zinc-roofed flour-mill sprang into sudden light, to be plunged almost instantly into the smothering darkness.

Ali had not moved. Buffeted by conflicting feelings, he lay on his back watching the tree blaze fitfully into traceries of light. He had never seen such a wonderful sight.

"Get up, Ali. Do something!" cried Elif, panic in her voice. "It's coming! . . . Ali! Please do something!" She ran about aimlessly, beating her knees in anguish. "Oh, my all-powerful Allah, did you have to bring this upon us too?" She rushed up to Ali and threw herself upon him. "You must do something, Ali. It's coming, worse than anything I've ever seen!"

Bursts of light were lashing the earth, revealing whirlwinds of dust that eddied furiously on the white road and in the valley to dash themselves against the darkness.

"What are you worrying about, woman?" Ali said at last. "Let it rain well and good. I hope the whole of the Chukurova is flooded. Come, get into bed with me. There's nothing we can do."

The skies rumbled. Deafening sounds came booming from far and wide to converge on the peak of the gum tree scattering into splinters over them.

"Curse you, man, get up! We've got to flee. Let's find a village, a cave, a shelter. . . ."

Ali was quite unmoved. "It's no use," he said wearily, "it'll be upon us before we take two steps. We've no choice but to stay where we are."

Elif began to tear at her hair in anguish. "Oh, my unlucky head!" she moaned. "What shall I do now? Where shall I go? Get up, Ali, and let's make a tent for the children at least. Get up, you're lying on the tent cloth."

"Are you mad, woman? What good would a tent be against

274

this torrent? This blessed rain . . . mightier than the great deluge of our Lord Noah! All the cotton spilled to the ground. . . . Oh, how heavy the cotton'll be then! I'll buy a young sprightly Cyprus donkey for Mother and a saddle too. . . . Don't be afraid, Elif. We're not made of salt that we should melt away with a little rain!"

In the glaring light she saw that he was smiling, almost laughing, with contentment.

"Monster!" she flared at him. "You're a monster. The murderer of my children, of your mother, of our horse. . . ."

She ran into the darkness. Some time later she was back with a pile of firewood which she quickly lit. Then she turned to Ali and started pulling madly at the goat-hair cloth on which he was lying. It jerked out of her hands and she fell sprawling on her back.

"Ali, for pity's sake," she pleaded weakly, "get up and let me have the cloth."

He smiled on, paying no attention to her at all. His dusty beard shone dully in the firelight.

A jagged streak of lightning split the dark sky asunder and almost simultaneously a thunderclap burst over their heads. Then huge warm drops of rain began to patter down.

Elif uttered a strangled cry. She began dumping the sacks, the basket, the tins and the bedding at the foot of the tree. Ali drew the blanket over his head and curled himself up. The rain quickened.

"Damn you, Ali, damn you!" She gritted her teeth. "A bloodthirsty monster, the unbeliever himself wouldn't do this. Mother, get up, help me pull this cloth from under him."

Ali sprung out of bed suddenly. "All right, I've got up!" he said crossly. "Why, you foolish woman, of what good is a tent against this lion of a rain?"

The fire had died down to a mere hissing glow. Meryemdje rose and seized one end of the cloth while Elif took the other.

Together, they held it over the fire and Elif bent down, scraping at the embers to rekindle them.

The rain was pouring down on them mercilessly now, like a dark stream. The ground about the tree had turned to mire.

"All right," said Ali, "we'll do as you say and see what comes of it, you witless woman. This cloth must be fastened to a branch, but how am I to climb trees with these bloated feet? And I have no rope either. . . ."

Elif shoved the corner of the cloth into his hand. "We've got rope and we've got everything we need! As for the tree, I'll climb it."

Strips of rope from previous years dangled from the corners of the cloth. She clambered up and secured one end to a branch. Scrambling down, she tied another of the strands to the trunk and the last one to a bush.

"A stake! Ali, you plant a stake here. Quick!"

Ali only looked on dreamily.

"A stake, Ali. . . ." She realised that nothing was to be got out of him. Rushing to the fire, she took a half-burnt stick and started hammering it into the ground with a stone.

"Mother, don't stay there," she cried, as she busied herself with the stake, "get under shelter."

The children were already under the tent near the fire. Then she saw that Meryemdje was moving away, into the darkness and the rain that was driving down now with the din of a loud waterfall.

"Mother! Where are you going? Don't go, Mother!"

She ran after her and tugged her by the arm. Meryemdje shook her off and plunged on into the night, with Elif hard on her heels. She seemed to be searching for something. Elif understood and set about gathering wood with her. They returned to the tree, wet to the bone, each carrying an armful of wood, and found Ali standing as inert as they had left him. The children were shivering. Elif began to feed the fire, wiping each branch dry as she did so. Meryemdje helped her, and together they managed to keep it burning. Water was streaming down the bark of the tree on to their bundles. She carried them into the shelter of the tent and spread the least wet of the blankets over the children.

When she sat down at last, Ali joined her, water dripping from his beard and his face still contorted in that demented smile. He stretched himself out full length, his elbow resting in a puddle.

As the wind and downpour gained strength a violent blast of rain swashed into the tent and drowned out the fire. Then the ropes started to snap, one after another.

"Didn't I say so?" Ali muttered. "Tents and fires against this rain? Why, it would sweep huge palaces away! Elif, put the matches where they'll keep dry. . . . In the empty bottle."

She found the bottle and handed it to Ali. "My hands are wet. The matches are here, in my breast." At the feel of his hand, a pleasant tremor flowed through her body, a flitting, hazy reminiscence of love and joy.

He wrenched the cork out and emptied the matches into the bottle. Then he tore off the side of the box and slipped it in too, replacing the cork carefully.

Then he drew the children to his breast and, covering himself with the blanket, bent over them trying to shield them as best he could. He pulled Meryemdje to him, and Elif crawled up and huddled against Meryemdje. They pressed closer and closer, almost cleaving to one another as the rain came drumming down, its deafening din swollen by the roar of the torrents that were hurtling into the valley.

First it was the children's teeth that began to chatter. Then Elif's. Ali tried hard to keep his mouth steady, but he too gave way in the end. Meryemdje was writhing incessantly. This terrified Elif. She held her in her arms and rubbed her, but Meryemdje's hands and face were like ice. Even by daylight, it would have been hard to tell that this shivering mound was really five human beings. They were as one trembling body, their teeth chattering in unison with clockwork precision. Even their armpits were wet.

At daybreak the rain slackened. Elif tried to extricate herself from the others, but her arms and legs would not obey her. Even her jaws clicked only spasmodically now. She broke away at last, falling back into the slush. Ali threw off the blanket and rose, drawing the children up after him. He could not straighten his back and his eyes had narrowed into slits. But there was an expression of bitter content on his face.

The clouds were receding in the north, revealing the blue translucent sky in all its limpid brightness.

As if seized by a fit of madness, Ali started skipping up and down. Elif stood watching him dazedly. She felt her wet clothes sticking to her body and revealing every line of it. Her hands went to her breast in embarrassment.

"Run," Ali panted, as he darted up to the children, "come on, run as quickly as you can. It'll warm up your blood. Run or you'll catch your death."

Elif broke into a run with them. Meryemdje lifted her head and stared at these dripping human forms who were scurrying about for dear life. She stirred feebly. Elif ran to her and pulled her up by the armpits. But Meryemdje crumpled back. Elif tried again, forcing her to take a few steps. This time, Meryemdje stood upright. She paused, facing the Chukurova, her eyes fixed on a distant spot on the plain. With her clothes clinging to her flesh, there was something about her of the bedraggled, wounded bird, its feathers dull, its neck drawn in mournfully. She looked at the others who were still running. Then she picked up her stick and walked off towards the path.

The clouds had rolled away now and a bright sun was warming up the steaming earth. The Chukurova plain was soon hidden in mist.

Elif set about packing again. "Everything's wringing wet!"

she wailed. "The flour, the bulgur, the bedding. . . . Soaked . . . and muddy too! They'll weigh like lead. We'll have to divide the load between us. . . ."

Ali stood by idly. Mother's a clever woman, he mused, she knows everything. She may be a little stubborn, but if it weren't for that one devilish failing, you could trust her instinct in all things. We haven't seen the last of this rain, and she knows it. This is the forty-afternoons rain of the Chukurova that only lets up in the morning. We can't afford to lag here. We must find shelter before the afternoon.

"I'm dying of hunger," whimpered Hasan, "I'm just dead. . . ."

"Shut up," snapped Ali, "the mill's only a little way down. We'll stop and eat there. Come on, Elif."

They lugged up the two packs, while Hasan struggled helplessly to lift his cherry shoots. Burdened as she was, Elif bent down and picked up the faggot which she placed on his shoulders.

"Off with you now," she said.

Ali was smiling as they dropped to the road. "Eh," he said, "God tempers the wind to the shorn lamb! He's sent us this blessed rain, that must have washed all the cotton into the mire. Look, Elif!" He pointed to the north where silvery clouds were gathering again. "See? It's coming. Hurray!"

He left them behind and plodded on, his feet sinking ankle-deep into the viscous mud.

The sun had dried their dank clothes. Larks flitted about them and bright-coloured hoopoes flew off in a whir of wings at their approach. Lizards were basking leisurely on the stones bordering the road.

They had gone down the slope, passing the three mulberry trees, and caught up with Meryemdje, when, far ahead, they saw a man suddenly emerging from the bushes. He seemed to be waiting for them, but it was only when they had drawn quite near that they realised this was Old Halil. His clothes hung limply about him and he had obviously been caught in the rain too. He peered at Ali with a prayer in his frightened, childlike eyes.

Meryemdje turned her head away in disgust. She swept by as if she did not know him.

Hasan nudged Ummahan. "Father's going to kill him, you'll see," he whispered, "he'll strangle him."

Ali just gave the old man an accusing stare and passed on. Old Halil was cut to the quick. He had never expected this from Ali. He glared after them until they disappeared around a bend. Then with an oath he fell into their wake and was soon trailing ten or fifteen paces behind them, not daring to draw any nearer.

Ali was upset. He knew his mother was watching to see what he would do. He silently cursed Old Halil for having appeared like a ghost before them. And indeed the old man had a spectral aspect. Who knows, though Ali, what hard fortune has befallen him, that he should be wandering thus, cut adrift from the rest of the village? His anger was fast melting into pity.

Old Halil had pinned all his faith on Ali, scanning the road for days as he waited for him. Now, all his hopes were shattered. He had nowhere to go, no one he could turn to. He longed to wave them all aside with a flourish and take himself off to a faraway land, but he was worn out and so he stayed this impulse and bent his unwilling steps after them.

By noontime they had reached the flour-mill. They unpacked the load and spread out everything on the grass to dry in the sun. Elif made a fire and put the bulgur *pilaff* to cook. They had no bread left at all, so she took some of the soggy flour and started kneading it. Then she noticed Meryemdje, still not talking but gesticulating over the flour-sack, trying to convey something to her. Elif remembered that wet flour was never any good when it dried. All of it had to be baked immediately. She placed three stones in the middle of the fire and covered them with a tin sheet. Then the two women busied themselves, Elif moulding small cakes of bread and laying them on the tin sheet, and Meryemdje turning them over and holding them for an instant over the embers so as to brown them thoroughly.

Hasan snatched the first cake that was baked. Ali took the next one and Elif handed the third to Ummahan. Old Halil sat farther off, his head bowed but covertly eyeing their every move.

When they had used up all the flour they laid the cakes of bread on the grass. Elif melted some butter in the skillet and poured it sizzling over the bulgur, and they all crowded hungrily about the saucepan.

"Give us an onion, Elif," said Ali. He cast an uneasy glance at Old Halil as he slowly chewed a spoonful of *pilaff*. It was against all rules and customs not to invite someone to share your meal, were he even your worst enemy. His brow darkened and suddenly his spoon clattered into the saucepan. He did not take it up again. There was a deep silence as he looked at his mother. Meryemdje's face was changing and that fierce expression of disgust had gone from her eyes. She lowered her head. Ali looked guiltily at Old Halil.

"Uncle Halil," he called softly, "what are you sitting there all alone for? Come and have a bite with us. Come, Uncle Halil."

Old Halil drew near apprehensively. Ali picked up the spoon and put it into his hand. The old man shakily broke a piece of bread, his eyes searching Meryemdje's face. Then he took a spoonful of *pilaff*. Ali split the onion and smilingly offered him a piece, which Old Halil took gratefully. Meryemdje never raised her eyes from the *pilaff*. She went on eating in obvious discomfort.

When the meal was over Old Halil pulled Ali by the sleeve and together they went to sit under the spreading mulberry tree. "They're gone to the colonel's plantation again," the old man announced. "No one stood up to that scoundrel but me. As for that mangy Tashbash of yours, he's become Sefer's own man. I was the only one to protest and I only barely escaped being killed. They all pounced upon me, but praise Allah it happened at night and I managed to give them the slip. Then I came down here to wait for you, you the child of my dear friend Ibrahim."

Ali smiled. "So that's how it is, eh?" he murmured. "Not one of them broke away, eh?"

"I broke away. Only I. . . . Ah, if only I were young and strong! Qow I'd have made him sweat. Old as I am, one night I crept up to him as he lay sleeping, bent on strangling the life out of him and ridding the village of such an infidel. I clamped my hands about his neck and squeezed and squeezed and squeezed for all I was worth while he writhed beneath me, but . . . Ah, this accursed old age! My strength failed me. I couldn't squeeze hard enough and he didn't die, the unbeliever. . . . And those shameless villagers all sided with him against me. All right, I shouted at them, you stick to that cur of yours. I've got my Ali."

Ali was gazing at the colonel's farm where it stood in the distance amidst a cluster of trees. Its corrugated-iron roof was shimmering wet after the rain. "To-morrow," he said, still smiling, "we'll join the villagers and start picking too."

Old Halil was stunned. "You mean, you too? You too following that pig? Why? Can't you leave the others and pick on another farm?"

"Oh, come on, Uncle Halil!" Ali chaffed him gently. "Isn't it a bit late in the day for that? Who'd have us now?"

"Well, I'm not joining those shameless villagers!" declared Old Halil doggedly. "I'm still a man, son, even if there's no other left in these parts. And I thought you were a man too. . . . Why, we'll be welcomed with open arms wherever we go. People will be proud to have us. What brave men, they'll say, who've held their own against a powerful Muhtar. Isn't that so?"

"We'll do that next year."

Old Halil thought bitterly of the wonderful visions he had conjured up as he had lain in wait for Ali. How the two of them would join forces and find a field in which every cotton plant carried a hundred bolls, how they would gather the cotton and become rich in no time, and the awe of the villagers when they returned. . . . He thought of the new black *shalvar* and of the embroidered sash and how he would perhaps magnanimously hand out ten liras to his son. . . . He cursed Ali silently.

"Are you really going to join the villagers?" he gasped out at last. Ali nodded.

"But you can't," the old man shouted angrily. "It's impossible. The Muhtar has got a warrant out for you. He's alerted all the gendarmes and the Government too, just as he's done for me, and worse even. How can you go and give yourself up? He accuses you of having killed your horse on purpose, as a ruse to shake off the rest of the village and be free to plunder all the Chukurova plain, to become a bandit, to stir up a big revolt against the Government. . . . And he's got all the villagers to sign up as witnesses against you and against me too. Allah protect us, this means fifteen years at least, if not the rope! You'd better do as I say and come with me to the cotton fields of Yüreghir which are always so bountiful. Anyway there's no cotton left to gather at the colonel's plantation. It was such a poor crop that the villagers picked the field clean in one day! In the land of Yüreghir the cotton blooms later than here. Come, let's go there."

Ali laid his hand on the old man's shoulder. "That Muhtar can't do anything to us, Uncle. Have no fear. Next year we'll go to the land of Yüreghir and gather heaps of cotton."

"Look, Ali," said Old Halil, driven now to play his last card, "if you come with me to the land of Yüreghir, I'll take you to Yasin Agha's farm, and all the money I earn I'll give to you so you can buy your mother a good sturdy donkey. After all, it's only fair. I killed her horse. You think I'm too old to pick cotton, eh? We're the old earth, my son. I can gather more than you and Elif put together! Come with me and see how rich you'll get. Yes, we'll even be able to buy your mother a three-year-old pure-bred, and all the villagers and that godless Sefer will be green with envy." He stopped and fixed his eyes expectantly on Ali. He was sure he had convinced him at last.

"Thank you, Uncle Halil," said Ali, as he put his arm about the old man affectionately, "I know you'll keep your word, but we'll do that next year."

For a while Old Halil struggled for more words. Then he fell back against the tree and remained there brooding sulkily till nightfall.

That night they gave Old Halil the goat-hair cloth to lie on. But the next morning there was no sign of the old man. The goat-hair cloth lay abandoned nearby.

Elif started packing, but she was arrested by Meryemdje, who had sidled up and was looking at her insistently. Elif noticed that she had lit a fire and had put some water to warm.

"You wish to wash your hair and henna it, Mother?" she asked.

Meryemdje produced a small pouch from her waist.

"Your green headkerchief is dry and ready too, Mother."

Meryemdje's eyes smiled. It was her custom every time they came to the Chukurova to henna her hair and adorn herself as best she could. She drew out a pair of ear-rings and held them out to Elif. The ear-rings were rusty.

"I'll polish them up for you, Mother," said Elif. She went to the fire and started rubbing the ear-rings with ashes.

In the meantime Meryemdje had taken out her bead necklace and was unravelling its tangled string. The green, red, orange and blue beads delighted her now just as much as they had when her grandmother had first given them to her on her wedding day. They were ancient, strangely-shaped beads, and nobody owned the like of them any more.

Elif had finished polishing the ear-rings. She brought the hot water over and holding Meryemdje's head down she carefully washed her sparse, soft-as-down hair. She was about to mix the henna when Meryemdje stopped her. The old woman had suddenly decided that this hennaing business would take too long and they had to be at the plantation as soon as they could.

Ali was watching her in amazement as she decked and preened herself. This year too? After all they had gone through? His own weariness, the pain in his feet, everything was drowned in a swelling wave of thankfulness. His mother was still alive and going strong in spite of her sallow face that had shrunk to the size of a tiny crumpled pouch. But why did she not talk at all? Would she never speak to anyone again? If it weren't for this misgiving and also for the disappearance of Old Halil, he would have felt entirely at ease now, for all their troubles were over. To-day they would be at the plantation.

At last Meryemdje was ready. With her green headcloth, glittering ear-rings, bead necklace and glass bracelet, she was her same old self. Only her back was a little more bent this year. She leaned on her stick for a moment and her eyes swept over the distant fields teeming with labourers picking cotton. Cars and trucks were rumbling along the road.

Suddenly a deep roar burst over them in the sky. A squadron of jets was zooming off towards Anavarza. The next instant it was out of sight.

They reached the cotton field in the afternoon. The air here smelled of burdock and dust and cotton, and from the nearby rice paddy there floated the rank odour of stagnant water.

Ali led the way to where the villagers had built their wattle huts. His eyes caught the tiny mounds of cotton that lay in front of each hut and then rested on a small group of villagers who were picking cotton at the far end of the field. He hurled his load down and slumped heavily to the ground, leaning against the pole of a hut. All the triumph and exultation of having arrived at last had dissolved at the sight of the field, with its stunted cotton plants overgrown with weeds. He closed his eyes, a searing fire in his heart.

The children paused uncertainly. Hasan still had the cherry

shoots on his back. Meryemdje and Elif came over and sat down beside Ali. Elif was nervously crushing a small cotton shoot in her hands.

One by one the villagers drew near, staring at them with wide eyes. They wanted to say something, some phrase of welcome, but the words stuck in their throats. They just stood there in a hushed circle.

Suddenly Tashbash came charging through the mute, frozen crowd. He stopped short, his eyes darting in alarm from Ali to Meryemdje, from Elif to the children. Then he moved like an automaton towards his friend.

"Welcome, brother," he murmured hoarsely, as though some hand were strangling him. "Well, you can see for yourself what he's got us into again. The crop's even worse than last year's. Don't worry because you're late. We're no better off than you are. A field full of weeds! Not a boll of cotton to a dozen plants. . . . Don't worry, it would have made no difference if . . . What's done is done. . . ." He broke off, unable to say another word, and stroked Ali's hand.

A deathlike silence had fallen, which no one had the courage to break. It weighed down heavily, thickly, unbearably.

Meryemdje began to drum the ground nervously with her right hand. Suddenly her eyes rested on a small, brilliantly pink cotton flower and with a jolt she remembered the ladybird. Quickly she drew the headcloth from her waist and untied the knot. The ladybird was still there, but long dead and dried up. She took the withered insect and laid it gently over the flower.

"Sleep," she murmured, "sleep, my luckless one, my lonely one, sleep here. . . ."

She lifted her head and ran her eyes slowly over the crowd in the all-encompassing silence. Then she pounded the earth violently with her right hand again and again.

"So what?" she cried. "We've arrived, haven't we? We're here."

Also in *The Wind from the Plain* trilogy
II IRON EARTH, COPPER SKY

"Yashar Kemal is one of the modern world's great storytellers"

JOHN BERGER

After a bad season the poor mountain villagers, who pick cotton for their livelihood, are unable to pay their creditor, the shop-keeper Adil Effendi. Such a break with age-old tradition causes them to be overwhelmed with a sense of guilt. They wait in terror for Adil to come, but he fails to appear and in his inexplicable absence his figure swells till it fills their minds and they become sick with the apprehension of some terrible disaster. In their despair they look to Tashbash, a brave man, one of themselves, who has always stood up for them against the tyranny of Sefer, their Headman.

They invest Tashbash with all the virtues, and to these miraculous power is gradually added. What this does to Tashbash, his innocent doubts and mental torment, the fate that comes upon him and the very apposite conclusion combine to make a moving story alive with acute observation of human nature, containing passages of lyrical beauty and deep compassion.

Iron Earth, Copper Sky is the second volume of the *The Wind from the Plain* trilogy, a sequel to *The Wind from the Plain*.

"This strange and lyrical book, beautifully translated by Thilda Kemal, has the compulsive power of a tale told to a wondering audience beside a flickering fire" *Daily Telegraph*

Also in *The Wind from the Plain* trilogy
III THE UNDYING GRASS

"Yashar Kemal is a cauldron where fact, fantasy and folklore are stirred to produce poetry. He is a storyteller in the oldest tradition, that of Homer, spokesman for a people who had no other voice"   ELIA KAZAN

Memidik, the young hunter, is obsessed by the urge to kill the tyrannous headman, Sefer, who has caused him much pain and humiliation. But each time he tries, the figure of Sefer looms many times larger than life, and Memidik freezes in fear. But his accidental slaying of another man fires him with renewed determination. Sefer, meanwhile, has been sentenced to solitude as the villagers refuse to speak to him. Sefer's taunting only strengthens their loyalty to their champion Tashbash whom they come to invest with mythical powers. The web of their fantasy becomes so extensive that when he returns to the village, a worn-out old man, they cannot recognise or accept him.

   The Undying Grass, the third volume in *The Wind from the Plain* trilogy and a sequel to *Iron Earth, Copper Sky*, also continues the story of Ali and his mother Meryemdje who, in their different ways, learn the difficult art of survival.

"He speaks for those people for whom no one else is speaking"
                                                      JAMES BALDWIN

Harvill Paperbacks are published by Collins Harvill,
a Division of the Collins Publishing Group